PRAISE FOR PR

"Oliveras has perfected the second-chance romance trope with Alejandro and Anamaría. Their anguish is so real that the book should come with tissues. The Key West setting is vibrant, adding a blessed touch of armchair travel to the current global circumstances. Wonderfully soapy, this is a romance to read in one sitting. A stunning romance of first love found again."

—*Kirkus Reviews* (starred review), *Anchored Hearts*

"The Florida island setting is only part of the appeal of this character-driven, second-chance romance between smart and badass Anamaría and sexy and artistic Alejandro as they slowly realize that successful relationships have room for both partners' professions and dreams. Another draw: Oliveras's portrayal of family and social media ties are reminiscent of Alisha Rai's romances."

—*Booklist* (starred review), *Anchored Hearts*

"A bighearted, beautiful book about first love, second chances, and finding one's place in the world. Oliveras writes with a rare warmth that not only brings her characters to life but also lets her readers sink into the gorgeous Key West sunrises she so lovingly describes. An exceptional getaway of a book!"

—Emily Henry, *New York Times* bestselling author of *Beach Read*

"Oliveras has been steadily growing her presence as a romance author, one with a knack for heartwarming family ensembles and a cozy sense of home. But *Island Affair* is her strongest work yet, perfectly calibrating its inviting family scenes with a sweet, heart-melting romance."

—E... *...ekly*

"I finished *Island Affair* with a big smile on my face. I can't decide what I adored more: Luis and Sara's love story; their relationships with their complicated and difficult and loving families; or the setting of Key West, which sounded so beautiful I wanted to jump on a plane. I can't wait to read more by Priscilla Oliveras!"

—Jasmine Guillory, *New York Times* bestselling author

"Oliveras's outstanding debut tangles romance into family life . . . The realistic, multifaceted characters have interesting nuances, and Oliveras never stoops to employing contrived misunderstandings, instead creating real obstacles with meaning and depth. Moving familial relationships and splashes of Puerto Rican culture round out this splendid contemporary and bode well for the future of the series."

—*Publishers Weekly* (starred review), *His Perfect Partner*

"Warm, sweet, and spicy in just the right amounts . . . A delicious read!"

—Kristan Higgins, *New York Times* bestselling author, *His Perfect Partner*

"Oliveras tops her excellent debut, *His Perfect Partner*, with this revelatory, realistic second romance set among the Puerto Rican community in contemporary Chicago . . . [Her] integration of cultural and class differences, familial expectations, and career objectives into the couple's romantic decision-making immeasurably enriches a moving plot about good people making difficult choices."

—*Publishers Weekly* (starred review), *Her Perfect Affair*

"Rising author Oliveras continues her excellent contemporary Matched to Perfection series featuring three Latina sisters, following the acclaimed *His Perfect Partner* (2017) . . . Oliveras infuses warmth, intelligence, and emotion into this refreshing read."

—*Booklist* (starred review), *Her Perfect Affair*

"The word I use the most often for Ms. Oliveras's writing is *warm*. I feel comfortable in whatever world she's created for me, and I usually love spending time with her people. You know those houses you walk into and there is something delicious-smelling in the kitchen, and you are welcomed with hugs and told to take your shoes off and within seconds you completely belong? That's Ms. Oliveras's writing . . . If you're a fan of second chances, I cannot recommend this enough. Warning, though, the descriptions of the warm breezes of the Florida Keys may just have you booking a flight!"

—All About Romance, *Island Affair*

"Delightful romance author Priscilla Oliveras offers an amuse-bouche of a holiday treat with this novella . . . Oliveras's own love for her family and passion for the great American pastime shines through as bright as a Christmas light."

—*Entertainment Weekly*, *Holiday Home Run*

"Priscilla Oliveras comes through with a sweet novella filled with charm and spirit, *Holiday Home Run*. *Holiday Home Run* gives us a beautiful peek into the vibrant lives of Puerto Ricans celebrating the holiday season, a memorably strong and smart heroine, and a hero who is charming and sexy."

—All About Romance, *Holiday Home Run*

"Such a sweet treat to get you in the upcoming holiday mood. Author Priscilla Oliveras has a hit to add to your Christmas reading list this year."

—*Mid-Life Goddess Books*, *Holiday Home Run*

"Oliveras's marvelous third Matched to Perfection contemporary (after *Her Perfect Affair*) tackles domestic violence and policing in Chicago's Puerto Rican community with superb nuance . . . Oliveras's tangled, topical conflicts between multidimensional characters blend with lovingly portrayed family life and an intricate, realistic plot, enmeshing the reader in her created world."

—*Publishers Weekly* (starred review), *Their Perfect Melody*

"Readers will feel utterly carried away . . . Whether you're well versed in Puerto Rican culture or completely new to it, Oliveras welcomes readers into a space that feels both familiar and new and exciting . . . A romantic, diverting melody."

—*Entertainment Weekly*, *Their Perfect Melody*

"Sexy, sassy, and overflowing with music, complex emotions, and family-loving Latinx American and Puerto Rican characters, this romance is a compelling, often joyful read and perfectly wraps up the Perfection trilogy."

—*Library Journal*, *Their Perfect Melody*

WEST SIDE LOVE STORY

OTHER TITLES BY PRISCILLA OLIVERAS

Keys to Love Series

Island Affair
Anchored Hearts

Matched to Perfection Series

His Perfect Partner
Her Perfect Affair
Their Perfect Melody

Paradise Key Series

Resort to Love

Novellas

Holiday Home Run, digital only

Anthologies

Summer in the City, "Lights Out"
A Season to Celebrate, "Holiday Home Run"
Amor Actually, "Meet Me Under the Mistletoe"

WEST SIDE LOVE STORY

PRISCILLA OLIVERAS

Published by Montlake, Seattle

www.apub.com

ISBN-13: 9781542031233
ISBN-10: 1542031230

Cover design by Faceout Studio, Jeff Miller

Cover illustration by Lucia Picerno

Printed in the United States of America

To the real Arturo and Berta: my paternal grandparents, Arthur and Bertha Hettler. Parents of nine children themselves, all raised on San Antonio's West Side, and grandparents and great-grandparents to many, who were showered with love and laughter and raised with your example of how familia cares for each other. Our dance parties in your living room on C Street are some of the best memories of my childhood. I love and miss you!

In the heart of San Antonio, a city lush and culturally rich,
A long-simmering rivalry heatens, rising to a fevered pitch.
Competition grows fierce; lines once boldly drawn, now foolishly crossed.
As lives become entangled, relationships once strong may ultimately be lost.

Two young lovers unwillingly swept up in the brewing storm.
One adolescent fraught from the circumstances in which she was born.
Around and between them a flurry of unwise decisions are made.
Before the howling winds can settle, consequences must be weighed.

Will blustery rage be calmed, its fires doused or remain ablaze?
Come, join our young lovers' tumultuous journey and boldly turn the page.

Prologue

The heavy bass thumping through strategically placed speakers around the rooftop club's indoor section pounded to the matching beat of Mariana Capuleta's throbbing headache and the syncopated strobe lights blinding her. Of course, it didn't help that the guy gyrating his pelvis into her backside had ignored the not-interested glare she'd given him. Twice. Nor did the girl on Mariana's right, repeatedly hip-bumping her to the *bom bom bom* rhythm of Maluma's latest hit.

"Ay, watch it!" Mariana yelled, ducking under the elbow of the husky guy flailing in front of her.

He flashed a smile, his chin jutting to the song's beat as he moved closer. He eyed her black, formfitting tank dress, his interest snagging on the amount of leg the midthigh hem exposed. She resisted the urge to tug down the material, which hit a couple of inches higher than she preferred. That's why she rarely borrowed from her shorter, petite-framed sister's closet. But earlier tonight, when Mariana had stopped by Cat's place after finishing her shift at the hospital, her younger sister had guilted Mariana into slipping on the stretchy dress to ring in the new year together.

"You rarely do anything fun," Cat had accused, before throwing her ace on the table. "C'mon, girl, you know you don't want me to go alone."

Ahhhh, the little sneak knew Mariana's weak spot. Since their teen years, she'd often been Cat's—or any of their sisters'—wingwoman. The responsible one making sure her younger siblings stayed safe.

That's why, instead of a quiet night of *The Great British Baking Show* streaming with a glass of cabernet, Mariana found herself a human pinball bouncing off her much more excited . . . more inebriated . . . fellow revelers.

The elbow flailer–turned-ogler licked his lips as he gave her body several once-overs, paying particular attention to her cleavage. Hunger glinted in his eyes. Biting his lower lip, he hip-swiveled closer, arm extended to place his beefy hand on her right hip.

No *Oye, wanna dance?* from this guy. Like everyone else out here, he took it for granted that braving the packed dance floor signaled her willingness to partner with anyone who approached her regardless of whether they struck her fancy.

Before she could put her palm on his shoulder to maintain some distance between her torso and his sweaty one, a young woman wearing a backless, sparkly halter dress slid in front of Mariana. Draping her arms around the guy's shoulders, the woman plastered herself against him. The guy's hand slid from Mariana's hip to the girl's. Grinning, he ducked his head to greet her with an openmouthed kiss. Seconds later, the couple bumped and grinded in a sensuous groove that would have had the nuns at Mariana's old junior high breaking out their rulers.

The DJ mixed into a popular J.Lo song, and the crowd swelled around Mariana in a claustrophobia-inducing crunch. She coughed, gagging under the cloudy mix of perfume, cologne, and perspiration.

Dios mío, at twenty-nine she was getting too old for this scene.

Then again, it had never really been her scene no matter her age. More like Cat's. Who had managed to get lost somewhere in the melee. When the blonde beside Mariana resumed her go-to hip-bump move, Mariana threw in the towel. Water and then fresh air were in order before she asphyxiated from the cloying atmosphere.

"Excuse me. Perdóname," she repeated as she pushed her way through the crowd. Lifting up on her toes, she craned her neck, searching for her sister's gold dress near the restroom area. Between the swarm of bodies, the glare of the strobe lights, and the blasts of fog billowing from the DJ stand, finding her pint-size sister proved a fruitless endeavor. This place had to be pushing the fire-code limit.

The line to order from the bar was three people deep, so Mariana wove her way to the far end, closer to the glass doors leading to the outside terrace.

"Water?" she called to the barback. She mimed taking a drink and mouthed the word at his raised-brow inquiry.

"Hey, mamacita, lookin' good."

The thick drawl and beer breath wafting along her cheek had Mariana ducking to the side. Mr. Dirty Dancing with the pelvic thrusts on the dance floor had followed her. Great.

She shook her head and waved him off with a flutter of her fingers. "Not interested."

"C'mon. We were having fun." His drunken slur garbled the words into one long string of syllables.

Despite the dim lighting, she noticed his glassy, bloodshot eyes, the constricted pupils dotting their centers. A sweaty sheen blanketed his flushed cheeks and pale face. Classic signs of inebriation she'd noted countless times over the years as an ER nurse.

"Lemme buy you a shot."

"No thanks. I'm good."

He listed to the side, falling against a tall, broad-shouldered man who stood with his back to them. The man pitched forward, amid complaints from others around them. Thankfully, the woman standing belly to the bar in front of Mariana turned, holding aloft two plastic cups with lime wedges teetering on their rims. As the woman eased by, trying not to spill her drinks, Mariana shifted to take her place. Pointedly ignoring the drunkard and the commotion he'd created behind her.

Rather than take the hint and get lost, the jerk made the mistake of palming her butt cheek.

Fuming, she spun around to plant her hand on his chest, stiff-arming him away. "Back off!"

Glassy eyes wide with shock, the jerk stumbled backward.

"Hey! I've been looking all over for you!"

Mariana blinked at the friendly greeting from the tall, broad-shouldered, and—now that he faced her, she noticed—really hot guy the drunkard had bumped into. His wide mouth curved with an amiable smile that had laugh lines crinkling the edges of dark eyes. Eyes that, unlike those of many around them, appeared clear. Lucid. And if she wasn't mistaken, they currently telegraphed an are-you-okay message at her.

She shied away as he reached an arm out, then realized he did so to take her cup of water from the barback.

"The rest of our group's outside. Wanna go find them?" The stranger tipped his head at the expansive windows overlooking the patio. An invitation, rather than an expectation that she would readily follow.

The drunkard started to complain, but the newcomer's features hardened into a fierce glare. The muscle in his jaw ticked as he rocked forward on the balls of his feet in a ready-to-pounce stance should the inebriated guy try a dumb move. Apparently not so sauced that he'd lost all ability for rational thought, the handsy jerk slunk away.

Intrigued—maybe even slightly charmed, though she could have dealt with the jerk herself—Mariana tilted her chin up to find her handsome savior staring at her. His worry-tinged expression softened the angular features of his deeply tanned face in a compelling combination that had her unable to look away. The sincerity in his dark eyes spoke to her. Calmed the pulse she hadn't even realized was racing.

He tipped his head toward the patio again. Another polite invitation for her to join him. Intrigued, she nodded. His lips curved in a tempting smile, and he shot her a flirtatious wink a second before dipping his shoulder to forge a path through the crowd. Mariana grabbed on to the back of his sports coat, creating a two-person chain that allowed her to stick close to him, as if doing so were natural.

Moments later, he pushed open the double-paned glass door, holding it and stepping slightly aside for her to exit first. Her bare shoulder inadvertently grazed his chest as she squeezed by. The friction sent pinpricks of awareness shimmying across her collarbone. A fresh breeze rushed over her, dispelling the oppressiveness of inside and gifting her with a hint of his woodsy, slightly spicy cologne. Desire curled in her belly. It spiraled lower with unexpected intensity, and she nearly dropped the cup of water he handed her.

"Th-thank you," she murmured.

Taking a hefty swig of the cool liquid, she led the way on shaky legs. A few steps onto the wide terrace, she halted to take in the trendy club's outdoor space, with its black leather love seats and ottomans and austere mood lighting provided by Edison bulbs in clear glass shades atop tall silver poles that dotted the space. Above them, a skyful of tiny stars sparkled like diamond dust tossed across an inky velvet. The downtown San Antonio skyline sprawled for miles, its buildings decorated with festive lights flickering their greeting. Her city throbbed with vibrant energy as the excitement of a new year, new goals, and resolutions approached.

The picturesque view had drawn a crowd outdoors, which meant all the seating options were taken. Mariana scanned the shadowy patio for a gap in the row of people gathered along the four-foot-high glass barrier lining the perimeter. Spotting an opening near the far corner, she picked up her pace.

Her stilettos tapped the white tile flooring as she cut a glance over her shoulder, hoping the intriguing stranger followed. Instinctively, she reached backward for him. He hooked his fingers with hers. Flashed his engaging smile. And, ay Dios mío, her heart fluttered in a way it never had before.

A delighted giddiness hummed inside her, and she jerked her head around to watch where she was going. At the same time, a tiny voice in the back of her mind cautioned her to pull herself together.

This reaction . . . her belly jittery, her breath quickening . . . it was . . . bueno, it was foolish. Nonsensical. Words few, if any, would ordinarily use to describe her. She must be more exhausted than she realized. Back-to-back-to-back shifts at the hospital filling in for fellow nurses traveling over the holidays had caught up with her. And yet . . .

Her fingers flexed, tightening their grip with his. The pad of his thumb brushed the back of her knuckles, and intimate parts of her body reacted as if he'd caressed their secret spots.

She swallowed, unnerved by her heated response.

By the time they made it to the railing, the gap she'd spotted had lessened while her anticipation had increased. Mariana tucked herself in sideways, leaving him room to do the same. Opposite elbows hooked on the glass ledge, they faced each other, mere inches apart.

Out here, the deafening noise of the music and rowdy revelers inside was dampened. Conversations buzzed at normal decibels while the DJ's tunes played softly in the background. Waiters carrying trays of drinks and fancy appetizers made the rounds, and the faint sound of car horns and traffic on the street twenty stories below drifted on the chilly air. For Mariana, it all melded into inconsequential white noise as she sipped her water and sneaked glances at the captivating stranger from under her lashes.

A dark sports coat skimmed the expanse of his broad shoulders. He had forgone a tie, leaving his pale-blue oxford unbuttoned at his throat. The shirt was tucked into a pair of relaxed-fit, straight-leg jeans that rode low on his trim hips, the pants' hem brushing his black cowboy boots. His more casual version of the "happy hour" dress code the bash required appealed to her as someone who spent most days in hospital scrubs and rarely wore much makeup except during mariachi band gigs and the occasional night out with coworkers or her sisters. Like tonight, when she'd reluctantly agreed to Cat's ministrations and wound up with sexy, smoky eyes and artfully tousled curls in the long black hair she usually wore pulled back out of the way.

However, it wasn't this man's attire that ensnared her attention.

No, it was the banked yet open interest glinting along with the reflection of a nearby Edison bulb in his sable eyes. The friendly smile tugging up the corners of his mouth again, the left side slightly—adorably—higher than the other. The polite distance he maintained but that she oddly found herself wanting to diminish.

Oddly because, ask any of her sisters, Mariana didn't *do* the pick-up-someone-at-a-bar routine. She didn't have time for uncomfortable morning-afters or the ill-advised walk of shame home. This pulse-sparking arousal he elicited? No doubt it led to T-R-O-U-B-L-E.

Although sometimes a little trouble could be fun . . .

No! If she were wise, she'd say thanks for his assistance, then head back inside to find Cat. It had to be close to midnight and Happy New Year hugs.

"I appreciate you helping me out back there," she offered, gesturing with her now-empty plastic cup.

"Looked like you had it under control. I was more like backup." His grin widened. Her traitorous heart fluttered again. "Nice stiff-arm move."

"Years of watching Cowboy football games and refereeing sister squabbles."

The low, rumbly chuckle that shook his shoulders played havoc with her resolve to keep their conversation short.

"Guys like that pendejo inside give the rest of us a bad rap." He grimaced with obvious distaste. The wind kicked up, teasing the short black waves in his hair. "I just had to deal with a kid sending inappropriate texts to my fourteen-year-old sister. Makes me leery to think of her being in a situation where another idiot like the one back there refuses to take no for an answer."

So, he had a little sister. One he obviously cared about, based on the worried frown creasing his forehead and angling his brows. As the oldest in her familia, Mariana could relate to that sentiment.

His beleaguered sigh endeared him a little more, and Mariana found herself wanting to press a fingertip to the tiny divot between his brows and smooth away his concern.

"The best thing you can do is teach her to stand up for herself. Enroll her in a self-defense class."

"Make sure she's got a strong stiff-arm, huh?" He bent one elbow as if cradling a football and extended his other arm in the classic Heisman Trophy pose.

Mariana laughed, charmed by his lighthearted teasing. She swatted playfully at his arm, and her fingers caught on his coat sleeve. Their gazes met. Held.

Their shared laughter slowly dissipated as a charged silence swirled around them. The wintry breeze whispered over them and Mariana shivered.

"Here, you've gotta be cold."

Quickly shrugging off his sports coat, he draped it over her shoulders, enveloping her with his warmth. His fingers caressed her neck as he adjusted the collar. Her breath caught, and his fingers stilled. She stared up at him, an irresistible pull drawing her closer.

"Thirty seconds!" The cry rang out through the club's speakers, setting off a flurry of activity as revelers hurried to prepare for the countdown.

Mariana remained rooted to her spot. Caught under a spell woven by attraction and a peculiar sense of shared kinship that she couldn't explain.

His eyes searched hers. Questioning. Almost . . . hopeful?

"Ten . . . nine . . . eight . . ." Revelers joined the DJ's countdown.

Mariana placed a hand on the man's chest, curling her fingers in his shirt.

"Seven . . . six . . . five . . ."

She licked her lips. Watched him track the motion. Felt his grip on the lapels of his coat tighten.

"Three . . . two . . . one!"

The city's fireworks burst in the sky above them. Cheers rang out. Pandemonium ensued as people embraced and couples kissed.

Mariana slowly rose up onto her toes. His head ducked closer, one hand sliding along her neck to cup her nape. His eyes drifted closed seconds before his lips touched hers.

Something brighter, more fiery, than any firework exploded inside her.

Dropping the cup, she slid both arms around his waist and pressed herself against him. He groaned, or maybe it was her, and their chaste peck morphed into a sensual, delectable, openmouthed kiss. He tasted of mint and rum and sin. A heady combination that left her woozy and wanting more.

Her palms explored his muscular back, reveling at the dips and curves that elicited a lusty moan deep in her throat. His fingers tangled in her hair, and desire pooled through her as he deepened their kiss. Hugging him tighter, she met his tongue stroke for delicious stroke.

Suddenly someone bumped into her from behind, knocking her off balance. Her ankle twisted, and she gasped. The sharp pain jolted her back to reality.

"Are you okay?" he asked, another worried frown sliding over his handsome face.

Dismayed at her behavior, she drew back and quickly divested herself of his coat. She winced as she stepped aside.

"I have to go. Here. Um, thank you." Evading his attempt to cup her elbow in support, she shoved his coat at him. "Happy . . ." Embarrassed heat crawled up her face. "Happy New Year."

Without waiting for him to respond, she turned and fled, her right ankle screaming at her to slow down. Other parts of her body screaming for her to go back.

"Wait! I don't know your name!"

Her gut clenched at his cry. ¡Dios mío! They hadn't even exchanged names, yet she'd plastered herself against him like they were old lovers.

Mortified, she wove through the crowd, praying she'd find Cat quickly.

"Don't sit at home. That's so boring. Let's start the Año Nuevo with a bang," her sister had suggested as part of her persuasive argument.

Ha! *Boring* wouldn't even begin to describe the start of Mariana's new year.

But with scholarship hunting and tuition worries and familia responsibilities hounding her, she couldn't afford bad decisions or any distractions. As delectable as the one she'd just left outside might appear.

She'd do well to think of tonight as simply a brief but pleasurable interlude with a beguiling stranger she'd never see again.

Chapter One

"Tell me the truth: Are you absolutely sure we're ready for this?"

The whispered question came from just behind Mariana's left shoulder. Barely audible above the din of their band's performance preparation in the largest of the community center's music rooms. Still, the inquiry was fraught with enough uncertainty, enough fear, that Mariana knew the "this" her sister referred to.

She angled her translucent-powder compact to catch her younger sister Blanca's bleak reflection in the round mirror. Ignoring the strum of guitar and violin strings, the *shush shush* of egg shakers, and the smattering of conversations, Mariana concentrated on the doubts looming like tornado-warning storm clouds in Blanca's hazel eyes.

Swallowing the *We sure as hell better be* response on the tip of her tongue, Mariana snapped her compact closed. The decision had already been made. Their application for the Battle of the Mariachi Bands had been submitted and, gracias a Dios, Mariachi Las Nubes had been selected.

As the oldest among the medley of girls who had landed on Arturo and Berta Capuleta's doorstep over the years, Mariana knew many of the others would take their cues from her. So, rather than voice her personal concerns about the bold plan their sister Catalina had managed to put into motion—one that required a bigger time commitment to the band just as Mariana was trying to figure out how to decrease her involvement when she started the physician-assistant program—she dropped her powder compact into her makeup pouch and zipped it closed. Schooling her features into the serene everything's-going-to-be-okay expression that soothed countless patients in her ER, she turned to face Blanca, the consummate worrywart among the eight Capuleta sisters.

Bueno, nine if you counted the most recent foster daughter their parents had opened their home to six months ago. The one currently grounded—a.k.a. on Capuleta house arrest, as Nina complained—after her ill-fated stunt. It remained to be seen whether, like the rest of them, the teen would eventually turn that all-important corner. The one taking her from being angry at the world to realizing her luck at joining the Capuleta familia.

"We can still back out, right?" Blanca asked.

The bordering-on-frantic question had Mariana squelching her frustration over Nina's impetuous act to deal with the problem in front of her.

"Even if that was an option, we can't. We won't. Think of the important example we're setting, Blanca. The first all-female band in the Battle. Plus, we need that winner's pot to help save the center."

"There has to be some other way to help Papo and Mamá, right?" Blanca pleaded.

"No, there isn't. Believe me, I've tried everything I can think of."

Even offering to put some of her saved tuition money toward the private loan company's ridiculous balloon payment. Papo had flat out refused.

"Entering and winning is the best way to get our hands on the cash we need. Fast." Mariana clasped her sister's shoulders and peered intently at Blanca, summoning every ounce of confidence she possessed. "All those young girls out there"—she jerked her head toward the music room's door and the quinceañera party out back in the courtyard—"they're counting on us to represent. We can *absolutely* do this."

Fake it until you become it. The mantra swiped from an old TED Talk her therapist had recommended wormed its way through Mariana's head. She didn't have the luxury of showing any sign of doubt. Far too many relied on her to be the voice of reason and reassurance.

And right now, minutes before Mariachi Las Nubes was set to hit the stage, Mariana needed Blanca focused on their gig. On doing their best to make Felicia Bonavilla's quinceañera memorable, in a the-band-rocked-our-world way. Not a the-band-sucked-rocks way.

With word out that Las Nubes had made the cut for the Battle, eyes and ears and cameras were more sharply focused on their band than usual. The naysayers, those who held fast to the patriarchal idea that the mariachi world was a man's world—like some of their Battle competitors—expected Las Nubes to fail.

That meant even less room for error once Mariana and her sisters took the stage. Even before that. Once they walked out of this room dressed in full charro, they had to be ready.

That's why, like always, she planned on ensuring nothing went wrong.

"We've got this," she assured the doubter among their group.

Blanca's frown deepened, her brow wrinkling like a Shar-Pei puppy's. She nibbled her lower lip, biting off the red tint that matched the shade each of the sisters wore for their show. "But you saw Papo's reaction when Cat first brought up the Battle. He doesn't want us having anything to do with . . . well, you-know-who."

The black coffee and protein bar Mariana had inhaled on her race here after her shift at the hospital churned in her belly. Her sister had a point.

Papo's rare show of machismo when he forbade them to enter the Battle was something Mariana and her sisters weren't used to. Not from him anyway.

From the day Mariana had arrived, a year before Cat and Blanca, with nothing but her beat-up rolling suitcase and the weight of sorrow mixed with pent-up fear heavy in her chest, Papo had proven himself to be patient and slow to anger. Except when it came to one person, and one person alone. The reason behind Papo's opposition to Las Nubes joining the competition.

Hugo Montero.

Papo's archnemesis and the leader of Los Reyes, the Battle's reigning champions.

The He-Who-Must-Not-Be-Named within the walls of Casa Capuleta. Both the first-floor community center owned and run by Arturo and Berta Capuleta and the familia's actual home in the apartments above the center.

The feud had begun decades ago after a betrayal by Papo's nemesis had destroyed their friendship, broken up the men's band, and put them on opposite sides when it came to gentrification efforts in San Antonio. The animosity eventually trickled down to the younger generation. At first, due to familia loyalty; more recently, because of Hugo and his band's insistence in joining the patriarchal cries that an all-female mariachi didn't hold with tradition.

"Are you absolutely sure going head-to-head against our most vocal critics is smart?" Ever the conflict avoider, Blanca winced at her own question.

Across the music room, Cat glanced up from helping their youngest sister with her guitar fingering for a new song Cat had written. She arched a brow, lips pursed in a wry should-I-step-in moue.

Resolve whooshed through Mariana, scattering her own unspoken, more personal—and thus unimportant—qualms about the competition. Her familia had to come first.

As the two oldest and barely a year apart in age, she and Cat had made a pact. Whatever it took to save Casa Capuleta and show the students in the community center's all-female mariachi music class that yes, they did belong there . . . Cat and Mariana would do it.

While Mariana shouldered the added responsibility of ensuring that her strong-willed, occasionally hotheaded sis didn't cross an inopportune line.

Cat shifted as if to stand, and Mariana gave the tiniest shake of her head. If Cat stepped in, her impatience would only fuel Blanca's unease. The two biological sisters might share the same heart-shaped faces, hazel eyes, pert noses, and petite builds, but like the guitar and the smaller vihuela—both members of the same string family—Blanca's and Cat's personalities sang decidedly different tunes.

None of them were sure how, but their mom had convinced Papo to grudgingly give his blessing for the girls to throw their collective mariachi sombrero in the Battle. In typical fashion, Blanca worried about the "grudgingly" while Cat grabbed on to the "blessing" and ran full speed ahead like Papo's favorite running back, Hall of Famer Emmitt Smith, racing with the football to the end zone.

With Cat focused on ways to jazz up their show, Mariana's job remained to ensure the rest of her sisters stayed mentally up to the task.

She gave Blanca's shoulders a tight squeeze. "We've been building to this point with each gig and festival we've booked. It might sound like a big step, but as our musical director, Catalina believes we're ready. Imagine the confidence boost for our students when they see us up on that stage. Plus, the prize money will get the loan shark to back off."

"Sí, pero only if we win."

"We will. I know we can."

"Oye, what are you two whispering about over there?" Jutting her chin in Mariana and Blanca's direction, Violeta set her guitar on the floor between her folding chair and her twin's. "Is Ms. The Sky is Falling still fretting about the Battle?"

The three teens, gathered in a horseshoe off to the left where they rehearsed with Cat, giggled at Violeta's teasing.

Blanca glared over her shoulder at Violeta. "Cállate. This is serious."

Violeta opened her mouth to fire a comeback, but her twin placed a hand on her arm. Sabrina's disappointed look silenced Violeta faster than Blanca's "shut up" could.

"Look, we know that this is serious." Cat strode toward Mariana and Blanca. Her black skirt, with its red-rose embroidery and gold Gala trailing down the sides, swished against her heeled boots. "We're the first all-female band to make it into the Battle. We all know the importance of who and what we represent. Plus, Mamá and Papo losing this building to that pendejo down the block who runs a scam of a business he calls a private lending company can't happen. I won't let—"

"*We* won't let that happen," Mariana interrupted. "We're a team. Siempre Capuletas." She emphasized their heartfelt battle cry with a fist raised high.

"Always Capuletas," Cat repeated, chin tipped up in a proud angle.

"Ven. Gather 'round." Mariana waved the others over to form a hand-holding circle. "The five of us older girls have been playing together for what seems like forever." Mariana looked from Cat to Blanca to the twins. "And you girls . . ." She smiled with encouragement at the three teenagers. "You came to us just a few years ago, and look how you've grown as musicians."

"You're welcome for that," Cat teased, lips curved with a self-satisfied grin.

Mariana rolled her eyes. "Humble much, hermanita?"

"Bueno, when they're taught by the lead mariachi music instructor at the famed Casa Capuleta Community Center, what more do you expect?"

"Oh, so we're 'famed' now, huh?" Mariana pointed at her younger sisters. "Did you girls catch that? Mind you, don't let it go to your head, you hear?"

"When you got it, flaunt it." Cat blew on her red-painted nails, then buffed them on her jacket's lapel.

A mix of groans and chuckles filled their circle.

"Yes, we will," Mariana asserted. "Papo and Mamá shared their love of music while giving each of us the home and familia we needed. For different reasons, but needed all the same. Now we have a chance to use our talents to positively influence others. And help save the place that's sacred to us and our comunidad."

"We wouldn't have to worry about saving Casa Capuleta if Nina hadn't started that stupid fire in the center's kitchen," one of the younger girls grumbled.

"Hey, enough of that," Mariana chided. The guilt on the faces of the three teens warned her this wasn't the first time the trio had shared a similar accusation with each other.

Disappointment tightened her chest. If the teens shut out their newest sister, it would be even harder for Nina to find her place here. And despite the fourteen-year-old's pissy attitude, Mariana sensed Nina's need to belong. To feel safe among people she could trust. Mariana had been there once.

She glanced at the music room's ceiling as if she could see through it to the two floors of apartments above them. "Yes, Nina screwed up by *accidentally* starting that fire in the center's kitchen. But it actually brought to light the building's faulty wiring. A problem that could have led to a much worse incident. We can't blame her for the loan Papo and Mamá needed to fix everything to code when the only other option was to kick out the tenants and shut down the community center."

"Yeah, we're blaming the cabrón private lender for demanding the balloon payment and threatening to sell the loan to the developer scum intent on erasing our comunidad with their gentrification plans." Cat's disgusted snarl mirrored the anger roiling in Mariana's chest. Such an injustice! And the jerk was from their own neighborhood.

Before, saying no to entering the competition because of the extra practice hours it demanded—hours that would cut into her physician-assistant shadowing and scholarship-interview prep—had been difficult enough. Doing so meant potentially disappointing the young girls who looked up to Las Nubes. Now, the prize money had become a necessity instead of a luxury. No way she'd back down or bow out like Blanca wanted. Mariana would simply figure out how to fit everything into her schedule.

Silently, she repeated the vow she had made the day Berta and Arturo had asked her permission to file for legal adoption—nothing bad would ever happen to her familia on her watch. Not if she could do something to stop it, as she believed would have been the case had her birth mother not hidden her illness.

"So, what's the plan?" Violeta asked, interrupting Mariana's troubled thoughts.

Blanca's hand tightened around Mariana's—Ms. The Sky is Falling signaling the doubts she still harbored. Based on the uncertainty shadowing Sabrina's face, she wasn't as on board with them competing as her twin appeared to be.

Damn, the last thing the band needed was a self-confidence problem.

Mariana glanced across the circle at Cat to gauge her reaction. Technically, Mariana was their group leader. The responsibility naturally fell to her as the eldest. Artistically, though, Cat held the reins. A powerhouse on the guitar, vihuela, and piano, Cat had musical skills that far exceeded the rest of theirs. She created the arrangements, wrote new material, and worked alongside their mamá teaching the music lessons the center offered.

"The plan is for us to win!" Cat said, her tone firm.

"I agree with Catalina," Mariana told the others. "We've got what it takes. We're the only first-time competitors, so they've never seen our act. More importantly, we're the first all-female group to make the cut. We've always known that we have an obligation to represent. To join other women out there proving that, as mujeres, we belong. The Battle of the Mariachi Bands gives us a higher platform to do that."

"It also means we can't afford to second-guess ourselves, because we'll be dealing with attitude from other groups. Especially Los Reyes. We know they're *all* asses with their machismo BS." Cat's red lips twisted with a sneer as she mentioned the band led by Papo's old nemesis.

"So, we quiet them by blowing them away with our talent," Violeta said. She bumped her shoulder against her twin's with a teasing grin, chasing away Sabrina's worry.

"Exactly," Mariana added. "Remember that festival in Austin? The judges and audience loved us! Ever since, Cat's been vying for us to book bigger gigs."

"And we can't get any bigger than winning the fifty-thousand-dollar prize and the chance to open for none other than El Príncipe Patricio Galán," Cat cried.

"A-ha-ha-haiiiiy!" Violeta let out a guttural grito of appreciation for the handsome crooner whose record label had agreed to sponsor this year's competition, doubling the prize money and adding the coveted opening-act spot for the internationally known mariachi singer's upcoming San Antonio concert.

The teens crumpled against each other in matching swoons, hands clutched to their chests. Even Blanca apparently got a little weak-kneed thinking about the well-known ladies' man, releasing Mariana's hand to fan her pink-flushed face.

Mariana shook her head as she snickered at their fangirl antics. "You all are too much."

"What? Even you, who says you never have time to date and probably haven't been out since I dragged you to the New Year's Eve bash, have got to admit that Galán makes your body tingle in all those places you learned about in anatomy class," Cat taunted.

New Year's Eve.

Mariana pressed a hand to her suddenly racing heart. Her sisters dissolved into laughter, probably thinking she was mooning over Galán with them.

Violeta and the teens wiped tears from their eyes, while Mariana . . . Bueno, she tried, again, to wipe the memory of her illicit NYE kiss with the handsome stranger. A kiss she hadn't divulged to anyone. A kiss she had relived over and over. No matter how often she told herself to forget about it.

"Doesn't matter who's the biggest fangirl here," Mariana told them. "What does is that we're gonna have to buckle down. Practice more. Not let ourselves get distracted by anything, or anyone, once the competition starts."

As if a switch had been flipped inside her, Cat instantly sobered. The gleam in her eye changed from playful to determined. "Sí. Think about all the music industry influencers who will be there. Or watching the videos. This is a chance to kick down the door far too many try to shut in our faces."

Cat jabbed a fist on her cocked hip, her expression fierce. Often, her tempestuous nature pushed the rest of them to try harder. Making their band even better. It also reminded Mariana that she'd have to be on her toes, ensuring her sister didn't snap at the wrong person in the heat of the competition.

"Okay, enough Battle chatter. We've got a show to do. Ven. Come on." Mariana wiggled her hand for Blanca to clasp. Once their circle was complete again, she bowed her head to begin their usual preperformance prayer.

A group "Amén" later, they scattered around the room for a final makeup check and to collect their instruments.

A few minutes later, her trumpet clutched tightly against her chest, Mariana strode to the door. "¿Todas listas?"

The tap of their black heeled boots against the aging linoleum answered her "are you ready" as the girls formed two lines. Two impressive lines of *puras mujeres fuertes*, as their mom liked to say. Pure strong women, dressed in their mariachi finery, honoring both their culture's history and the feminist changes many before and now many alongside them pushed for.

Shoulders back, head high and proud, Mariana trailed her gaze from one sister to the next. Willing them to see and feel her confidence in them.

"Bueno. Let's go make Mamá and Papo and our Casa Capuleta students proud. Here comes this year's Battle of the Mariachi Bands champions!" she cried.

A smattering of "hell yeahs" and "sí's" answered her. Along with a "you bet your ass" from Cat.

As Mariana reached for the cool metal doorknob, she sucked in a deep, cleansing breath and sent a prayer above. The personal sacrifice the competition might demand from her didn't matter. Mariachi Las Nubes *had* to win.

She'd do whatever it took to make that happen.

Chapter Two

"We shouldn't be here." Angelo Montero shot his best friend a dubious side-eye as Marco slowed his beat-up Chevy truck for a red light at the intersection of South Las Moras and West Commerce.

"Why not? It's research, man."

Angelo huffed a breath between his teeth at his buddy's twisted rationale. "Yeah, right."

"Hey, you're into numbers and percentages and crap like that." Marco shrugged, clearly at ease with what Angelo considered a foolhardy idea. "Think of tonight as a way to increase our odds of winning the Battle."

"I shoulda stayed home."

"And make me do recon alone? C'mon, man, that's not cool!" Marco complained. "What the hell happened to 'womb to tomb, with you to the end'?"

"We were kids back then, güey. Back before everything . . ." Angelo shook his head, pushing away the past. "Forget it. I'm here. Still letting you talk me into harebrained ideas and praying they don't get us into trouble. Knowing they probably will."

He shifted in his seat to gaze out the passenger-side window at the three-story brick building looming on the far-right corner. Casa Capuleta. Enemy territory, if you asked his uncle.

A faded red-and-green awning shaded the cracked sidewalk in front of the entrance. The words Casa Capuleta were scrawled in black script on the top half of the glass door. Fanning out along the weathered bricked facade, under the length of wide windows on either side of the door, a hodgepodge of planters with brightly colored flowers valiantly tried to give the aging building a welcoming feel.

Even with its run-down appearance, the modest neighborhood community center with its two stories of apartments above garnered raving online reviews for the public and private events and various arts classes it offered. This despite the slightly dilapidated neighborhood with its shabby storefronts, cracked sidewalks, and dimly lit back alleys probably best left untraveled late at night.

As the CPA for his tío Hugo's property brokerage firm, Angelo knew the Pearl District and other projects on the east side of San Antonio had already proven worth his uncle's investment. With gentrification efforts now moving into the west side, Hugo had been eyeing and acquiring properties over here, intent on getting himself a piece of the action.

Angelo slowly glanced up and down Las Moras Street. His tío was right. This part of town could use some sprucing up. When that happened, Casa Capuleta would only benefit. Business would surely pick up, even though word around town and in their close-knit musical circles was that Casa Capuleta's monthly mariachi night regularly packed the center's back courtyard already. Supposedly people of all ages came in droves, eager to pay five bucks a head to benefit various neighborhood causes. Food trucks parked out front or people brought their own snacks and drinks, then spent the evening dining and dancing outdoors, enjoying the music of Casa Capuleta's all-female band, Mariachi Las Nubes.

A band that had been making a name for themselves in recent years, booking larger gigs, winning or placing in festival competitions, even when faced with pushback from people holding fast to traditional views. Like his tío. Based on their growing reputation, Angelo wasn't surprised that Las Nubes was one of the eight contestants in this year's Battle of the Mariachi Bands. The same could not be said for his uncle.

Shortly after the news went live online yesterday, his tío Hugo had stormed into the downtown office, red-faced, steam practically blasting from his ears like one of those old cartoon characters.

"I don't know what the hell Arturo Capuleta's pea brain is thinking, pero that cabrón entered his daughters into *my* competition!" Tío Hugo had roared, slamming the office door behind him.

Angelo hadn't bothered pointing out that Las Nubes had been gaining in notoriety the past couple of years, so them entering the contest wasn't a far-fetched idea. His tío didn't care.

Not to mention, the competition didn't exactly *belong* to Hugo. Los Reyes had won for the first time only last year. That didn't matter to his tío either. Since the competition's inception five years ago, Hugo had coveted the Battle's top spot with a fervor that would have their parish priest making a sign of the cross and mumbling a prayer for his tío's soul.

It wasn't the prize money that drove Hugo's coveting. His property brokerage firm was thriving. Angelo should know; handling the accounting at El Rey Properties had been his job since he'd graduated from UT San Antonio's five-year Master of Accountancy program after transferring from UT Austin when his parents died. A move that had been Tío Hugo's strong "suggestion." Besides, the eight members of their band, Los Reyes, always split the pot they earned from gigs and competitions.

What his uncle desired, with an intensity rivaling the one felt by admirers of Frodo's infamous ring, was the bragging rights. It's why the gold trophy sat in a place of honor on their living room mantel while a framed photo of Los Reyes being crowned champions graced the firm's lobby wall.

For Angelo, winning had simply meant a modest bump in his monthly savings. But this year, with the jackpot doubled in size, winning meant a larger sum added to his secret house fund. An amount that would bring him one step closer to a down payment on a home for him and his little sister.

One step closer to opening his own consulting business.

One step closer to achieving a small sense of freedom and finally standing on his own. Out from under his tío's large shadow.

Guilt pricked Angelo's gut like cactus thorns poking his side. Embedded there ever since the first time he'd wished for his old life. His old dreams. Before parental responsibilities for his little sister had taken precedence over everything else.

Man, he hated sounding ungrateful for his uncle's assistance all these years. But Angelo was no longer a clueless college sophomore thrust into the role of guardian to his four-year-old sister after their parents were killed by a drunk driver. Back then, he'd been a kid himself, struggling with how to comfort a child who cried for her beloved mamá and papá in the middle of the night. Unsuccessfully juggling classes and a part-time job and the financial mess his parents had unwittingly left behind.

As Angelo's father's older, and only, brother, Tío Hugo had stepped in to handle everything. His support these past ten years had been a blessing. No doubt about it. Yet lately, more and more, Angelo couldn't help but feel that support came with strings. Ones that bound him to a career he had never intended to pursue until his uncle had brought it up. Then pushed.

"Familia helps familia, no?" Tío Hugo had insisted.

He had needed someone he could trust to manage the books as El Rey Properties continued flourishing. For Angelo, accounting wasn't a complete departure from his international business and finance degree. Plus, Hugo had offered to pay his college tuition. It had sounded like the right decision. At the time.

In more recent years, not so much.

But . . . familia helps familia.

Sometimes, the adage felt like a double-edged machete.

Saving money for his move out of his uncle's house was easy. Figuring out how to make the change without creating a rift between him and the prideful man who'd become his father figure during the most difficult time of Angelo's life . . . that all-important piece of the puzzle continued to elude him.

"You coming or what?" Marco tapped the roof of his truck and bent down to peer back inside.

Shaking off the stressful conundrum, Angelo realized that while he'd been lost in thought, his buddy had made a left turn and snagged a parking spot a block down. Now Marco stood on the worn asphalt, waiting for him.

"I sure as hell hope we don't regret this," Angelo muttered. "If Tío Hugo hears about our little visit—"

"Güey, if that happens, he'll slap us on the back, buy us a round, and praise our sneaky maneuverings. He'd probably take credit for the idea."

Angelo scowled at Marco's sly grin. "Cut it out. You know it annoys me when people imply there's something shady going on with the company. My tío's not like that."

"Man, chill." Marco tapped the truck's roof again. "We're just comin' to hear some música. Eso es todo."

"Yeah, that's all," Angelo repeated grimly.

He couldn't explain it. But ever since he'd learned that Las Nubes was in the competition with them, a weird sort of antsiness had twitched inside him. Like something was in the air. Something was coming. He just hoped it was something good.

Mumbling a curse, Angelo pushed open the passenger door. The rusty hinges groaned in protest. When they reached the intersection with the community center, the strains of a Mexican polka floated on the crisp March air. The large plate glass windows on either side of the front door revealed an empty, dimly lit lobby. Looked like the party was confined to the center's well-known back patio area, where online pics showed a small stage and dance floor holding court. Perfect for celebrations like the quinceañera Marco had heard about through the grapevine.

Angelo had never crashed a fifteen-year-old's birthday party before. Too bad his best friend remained undeterred.

Marco shoved his keys in a front pocket of his Wranglers, then jerked a thumb at the low wrought-iron gate on the left side of the building. A light pink sign with dark purple lettering announcing Private Event: Felicia Bonavilla Quinceañera Fiesta hung over the gate. A bouquet of white and purple helium-filled balloons floated above, bobbing in the slight breeze.

"It's invite only," Angelo tried again, still looking for an out.

"No one's gonna question us," Marco tossed over his shoulder. He gave a quick double take, then stopped with his hand on the metal latch. "Unless you don't wipe that something-smells-like-crap look off your face. It's a fiesta, not a funeral. Where's that handsome smile of yours?"

Marco made to pat Angelo's cheek, but Angelo ducked and swatted his buddy's hand away.

"C'mon, man. When was the last time you went out on a Saturday night?" Marco challenged.

"Last weekend."

Marco scoffed. "I mean on a date. Or a night of pool with the guys. Not the movies with your kid sister."

"I don't have time for stuff like that. With Tío looking to turn West San Antonio into a mini East Austin, I'm busy running numbers and combing through investment documents. Plus, Brenda's getting to that age when boys start sniffing around. You remember that mess back in January."

The wind whipped up, sending an aluminum can rattling down the sidewalk into the empty street. The jarring clatter matched the alarms clanging in his head at the memory of the kid from Brenda's school who had repeatedly texted, pushing her to send him a "sexy pic."

"Every time I think about that punk, I don't know whether I'm pissed or scared. Hell, it's usually both!"

Marco's bushy, dark brows rose to a comically surprised level. "Daaaamn. That's messed up."

"You're telling me! I damn near—" Angelo broke off when an older couple approached them from the building's side parking lot.

Underneath her open coat, the plump woman wore a long, lacy blue dress with shiny beading circling the neckline. Fancy attire that at first seemed out of place among the sun-worn storefronts, graffiti-splattered trash cans, and dingy streets. Obviously, she and her partner were headed to the quinceañera Angelo was about to crash.

The older man sported black slacks and a white oxford with a thin black tie, a black leather vest, and matching cowboy boots. Typical cocktail attire for many men in their comunidad. He tipped his cowboy hat in greeting at the same time the woman gave Angelo and Marco a polite smile.

"Buenas noches." Angelo tucked his chin in deference as he wished them good evening.

Once the older couple had passed through the wrought-iron gate and moved out of earshot, Marco spun back around to Angelo. "You never told me, did Hugo blow a gasket when he found out or what?"

"Are you kidding? I kept him out of it to avoid him blowing up and making it worse. I had Brenda snap a screenshot, then I called the kid's parents and reported him to the school principal. The punk wound up with only a week of in-school suspension."

Marco clapped a hand on Angelo's shoulder in a show of solidarity. "Your sister's a good kid, güey. But you're gonna have your hands full keeping young pups from sniffing around her. No doubt about it, that kid crossed the line. But you remember how we were at that age."

No, not really. Until the enticing, enigmatic woman and their brief but memorable make-out session on New Year's Eve, Angelo had rarely recalled those old days of mischief. Back when his main concern had been earning enough money busing tables at a local restaurant after school so he could treat Rosalina to dinner and a movie. Back when college plans had been about the two of them heading off to UT Austin, intent on studying abroad together.

They'd done the first and were planning the second with the help of their advisers. Until his world tilted on its axis, forcing his priorities to change. He couldn't really blame her when she decided hers didn't have to.

"That's why dating and pool nights with the guys are the last things on my mind," he told Marco.

Unless they involved a certain mystery woman. But the odds of Angelo finding out her identity were slim to none.

"I'm more worried about when Brenda starts dating. As it is now, when she comes to our gigs, I spend most of my time onstage either keeping watch over her or scanning the crowd for any punk who might be eyeing her, thinking he's smooth enough to make a move."

"I do not envy you. That's some stressful shit." Marco shook his head woefully and unlatched the gate. "C'mon, let's get this spy mission underway. I gotta have you home before you turn into a pumpkin at midnight."

Angelo shoved Marco's shoulder but followed behind him anyway.

They strolled down the path that ran the length of the building, lined on the other side with a tall hedge that shielded their view of the small parking lot and strip mall on the left. A row of low lights dug into the soil every few feet illuminated their way. Up ahead, the sidewalk ended at a larger concrete slab, where Angelo pulled to a stop, awed at the unexpected grandeur of Casa Capuleta's back courtyard.

Tables packed with people and draped with white cloths and pink floral centerpieces framed three sides of the dance floor area, with the slightly raised stage on the other. The eight-foot hedges continued along the courtyard's perimeter, blocking out the chain link fence and the neighborhood to provide an air of privacy. Tall potted trees with twinkly lights strung through their branches and leaves were scattered throughout the area with strings of the same tiny white lights crisscrossing overhead to give the space an ethereal, fairy-woodland feel.

As Angelo entered Casa Capuleta's hidden oasis, the odd sensation of having wandered into another world niggled at the back of his neck. The tension knotting his shoulders over venturing into forbidden territory slowly loosened.

Brenda would love hanging out back here if the two of them lived in one of the upstairs apartments. Reading a book while sprawled on one of the wooden bench swings, humming along while he played his guitar under the twinkling lights. Neighborhood dance parties and cultural events in your backyard.

So different from Hugo's estate, with its interior decorator's touch and manicured landscape. The house was a showroom of riches from his uncle's years of hard work, the large acreage an investment. But it wasn't the same as Brenda and Angelo's modest childhood home. The one they'd been forced to sell to pay off their parents' debt.

"Oye, what the hell are you doing?" Marco hissed. He grabbed Angelo's elbow, dragging him out of his mental stupor and toward the shadowed edge against the building. "First lesson in spying on a competitor, güey: blend into the crowd. Don't draw attention to yourself."

Angelo squinted up at the bright floodlight mounted on the roof corner above them, its beam aimed directly at the spot where he had stood gawking at their surroundings.

"Sweet, we're right on time. Here they come." Marco gestured to the double glass doors leading from the community center to the courtyard.

Two lines of women wearing black mariachi outfits marched out carrying their instruments, the clack of their black heeled boots on the concrete announcing their arrival. Heads high, dark hair sleeked back in low buns decorated with red roses, they made a striking entrance.

The deep-red material of the silky bow at each woman's throat matched the slash of color on their lips and the vines of red roses embroidered down their sleeves, along the edges of their short jackets, across their waistlines, and trailing down the outside seams of their ankle-length black skirts. A captivating mix of the strength and pride of their mariachi tradition along with an alluring feminine flair.

Murmurs of recognition rustled among the partygoers. Their anticipation matched a zinging sensation that shot through Angelo's chest. More than mere competitor interest had him suddenly anxious to hear whether the sisters' sound would match their visual magnetism.

"And now, the moment you've all been waiting for," the DJ announced. "Heeeere come Mariachi Las Nubes!"

The crowd erupted in cheers.

The eight members of Las Nubes bowed their heads in a show of thanks, but they didn't break stride, heading straight for the stage.

"The Capuleta girls are some fine-looking mariachis," Marco murmured. Arms crossed, he leaned against the side of the building next to Angelo.

Eyes glued to the band weaving through the tables, Angelo tucked his hands in his front jeans pockets. They had marched out so quickly, he hadn't really gotten a good look at all of them, but *girls* wasn't quite the right word. The last three were clearly teens, but the other five had to be older. Probably mid-to-late twenties. Closer to his and Marco's ripe old twenty-nine and thirty.

The mariachis trailed each other up the two steps on the right front corner, then spaced themselves across the stage. The guitarrón, vihuela, and guitar held down the right side, two trumpets and a percussionist clasping a pair of egg shakers filled center stage, and the two violinists completed the group on the left.

The sister with the vihuela tucked the small guitar-like instrument under one arm and shared a nod with the taller trumpet player. Together they stepped toward two of the multiple microphones that zigzagged across the front of the wooden flooring.

Something about the way the trumpet player carried herself as she approached the mic seemed familiar. Maybe they had run into each other at a festival in street clothes without him realizing who she was. In full charro he would have recognized her as a Capuleta and steered clear.

"Mmm-hmmm, Cat Capuleta can play my vihuela a-n-y-time she wants," Marco crowed, proof of the player reputation he regularly lived up to.

"Oye, respeto." Angelo elbowed him. "You're practically in her parents' house."

Despite the bad blood between their familias, he couldn't help but be impressed by how Arturo and Berta Capuleta had taken in so many young girls over the years. It spoke of good character. Which didn't align with the picture Tío Hugo painted of the troubled history between him and the Capuleta patriarch.

Former best friends. Business partners decades ago. Until Arturo betrayed Hugo by stealing the woman he loved. To this day, Hugo's bitter reaction to even the name Capuleta was enough to have always made Angelo give his uncle's nemesis—and the man's entire family—a wide berth.

That's why Angelo had never set foot on Casa Capuleta's premises. Or attended any of Las Nubes's public performances. Standing here in the shadows mere feet away, impressed by the sisters' entrance, it was the closest he'd ever purposefully been to a member of their familia. He would have sworn the same was true of Marco.

"You know Cat Capuleta?"

"Naw, man, Cat and I've never met." The edges of Marco's mouth tipped down under his black mustache. "Doesn't mean I wouldn't like to merge our musical skills, if you get my drift. But with the bad blood between their dad and Hugo and the way the viejos in our band complain about the girls' nontraditional show . . . Uh-uh. Sniffing around any Capuleta ain't worth the grief. But that don't keep me from dreaming."

His tongue practically hanging out of his mouth, Marco stared at the stage with a besotted expression.

Chin high, shoulders proudly back, red lips spread in a wide smile, Cat Capuleta faced the crowd with an air of supreme confidence. She winked playfully at someone in the audience, and Marco murmured a lovesick "Ay-yi-yi."

While his best friend mooned over one Capuleta, Angelo studied the taller sister standing beside her.

That niggling something's-coming sensation on the back of his neck from earlier returned. This time it tingled across his shoulders, traveled down his arms, leaving a trail of goose bumps.

"¡Bienvenidos, amigos!" Cat's sister greeted the crowd.

Angelo flinched at the familiar velvety voice.

Was this? Could she be his . . . ?

"Welcome to Casa Capuleta and Felicia's fabulous celebration. I'm—"

"Mariana Capuleta," Marco whispered along with her.

Surprise galvanized Angelo, and he pushed off the building. He squinted at Mariana Capuleta, imagining her with that tight bun loosened. Wondering if her dark hair would cascade in sexy waves past her shoulders.

His mind whirling with the possibility, his pulse thundering in his ears, he stared at the oldest Capuleta. Could she be the mystery woman who had dazzled him on New Year's Eve? The one who invaded his nightly dreams?

Taller than her petite sister by a good four inches, Mariana probably stood five foot six or seven. It was the same height.

Her lightly tanned skin stretched smoothly over high cheekbones, an angular jawline with a slightly pointy chin, and a straight, almost hawklike nose. Individually, her features might appear too harsh. All together, they created a fascinating combination that easily made her the most stunning woman he had ever laid eyes on.

The same woman who had captivated him with her fierce stiff-arm, her charming smile, and a scorching kiss that left his body aching for release.

"We're proud to honor another Latina with our performance tonight," Mariana continued, her dulcet voice calling to him.

Cat held an arm out toward the guest of honor holding court at a large table to the left of the dance floor. The birthday girl grinned, showing off a mouthful of braces.

"Another *fierce* Latina," Cat added.

As if on cue, each of the Las Nubes band members raised a triumphant fist. The one playing the guitar threw her head back and howled a loud, guttural grito that had more of the traditional Mexican joyful cries echoing across the courtyard.

"We'll start things off with a special request from Felicia and her mamá," Mariana said once the crowd started to settle down.

But Angelo no longer cared about their performance. He wanted to clear the courtyard, leaving them alone. He wanted to talk to her, ask her a million questions. Wrap her in his arms and pick up where they had left off.

Cat bent toward the microphone with an impish smirk. "A request that shows their excellent taste in música y artistas!"

"Definitely," Mariana agreed. She sent a secret smile toward the birthday girl, and Angelo found himself desperate to be the recipient of one, too. "In their honor, we created a medley of songs from the Queen of Tejano Music—"

"Selena!" The boisterous shout rose from all the members of Las Nubes in unison. Dozens of others in the crowd echoed the beloved singer's name.

Mariana's smile lit up her face as she scanned the audience. Her delightful glow kindled a warmth inside him like the early-morning sun peeking over the horizon at the ranch his tío owned several hours west of San Antonio. The gold rays spreading hazy light over the land, dispelling the darkness.

The two sisters' banter continued for several minutes as they introduced their set. Cat teased, winked, and basically had the entire audience eating out of her palm thanks to her combination of beauty, wit, and cheeky personality. But it was Mariana who ensnared Angelo's attention. Just as she had during their brief time together.

The way she seemed to pick people out of the crowd, speaking directly to them, as if they shared an intimate conversation, drew him. Her husky laughter each time Cat made a wisecrack. Her infectious smile. Everything about her strummed a chord deep within him. Plucking strings he swore had been out of tune for years.

Cat's boldness inched toward the line of brash, though she clearly attracted the most attention. Case in point: Marco, who stared at her with adoration.

Mariana . . . she wore her confidence with a subtlety Angelo preferred.

It was there in the sincere smile curving the edges of her full red lips.

In the pure delight shining on her striking face.

In the comfortable way she held herself, her carriage proudly erect while exuding a warmth that welcomed you.

The combination urged him to move closer to her, witness the sparkle in her eyes again. Confirm his memory of the gold flecks swimming in their depths.

When they first met, she'd worn a skimpy, figure-skimming black number. Tonight, her mariachi charro covered her from head to toe like a nun's habit. Even the large silk bow at her throat hid the bottom half of the elegant neck he had imagined himself kissing.

His fingers twitched with the urge to trace the roses embroidered along the curves of her hips. Brush the smooth skin on the back of her hand as it cradled her trumpet. His lips longed to taste her sweet mouth again. Moves that, in their world of feuding sides, would be considered a sin.

At the moment, the threat of the feud wasn't strong enough to dull her appeal. Though he knew it should.

He watched, entranced, as she lifted the instrument to her pursed lips. Eyes closed, her chest expanded as she sucked in a deep breath through her nose. The opening notes of Selena's "No Me Queda Más" trilled from Mariana's trumpet, piercing the night air. Her fingers expertly worked the valves as she played the song's intro, one foot tapping out the beat while the audience cheered their approval.

Man, she was good. *Better* than good. Her talent, her charm . . . everything about her had him absolutely enthralled.

The rest of the band soon joined in. Cat plucked at her small vihuela and edged closer to the microphone as she crooned the words to one of Selena's beloved hits. Lowering her trumpet, Mariana came in on the harmony, and Angelo leaned forward, greedily picking up her notes, soaking in her rich alto voice.

Every argument he had thrown at Marco earlier about why they had absolutely no business being here vanished under Mariana Capuleta's spell.

The song transitioned to another Billboard number-one hit, and the birthday girl hopped up from her seat with a delighted shriek. Mariana motioned toward the area in front of the stage, encouraging the teen to show off her moves. A middle-aged woman in a purple, one-shouldered cocktail dress joined hands with the girl. Hips swaying, they dance-walked around their table to the open floor.

On the stage, the sisters sang, played, shimmied to the music . . . and Angelo couldn't tear his gaze away from Mariana. The medley transitioned into "Amor Prohibido," and the crowd went wild. Mariana's face flushed with excitement as she swiveled her hips to the rhythm.

Raw lust shot low in Angelo's body. Ay, the irony of this stunning woman sparking his desire while singing about prohibited love.

"Man, they're incredible. We're gonna have to really up our game," Marco muttered when the five-song medley finally drew to a close. His slack-jawed expression told Angelo that his bandmate shared a similar admiration for Las Nubes's rich harmonies, talented instrumentation, and vibrant stage presence.

The unpleasant reality that the Battle would add fuel to the long-standing rivalry between Las Nubes and Los Reyes—another line in the sand separating him from Mariana Capuleta—hit Angelo like a gut punch. As he reeled with the unpleasant reality, one of Casa Capuleta's back doors pushed open. A skinny teen trudged out, precariously balancing a large tray filled with plated chocolate cake pieces on his shoulder. The tray wobbled, and the kid bent his knees, his torso twisting as he fought to balance his load.

Angelo hurried over to steady the tray with one hand while holding the door open wider. The pimply-faced teen murmured a "gracias" before stumbling toward a nearby table.

Las Nubes kicked off their next song amid more raucous cheers, and Angelo mentally tipped his cap to the sisters. They sure as hell knew how to please a crowd. That boded well for them in the audience-voting portion of the competition.

He was a few steps away from his and Marco's shadowy recon corner when someone clasped him on the shoulder and spun him around.

"¿Qué carajo?" he complained, stumbling back a step.

A thin, wiry man wearing a brown ball cap with the Casa Capuleta logo shoved him in the chest with a glare.

"That's my question, cabrón," the guy growled. "What the hell are you mangy Monteros doing here?"

Before Angelo could respond, Marco stepped in between him and the other guy. "This is a public place. We got every right to be here, Tonio."

Tonio! Arturo Capuleta's right-hand man.

Shit, this was nearly as bad as running into Capuleta himself. Dread dripped over Angelo like butter melting on a toasted pan dulce right after the sweet bread had been pulled from the toaster oven.

Tonio's pockmarked face scrunched in a pissed-off scowl. He jerked his chin and spit on the ground, barely missing Marco's left boot.

Marco's fists clenched at his sides, and Angelo's dread turned from a trickle to a fire hydrant burst open on the street. His best friend's reputation as a player was as infamous as his tendency to be a hothead.

"We don't want any trouble, man," Angelo said, pointedly keeping his tone calm.

He eyed Tonio over Marco's shoulder. The man might be pushing his midforties, but his fierce scowl seemed to say he wouldn't mind finding trouble if it involved kicking their asses.

Mariana introduced their next song, her rich voice brushing over him, and all Angelo wanted was to turn back to her. Let himself get lost again in the otherworldly aura of the courtyard, with her like a beautiful fairy casting a spell over him that left him feeling exhilarated. Something he hadn't felt in ages. Until he'd met her.

"If you weren't looking to cause any problems, you shouldn't have come crawling in here tonight," Tonio growled.

"Oye, pende—"

"No!" Angelo grabbed Marco's arm to keep him from taking a swing at Casa Capuleta's assistant manager.

Tonio glared at the two of them.

Marco growled low in his throat.

"We were ready to go anyway," Angelo said flatly. "There's nothing here we need to see."

Liar.

"The trash belongs out on the corner," Tonio sneered.

Marco lunged toward the older man, making Angelo tighten his grip on his buddy's arm.

"I repeat: no one wants any trouble," Angelo affirmed. "There's no need to ruin that young lady's special night. ¿Me oyen?"

If Tonio and Marco did hear Angelo, they ignored him. Instead, their death stares sharpened, neither willing to give in first.

"You are not welcome here," Tonio finally ground out.

"We're going," Marco spat back. "Only 'cuz I can't deal with your stench."

Tonio's eyes narrowed to reptilian slits.

Angelo would have laughed at their adolescent barbs, if Marco weren't prone to throw punches first and think rationally later. A habit Tonio seemed likely to possess as well. Without waiting for any more of their machismo posturing, Angelo tugged his friend and stepped around Tonio.

Marco made sure to jam his shoulder into the other man's but kept his mouth shut as Angelo dragged him down the path toward the wrought-iron gate.

Behind him, Mariana thanked the crowd for coming to celebrate the birthday girl and invited everyone to "visit Casa Capuleta again."

If only he were free to take her up on the offer.

To do so would be absolute foolishness.

Disappointment had his boots pounding the sidewalk with more force as they neared Marco's truck.

"Pendejo, trying to kick us out," Marco grumbled, shaking off Angelo's grip. "At least we got to hear most of their set. Get a taste of what we can expect in the competition."

The Battle!

Mariana would find out who he was—who he was related to—at the first all-teams meeting next week. Damn it! He didn't want their reunion to go down like that. Poisoned by an animosity that others had created.

Outrage blew through him.

Before he thought twice about it, Angelo pulled out his phone and pretended to read a text. "Orale, güey, looks like Brenda decided not to sleep over at her friend's place. I gotta go pick her up."

"Get in, I'll drive you." Marco hit the automatic unlock button on his truck key fob.

"No, that's okay. Your place is in the opposite direction. I'll get a car to take me, then reroute us home."

"You know I don't mind—" Marco broke off and dug his cell out of his back pocket. A wolfish smirk curved his lips as he scanned his screen.

"Let me guess," Angelo said, relieved he might have been given a reprieve from his lie. "Wanda?"

"Love calls."

"Love? You? Ha!"

"You're one to talk, Mr. Pumpkin at Midnight." Marco paused, one foot already inside the driver's side of his truck. "You sure you're good if I head out? Wanda can be impatient. But I don't wanna leave you stranded."

Angelo waved him off. "Go. I'll be fine."

As long as he didn't follow through with his reckless idea.

But really . . . if he ran into Mariana alone on her way out, it wouldn't hurt anyone.

As long as he didn't get caught.

Chapter Three

"Are you sure you don't want to stick around the fiesta with us?"

Mariana shook her head at Cat's question.

"It's a Saturday night," Cat pressed. "Girl, you gotta live a little. Try having some fun for a change."

No gracias. The last time Mariana had followed her sister's advice, she'd wound up making out with a guy whose name she didn't even know. Worse, she'd spent the past few months mooning over him when she had no way of figuring out who he was. Not that she had time for dating anyway.

Wrinkling her nose at Cat's come-on pout, Mariana shook her head again. Adrenaline from the high of performing still hummed in her system, but she needed to start winding down, not partying. If the ER was slammed, she'd be running all day tomorrow.

"Your sweet disposition is tempting," she teased Cat. "Unfortunately, I have a shift in the morning. I'm sure you'll have enough fun for both of us."

"Ha! Suit yourself." With a sassy hitch of a shoulder, Cat sauntered toward the coolers of beer and wine.

Mariana waved bye to the rest of her sisters on her way to the side path. With an hour or so left of the quinceañera, her father was probably in the kitchen wrapping up with the caterers, ensuring everything was in order. Later, her mom would come down to assist him, the Bonavillas, and any others who stuck around for cleanup.

Felicia's parents, like so many others in their neighborhood, were familia. By choice, but familia all the same. The Bonavillas had held their wedding reception at Casa Capuleta. Baby showers and First Communions for all three of their kids had warranted fiestas in the courtyard. The fact that the Bonavillas now celebrated their oldest's fifteenth birthday here was a proud moment for Mariana's parents. A testament to Casa Capuleta and its place in the history of their comunidad.

A history those gentrification-focused property brokers didn't appear to understand. As if they saw only the dollar signs they might gain by closing down the center and turning it into some random designer-name baby store, hot yoga gym, or whatever else happened to be the flavor of the month.

No way. Not here. Whatever it took to keep the developers away from her sanctuary, Mariana vowed to do it.

Reaching the front of the building, she pushed through the metal gate, letting it clang shut behind her. She squinted under the garish yellow streetlight and scanned the line of parked cars up and down the road.

Darn. They liked to keep the side parking lot open for event attendees, but it'd been a mad dash from the hospital to Casa Capuleta, then a race to change for the show. Now she shifted her trumpet case from one hand to the other and tried to remember where the heck she had parked.

Across the street, a figure rose from the bench in front of Silva's corner bodega. Tall and broad shouldered, a man in jeans and a pale cable-knit sweater stepped out from under the awning's dark shadow. Reaching the corner, he crooked an elbow to wave at her, the motion tentative. Mariana barely checked the reflex to see if he might be waving to someone behind her.

The stoplight changed, and the man stepped into the crosswalk. The play of shadows over his face made it difficult to see him clearly, but something about him . . . something felt familiar.

One hand tucked in his front jeans pocket, he tipped his head back to finger-comb his wavy hair off his forehead. The motion allowed the corner streetlight to shine directly on his face, giving her a good look at—

Mariana sucked in a sharp breath. Dios mío. It was him. The stranger.

Her stranger, from the rooftop bar New Year's Eve.

A hesitant smile curved his lips, tilting the left side of his mouth the tiniest bit. Hinting at the wide grin she pictured in her mind when she closed her eyes and let herself travel back to that dreamlike night.

She swallowed nervously, her grip on her trumpet case handle tightening and loosening spastically. Elation clamoring in her chest, she drank him in as he drew near. The soft blue of his sweater stretched across his shoulders and chest, his face a mix of shadows and bronze skin and the flash of straight white teeth in the gloomy light.

He stopped several feet away from her, his boots landing just inside the edge of the streetlight's luminous glow. Back in the courtyard, the DJ switched to a well-known Bad Bunny tune, and a chorus of teens sent up a raucous roar.

The stranger glanced at the gate behind her, then back at her. "Hola, uh, hi. It's great to see you."

"How did you . . . ? What are you . . . ?" She broke off, the questions tumbling helter-skelter in her head and twisting into nonsense on her tongue.

"I was at the party earlier and heard your set with Mariachi Las Nubes."

"Really? So, you know the Bonavillas?" What were the odds of that?

"Uh. Well . . . it's . . ." He scratched at his temple and frowned. "Not really."

"But you were at the quinceañera?" she prodded, confused by his hesitance. So different from the man who had jumped in to help her when others in line around her hadn't.

He rubbed a hand across the back of his neck in a nervous swipe. His gaze slid off to the side, then back to her. A classic avoidance move. Based on her experience with many gunshot or stabbing patients in the ER, she had a sneaking suspicion that he was more than likely about to either lie or, at the very least, skirt the truth.

"Yeah, I was there. Bueno, for part of it anyway," he answered.

"So, if you don't know the Bonavillas, you, what? Party crashed?" A bark of surprised laughter escaped before she could stop it. "A fifteen-year-old's fiesta?"

A pained expression scrunched his handsome face. "Kind of. But for good reason. I mean, we got to hear you and Las Nubes."

"We?" She shot a glance at the shadowy but empty bench across the street. "Is someone with you?"

"What? Oh no! My bandmate left after we—"

"After you?" she prompted when he didn't continue.

He jabbed a hand through his hair again, leaving it sexily mussed. "After we, uh, cut out earlier."

Uh-huh. Something was off. As cute as this guy might be, he wasn't giving her the whole story. And dream-worthy strangers were, unfortunately, still strangers. Even if this one made her pulse kick into an off-to-the-races pace.

"Okay, well, it was nice running into you, but . . ." Her heart—fine, her libido—begged her not to do it, but her head compelled her to play it safe. "I should probably go."

She took a tentative step backward. Then another.

"Wait!" He leaned forward on the balls of his feet as if she were pulling him with her.

"Yes?"

Hope unfurled in her chest as she searched his eyes, looking for the humor and compassion that had charmed her. For the heated interest that had lured her into behaving rashly. Behavior she had taken further in her lusty dreams.

His shoulders rose and fell on a rush of breath that seemed painful based on his uncomfortable grimace.

"Here's the thing. My buddy and I got thrown out by Tonio because we shouldn't have been here. But when I saw you onstage and recognized you from New Year's Eve, I . . . I couldn't just leave. Not when . . ." He jabbed a hand through his thick hair again in a move she now cataloged as a tell of his unease. "Not when I haven't stopped thinking about that night at the rooftop club. Wondering how you are. *Who* you are. Once I knew, I—I had to at least try to meet you, especially before the all-teams meeting for the Battle of the Mariachi Bands and the added stress the competition brings."

He edged a half step closer, a sense of urgency vibrating off him. "Before everything else, every*one* else, gets in our way. I was hoping we could talk."

Mariana held her breath, transfixed by his earnest plea. Hanging on to the hope that she hadn't read him wrong that first night. Thrilled that him finding her might be a good sign.

"Are you saying that you're in the competition, too?"

He nodded.

Excitement skittered up her spine. That meant they'd definitely be seeing more of each other. They'd be competitors, of course. And Las Nubes needed to win. Nothing was more important than that. But still, knowing she'd get to spend more time with him was fantastic news!

"So, you're a member of—Wait!" The command was more for her own tumultuous thoughts than for him as something he'd first said circled back in her head. "Tonio actually threw you out?"

He nodded again, and she shook her head, shocked by Tonio's behavior. Their assistant manager could be a bit overprotective, acting more like an older brother / younger uncle to Mariana and her sisters, but unless Angelo and his friend had caused a problem, Tonio wouldn't normally make a big deal about two extras being at the fiesta.

"Why? I mean, how did he even know you were party crashing?"

Angelo rolled his lips between his teeth like Blanca did when she had something to say but wasn't sure about your response.

A premonition tickled the back of Mariana's neck as she watched his chest rise and fall on another deep sigh. Then he surprised her by extending his hand to shake.

"I'm Angelo Montero. Guitarist with Los Reyes."

Her trumpet case slid from her fingers, landing with a heavy thunk on the sidewalk.

Mon-Montero? As in . . .

She gasped, the revelation of her handsome stranger's identity shocking her system like a jolt from a pair of defibrillator paddles. This had to be a joke.

Only, his serious expression—mouth pinched, concerned eyes hooded by the frown puckering his brow—confirmed her fear.

One hand pressed to her racing heart, she hurried to the metal gate, peering down the shadowy path to the courtyard. Dios mío, what if Papo walked out here? Or, probably equally as volcanic when it came to the Montero name, Catalina? Talk about a freak-out waiting to happen!

Her head reeling, Mariana grabbed the metal rail, squeezing until the edge bit into her hand. Why? Why did he have to be a Montero? Why couldn't, for once, life be fair?

"Mariana?"

Hearing her name in his husky, hesitant whisper made her ache with regret. It didn't matter that she'd spent the past few months wishing she could somehow cross paths with her intriguing stranger again. Mariana knew what she had to do. What her familia would expect her to do.

"You shouldn't be here." The words scraped her raw throat.

"Don't say that. C'mon, give me a chance."

Mariana swung back around at his gruff plea.

He held out his arm, palm up. An invitation for her to join him. Just like that first night.

She wanted to. Dios, how she wanted to. But she'd been conditioned to expect antagonism from members of Mariachi Los Reyes, especially Hugo Montero. Would his only nephew be any different?

No matter how much she wanted to believe so, she couldn't be sure. And no way would she put her own pleasure before her familia's well-being.

"You have to go, please. If someone else sees you . . ." Dread flooded through her. It was only a matter of time before people started leaving the fiesta. If Papo or Cat caught him, they'd likely blow like the fireworks that had lit the sky on New Year's Eve. "I'm sure Tonio plans to tell my father what happened. If he hasn't already. Papo will not be pleased."

"Because of the feud."

"Yes!"

"The one you and I have nothing to do with."

A harsh laugh burst from her at Angelo's naivete. "You're a Montero. I'm a Capuleta. Many Los Reyes members have made it clear where they stand when it comes to my sisters and me and our band."

"Not all of us," he qualified.

She arched a dubious brow.

Disappointment joined the shadows flickering over his face. His fingers curled into his palm, and he slowly lowered his outstretched arm. Remorse spread through Mariana like an oil slick, smothering the budding hope that had sprouted when she first recognized him.

This awareness of him, the attraction refusing to be denied, made no sense. Not now that she knew his identity.

They eyed each other in silence.

Her, anxious for him to leave, keenly sad for the loss of what might have been.

Him, lips pressed in a firm line, his gaze boring into hers, as if willing her to change her mind.

"Fine, I get where you're coming from." One of Angelo's bootheels scraped the sidewalk, a frustrated punctuation to his muttered words. "And next week, when the mariachi competition starts, more battle lines will be drawn."

"Exactly."

"But, until then, no one knows that the two of us have met. Right?"

She frowned, puzzled by his question. "Right."

"So, if we, let's say"—he tilted his head from side to side as if mentally weighing an idea, maybe as desperate as she to not end things between them this way—"accidentally met up on the street and decided to spend some time together . . . it could stay that way. Our secret, I mean."

"Ahhh, I don't normally . . ."

Don't normally what? Keep secrets from her familia?

Ha! Then how come she hadn't told anyone about New Year's Eve? The kiss she hadn't been able to forget. The man she wished for more time with.

The man who stood right here. Her prayers come true!

Out back in the courtyard, the music slowed to a romantic ballad. Couples would be pairing up. Cuddling on the dance floor, stealing kisses under the strings of lights and starry night sky.

Girl, you gotta live a little.

Cat's taunt whispered in Mariana's ear. Ay, did she dare?

As if sensing her indecision, Angelo held out his hand again, palm up.

"Look, I know I shouldn't be here. Shouldn't be talking to you or thinking about asking if you'd like to go get a drink or a bite to eat. But I am. Here. Asking. Hoping your answer will be yes."

Chapter Four

"You sure this is okay?" Angelo settled into the hard plastic booth in the busy Whataburger dining area. Not exactly the place he had expected Mariana to suggest when he'd invited her for a drink at nine thirty on a Saturday night.

Not that he'd expected her to say yes after finding out who he was in the first place. But no way could he have walked away without trying.

"I'm good. Starving, actually."

He caught the curve of her smile across the white laminate table before she ducked her head to glance down at the hand pressed to her stomach.

Earlier, while he filled their drink cups, she'd done a quick change out of her charro. She had exited the bathroom minutes later in black leggings and a red V-neck sweater dress that hugged her figure, hinting at her cleavage and treating him to a spectacular view of her shapely legs. Good thing he'd already been seated at their booth, because the woman left him weak-kneed.

Her dark hair remained swept back in the slick, low-bun style. The one his sister had called a chig-something or other on their way to mass a few Sundays ago when she'd asked what he thought of her new look.

Funny, on Brenda the low bun had warranted a brotherly "nice."

On Mariana Capuleta, the sleek style highlighted her high cheekbones and striking features. The red flowers that matched the rose embroidery on her charro and now the color of her sweater remained tucked into the knot low on the back of her head. As they had earlier, his fingers itched to pull the flowers and pins from her hair, loosen the tresses to watch them tumble over her shoulders again. Find out if their dark luster felt as silky as his memory promised.

The clatter of plastic food trays slapping onto the table behind him jolted Angelo out of his hair-fetish stupor. A group of teens jostling and laughing plopped into the booth, unaware of the precarious state of affairs on this side of the shared seat back.

"So, here we are." Mariana's breathy announcement accompanied her slow glance around their surroundings. Not quite nervously, but definitely with watchful intent.

"Yes, here we are."

Surprisingly. Probably foolishly. Hopefully not regrettably.

"Remind me again, why was it that you and your bandmate decided to crash the party tonight?" She reached for her supersize cup of Big Red and eyed him as she sipped from her straw.

His thumb tapped the tabletop with nervous energy as Angelo forced himself to look away from her lips puckered around the orange plastic. To stop thinking about their hot kiss and his desire to relive it.

Admitting to Marco's harebrained idea of spying on Las Nubes sounded as underhanded as . . . hell, as it actually was. It had been hard enough convincing Mariana to join him. Angelo doubted she would stay if she questioned his intent. Especially if she tied it to the long-running feud. But he didn't feel comfortable starting their short time together with anything less than the truth.

Honestly, as soon as he had recognized her onstage, he'd forgotten about the Battle, the feud. Their warring father figures. His decision to stick around and wait for her had been a move made out of desperation. And the all-consuming need to connect with the woman who had captured his attention in a way no other had in years.

He hadn't been sitting on that bench long when Mariana burst from the shadowy pathway and stopped on the sidewalk. The streetlamp had bathed her in its spotlight, the pale glow glinting off the gold gala on her bolero jacket and skirt. And he . . . he'd been like a moth drawn to her brightness. Unable to resist the urge to speak with her again. On their own terms, not everyone else's.

One meal before reality stepped in again. One stolen moment to see if their connection was as strong as he remembered. That's all he wanted.

What could it hurt?

"Earth to Angelo." Mariana jiggled her cup in the air, and the tumble of ice snagged his attention.

A bemused smile tipped the corners of her mouth. It plumped her cheeks and teased a glimmer in her hazel eyes. Eyes he now confirmed were indeed tinged with shades of green and flecks of gold.

He cleared his throat and carefully picked his words. "Marco heard there was something going on at Casa Capuleta tonight. Thought we might want to check it out."

"And the Private Party sign on the side gate didn't give you pause?"

"Well, yes. I did have—" He broke off. No way would he throw his buddy under the bus by tagging Marco as the instigator. They had walked into Casa Capuleta together. "We were already there, and—"

"And it seemed like an easy way to check out the competition."

Angelo winced at her bald statement. Surprisingly, her expression leaned more toward impressed than pissed.

"Pretty much. Mariachi Las Nubes is the new kid on the block, at least when it comes to the Battle." He tipped his cup in salute. "You ladies put on an impressive set."

For the first time since he had introduced himself in front of Casa Capuleta, Mariana grinned. One of those wide, brimming-with-pleasure smiles she'd flashed for the audience earlier. Only this time, it was for him. Just like on that rooftop.

A knot tightened in Angelo's chest.

"My sister Cat would love hearing that," Mariana teased.

The restaurant's main door opened, and she sat up, eyes wide with trepidation.

A middle-aged couple entered, then made their way to the line at the counter. Mariana sank into her booth seat. A relieved sigh whooshed from her lips.

"Hey, we drove to this location for a reason, remember?" he told her, lowering his voice to maintain their privacy.

She fingered the gold crucifix dangling on her delicate necklace. Gave him a slight nod, softened by a chagrined roll of her eyes. "Guilt. The bane of every Catholic school student everywhere, I suppose."

Angelo chuckled, pleased that she could joke when still clearly worried about the ramifications of their dinner date. He understood her caginess. If someone who recognized them showed up, they'd both have some uncomfortable explaining to do to their familias. And in his case, band members.

Frankly, though, that didn't matter. The excited energy coursing through him now that he'd found her zapped any care he might have about the trouble sitting here with her could bring.

"Pretty gutsy of you and your friend, showing up at our performance like that," Mariana said. "On our turf, no less."

"That's one description."

"You've got another?"

"Lucky."

A corner of her mouth curved with a ghost of her charming smile. He'd take it.

Silently, she traced the wording on her cup with a short, red-painted nail, pausing when she reached the end of the script.

"Did your uncle put you up to this?" she asked softly, peering at Angelo from under her long lashes.

"No!"

The uncertainty looming in her expressive eyes had him leaning across the table to lay a hand on her wrist.

"He doesn't even know we were there," Angelo insisted. "Much less that I stayed behind. And Marco thinks I left to go pick up my sister, Brenda. I swear."

She worried her bottom lip, nibbling off the red lipstick stain. Gently he swiped his thumb along her wrist, seeking to soothe her misgivings. Wishing they weren't stuck in this strained limbo between a world others had created and one in which he could simply be a guy interested in getting to know a girl he found incredibly intriguing.

The chatter from people around them seemed to hush. The squeak of sneakers on the linoleum from a group of kids horsing around and a timer buzzing back in the kitchen faded. Angelo's sole focus remained on her and their stolen time together.

It was ill advised. Dangerous. *Liberating.*

For years he'd lived under his tío's watchful eye. Following Hugo's advice, thankful for the support during the most difficult time of his life. Biting his tongue when his tío's old-school views and strong personality chafed.

But when it came to Mariana, somehow Angelo knew she was worth the risk.

Her brow puckering, Mariana slid her arm away from his touch and reached for her purse strap.

Angelo's spirits sank.

"I'm sorry. I really wanted to do this. But—"

"Three fifty-five!" The Whataburger employee's cry from behind the counter interrupted her goodbye. "Order number three fifty-five!"

She looked at the receipt on the table. At the bottom of the paper, 355 was printed in large, bold font.

"I promise you. There was no underhanded strategizing going on," he told her. "Marco and I just wanted to hear your band play. That was the extent of our plan. Nothing else. Only, I saw you. Recognized you from New Year's Eve. And I . . . I couldn't walk away. I *had* to talk to you. Before all of that, out there, got in our way."

He gestured toward the entrance, the cars buzzing by on the road and the world carrying on outside without them.

The kid behind the counter yelled their number again.

Frustrated that she might be slipping away when he'd only just found her, Angelo drove a hand through his hair. "Just . . . just give me a chance. *Please.*"

Her pensive expression softened. Releasing her purse strap, Mariana settled back in her side of the booth. "Dios mío, you certainly know how to sweet-talk a girl, huh? Plus, like I said, I'm really hungry. But that doesn't get you off the hook." She waggled a finger at him in warning. "I have more questions. So, can you hurry up before they give our food away?"

He barked out a laugh, satisfaction zinging through him as he grabbed the receipt and slid down the plastic seat.

~

Angelo dipped a fry in the glop of ketchup holding down a corner of the hamburger wrapper he'd spread out like a placemat in front of him. "So, you're an ER nurse, but you're starting the physician-assistant program at UTSA this fall?"

"Mmm-hmmm. That's the plan."

"And you've—"

"Eh!" Mariana set down her half-eaten single burger and grabbed a napkin to wipe her mouth. "My turn."

"Hey, that wasn't really a question. More like, restating information."

"Phrased as a question. So, my turn." He started to object again, and she quickly added, "You made that rule, not me."

And apparently, she was a rule follower. A trait he identified with. Most of the time anyway, seeing as how the two of them were breaking bread together. A cardinal sin according to his uncle and her father.

"Look, you seem like a nice guy."

"Aw man," he complained on a groan. "Not the dreaded nice-guy designation."

A smile flirted with her lips as she leaned toward him in that appealing way she had. The one that made him feel like he had her undivided attention. Like no one else mattered except him and what he had to say.

"I mean that as a compliment." Her smile dimmed. The worry that never quite left her eyes for long returned. A hint that their détente neared its end. "Those are words I wouldn't normally associate with someone who shares blood ties with the owner of El Rey Properties."

His uncle. A topic they had agreed to steer clear of when Angelo had returned with their meal earlier.

As if she read his thoughts, Mariana tipped her head in acknowledgment.

Angelo took a swig of his Coke, swallowing his distaste for the bitter truth that, until tonight, he had allowed his tío's views to sway his own so strongly. Arturo had betrayed Hugo. Thus, the Capuleta name was not to be trusted. Angelo had accepted this as gospel for most of his life. But as he learned about the Capuletas and the rest of the comunidad on the West Side, his uncle's version didn't add up in Angelo's facts and numbers–driven brain.

"It's no secret that many of your band members are some of Las Nubes's staunchest critics. But you . . ." Mariana's nails thrummed the table as she eyed him, making no secret about her interest in sizing him up. "You don't give off the same egotistical vibes I expect from a Montero. More like, bueno, appealing, nice-guy ones."

"Well, when you frame it like that, I guess I'll take the compliment." He winked as he bit into another fry, and her bemused chuckle teased an answering one from him. "My tío isn't a bad guy."

Her arched brows telegraphed an "I beg to differ" sentiment as she sucked on her straw before responding. "Look, I get familia loyalty. That need to hold tight to those ties. Especially if, like me, you don't have many."

"Same here."

"Everyone knows that my sisters and I came to Casa Capuleta through the foster system. With me, my birth father was never in the picture, and my mom died when I was eight," she continued. "Arturo and Berta not only opened their home, they invited me to make it my own. Gave me nearly two hands full of sisters, who, while at times annoying, I wouldn't trade for anything. My familia loyalty runs as deep as yours. So, we'll have to agree to disagree about who we think is a 'bad guy.'"

And there it was. Their shared threads of responsibility and allegiance made them alike while also tying their hands, keeping them apart.

But they shared something else. A painful experience Angelo truly wished they didn't.

"When your mom passed, you were only a little older than my sister, Brenda, was when our parents died." The words tumbled out before Angelo could stop them, surprising him. He rarely spoke about that time in their lives. Definitely not with someone he'd just met.

Chalk it up to Mariana's candor in sharing her past so easily. Maybe also the ticking clock in his head pushing him to make the most of their short time together.

"How old was she?"

"Brenda was four." A heartbroken, confused, needy four.

"And you?" The empathy in Mariana's gently voiced question, the tender expression on her face, had Angelo setting aside the last bit of his hamburger as his story came pouring out of him like a hose gushing water.

"It was fall semester my sophomore year at UT Austin. When I was declared her guardian, I moved back home and transferred to UTSA. Tried, mostly failed, to make things as normal as I could for her."

"That's a lot of pressure for a . . . what . . . nineteen-year-old?"

Damn, those ten years had flown by. It felt like a lifetime ago. Someone else's lifetime. The old him he barely recognized anymore.

"Raising your sister couldn't have been easy. It's pretty freaking admirable how you stepped up."

Uncomfortable with her praise when, in reality, it was his uncle who had saved them, Angelo cleared his throat and crooked a finger to tug at his sweater's scoop neck. "I've screwed up more than I would have liked. Especially in the beginning. But at least Brenda and I had each other and our tío's support. You didn't have any other relatives?"

"Uh, no. I wasn't as lucky. I went into the system and landed at my first foster home, which wasn't exactly the best situation."

Her voice trailed off, and a tiny V wedged between her brows as she recalled what seemed like an unpleasant memory from her past. She took another sip of her Big Red, slowly swallowed, and he was left wondering what part of her story she would keep locked away. What part she would reveal to him. He wanted it all. Wanted her to feel comfortable enough to share everything about herself with him.

"Let's just say that moving to Casa Capuleta was a true blessing. I owe the life I have now to my parents. They saved me. And my sisters." The staunch certainty in her voice told him she didn't speak those words lightly.

Based on the little he had gleaned from others outside his tío's immediate circle and what Mariana had divulged tonight, Arturo and Berta Capuleta sounded like real-life guardian angels for the girls they took in as their own.

Far different from the "traitorous double-crosser" label Tío Hugo had always stamped on Arturo Capuleta's character.

Reconciling the two "truths" didn't seem possible. Especially not when in the company of the captivating, loyal daughter the Capuletas had raised.

In the short time since Angelo had suggested they set aside talk of the feud and let themselves enjoy their meal over general dinner conversation, Mariana had played along. They had chatted about topics from the mundane—their careers and alma maters—to the more personal—why they'd chosen the instruments they played, how music connected them to their parents, and their siblings. A lot about her siblings.

How could he not be enthralled by the way her eyes lit up or the throaty chuckle that accompanied a story about one or another of her sisters? The devotion that oozed from her pores when she spoke about growing up within the welcoming walls of Casa Capuleta. A place vastly different from the rigid confines of his uncle's lavish estate with its often stuffy, country-club air.

"I'm impressed by how you all bonded and seem to get along so well," he told her. "Brenda hit adolescence, and I swear, there are days I can't do anything right."

"Oh, we had our skirmishes. Still do!" She popped a fry into her mouth, chewing and swallowing as she smirked at some sister squabble her faraway gaze envisioned.

He wanted to ask her to share it, allow him to relive the moment with her. But she blinked as if clearing it away, her eyes refocusing on him.

"We were five teenage girls under one roof back then. I often wonder how our parents did it. Still do, with the four younger girls now."

"I've only got one moody teen at home, and I feel outnumbered."

Mariana's laughter rippled over him like refreshing lake water lapping at the shore.

"Seriously, if that doesn't make your parents worthy of sainthood, I don't know what does."

Humor plumped her cheeks. "So, it's just you and Brenda at home?"

"And my tío. The three of us live at his place out in Fair Oaks."

"Ay, the number of times one of us complained about wanting our own room. We were crammed together in two apartments remodeled to make one above Casa Capuleta. You wouldn't believe the fights we had over the bathroom."

She bit into another fry, snickering at another memory he hoped she would share.

"Cozy and filled with love, my mom likes to say. But believe me, there are times it's more like cramped and swarming with chaos!"

He laughed at her wide-eyed horror. "Isn't that how you perfected your stiff-arm move? Refereeing sister squabbles."

"Exactly!" Mariana shook a fry at him, then popped it in her mouth. "I can't believe you remembered that."

Oh, he remembered everything about the night they'd met.

They shared a grin, and damn if the urge to lean across the table and kiss her didn't have him nearly lifting off his seat. Forgoing the last of his food for a taste of *her*.

The more he heard about life growing up at Casa Capuleta, the more time he spent with Mariana, the more he found himself wondering what it must feel like to be included in the close-knit group she welcomed and loved as familia. Silly wonderings he would never know the answer to because this fast-food dinner together was as far as any relationship between them could extend.

A sobering reality.

"Kidding aside, we've endured hardships, before and since arriving at Casa Capuleta." She reached for a napkin, her lips slipping to a serious line. "I'll do anything for them. Familia by choice or by blood, sometimes you can't tell the difference, verdad?"

He nodded, enthralled by her strong conviction. It spoke to him on an innate level he couldn't quite define. But it felt right. *She* felt right.

"Our parents have always told us girls that there are no limits to what we can accomplish. That it's not only 'a man's world' out there."

She jutted her chin at the restaurant's main entrance and filled parking lot. "Mariachi Las Nubes wanted to enter the Battle because we believe it's important to represent. To prove that we, and musicians like us, do belong onstage. Now there's extra pressure to win so we can help save Casa Capuleta."

"Save it? What do you mean?"

Wrinkling her nose, she waved off his question with the napkin, then wiped her fingers.

"Is something going on with the center?" he pressed.

"Yes, in a way. But I shouldn't have said anything. Especially not to—" She winced, and he realized she didn't need to finish the rest of her sentence.

"Especially not to a Montero?" He hated even having to ask. Dreaded hearing the answer he fully expected.

She nodded, and just like that, their momentary truce was over. The feud, forged by her father and his uncle and maintained by some of their band members, might as well have pulled up a chair at their booth. Her hamburger wrapper crackled as she gathered it into a ball, crushing it along with his spirits. Frustration roiled in Angelo's gut.

"Because of the feud, my parents didn't even want Las Nubes to enter the Battle. Cat and I felt we had to. As an all-female mariachi *and* for the winner's pot. I promised my mom that I'd do my best to keep the animosity between our familias from hurting my sisters or upsetting my dad. Or ruining Mariachi Las Nubes's chances of winning. That's why I shouldn't be here."

Her troubled gaze flitted around the bustling dining area like a bee searching for a spot to land. When it finally did, on him, the disappointment clouding her hazel eyes pricked like a stinger. "Being with you is kinda like . . . I don't know."

"Fraternizing with the enemy?"

Guilt tiptoed across her face at his description. And yet she had agreed to join him.

"Why did you say yes?" he asked.

She bit her lip, its red tint now a faint stain.

"Wait a second." A terrible thought snaked its viperous way through his head. "Were you the one with the sneaky intentions here? Trying to see what kind of Los Reyes insider info you could get out of me?"

"No! It wasn't like that."

Forget tiptoeing—guilt set up camp in the frown lines crossing her forehead and pinching her lips. Shame over potentially being played for a lovesick pup burned the back of his neck.

"I've been up front from the beginning, Mariana." Angelo spread his hands palms up on the table. "Have you?"

Her throat moved with a swallow as she stared at his outstretched arms; then she slowly reached out to link her fingers with his. "Just so you know, I don't normally go around kissing strangers I meet at bars."

"You don't really strike me as the type." Her fingers tightened around his. Encouraged, he shared a truth he hoped she already suspected. "For the record, I don't either."

"That's a relief." A corner of her mouth hitched with chagrin. "That night at the rooftop club. The way we met and connected. Every time I thought about it, about you . . ."

"So, I wasn't the only one replaying that night in their head?"

Her fingertips swept across his palm in a barely-there caress, and damn if it wasn't the most titillating sensation. Lust sparked, hot and demanding.

"No, you weren't the only one," she admitted softly. "Which makes this even harder, because now that we know who the other is . . ."

He sandwiched her hand between both of his, not ready for the outside world to intrude.

Her eyes drifted closed, and he sensed the tug-of-war inside her. The same one he'd been waging since he recognized her earlier. Eventually, when she gazed back at him, the strength of character he was coming to associate with her shone in her eyes.

"I'm sure both sides of this feud have their own version of the truth. I'm not naive enough to believe that my dad was or is a saint," she said softly. "But I'm hoping my instincts about you are right, and you're with me in wanting to avoid a bloodbath in the midst of the Battle."

"They're one hundred percent right."

"Las Nubes will fight hard to win the Battle, but I can promise that we'll fight fair. What I have to ask is, can you say the same?"

On his part, yes.

When it came to his uncle and some of the others, Angelo couldn't make any guarantees. Even though he carried the responsibility of filling his father's boots by stepping into his spot in the band, the generational age difference between Angelo and his uncle remained. As a sign of respect, Angelo had never called out his uncle when it came to his antiquated views on gender roles. He was beginning to think that may have been a mistake.

The possibility had his double burger churning in his stomach as if he'd just gotten off a roller coaster at Six Flags.

"I have nothing but respect for Las Nubes," he said.

"But others on your side won't keep quiet about not feeling the same."

Unwilling to lie yet unable to voice the distasteful truth, he nodded.

Water murkier than the San Antonio River ran between the banks separating their two familias. The bridge that once connected them had been demolished when Arturo stole Berta away, leading Hugo to close their property deal on his own and push his former best friend out. Hugo had never gotten over being jilted and having someone he'd considered a brother betray him. Today, shots were exchanged in the fight between sticking with tradition and changing with the times.

As much as Angelo may want to rebuild a connecting bridge for him and Mariana, he didn't see how. Not yet.

"Well, then. I appreciate your candor." The words were delivered on a rush of air as Mariana sank back in her bench seat, dragging her hand out from between his to rest on the table. The inches separating them somehow felt like miles. "I'll have my work cut out for me, but this competition cannot become another stressor for Papo. Not with property brokers circling Casa Capuleta like buzzards."

"Buildings and land on the west side of town are hot commodities. Your parents could get a great deal if they're thinking about sell—"

Mariana's palm smacked the table. "Casa Capuleta is *not* for sale!"

Startled by her vehemence, he nearly knocked over his drink cup. Several heads turned in their direction. Inquisitive stares shot their way. Angelo sent a hesitant smile to an older woman giving him a parental glare from several tables away.

"I was simply making a general statement. Not a sales pitch." He held his hands up, warding off the daggers Mariana's eyes fired at him.

Her chest rose and fell with a huff of breath. Her tan cheeks flushed with an anger that tightened her jaw. Forearms on the table, she leaned toward him.

"Are you involved with them?" she asked in a harsh whisper. "Is your uncle behind the private lender who's trying to screw my parents with his bogus ultimatum?"

Angelo blinked in surprise, his thoughts scrambled by her staggering accusation. "Uh, I'm not sure who the 'them' is you're referring to. I don't handle any property acquisition or management, remember? Only the books and taxes."

Her eyes bored into his. Penetrating. Searching.

He couldn't look away. Hell, he could barely even breathe. All he could do was will her to believe him. To stop seeing him as the enemy.

Several tension-filled seconds passed; then the air suddenly whooshed out of her, her body sagging against the backrest like a deflated balloon. She buried her face in her hands, and his chest tightened with remorse. Brenda's tears always cut him off at the knees, pulling him back to those heartbreaking nights when she had sobbed for their parents. If Mariana started crying . . .

"Dios mío, I'm a mess," Mariana mumbled. Her hands dropped to her lap. Chin tucked, she sucked in and released a deep breath that tugged at his need to comfort her.

"You're not a mess. Not from my perspective."

"Gracias, but clearly, I need to go. It's late, and I have to work in the morning." She slung her purse strap over her shoulder, then started to slide out of the booth. "I'll figure things out."

"I'll do whatever I can to make sure our guys are on their best behavior. And I'll talk to my uncle." Exactly what Angelo would say that might actually resonate with his hardheaded tío remained to be seen. But he would do his best. For her.

She rose to stand at the foot of their table. Her lips curved in a tremulous smile, and damn if he didn't feel a compulsion to pull her into his arms, promise her that everything would work out. Instead, he joined her, making himself maintain a polite distance when he itched to hug her.

"I appreciate that," she murmured. "You really are a—"

"Nice guy," he finished.

A puff of laughter blew from her lips. "Yes, despite everything, you definitely seem like one of the good ones. Thank you for dinner. And the conversation. Makes me wish . . . bueno, if only—"

With a sad shake of her head, she moved to step around him, but he wasn't ready for her to go yet. Wasn't ready for tonight to end.

"If only our situation was different?" he asked, the words a foolish plea from the lonely corner of his heart where she had started to take up residence.

Mariana stopped, their shoulders millimeters from touching. Indecision and dashed hope clashed in her eyes.

Angelo studied her beautiful face, committing her striking features, even the speck of a little mole on her left temple, to memory.

"If only our situation was different," he repeated. "I wouldn't have wanted you to leave—again—without me asking for your number."

The gold flecks in her eyes sparkled with interest.

"Which I don't normally give out. But . . ." She paused. A corner of her mouth tipped up in a sheepish half smile. "But I would have taken yours. Then tried, and more than likely failed, to not text you."

Satisfaction strummed a glorious song inside him. Followed quickly by the discordant notes of disappointment at the regret that slipped over her features.

"But it isn't different." A statement, not a question, because he knew it to be the truth.

"No, unfortunately, it's not," she answered.

Damn, the unfairness of the sins of others tainting the world around them.

They stared at each other in heavyhearted silence until a young teen excused herself to pass by, severing their fragile tie. An insatiable need Angelo hadn't even known existed until it burned in his chest.

"Gracias for a memorable evening. Two, really. They were a pleasure." Mariana cupped his cheek gently, the warmth of her palm spreading down to wrap around his heart. "Cuídate, okay?"

With a sad smile he knew he'd see in his dreams, she walked away.

By the time he found himself murmuring a "take care of yourself, too," Mariana was pulling open the main entrance door. He watched as she crossed the parking lot, then slid behind the wheel of her sedan. Once she had safely made the turn into the street, he sank onto the booth seat.

His thoughts spun like tires burning rubber as they gained traction on the pavement. He might not be involved with property transactions at El Rey, but that didn't mean he couldn't poke around. Secretly ask some questions. Find out whether his uncle had a connection to whoever was eyeing the Casa Capuleta building.

Gentrification efforts had been trickling over from the successful Pearl Brewery area on the east side of town, slowly making their way to the west. It was only a matter of time before offers were made on land and properties.

Still, Mariana had made it sound like someone was trying to strong-arm her parents into selling. Years ago, his parents had been misled, then swindled by a bad financial decision. The idea of the Capuletas being taken advantage of in a similar manner made Angelo's blood boil.

No way his uncle would be involved in something like that after what had happened to Angelo's parents. But given Hugo's competitive streak and the fiery history between him and Arturo Capuleta, Angelo was beginning to fear that might not be the case.

He sure as hell hoped not. Because after tonight, another evening that left him more enamored by Mariana Capuleta, Angelo knew he'd do whatever he could to protect her.

Chapter Five

"Hey, Nina, how's your test prep coming along?" Mariana asked, setting her trumpet case on the familia's old oak dining room table late Sunday evening with a tired sigh.

Nina grunted, pairing the annoyed response with a teen-appropriate shoulder hitch. Like she couldn't be bothered to give a full shrug. The moody teen didn't look up from the thick text and spiral notebook spread out in front of her.

Mariana pressed her lips together to keep from reminding Nina that her current situation was her own doing. What had her newest sister expected after breaking into the community center kitchen and having the bright idea to light a cigarette with the gas stove? Only, she also inadvertently managed to catch a pile of hand towels on fire. An oh-shit mistake she compounded by attempting to swat out the flames with her sweatshirt instead of grabbing the extinguisher. Then, in her flailing freak-out, she knocked the lid off the deep fryer, setting the oil aflame and making things even worse.

Of course, as the fire marshal had pointed out, the kitchen-fire debacle had clued them into the building's wiring problem, which could have led to a much grimmer catastrophe down the line.

That "silver lining" helped soothe Mariana's aggravation with Nina's propensity to long jump over the do-not-cross line when it came to rules, then later claim she hadn't meant it.

"I imagine being grounded still sucks as much as it did when I was younger," Mariana said, making another attempt to lure Nina into more than monosyllabic responses.

"Like you've ever been grounded," Nina scoffed, her focus still glued to her notebook. "You? Ms. Straight and Narrow? Yeah right."

The silly nickname Nina had given her and the memory of that one time back in high school Mariana had been punished had her smiling. "Oh, even me, the rule follower, managed to earn a stint on Capuleta house arrest."

Mariana's answer had Nina peeking up from under her lashes. Skepticism and interest warred in her expression. The latter a new reaction from the teen, who typically kept herself at a distance.

Progress. It had Mariana considering how much to share of her one walk on the degenerate side. No need to give the kid more ideas of how to get herself into trouble.

"One night, Cat wanted to meet up with friends after curfew," Mariana said, leaving out that the friends happened to be the two Perez brothers.

Cat had been crushing hard on the youngest and begged Mariana to pleeeeease sneak out with her to meet up with the boys. Knowing Cat would go either way, and unwilling to let her sister do so alone, Mariana had agreed. Sure, the brothers usually kept out of trouble, but she wasn't taking any chances.

"It was supposed to be a stroll around the block. But it turned into grabbing fries at the Whataburger a few streets over." Later, she and her sister had crept up the back stairs, giggling over Cat's awkward good-night kiss with her wannabe beau. Shushing each other at the front door, Mariana heady with the high of sneaking out for the first time.

It'd been fun. Right up until Papo caught them tiptoeing through the living room and Mariana dropped her supersize cup of Big Red in mortified dismay when he turned on the lamp by his recliner. That red-dye soda stain had never completely come out of Mamá's pastel floral area rug. And Mariana had never forgotten Papo's disappointment in them. In her.

But Cat and Mariana had suffered those consequences together. Nina was alone. A situation she had experienced far too much in her young life.

"Let me get this straight," Nina scoffed. "You snuck out to meet up with a guy and all you did was hang out at Whataburger? Losers."

"Who said anything about a guy?" Mariana hedged, letting the "loser" comment slide.

Her sourpuss expression screaming "Get real!" Nina practically dared Mariana to refute the accusation.

Mariana worked to keep her own expression blank as irony smacked her on the forehead. Forget any tomfoolery she had committed in high school. Last night, she, Ms. Straight and Narrow, had engaged in *another* clandestine meal at yet *another* Whataburger. This one purposefully miles from here to avoid being caught. This meal with far worse ramifications if her familia found out.

Once again, her evening hadn't ended in a kiss. Though she'd be lying if she said she hadn't wanted to kiss Angelo Montero. Imagined it while alone in her bed. The warmth of his hand cupping the back of her head, his fingers splaying along her neck. His lips covering hers, teasing and tempting her to open for him. The taste of his tongue—

"Why is this crap so boring?"

The slap of Nina roughly turning the page scattered Mariana's heated musings like a dandelion's white fluff on a wish-filled puff of breath. The odds of that wish coming true were about as high as the odds of her having another date—a real one this time—with Angelo. She'd be smart to remember that and forget him.

"Whatcha working on?" she asked her sister. "Need some help?"

"Stupid algebra," Nina complained. "I don't know why the hell we have to learn this. It's fuc—"

"Ah-a-a-a! You know the rule. No cursing." Mariana glanced through the arched opening to the kitchen and living room beyond, making sure their mom wasn't within earshot.

Using her favorite form of communication, Nina rolled her eyes at the reminder.

"In response to your rhetorical question, you learn algebra because it'll help you get into college and train your brain to problem solve. A skill that'll help you with life in general."

Nina answered with a mature *pffft*.

Mariana stepped closer to rest her hand on her sister's shoulder in a show of support. Nina ducked out of reach, sending her notebook sliding across the table, where it *thwacked* against the black trumpet case. Her face scrunched with a fierce scowl that screamed "back the eff off."

But Mariana saw it. The fear shimmering underneath the gruff veneer, widening the teen's dark brown eyes. Turning her tan face a pallid gray.

White-hot anger shot through Mariana's chest. Damn those people who had conditioned Nina to flinch from another's touch. To expect punishment instead of love or compassion. Especially from her familia. Blood or found, familia shouldn't inflict harm. Unfortunately, Mariana knew that wasn't always the case. She also knew it would take time to build and earn Nina's trust.

"What the hell's up with you?" the teen accused. Her anxious gaze darted back and forth between Mariana's extended hand and her face.

Mariana held up both palms in a conciliatory gesture as she backed up a step. "I didn't mean to startle you. Just wanted to say that I'm pretty good at algebra. Ask Cat or Claudia. They would have bombed without my tutoring. Maybe I can help you pass, too."

"I got it. You don't hafta bother."

"It's not a bother."

"Whatever." Nina tossed her ponytail over her shoulder, then stretched across the table to grab her spiral notebook.

"Let me know if—"

"I'm good."

Mariana didn't push again, but if Nina thought her snarl might get Mariana to back off for good, a move that would disappoint their parents, the kid had another think coming. Working in the ER, Mariana had learned how to handle pissy attitudes or worse from patients and doctors alike. Teen moodiness? Ha! No problem.

Leaning her hip against the table's edge, Mariana pushed up the sleeves of the sweatshirt she'd thrown over her scrubs after her shift earlier. "Okay, so you don't need math help. But here's a notification for you since your cell phone use is currently limited: I'm not going anywhere. None of us are going anywhere. We're all here to stay. That includes you. If you want."

Nina's mechanical pencil stilled for a beat, then continued jotting down the numbers and letters in her next math problem.

"You messed up. News flash, we all do. It's how you handle things moving forward that counts. But you're a Capuleta sister now, and that means even when you pull a stupid stunt like the one you did, we all have your back."

The snap of the pencil lead breaking was the only indication that Nina had heard Mariana's promise.

The teen jabbed the eraser down several times with her thumb. Then, after a cagey, side-eyed glance at Mariana, she went back to work.

"Oh-kay then. I've had my say. The ball's in your court. You want some algebra help, maybe some company while you're experiencing the thrill of Casa Capuleta confinement, give me a call." Hooking her fingers through her trumpet case handle, Mariana turned to leave, then changed her mind and about-faced.

"I won't hug you adiós, *not* because I don't want you to bite my head off, but because I'm respecting your boundaries. Just know, I'd like to. And someday, you're gonna wanna hug me, too."

Nina's puff of breath might have been a show of irritation, but one side of her mouth twitched in a half smirk Mariana took as a positive sign. Satisfied, she turned to go, striding from the dining room, through the kitchen, into the second half of the Capuleta home.

Years ago, Arturo and Berta had converted two of the two-bedroom, one-bath apartments into one large home for themselves and the girls they hoped to start fostering. An arched opening had been carved into the wall separating the apartments, and one kitchen had been gutted to create the large living room area where the familia gathered for sing-offs, game nights, movie watching, and the occasional all-familia meeting.

Dressed in a Hawaiian-print bata, their mom gave a tired smile from her seat curled up on the faded, olive-green sofa. She paused her telenovela on the TV, then moved aside the skirt of her housedress and patted the cushion beside her.

"Siéntate for a bit," her mom invited.

"Ay, I'd love to sit and relax," Mariana answered. "Pero if I join you, I may not be able to get up later. I've been pulling extra shifts, including both days this weekend and next, so I can get off for the Battle. I'm beat. There's a glass of cabernet and a bubble bath in my near future. Maybe an episode or two of a baking show filled with delicious recipes I'll probably never attempt pero enjoy pretending I will."

She and her mom grinned at their familia's inside joke. With Mariana's busy schedule, her idea of baking snacks for rehearsal involved picking up a box of her favorite sweet breads from the panadería.

"Pobrecita, mija, you work so hard." Her mom rose and opened her arms for a hug, repeating her "poor girl" lament.

Several inches taller, Mariana bent to lay her head on Mamá's shoulder. The comforting sense of home and safety enveloped her. She'd been lucky enough to have experienced a devoted mother's love before coming to Casa Capuleta. For Nina, it was the opposite.

Mariana wasn't sure which was worse—knowing the blessing you have and losing it or not knowing what you had missed out on until it presented itself, but being too afraid to trust that it was real.

"Gracias for trying with her," Mamá whispered.

"She's a tough nut, but we'll crack her shell. In a good way, te prometo," Mariana promised. Her mom squeezed her a little tighter in response.

When they eased apart, the worry that had shadowed her mom's darkly tanned face lately had lightened. "I didn't see you after your performance at the quinceañera last night. I opened the windows to listen. You girls sounded beautiful, mija. Felicia and her parents were so happy."

Pride for her sisters and the musical gifts they shared buoyed Mariana's tired spirit. "The audience loved Cat's new song mash-up. As much as I don't like feeding her ego, I have to admit, she's freaking talented."

"Ay, no seas mala," her mom chided.

"I'm not being mean, I'm complimenting her." Mariana grinned at her mother's arched-brow, I-know-what-you're-up-to expression.

"Sí, your sister is talented. As are *all* my girls."

"You have to say that, you're our mamá."

"It is also the truth." Her mom's levity dulled, gravity looming in her brown eyes as she clasped Mariana's arms. "That is why I agreed with Catalina and you about this competition. Tengo mis dudas, pero I also have faith. And my faith in Him and you girls outweighs those doubts. I am counting on you, mija, to keep an eye on your sisters, especially the three younger ones. And your father. He may no longer be the band's manager, but you know he intends to be at those meetings, watching over his girls. You must be the calm in the storm that may brew if we are not careful."

The ever-present knot of resolve and desperation in Mariana's chest tightened. "You know I will look out for them. Siempre."

It was a promise she made to her mother as much as to herself. She would protect her loved ones. *Always.*

For that very reason, last night had to remain an anomaly.

So what that she had really enjoyed Angelo's company? Their surprisingly easy conversation, even while exploring a common bond in the loss of their parents. Their shared understanding of the sacrifice of putting familia before self. His unexpected humility in admitting his struggles with parenting his sister. How right it had felt to simply hold his hand, see her interest and longing mirrored in his eyes.

None of it mattered. He was a Montero.

And yet something inside her felt sure that Angelo was nothing like his tío.

"Mamá, do you really think El Rey Properties is behind the sudden demand for the balloon payment on the loan? Would this antagonism between Hugo Montero and Papo go that far?"

"Ay, mija, I really don't know. I've always wanted to believe that somehow your father and Hugo would mend their rift. That Hugo would come to accept that Arturo and I never meant to hurt him. But the more time that passes, and with gentrification creeping into our neighborhood, I am not so sure." With a heavy sigh, her mother reached for the crucifix dangling at the end of her gold necklace, a larger replica of the ones Mariana and her sisters had received for their quinceañeras. Her mamá's thumb rubbed at the tiny, raised figure, a talisman from which her faith drew strength. "I do know that we cannot let the past misshape our future."

"But it can guide us. Keep us from making the same mistake, right?" Mariana asked.

Only, which of the many mistakes made on both sides should she avoid? Trusting Angelo, desiring him, pushing him away?

As if she sensed Mariana's inner turmoil, her mom softly cupped Mariana's cheeks. "Remember, mija, sometimes there is a thin line between love and hate. The Hugo Montero I knew as a young woman, the one who introduced me to your papo, was not a bad person."

Her mom's claim echoed Angelo's from last night. And yet, Hugo Montero's actions continuously spoke differently.

"Hugo chose his path. Your papo and I chose our own," Mamá continued. "What matters now is protecting our familia and Casa Capuleta. If Las Nubes wins the Battle, our comunidad and students win, too. Me entiendes?"

"Sí, I understand. You can count on me." The familiar weight of responsibility settled onto her shoulders and Mariana straightened, accepting it with pride.

"Muy bien."

Her mom patted her cheek, then turned away. Her house slippers shuffled on the laminate wood flooring as she made her way to the sofa. A satisfied smile curving her lips, she settled on the cushions and reached for the remote control to continue watching her telenovela.

"Now vete, go." She shooed a hand at their "back" door, what used to be the entrance to the second apartment. "Get some rest. I am worried about the time commitment for this Battle and your already busy schedule."

That made two of them. But Mariana kept the concern to herself. She had to. The competition prize money would be the solution to her parents' financial woes, even if the mandatory participant meetings, extra rehearsals Cat would rightly demand, and actual performances would be a major time suck.

Instead, Mariana smiled, lied through her two-years-of-braces straightened teeth, and assured her mom she had everything under control.

She would, as soon as she figured out how to squelch her irrepressible attraction to a certain mariachi with a knack for surprise date nights and toe-curling rooftop kisses.

Chapter Six

"This is like, big-time," Teresa murmured, awe and unease coloring her words.

Mariana glanced at her youngest sister, thirteen as of last month, seated beside her in the third row of the historic Majestic Theatre.

Doubt pinched Teresita's face as she craned her neck to gaze around the site of the Battle of the Mariachi Bands' first meeting Thursday evening. Mariana followed suit, taking in the famed theatre's grandeur, equally as awed by the lush design and intricate details that had landed the Majestic on many "must-see while in San Antonio" lists.

Inspired by a mix of Spanish Mission, Baroque, and Mediterranean architecture, the building's every nook and cranny begged to be appreciated. From the vaulted ceilings with twinkling lights and drifting clouds to the side balcony seating designed to replicate a Mediterranean villa, grapevines and foliage clinging to the walls and adorning the colorful glass windows. From the elaborate peacock perched on a balcony railing to the decorative arches and statues, and countless other ornate touches that gave visitors the illusion of having been transported to a European villa carved into the side of a mountain.

Tonight, a nervous energy hummed among the competition participants seated in the orchestra level.

"I'm the youngest one here," Teresa mumbled. "What if I'm not ready?"

Elbow perched on the padded armrest between them, Mariana leaned closer. "Being the youngest makes you even more impressive, Teresita. Some of those other musicians have been playing for years, and they're still no match for you. Your guitar skills on Cat's new song? Increíble."

"You really think I'm that good?"

"Girl, I don't think it; I *know* it!"

Mariana held her fist up for a bump. Relief curled through her when Teresita tapped knuckles, then splayed her fingers to mime an explosion. Exactly like what Mariachi Las Nubes planned to do—blow the other bands and the judges away.

Teresa grinned, and Mariana hoped her sister recalled the words of Mariana's pep talk before they'd left home earlier.

Juntas podemos. That's all they needed to remember. "Together we can."

"Hey!" Cat tapped Mariana's shoulder from her seat in the row behind them. She tipped her head toward the older gentleman who had introduced himself as the director and a group of others from his team gathered in front of the stage. "Do you think they'll start on time, even if all the bands aren't here yet?"

Mariana checked her watch. Ten minutes to six.

"No idea," she answered. "Frankly, I'm surprised anyone would risk being late, especially with the carrot dangled that Patricio Galán might make an appearance."

"Oooohhhh!" Twin swoony sighs from Cat and Teresita met her reminder.

"What's going on with you girls?" Violeta asked from two seats down.

Cat feigned a verklempt faint, pressing the back of a hand to her forehead and collapsing into her cushioned auditorium seat. "¡Ay, mi corazón!"

"Your heart? *My* heart! He's my crush!" Teresita teased.

The other girls pressed toward them, and the conversation turned to Patricio and their adoration for the handsome, internationally admired mariachi.

Scooting to the edge of her seat, Mariana twisted around to get a better look at the rest of the bands spread out behind them. Papo waved to her from where he stood in the aisle halfway up, chatting with José Alfredo, the leader of Mariachi Mi Corazón, the third band from San Antonio. He and Papo had known each other for years. They often recommended the other's band for gigs they couldn't book. Unlike Mariachi Los Reyes, who'd been known to horn in on potential opportunities that might have come the sisters' way.

Mariana knew the two Houston bands from small festivals they had played together. She and Cat had hung out with one of the ladies from Mariachi Luna y Sol, the only coed band. Las Nubes had never come across the mariachis from McAllen and El Paso, but Cat had done extensive research on all the competitors. Now she and Violeta wasted no time in exchanging snide whispers about who was known for their sound-the-alarm level of machismo and old-school thinking.

With the meeting start time nearing, only a few stragglers like Papo and José Alfredo continued intermingling. The rest sat in distinctly separate groups, all the bands present and accounted for, with one notable exception. The reigning champs.

No one from Mariachi Los Reyes had checked in yet when Mariana had done so for their band twenty minutes ago. With San Antonio's infamous traffic snarls, especially on a workday, they had opted to leave Casa Capuleta early rather than risk arriving late. She had a hard time believing Mariachi Los Reyes wouldn't have anticipated the same potential delay.

Still, she didn't mind putting off the impending unhappy reunion between Papo and Hugo a little while longer. Nor her need to pretend that she and Angelo had never met. Both had her heart racing for completely different reasons.

Mariana had been waiting for Papo to complain about Angelo and Marco getting kicked off the premises Saturday night. But that boot had never dropped. Either Tonio had kept the incident to himself, which didn't make sense, or Papo was keeping it from Mariana and her sisters.

That was fine. She had a whopper of a secret herself.

One with the propensity to knock her off her game if she wasn't careful. As if she didn't have enough stress already. Between her promise to her mom, her compulsion to do all she could for those who relied on Casa Capuleta, while still finding the time and energy for work and PA shadow hours, she shouldn't be losing sleep over someone she wanted to be with but couldn't.

"Five minutes, everyone!" the stage manager announced.

"I can't believe no one from Mariachi Los Reyes is here," Cat said. "Talk about a dumb move on their part—and lucky for us if it gets them disqualified."

"Dumb" was not a word typically associated with Angelo's uncle. Everyone knew about Hugo's determination to take home the title a second year in a row. No way he would miss—

"¡Buenas tardes a todos!" The booming "good afternoon, everyone" reverberated off the theatre walls as Hugo Montero strode down the center aisle, arms spread wide as if welcoming all to his humble abode.

"Speak of the two-horned devil." Cat's upper lip curled with distaste.

Mariana ignored her sister. Instead, her gaze remained glued to Papo, still standing in the center aisle, even though José Alfredo had stepped aside to make room for Montero and the rest of his men, who filed in behind him.

With Papo's back to Mariana, she couldn't see his expression, but his stiff shoulders and arms, hands splayed at his sides like a gunslinger ready to make a quicksilver grab of his gun, told her Papo was in pissed-off mode, still seething from the unexpected house call the private lender had made earlier today. Based on the narrowing of Hugo's dark eyes as he drew to a halt, she'd guess her father wasn't offering a friendly hello.

Brow furrowed with a what's-up frown, Angelo peered around his uncle. Surprise, followed quickly by dismay, registered on the handsome face that had invaded her dreams far too often over the past few months.

Angelo murmured something that made his uncle give a firm shake of his head.

"Ay Dios mío, Mamá said to watch out for this," Blanca fretted.

Cat sucked her teeth in obvious annoyance and slid Mariana a look that asked whether they should step in to defuse the standoff or wait.

Before she could decide, Papo gestured to the last rows of the orchestra level, ushering Los Reyes to the back of the theatre. As far away from Mariana and her sisters as they could get without relegating the other band to standing-room-only status.

Booted feet spread in a wide stance, Hugo glared at her father. The muscles in Hugo's square jaw tightened. The thin slash of his black mustache mimicked the hard line of his lips, evidence of his displeasure with Papo's one-man blockade.

"It's fine, Tío. C'mon." Angelo put a hand on his uncle's shoulder. "Sitting back here gives us a better view of the entire stage."

Neither Hugo nor Papo moved.

Frustration billowed inside Mariana. The competition had yet to begin and already the two patriarchs were flexing their muscles like prizefighters in a ring.

This had to stop! Any fighting should take place onstage, with their instruments, choreography, and vocals as their weapons.

Hands clenched with resolve, Mariana pushed to her feet. The padded seat sprang closed with a muffled *thwack* against the back cushion. Cat followed suit. Before either one could intervene, the director beat them to it.

"Looks like everyone's here. If you'll take your seats, we can get started. There's a lot to cover."

A beat passed and the standoff continued.

"Papo, come," Mariana called. "Blanca saved you a seat on the aisle."

Angelo's gaze met hers. The apologetic understanding in his dark eyes transported her back to their booth at Whataburger. His promise from the other night whispered through her mind.

I'll do whatever I can to make sure our guys are on their best behavior.

She had warned herself not to hope. Apparently, she'd been right. There were few, if any, who could hold Hugo Montero in check. Not when Papo stood there practically egging the other man on.

Angelo tipped his head in an infinitesimal greeting. So different from his sheepish grin the other night when he admitted that he'd waited for her in front of Casa Capuleta, even though he'd been tossed to the curb. Or the relieved smile when she'd agreed to grab a bite. Or the slightly crooked smile when he joked about the trials of being the guardian of a teenager.

Determined to ignore the strange pull between them, Mariana forced herself to look away, severing their connection.

"Papo, por favor," she pleaded.

Angelo tucked his hand in the crook of Hugo's elbow to pull his uncle toward where the rest of their band now sat in the back rows.

Moments later, her father plopped into his seat beside Blanca. Mariana sat down and leaned across her sister's lap toward him. "We will beat them where it counts, Papo. Up there." She jerked a thumb at the stage a few rows in front of them. "Where Pepe Aguilar and Mariachi Tecalitlán and others have inspired us with their performances."

The hard set to his craggy features, so unlike the mild-mannered man she knew him to be, softened. Blanca laid her head on his shoulder, and the last dregs of his anger dissipated from his nearly black eyes.

"Sí, we can do this." Cat leaned forward to grab the back of Papo's seat. "I've been working on rearranging our set for the first round. We'll show Montero where he can stick his archaic no-women machismo."

Even worrywart Blanca snickered at Cat's brash claim.

"You see? Mariachi Los Reyes and the others don't stand a chance," Mariana promised.

Of course, changing their current lineup of songs and adding to their choreography meant more, and probably longer, rehearsals. She bit back a tired sigh. Never underestimate the value of power naps in the ER break room.

"Were you able to switch your shifts to days?" Cat asked, as if she had read Mariana's mind. "I'm adding two extra rehearsals this week so we'll be ready for next Saturday."

"I might be a zombie by the end of the week, and it took a little bribing, but yes."

"That's why they invented concealer," Cat shot back, showing no sympathy for Mariana's predicament. "No rest for the weary. We got a Battle to win."

Blanca pressed a finger to her lips to shush them as the competition director kicked off staff introductions.

Mariana slid a notebook from her satchel, then settled into her seat. She put an asterisk beside the stage manager's name, planning to introduce herself before leaving today. The middle-aged woman tasked with assigning dressing rooms and rehearsals could help with Mariana's plan to keep as much distance between Los Reyes and Las Nubes as possible.

Nearly forty-five minutes later, the staff had gone over the schedules for the three rounds of competition, the availability of practice space for those from out of town, and the required and optional publicity involving Nuestros Niños. Also known as "Our Children," the charity founded by Patricio Galán was this year's beneficiary of the two ticketed competition rounds.

"We have one final speaker, who was delayed briefly but is now on his way. Let's take a short break and reconvene in ten to wrap things up," the director announced.

The rumble of conversations rose as most of the participants stood. Some moved into the aisles to converse with musicians from other bands.

"What do you think?" Cat asked.

Mariana swiveled to face her sister in the row behind her. Over Cat's shoulder, hands on the waistband of his light-wash jeans, Angelo twisted from side to side, stretching his back. The motion pulled his navy sweater snug across his torso, teasing her with memories of New Year's Eve, when her palms had greedily traced the muscles along his back. Savoring his steely strength.

"Think about what?" she murmured, unable to tear her gaze from Angelo. Willing him to turn in her direction, seek her out. Reminding herself it was best if neither of them did.

He dug the fingers of one hand into the juncture of his neck and shoulder. Eyes closed, he massaged the area, wincing with discomfort. She wondered whether, similar to the "regular day" he'd described the other evening, he'd spent today stuck in front of his computer crunching numbers and reviewing financial reports for El Rey Properties.

"Do you think Patricio Galán will actually show up?" Cat clarified. "The man's only got a short break in the middle of an extended tour. I'd think he'd want to spend it relaxing. Not dealing with all of this." She circled a hand in the air, indicating the eight bands and staff.

"Ay, I sure hope he comes." Blanca's swoon was met by Claudia's fervent, "He has to! I even wore my favorite lipstick!" a couple of seats down.

Teresita made a kissy face and batted her eyelashes, eliciting giggles from the other two teens. Relieved to see that the nervous qualms Blanca and Teresita had struggled with when they first arrived had finally quieted, Mariana grabbed her purse and excused herself to use the restroom.

Halfway up the aisle, she stopped to exchange hugs and cheek kisses with the girl from Houston's Mariachi Luna y Sol. When

Mariana turned to head toward the lobby, she found Angelo standing on the edge of the aisle several rows up. Some of his band members milled about, but he had clearly separated himself from them. His thumb scrolled over whatever held his attention on his phone screen.

He glanced up. For a hot second that scorched her lungs as she sucked in a breath, his gaze connected with hers. Held a beat. And another. Then he looked back down at his phone.

Mariana continued up the aisle, telling herself to simply pass by him. To not tempt fate.

"It's good to see you," Angelo said, his voice pitched low.

Her feet slowed to a stop. "You too."

She angled to face the left side of the theatre, pretending to search the crowd for someone.

He mirrored her, turning in the opposite direction, pretending, she now realized, to read something on his screen.

For all intents and purposes, they were simply two competition participants who happened to be standing near each other.

Or not.

"For a while there it seemed like Los Reyes was pulling a no-show," she said.

"Tío Hugo always likes to make an entrance."

"I would have never guessed."

His warm chuckle sent tantalizing shivers sizzling through her. She called herself all kinds of foolish for daring to talk to him. Even more for reveling in her body's reaction to what it couldn't have.

"It's pretty wild that we get to perform up there," he said, motioning toward the stage.

"Unbelievable, really. Though only if we make it to the second round."

"Oh, Los Reyes will make it."

A laugh bubbled up her throat at his smug response. She tried to smother it with a hand over her mouth, but her laughter slipped out. "My sisters and I look forward to joining *and beating* you there."

Angelo shifted toward her, negating the pretense of them as uninterested bystanders by gently clasping her elbow. "About the other night—"

"¿Mariana, estás bien?" Papo called from where he stood talking with a group off to the right. Eyes narrowed with suspicion, he strode down the row.

Angelo eased back a step, his fingers sliding to her forearm as if he was loath to release her.

"You were told the other night to stay away from my girls," Papo barked, chin jutting at a pugnacious angle.

"I was simply making small talk, that's all." Angelo held up a hand in polite apology.

Her father answered with a disbelieving *humph*.

"Papo, it's okay. Really." She clasped his arm to lead him back to their seats. To her dismay, Papo's feet planted like stakes in the ground, and he refused to budge.

In her peripheral vision, she caught Hugo descending on them from the other direction. His face was blotchy with anger, his jowls quivering like an angry bulldog's. "You have a bone to pick, Arturo, you pick it with me."

"Oye, there's no need for any of this." Angelo stepped in between her father and his uncle, palms out as he tried to hold them off.

Papo shoved Angelo's raised arm aside. Hugo snarled and lunged forward, pushing Angelo out of the way. As Angelo tried to intervene, his uncle's elbow connected with Angelo's cheekbone. He staggered back with a muttered curse.

One palm pressed to his right cheek, he glared at the two older men. "Enough! No one wants to create a scene here."

"I could *not* agree more!" Patricio Galán's cry from the top of the center aisle shocked everyone into silence.

Dressed all in black—from the Stetson on his head to his long-sleeve button-down, designer jeans, and custom-made boots—the famed musician made a striking figure. He crooked a thumb on his black leather belt with his signature ornate silver buckle. Swap his indignant expression for a bedroom-eyed smolder and the man was the cover of his latest platinum album come to life.

"The only story we want the press covering is the one about the much-needed funds we plan to raise for Nuestros Niños." Galán's indignant gaze swept the room like a king surveying his subjects. "Any outside animosity ends ahora mismo. And I mean, *right now*. Or it is paused until we are done. If anyone has questions about how serious I am about that, I direct you to the morality clause in your contract that stipulates behavior constituting grounds for disqualification."

Nervous glances were exchanged between some of the mariachi. No one ventured to protest.

Galán gave a brisk nod. "However, I am sure we will not have to worry about any of that. Right?"

The question was obviously rhetorical because, without waiting for a reply, like Moses parting the Red Sea, he lifted a hand and the participants backed out of the aisle, scurrying for their seats.

Angelo led his uncle to where other Los Reyes members had gathered near the back.

Mariana clasped Papo's elbow and drew him down the aisle to their seats with the girls. Embarrassed heat stung her cheeks. She doubted whether Galán's warning could actually hit pause on the feud between the Capuletas and Monteros. But if his commanding presence could muffle the tension long enough for Mariachi Las Nubes to win the money and pay off the slimy private lender, and raise that trophy high for all young female musicians to see, even she, the last holdout among her sisters, would join Galán's fan club.

Just as Galán passed her row, Mariana's cell phone started vibrating with an incoming call. A quick check showed one of her coworkers' names flashing across the tiny screen. There was only one reason Suzy Gomez would be calling. The little girl who was the lone survivor of a car accident with her parents yesterday must be out of surgery. Unless she didn't . . .

Mariana cut off the thought.

"Papo, this is about a patient. I have to take it," she whispered, holding up her phone for him to see.

He frowned and shot a hard glare over his shoulder in the direction of Los Reyes.

"I'll be fine," she assured him. "This shouldn't take long."

Hunkered down to avoid drawing attention to herself, she scurried to the side aisle that ran along the ornate wall, then ducked into one of the deep green–painted alcoves that would lead to the lobby. Once out of view, she glanced back to catch Galán hoisting himself up onto the stage.

His trademark grin flashed white against his deep bronze skin as he rose from his haunches. "Thank you for your patience while I wrapped up another meeting. I am Patricio Galán, the host for this special Battle of the Mariachi Bands anniversary year. Which, gracias to my record label, will award a special grand prize."

Applause and guttural gritos met his mention of the higher stakes this year.

Mariana's phone stopped vibrating, then immediately started again. Crap! That couldn't be good. If everything had gone okay, Suzy would have left an "all's well" voice message.

Unease quickening her footsteps, Mariana hurried to the lobby. If-onlys tripped over themselves in her head. If Mariachi Las Nubes weren't in the competition, Mariana would have stayed after she clocked out. Waited and been there when the child woke up from surgery, knowing the little girl would be afraid. If they were lucky, Child Services had finally located a family member. If not, once she recovered, the sweet child would be shuffled into the system. Alone and scared.

Empathy welled in Mariana's throat. Unfortunately, tonight's all-teams meeting meant no going above and beyond for her patients after her shift ended. Instead, she'd left on time, something she rarely did. Unless familia duties called.

The juggle of responsibilities seldom weighed on her. But as another round of applause for something Galán said carried into the lobby, Mariana found herself torn between familia and her own dreams. Wanting to be here with her sisters, sharing the love of music and culture that bonded them, and also at the hospital, helping those who struggled to manage the bureaucracy of the system on their own, like her birth mother had all those years ago.

The internal tug-of-war between familia responsibility and her own goals was nothing new. But there *was* something different this time.

The addition of a certain dark-eyed, appealingly likable guitar player was definitely something different. In the midst of the chaos around her, seeing Angelo again, even if she had to keep her distance, was a secret little treat that had her pulse racing and her imagination creating what-ifs. At least until reality stepped in to remind her of her folly.

Chapter Seven

Angelo watched Mariana hurry up the side aisle, her cell clutched in her hand like a lifeline. Guilt for his part in causing the concern pinching her full lips and furrowing her brow burned in his stomach.

He should have left well enough alone. Kept pretending to ignore her rather than give in to his need to talk to her, tease a smile from her, again.

A mistake that had only compounded their problem.

Thankfully, Patricio Galán's arrival had forced her father and his uncle back into their respective corners. Though Mariana's quick exit shortly after left Angelo surmising that she was still upset.

Angelo listened with half an ear as Galán shared his vision for the competition: celebrating some of Texas's best mariachis, raising needed funds for Nuestros Niños, and giving one band a chance to shine on the big stage with him.

When ten minutes had passed without Mariana's return, Angelo began to worry that maybe she'd been more shaken by the confrontation than she wanted the others to know. Sibling responsibility could weigh on you like Atlas's globe. Angelo felt it with Brenda. As the oldest, Mariana had eight sisters counting on her.

"I gotta check on something. I'll be back," Angelo whispered to Marco.

Without waiting for his buddy to ask any questions, Angelo excused himself and squeezed past the other Los Reyes members in his row. Then, taking a similar route as Mariana had on the opposite side of the orchestra level, he hugged the wall and headed to the lobby, where he hoped to find her.

Moments later he reached the open area with its elegant, often photographed chandelier and hit pay dirt.

Huddled in a corner, chin tucked, phone pressed to her ear, Mariana bit her lip and scowled at whatever she heard on the other end of the line. The fingertips of her other hand pressed into her forehead, moving in slow, tiny circles as if massaging a headache.

He edged closer. Not wanting to eavesdrop yet wanting to alert her of his presence, that he hoped to . . .

To what?

Crap, once again where she was concerned, he had reacted without any real plan. He probably shouldn't have followed her. If the wrong someone else walked through one of the archways, him being here could very well make the situation worse for her.

"And they haven't located a single family member yet?" Frustration tinted her question. The toe of her dark brown ankle boot *tap tap tapped* at the corner where the carpet butted up against the wall.

Her scowl deepened, broadcasting her displeasure with the response she received.

"You're sure her vitals are steady?" she asked, then hummed a dull "mmm-hmmm" at the answer. "And you promise you'll call me if anything changes? If she wants some company, I can head . . . I know I don't have to . . . ay, Suzy, por favor, she's six, and her parents just died in the same accident that put her in our care. If DFPS hasn't . . . okay, but . . ."

The speed of Mariana's frustrated boot *tap tap tapping* increased.

Angelo didn't have to be a trained therapist to understand why the patient in question struck a chord in her. Why she identified so strongly with a child who had suddenly lost her parents and was reliant upon the Department of Family and Protective Services. Or why he felt compelled to stick around and offer whatever solace Mariana might accept from him.

"Ugh, you know I can't . . . fine," she grumbled into her phone. "At least text me with any updates, okay?"

Her shoulders rose and fell on a heavy sigh as she slipped the phone into the satchel hanging across her body. Angelo waited for her to turn around and notice him before he approached. Instead, she slumped forward to press the crown of her head against the wall.

Face shielded from view by the curtain of her long, black hair, back hunched against the unfairness of the world, she was the picture of dejection.

His brain warned him to leave her alone. Let her sisters comfort her when she returned to them.

His heart had other ideas.

He stepped to her side, his bootheels muffled on the carpet, and gently cupped her shoulder.

Mariana spun around, her hazel eyes widened with shock, and nearly smacked him in the face with the butt of her palm as she tried to stiff-arm him. Angelo dodged the blow and stumbled back.

"Perdón, I didn't mean to surprise you," he apologized.

She splayed a hand over her heart, her short red nails vivid against the soft blue of her cashmere sweater. "You didn't . . . bueno, yeah, you did."

"Everything okay?"

"Mmm-hmmm." Her head bobbed yes, but the shadows clouding her eyes told a different story.

"I couldn't help overhearing. Sounds like you're worried about a patient?"

"Comes with the job description."

Man, she was an expert at putting on a brave face. "If you want to talk about—"

"Angelo, what are you doing?"

Her blunt question stung. Though, admittedly, he was experiencing some of the same confusion stamping her face. He had no business seeking her out. And yet, he couldn't resist.

While he grappled for an answer that made sense, she pressed a palm to her forehead, her eyes fluttering closed momentarily on a soft exhalation of breath.

"We're not friends. We can't be. That bruise on your face is evidence enough that this conversation shouldn't be happening."

She swished a hand in the space between them, a resignation he wasn't ready to accept twisting her lips. He clasped her hand, unable to ignore the compulsion to recapture the connection they had made on Saturday night. The indefinable something that had ensnared him since New Year's Eve.

When she didn't pull away, instead letting him flirt with the edge of her personal space when he stepped nearer, relief winnowed through him.

He waved his other hand toward the stage and seating area beyond. "Maybe out there we have to play by their rules. But here, it's just you and me."

Her expression softened. Encouraged, he continued.

"If not friends, then respected acquaintances. At the very least, late-night hamburger-craving companions."

She rolled her eyes, but he caught their flash of humor at his weak attempt to lighten the mood.

"And when a friend, *an acquaintance*"—he amended before she could argue semantics—"is upset, my parents taught me it's important to try and help."

"Bueno, I appreciate that, but it seems like I should be worried about you."

It was her turn to step closer. Her turn to surprise him by fluttering her fingertips over his cheekbone. He flinched, the motion bringing a stab of pain to the tender area.

"You should get some ice on this as soon as we're done here," she advised.

"Yes, Doc."

"Nurse," she corrected, her tone smug. "We do all the really important work."

His chuckle caught in his throat as her fingertips continued their exploration of his cheek. His temple. A whisper of a caress along his jawline. The innocent touch had lust blazing a fiery trail down his body.

"I'm sorry this happened," she said softly, dropping her hand to her side. Leaving him craving more of her gentle ministrations.

"It's not your fault. You weren't the one who elbowed me."

"I know. But I can't help feeling partially responsible. My dad's normally not so hotheaded. I didn't expect him to egg your tío on like that. It's just . . ." She drove her fingers through the length of her silky hair, her troubled gaze flitting to a gold-framed floral painting on the wall beside them. "The guy who lent my parents the money for the building repairs stopped by Casa Capuleta this afternoon. He's giving them a hard time about a balloon payment they hadn't expected. We think it's because he wants them to default on the loan. They really shouldn't have trusted him in the first place."

"Are you sure the guy's legitimate?"

"Supposedly, but he doesn't seem like it. I was still at the hospital when he dropped by today, but apparently he and Papo got into a pretty loud argument." She sighed, her troubled expression softening with remorse as she eyed his sore cheek. "I'm guessing seeing your uncle, then the two of us talking, tipped my dad over the edge."

"What are the loan terms?" Angelo asked. "Maybe I can take a look at the paperwork, or run it by one of our lawyers?"

"Are you kidding me?" Her harsh scoff made it seem like Angelo had offered to drag the loan guy out back and rough him up or something equally ridiculous. "No offense, but I can*not* involve you. I shouldn't have said anything about it. We're not even sure that El Rey Properties isn't a player in whatever illegal deal this guy's cooking up."

"We wouldn't do something like that."

Mariana's arched brow told him she thought otherwise.

Angelo hooked his thumbs in his jeans pockets and met her stare for pointed stare. If she couldn't bring herself to trust him on this—

"Fine," she finally said with a moody huff. "'Illegal' might not be the right word. But 'unethical'? 'Underhanded'? Maybe."

Anger flared in his chest. For years there'd been rumblings about Tío Hugo and his luck—what Hugo called "savvy business sense"—at getting in on the right property deals at the right time. But Angelo had never come across anything illegal while managing the books for his tío's company. If Mariana truly believed El Rey Properties engaged in unethical practices, that meant she painted him with the same unsavory brush.

"I guess, right or wrong, you're going to believe what you want to believe," he said, disillusioned by her inability to at least give him the benefit of the doubt. "Or what you've been taught to believe is true anyway."

"Like it's any different for you and whatever your uncle has preached in your house?" she shot back. "Sure, you seem like a nice guy, but—"

"*Seem* like? Are you kidding me?" Upset by her use of the qualifier, he spun away.

"Angelo, wait!" She grabbed his wrist, stopping him. "I didn't mean it like that. I'm sorry."

Her softly spoken apology had him turning back. "You can't have it both ways, Mariana. I'm either some unethical property grabber with ill intent or one of the good guys who believes in playing fair."

Her gaze connected with his. Earnest. Searching. Flickering with . . .

Damn, he would swear she wanted to trust him. Believe in him. Or maybe this inexplicable pull he felt had him so mixed up he only saw what he wanted to see.

"Therein lies the conundrum of Angelo Montero," she murmured, gently caressing his bruised face again.

Reacting on instinct, Angelo clasped her wrist, holding her hand against his cheek. Reveling in the sensation of her cool palm on his heated skin.

Her lips parted on a soft gasp. Her eyes widened with surprise and . . . blessedly . . . desire.

"There's no conundrum here. I am exactly what you see," he told her.

A furrow wedged between her brows again. More puzzled than worried this time.

"Whatever's going on with Casa Capuleta, I'm not aware of it, but I'll find out if El Rey Properties is involved. You have my word," he promised, lowering their joined hands to sandwich hers with both of his.

Her puzzled frown remained, but she nodded mutely. More importantly, she didn't pull away from him.

"I don't want us to continue the fight that happened out there. I came looking for you because I wanted to make sure you were okay."

"I'm fine."

"Based on what I overheard of that phone call, you're concerned about a young patient. Which, I'd say, happens often with you because you care so much about those around you. It's admirable. And stressful. I'm a good listener, if you need one."

Her mouth opened as if she were about to respond. As if she might trust him enough to confide in him. Anticipation held Angelo's breath hostage. But then she pressed her lips together and shook her head. Tugged lightly against his grip. He obliged, releasing her hand, disappointment settling uncomfortably in his chest as she backed up a step. And another.

"Um, thanks, but . . . I'm used to juggling things on my own. Seems like there's always any number of glass balls in the air. But I've got it under control."

Fingers death-gripping her satchel strap, shoulders erect, she talked a good game, but he had witnessed her dejection moments ago when she was on the phone. The image of her slumped against the wall was emblazoned in his mind. Wavy dark hair draping her hunched shoulders and back, frustration evident in her voice, and anxious boot taps. The picture joined a collection of mental snapshots from their brief moments together that constantly shuffled through his memory on auto-replay.

But this rare glimpse of her vulnerability. Of her trying not to crumble under the pressure coming at her from so many directions. It echoed a private struggle of his own.

That drive to do or be what others expected. Sacrificing self for what was supposed to be the greater good. It didn't come without a price. Between her family and her job, Mariana seemed to take care of everyone else. But who looked after her?

"Every once in a while, it might be a relief to have someone lean in and catch one of those glass balls for you," he ventured. "Or with you."

"When I'm really in a bind, I've got my sisters and my mom and dad. Coworkers."

No significant other. The satisfaction that came with that knowledge was tempered by the reality that she didn't plan on including him on that list either. He'd do well to hold a similar stance and quell this infatuation with her. It wasn't like he didn't have his own glass balls, as she referred to them, hovering in the air. With the added burden of knowing that in pursuing one for himself, another might shatter.

"Sounds like you're all set with empathetic listeners then." So she didn't need him.

"I am, gracias."

"Bueno, pues . . ." Well then . . . what? There was really no reason for him to stick around. "I should go."

She gripped her satchel tightly and gave him a jerky nod.

"I hope your patient's okay and you're not too stressed. Good luck with your juggling and . . . everything else, Mariana."

He eased a slow step backward, wishing for just one more of her engaging smiles. Settling for the wistful longing in her soulful eyes.

"Well, what do we have here?"

Patricio Galán's question, coming from behind Angelo, stopped him like a thief trapped in a spotlight. Mariana's face went slack, her jaw dropping open.

"Is he talking to us?" Angelo whispered.

"Uh-huh," she squeaked, her face stamped with the petrified disbelief of a teen caught in the midst of something illicit.

Madre de Dios. Angelo squeezed his eyes shut and sent a prayer that his tío or Arturo Capuleta wasn't following the competition's esteemed host.

"Alberto, give me a minute. I'll meet you out front," Patricio said.

Spinning on his bootheels, Angelo found the superstar making short work of the distance from the decorative lobby archway to the corner where Angelo and Mariana stood. Galán's custom-made boots with their one-of-a-kind stitching thunked ominously on the carpeted floor as he drew near. Behind him, the older gentleman who had entered with the singer earlier beat a hasty retreat in the opposite direction.

Galán reached them, and Angelo held out his hand in greeting. "Good to meet you. Angelo Montero a su servicio."

"A pleasure. I recognize you from last year's champion photo," Galán said, squeezing Angelo's hand in a firm handshake before turning his infamous charm on Mariana. "And you, a Mariachi Las Nubes Capuleta, verdad?"

"Sí, that's right. Mariana. Codirector of our band. Ready to unseat the champions and claim this year's title."

Galán threw back his head with a hearty laugh. Mariana's pleased smirk replaced her momentary shock at the superstar's entrance.

"Your competitive nature is commendable. Las Nubes has certainly garnered my rapt attention." Galán tipped his head at her with approval, his smoldering charm at megawatt level.

Mariana's tan cheeks turned a rosy shade. The welcoming smile she flashed onstage made an encore appearance, a raspy chuckle joining the act. Watching her swoon under Galán's charm like one of his groupies had jealousy jackhammering through Angelo.

Then, as swiftly as it burst out of him, Galán's laughter sobered. Hands clasped behind him, he rocked back on his heels, his eyes tracking from Mariana to Angelo. "I've done extensive research on all the bands who made our top eight. And I am aware of the bad blood, so to speak, between your father"—his piercing gaze homed in on Mariana, then moved sharply to Angelo—"and your tío. As well as the traditional-versus-contemporary rivalry between your bands. That's a hot topic in our industry and among our selection-team members. Trust me, we weighed the potential drawbacks of having both Mariachi Los Reyes and Mariachi Las Nubes competing together. You both deserve to be here. However, after what I almost witnessed earlier, I don't want to think I may have miscalculated."

Galán paused, letting the gravity of his words sink in.

Mariana's shoulder bumped Angelo's as she straightened and cleared her throat. "Señor Galán, I can assure you that you made the right choice."

"Definitely," Angelo added.

"That's good to hear. And please, call me Patricio," the singer answered. "We couldn't see breaking with tradition by denying the reigning champions the chance to compete again. Pero con Las Nubes—with Las Nubes we see a novice entry with strong musicality and raw talent. The sample video you submitted proved you and your sisters deserved a spot. It convinced me that any potential conflict due to the rivalry would be outweighed by your bands' professionalism. Was I wrong?"

"Not at all. Mariachi Las Nubes takes this opportunity seriously," Mariana replied.

"As does Los Reyes," Angelo added. "Holding the champion title is an honor we regard with much respect. Along with the respect we have for our fellow competitors."

In a show of solidarity, Angelo looped an arm around Mariana's waist. He felt her stiffen, but she didn't shy away.

"Muy bien. Let me be clear, though. What happened earlier, or worse, cannot occur again," Galán warned. "We want publicity focused on the kids the charity assists. On the funds we are trying to raise for them with a celebration of our music. Since the two of you appear to have cooler heads, I will count on you to find a way to keep the peace between your bands."

"Wait, what?" Mariana's shocked question echoed the one Angelo was ready to ask.

Twisting to face him, she shot him an incredulous glare, and he quickly dropped his hand from where it nestled comfortably on her lower back.

"Do not disappoint me. Got it?" After delivering his ultimatum with a finger pointing at the two of them, the Legend in Black strode away, leaving Angelo and, by the looks of her pale complexion, Mariana, thunderstruck.

"Wh-what the hell just happened?" A dumbfounded expression widened her eyes.

Angelo stared at the now-empty archway through which Galán had entered and exited like a tornado, his strong winds leaving them storm-tossed and rattled. "It looks like he thinks we can work together somehow to defuse the situation."

"Uh-uh." Mariana shook her head, her long hair swinging along her back and shoulders. "Galán couldn't possibly expect us to pair up like this."

Not "could"—the mariachi expected it.

Suddenly, like a pecan falling from one of the trees out on his tio's sprawling ranch and weekend-getaway property, a realization hit Angelo on the head: Galán had unknowingly handed Angelo the opening he'd been seeking.

Grabbing at his chance, he pulled his cell phone out of his back pocket, unlocked the screen, then held it out to Mariana. "Here, if we're working together like Galán wants, it'll help if we exchange phone numbers."

"This is not a good idea. You already know that I'm not a fan of sneaking around."

"It doesn't have to be like that. Maybe we simply share basic logistics info. Like, when our band plans to schedule stage rehearsal or volunteer for a publicity event. That way, the other can choose different times, decrease the chance for uncomfortable band mingling."

Eyes narrowed, Mariana studied him as he imagined she would a patient being evaluated in her ER.

"C'mon. If we merge our juggling acts when it comes to the Battle, we might avoid any potential drops. That's what you want, isn't it?"

Angelo wiggled his cell for emphasis when she didn't answer.

Several anxious—leaning toward hopeful—heartbeats later, Mariana let out a weighty sigh. Lips teasing him with a Mona Lisa smile, she snatched his phone and tapped in her contact info.

"Are you sure you're not in sales? You talk a pretty good game," she grumbled.

Angelo grinned.

That quickly, what had started out as a disastrous beginning to the competition had morphed into the unforgettable night Mariana Capuleta finally gave him her digits.

Chapter Eight

"You don't have to sit here with me. I don't need a babysitter."

Seated at the familia's dining table late the following week, Mariana let Nina's snark slide off her like one of the sweat drops beading a path down the side of her iced tea glass. "After the long week I've had, I am off the clock tonight. Believe me, Papo and Mamá couldn't afford my babysitter rates anyway."

"Pfff. Whatevs."

"Call it habit." Mariana shrugged, nostalgia a comfortable companion. "Years of studying at this table ingrained the idea that work happens here, vegging happens over there."

She glanced through the open kitchen area to the sala where Claudia and Teresita currently lounged, sprawled on the faded sofa, watching some reality show. Papo dozed in the recliner, the book he'd been reading resting on his belly.

In the kitchen, their mom busied herself with putting away the leftover enchiladas and rice from dinner. She held up a plastic container, wiggling it in the air at Mariana to indicate it was the one she should take home with her for lunch during her shift tomorrow.

"What are you studying for anyway?" Nina asked.

The teen's interest, or the fact that she expressed it, was something new. Maybe she was finally starting to lower the barbed wire fence she wrapped around herself for protection.

"Not that I care or anything," Nina added with a surly one-shouldered shrug.

Mariana bit her bottom lip to hold back a snicker. So much for the fence lowering. She swiveled her laptop around to show Nina the screen across the dining room table.

"Gentrification and your comunidad," Nina read. Her top lip curled. "Sounds boring. I figured you'd be into A&P or something health science-y like that."

"Anatomy and physiology?" Mariana repeated, surprised that Nina used the acronym with familiarity. "Is that a subject you're thinking about taking next year?"

"Maybe. The school's guidance counselor mentioned it in her litany of advice. But who knows if I'll even be at that school next year. If I wind up back at my old school again, the only postgraduation plans they preached was stay out of jail. It's all a joke."

Tough-girl words spoken by a teen with her shoulders hunched against the world. Her black-painted nail flicked the top corner of her spiral notebook, feigning a nonchalance Mariana was convinced was mostly for show.

"You could still be at your current school. If you wanted."

"It's never about what I want. It's all about the adults. The system and all its rules and crap. They don't care about girls like me."

Regret for a system, a past, that had forged the chip on Nina's shoulder, burned the back of Mariana's throat. She chose her words carefully, tiptoeing closer to that barbed wire. Knowing if she pushed too much, Nina might flick the switch, turning that fence into an electric one.

"Whoever that nebulous 'they' is, bueno, *they* don't matter here. You do. We do. But that's something you have to believe on your own. Me telling you won't change your mind. I know that. Those two . . . oh, those three know that." She jerked a thumb at Teresita and Claudia, now joined by Fabiola, who had squeezed in between her two sisters on the sofa. The trio laughed at whatever antic the rich and famous were embroiled in on the TV. Papo stirred in his recliner.

"I'm not like them," Nina grumbled.

"Me either. Same with Catalina and Blanca, or Violeta and Sabrina. We're all different. Even the ones related by blood. And yet, we each eventually found a way to fit in. Make our place here."

"That's good for you. But I already have a place. With my mom. As soon as she gets out of jail, I'll be back with her."

Spoken with inevitability, not joy. As if Nina was resigned to the idea that her old life was all she could know. All she might deserve.

"Casa Capuleta isn't going anywhere. You'll always be welcome here. That's why I'm reading this." Mariana tapped the top of her computer screen. "Because gentrification is a reality we have to deal with, and I plan to figure out how we can protect this place."

Across the table, Nina eyed her with a look that, in a way only moody teens the globe over managed, somehow meshed snark with wonder.

Mariana's cell phone buzzed, the reverberation amplified by the oak tabletop. She picked it up and her stomach did a little flip as she read the sender's name flashing across the screen.

"Is that your novio?" Nina asked.

"Wha—No!" Mariana's cell slipped from her grasp, tumbling over to Nina's side of the table. "Everyone knows I don't have a boyfriend. Who has time for that?"

Nina's scoff accompanied her rolling eyes. "Most girls your age, that's who. Look at Cat. You should get out with her more. What are you, pushing thirty? That's like, what's it called . . . spinster age!"

"Uh-uh-uh!" Mariana waved a finger at Nina. "Don't you go falling for that patriarchy bull. A woman does not have to be married off to have a fulfilling life. Cat would be the first to agree with me on that. She may have fun playing the field, but her sights, and mine, are focused on our careers."

"Yeah, well, at least she's having fun. The girl headed out on a date after band practice tonight. You . . ." Nina's lips puckered like a duck's bill, her expression clearly emoting a sucks-to-be-you sentiment as she waved a limp hand at Mariana's laptop. "You're sittin' here reading 'Gentrification blah blah blah.'"

"To each her own. I—"

Her cell vibrated a second time. With the screen facing up, the sender's name flashed in the brightly lit notification box: WHATABURGER, 210-555-1970.

"You got Whataburger in your contacts? That's some serious junk food fetish." Nina laughed, her dark ponytail swishing behind her as she shook her head.

Mariana snatched up the phone, thankful that Nina turned the page in her American history book and went back to note-taking.

Angling the device for her eyes only, Mariana tapped open the message app, anxious to see what Angelo had sent. Seconds later, laughter rumbled up her throat. She tried, but failed, to stop herself from grinning at his adorable humor.

Whataburger: My day . . .

Followed by a GIF of a guy wearing khakis and a white oxford, standing in the middle of a cubicle-filled office, frantically shooting a fire extinguisher at various fires around the room.

Whataburger: How about yours?

She thumbed in her reply—About the same—then snickered as she scrolled through a string of young-George-Clooney-in-scrubs GIF options that came up when she searched "ER."

Nina's pencil stilled.

Mariana felt the girl's suspicious gaze laser beaming on her, scanning for info. She rolled her lips between her teeth to keep from broadcasting her pleasure at hearing from him again.

Angelo had started this GIF game via text a week ago, after Patricio Galán had issued his bizarre mandate in the lobby at the Majestic during last Thursday evening's Battle meeting. The texts were typically mundane—how was work, are rehearsals going well, are your sisters driving you bananas like mine, all's quiet on my home front what about yours? Usually accompanied by a GIF or meme that often made her giggle with amusement. Or in the case of the bananas comment, belly laugh out loud in the middle of the break room at the hospital.

His cheesy thoughtfulness over the past week had brought a refreshing frivolity to her demanding schedule. She found herself anticipating his texts, her tired spirits lifting when she thought of them. Picturing his crooked grin when she responded with her own silly GIF.

Chuckling, she nixed the sexy Clooney GIFs. Instead, she sent a wide-mouthed, bug-eyed panda bear image captioned "Pan-da-monium!"

"You must really like hamburgers," Nina mused, head bent over her textbook.

"Sure, who doesn't?"

"Vegans. Vegetarians. Doubtful you'd find them saving Whataburger's number on their phone." Nina glanced up, her eyebrows raised in question. "How long you been talking with 'Whataburger'?"

The cheeky girl even finger-quoted the restaurant name. As if she knew it was code for something . . . someone . . . else.

Was Little Miss Leave Me Alone actually digging for details?

The self-satisfied smirk on Nina's mouth said yes.

Wonder of wonders. The teen clammed up like an informant who hadn't been slipped any money when it came to talking about herself. Yet here she was poking and prodding and innuendo-ing in Mariana's business.

The phone vibrated again.

Whataburger: Any chance you're free to grab a bite tomorrow night?

Mariana's pulse skipped. Last night she had hesitated to answer when he called instead of texting. Then they'd spent over an hour talking. Afterward, she'd fallen asleep feeling relaxed instead of stressed. But dinner . . . a date . . . did she dare?

Whataburger: We could go over Saturday's Round One competition lineup at Market Square. Strategize together.

"Talk about great customer service."

"Hmm? Uh, yeah, sure," Mariana murmured, caught in her internal do-I-don't-I tug-of-war.

"Who knew Whataburger had text-ahead ordering. Which location is that again?" Nina asked.

The *thump thump thump* of Nina's pencil on her notebook had Mariana glancing up. She blinked several times, trying to switch mental gears from Angelo's tempting invitation to Nina's unexpected nosiness. Both had Mariana's pulse quickening.

Guilt burned through her like lava droplets spitting from a volcano threatening to erupt. Which was exactly what would happen if she went on a date with Angelo and got caught.

However, Angelo did raise a good point. It'd be wise for them to review the individualized itineraries the show organizers had sent for the competition's first round this weekend. See how they could best ensure their band members stayed separated as much as possible. Especially Papo and Hugo.

On the other hand, strategizing with the enemy didn't have to involve dinner together. As enticing as the idea might be. No way should she meet up with Angelo. And absolutely no way should she reveal to Nina, or any of her sisters, that the guy causing her goofy smile in the bathroom mirror when she read his buenos días, have a kick ass day message—sent with a GIF of a donkey kicking its hind legs in the air—was a member of Los Reyes. Worse, a Montero!

Talk about making the feud go nuclear.

Pushing her laptop screen closed, Mariana slipped the computer into her satchel and pocketed her phone. "I better get going. Don't want my fries to get cold."

"Yeah, that's what I thought," Nina grumbled. Leaning back in her dining chair, she crossed her arms, covering the bottom half of the Dallas Cowboys logo on the front of her navy-and-white sweatshirt. A classic closed-off body-language pose the teen had perfected during her six-plus months here.

"Meaning?" Mariana asked.

"Meaning, you, the nosy therapist, the lady from DFPS, even them"—Nina flung an arm out toward the kitchen and living room, then gruffly crossed her arms again—"y'all want me to spill my guts all over the place like I'm a problem you gotta fix. Doesn't matter how many times I freakin' say I'm sorry and that the fire was an accident. No one listens. No one cares. You're all too busy labeling me as 'prone to detrimental behavior.'" There went the finger air quotes again. Accompanied by a lip-curling sneer. "Pues, news flash, *hermana*, it's clear I'm not the only one with secrets here. Only, I don't see you coughing up any of 'em."

Nina's snarl turned "sister" into a derogatory word. The unfair connotation had exasperation and anger mixing with Mariana's earlier guilt shooting from that emotion volcano she worked hard to keep dormant.

Splaying a hand on the table for support, she leaned across it. Not quite invading Nina's personal space, but close enough to leave no room for doubt as to the seriousness of Mariana's words.

"None of us is a problem that has to be fixed, Nina. Including you. We're all just trying to do the best we can. For each other. For ourselves.

For the community Casa Capuleta serves. I can promise you, everything I do comes back to that. We want you to be a part of our familia. I'm praying that eventually you want that, too."

Mariana remained still. Bent across the table. Face level with Nina's, staring into the girl's dark eyes. Searching for a hint of understanding, of acceptance.

Canned laughter from the television show filled the tense quiet.

Nina broke the staring contest first. With a huff, she slammed her history book closed, gathered up her notebook and pencil, then shoved her chair away from the table. The wooden legs screeched against the worn linoleum.

"Look, I know exactly who I can count on. Me, myself, and I," Nina said, chin high, expression resolute.

One step forward, two steps back. A sometimes tiring, patience-testing dance when it came to dealing with your past. Creating a new future for yourself. Mariana understood it. Had lived it. At times she still did.

Rather than allow the embers of exasperation to blaze and burn, she stamped them out and straightened away from the table. "Me, myself, and I, huh? That can get to be a lonely trio. Believe me, I speak from experience."

Nina didn't soften. Her jaw stayed equally as tight. Her lips pressed in the same firm line.

Fine. Mariana could wait her out. She had learned from the best. Dios knew Mamá and Papo had the patience of saints when it came to waiting out teen attitude fueled by life's unfairness.

"What's happened to you so far, those wrongs you've been dealt. It all sucks. And I'm not going to pretend that I can one hundred percent empathize, because while our childhoods have similarities, they also have big differences. But I do know what it's like to feel alone in the world. Scared to admit it because saying it out loud makes it somehow seem true. More real."

Nina flinched and Mariana paused, cognizant of the precarious line between extending a helpful hand and pressuring someone who wasn't ready. But Nina didn't storm off to hole up in her room as she'd been wont to do. Stoic, hands-off vibe and all, she was listening.

Encouraged, Mariana gave Nina what she wanted by picking open a wound she had spent years trying to heal.

"Unlike the others, I didn't have a sibling to lean on or cling to. I get how hard this is. When your life feels like it's spinning out of control. Wanting but also afraid to trust. To believe. To hope." Mariana pressed a palm to her racing heart, a lingering symptom of the panic attacks she had learned to calm thanks to hours of therapy.

"It's okay to take your time, Nina. Feel things out. All I'm asking, all any of us is asking, is that you be open to something different. Something better. Something you, I, and the rest of the girls deserve. Because you do, Nina. You do deserve better. And we want to help you get there."

Tears pooled in Nina's eyes. Her pointy chin trembled. Then, strong-willed fighter that she was, Nina swallowed the emotions she visibly battled and tightened her crossed arms. As if giving herself the hug she couldn't bring herself to accept from Mariana.

Not yet anyway.

Mariana refused to believe that day wouldn't come.

Her phone vibrated in her back pocket, then stopped. Another incoming message. She ignored it. "When or if you want some company to spill your guts to or watch a movie in total silence, give me a call."

Nina didn't respond. Which meant she also didn't dismiss Mariana's offer. Small victories.

"Okay then, I'll catch you tomorrow when Las Nubes has yet *another* rehearsal." They'd had one every night this week. After a quick double rap of her knuckles on the scarred tabletop, Mariana headed into the family room to say her goodbyes.

Two steps into the open kitchen, her phone vibrated, the motion continuing this time, signaling an incoming call. Her mom's cell chimed on the counter next to the fridge. Over on the sofa, Claudia mumbled, "Oh crap," at something she read on her phone's screen. The sixteen-year-old sat up, elbowing the other two girls, who leaned in and peered at whatever had snagged their older sister's attention.

"This is not good." The doom and gloom in Claudia's words matched the grimaces on the faces of all three teens.

Mariana's cell quieted, then immediately started vibrating with an incoming call again. The sisters' SOS. Something was up. She dug the device out of her back jeans pocket to find a picture of Cat in full charro, snapped before a performance last year, filling the screen. Mariana slid her thumb across the icon to answer the call, but before she could even say hello, Cat's panicked voice blasted through the speaker.

"Ay Dios mío, I think I really effed up!"

Mariana blinked in surprise. Cat wasn't usually one to readily admit a mistake without putting some kind of spin on it. "Whatever happened, we can fix it."

"No, this is bad. Like, really bad. Pero te lo juro, I mean, like, cross-my-heart swear, I did not expect my post to go viral!"

The fear in Cat's wail had Mariana instantly switching into crisis-management mode. "I'm sure it's not as bad as you think."

"Not as ba—you haven't seen it, have you? ¡Ay! Why am I not surprised?" Cat let loose a litany of curses that would have had their mom waving her chancla.

Instead, several feet away, hip leaning against the kitchen counter, their mom looked up from whatever she read on her own phone. The dismay pinching her features matched Cat's tone on the other end of the line as she continued lamenting.

"The Battle Instagram account posted a series of pics introducing the Round One bands, reminding people to attend this weekend. And some imbecile commented that female mariachis can't measure up."

"We've heard those cheap shots before," Mariana reminded her sister. "You've said yourself that we should ignore them."

"I did."

"Good!" Surprising, actually. Cat practicing self-restraint when it came to her music didn't happen often. "So, what's the—"

"At first."

"Caaaaaat . . ."

"When they tacked on a new reply specifically calling out Las Nubes, then added several crown emojis, I realized the pendejo had to be someone connected to Los Reyes. That's when I lost it."

At the mention of Angelo's band, dread oozed over Mariana like hot wax dripping down the side of a candle. "Por favor, tell me you did *not* take the bait."

Her question was met by silence, and Mariana pressed a palm to her forehead, anticipating an impending social media headache. This was exactly why she avoided those sites and left promo to the other girls.

"What did you post, Cat?"

From her perch on the edge of the sofa, Claudia held her phone out. The living room was too far away for Mariana to see much of anything other than Cat's face, more than likely evidence of her hotheaded nature captured on the screen. Available for the entire globe to see. Mariana motioned for her younger sister to come to the kitchen.

Their mom hurried over to Mariana's side, too. Worry clouded her eyes as she handed Mariana her phone, open to a story on a local news station's website. The headline—**Gentrification & Women's Rights Battle It Out in Annual Mariachi Competition**—in bold black font achieved its intended goal, snagging her attention and compelling her to scroll to find the short article.

"I swear the idea of someone copying the video and posting it in other places didn't hit me until—crap—until my phone started blowing up! I—"

"Hold on, give me a sec," Mariana demanded. "I'm reading an article on Mamá's phone. I haven't even gotten to your video yet."

"Are you still at Casa Capuleta? Is Mamá there?" Cat asked.

"Sí, estoy aquí," their mom answered.

Cat groaned. "Am I on speakerphone?"

"No, you're just yelling that loud!" Mariana told her. "Hold on, I'll switch you over, but Papo's dozing in his chair, so lower your freak-out voice." She cut a quick glance at Papo, blessedly still napping in his recliner.

The other three girls scampered from the sofa into the kitchen, where they huddled around Mariana, who stood with their mom's phone and the article in one hand and her cell with Cat on speaker in the other.

Nina suddenly appeared on Mariana's side, pressing close to read the news article. Mariana shot the usually recalcitrant teen a puzzled glance. Nina responded by grasping Mariana's hand to get a better look at Mamá's cell screen without the glare from the overhead light.

"Mamá, I'm sorry. I hope this doesn't cause any problems for Casa Capuleta. Or the competition." Cat's tinny voice over the speaker was laden with uncharacteristic remorse. "What does the news station say?"

Mariana scanned the short article, sharing a few sound bites aloud. "'Leader of local all-female mariachi puts competitors on notice'—that's not so bad," she mused. "But then it goes on with 'decries the patriarchy and questions the commitment to culture and tradition of some profiting from gentrification efforts in the city.'"

Mamá visibly winced, and the two youngest girls shot pained expressions around their circle.

"Ay, Cat, why would you bring that up?" Mariana complained.

"I just started talking into the camera, and then I hit 'Post' without thinking."

"This last quote of Cat's is pretty kick ass." Nina pointed at the final paragraph; then her hand drifted back to her side as she continued reading. "Bueno, until the reporter puts her pinche two cents in."

"She makes a cheap shot? Read it to me!" Cat demanded.

Mariana obliged: "In the words of Las Nubes's leader, 'Mujeres like us, women who work hard and honor those before us, deserve to be heard. And believe me, we will be when we hold up that trophy.' Stay tuned for more on the Battle, and how the other competitors feel about this blatant throwing of the gauntlet."

Underneath the last sentence, along with clips from Cat's video, were the words "developing story." A sure sign the reporter would continue digging for more dirt.

"Can you take your post down?" Mariana asked.

"I did, pero I'm already seeing copies of it all over social media and who knows where else."

Mariana bit her tongue to keep from cursing. While she'd read the article on Mamá's phone, Mariana's had continuously vibrated with incoming messages from Blanca, Violeta, and Sabrina. Another notification from their "Big Sis" text thread flashed in a banner at the top of the screen. Needing calm rather than more drama from the others so she could think, she tried swiping the notification away with her thumb but couldn't reach. Nina did the honors for her.

"Is Las Nubes going to be in trouble?" Teresita whispered. "We all heard what Patricio Galán said at the meeting."

Mariana had missed the bulk of his speech because she'd been in the lobby. With Angelo. The guy Galán had told her to work with to keep the peace. A job she was currently failing at.

The famed singer would be less than pleased with the negative press created by Cat's viral word vomit. Especially after having stressed his desire to keep the focus on Nuestros Niños and the good the organization did for local children.

"That's what I'm afraid of," Cat admitted. "The first round is in two days. What if we're kicked out before we even get a chance to compete?"

The question elicited a horrified gasp from the others, including Nina, who'd shown no interest in being part of the band.

"Hold on, let's not get ahead of ourselves," Mariana advised. "Let me watch the video. And let's see if there are any more news reports. I'll come up with a way to spin this . . . mess."

"I can think of a few other choice words for what I've done," Cat muttered.

"Ones you will not share," Mamá reprimanded.

Despite the stressful circumstances, the teens grinned at Cat's grumbled complaint. Even Nina, who remarkably remained huddled with them, smiled at the fact that no matter your age, Capuleta House Rules still applied.

How-best-to-handle-this thoughts tumbled through Mariana's head while messages from the other older sisters continued flashing at the top of her phone. The buzzing vibration traveled up her wrist and into her forearm, tiny shocks to her fraying nerves. She could practically sense Blanca's worry gene kicking into overdrive. No doubt the twins were in their shared apartment, Violeta muttering snarky what-the-hell complaints while Sabrina shushed her.

"Cat, will you please text in the thread and tell the others to hang tight. And to stop blowing up my phone! It's distracting."

The harried edge in Mariana's voice had Fabiola, Claudia, and Teresita gaping at her with fear-filled eyes. Nina pressed against her side and leaned her head against Mariana's shoulder. The unexpected show of support brought a tightness to her chest. A thick wad of tears jammed her throat. They all looked to her for guidance. That meant she couldn't afford a misstep or her own freak-out.

She was good at problem-solving and calming ruffled feathers. She'd done that most of her life. In her first foster home, where one wrong move meant the threat of a smack or a meal withheld. With her sisters growing up, where she played referee to their disagreements. Mostly because of her need to keep the peace within their sanctuary. She could find a way to do damage control here.

Her phone buzzed with Cat's give us a minute to the others. Nina swiped the message off the screen without Mariana even asking.

"Maybe we should call the competition director, tell them—"

"No!" Mariana interrupted Cat. "Not until we have a plan. Right now, we'd simply be pointing out the problem. We need a solution. Give me a bit to think. I'll circle back with everyone later tonight or first thing in the morning. Okay?"

Their mamá nodded. "I will let your father know. Assure him that you girls will handle it. And remind him to hold his tongue about the Monteros until the competition is over."

"Gracias," Mariana whispered.

Mamá pressed a kiss to her cheek in answer.

Mariana's phone buzzed again. Groaning her frustration, she looked down expecting to find another Big Sis message. Her breath caught when she saw the notification banner, lit up like the Majestic Theatre marquee for their entire huddled group to read.

Whataburger: I saw the article and social media posts. We need to meet.

Nina slanted her a wide-eyed "oh shit" glance, then quickly swiped the message away without a word. Shifting slightly, she laid a hand on the center of Mariana's back. The gentle pressure of Nina's open palm seemed to say *I got you.*

Even in the midst of darkness, there was always a glimmer of light. One of their mamá's favorite sayings. Nina coming to her rescue was a definite glimmer of light.

"Cat, I'll call you later," Mariana said. She thumbed the "End Call" icon, then pocketed her cell. "I'm heading home, but you girls—" She waved a hand to indicate all four younger sisters, purposefully including Nina in the mix. "If anyone says anything at school tomorrow or on social media, deflect, ignore, and give the line Galán used: 'We're excited to be part of raising money for the charity.' Got it?"

As a group, the girls nodded.

Minutes after the round of tight hugs and cheek kisses goodbye and her don't-worry-I'll-figure-something-out assurances, she sat in her car in the darkened parking lot alongside Casa Capuleta. The streetlight in front of the building shone through her windshield, casting the interior in a mix of gloomy shadows. Her cell cradled in her palm, she read through Angelo's last few messages.

Whataburger: Any chance you're free to grab a bite tomorrow night?

Whataburger: We could go over Saturday's Round One competition lineup at Market Square. Strategize together.

Whataburger: I saw the article and social media posts. We need to meet.

Anyone could tell the difference in tone.

If Angelo had seen everything, no doubt Hugo Montero had as well. She didn't even want to imagine the older man's thunderous reaction.

Wistfully she scrolled back through the entire text thread, delaying her response. Unsure what it should be. The silly GIFs and memes had done more than make her laugh and brighten her mood this past week. Each exchange with Angelo had made her yearn for the simplicity of a relationship without their familia drama hanging over them. For the ability to give in to her attraction without guilt interfering.

Any chance you're free to grab a bite tomorrow night?

Half an hour ago, she'd been oh-so-tempted to say yes. Allow herself the treat of spending a couple of hours in the company of a man whose sense of humor made her laugh and relax. Whose deep, soothing voice over the phone last night had wooed her into sharing private details about why being a PA was so important to her. Whose kiss made her heart race, while his husky "sleep well" as they hung up made her feel cared for, wanted.

Any chance you're free to grab a bite tomorrow night?

Dios, now it was even more ludicrous for her to consider his invitation. There was no way they'd be able to avoid the fallout that would inevitably come if they continued their forbidden dalliance.

At best, they could try for a friendly alliance, along the lines of what Galán expected, for the duration of the competition. If she were lucky, Angelo wouldn't be pissed about Cat's rashness and, instead, would agree to help by dousing the flames of fury her sister had undoubtedly fanned among Mariachi Los Reyes.

Involving a Montero might not be the idea her familia anticipated her coming up with, but they didn't have to know. She'd take Angelo's assistance if he was still willing to offer, leaving her to concentrate on how to turn the reporter's "developing story" into one that focused on the competition benefiting the charitable organization.

Decision made, Mariana fired off a reply to Angelo.

Wrapping up at Casa Capuleta and heading home. Will call in 25-30 min.

Three little dots immediately floated at the bottom of the text thread. As if he'd been waiting to hear from her. Unable to stop thinking about her. Wanting her. Just like it was for Mariana when it came to him.

Nervous anticipation hummed through her as the dots danced on her screen. A jittery, tingly sensation that had little to do with Angelo's potential problem-solving help. And far too much to do with the thrill of having a justifiable reason for connecting once more with the last man her familia would accept.

Chapter Nine

An ice-cold bottle of Shiner Bock cradled in one hand, his cell in the other, Angelo sank into the love seat squared off in front of the library fireplace. With Brenda holed up in her room streaming a show until her school-night lights-out curfew, all was quiet on his and his sister's side of their tío Hugo's sprawling Fair Oaks Ranch mansion.

Nearly an hour had passed since Angelo had left his uncle brooding in his home office after giving one final consejo to the older man—leave the situation alone. Don't risk causing negative repercussions for Los Reyes by responding. Or having someone else who could be tied back to them respond. Mariachi Las Nubes would pay whatever price Galán and the competition organizers warranted for Cat's viral gauntlet throwing, as one reporter had called it.

Not that Angelo's ornery uncle would take his advice.

Cat hadn't only questioned Hugo's business ethics or thrown shade on his cultural pride. She had issued a clear challenge: we're coming for you in the Battle.

Talk about waving a red flag in front of a bull.

Of course, Angelo wasn't taking his own advice and leaving the situation alone either. He couldn't. Not with Mariana involved.

Tipping the bottle to his lips, he sipped the rich, dark brew. Its lightly hoppy aftertaste danced on his tongue, and he thought of another Texas-made beverage, Tito's Vodka. According to their conversation at

Whataburger, Tito's paired with soda and a lime was Mariana's drink of choice. He'd tasted hints of it when they kissed New Year's Eve. Had found himself ordering it a few times since because it reminded him of her.

He scoffed at his own foolishness and checked the time. Her thirty minutes were almost up.

It'd be a helluva lot easier if he backed off, let her and her familia deal with their own mess. Easier. Not necessarily better.

Granted, there was always a chance that she would blow him off. Too busy circling the Capuleta wagons, game-planning their strategy for calming the waves Cat had stirred up. But, among her many enticing traits, Mariana's sense of responsibility held sway, and Galán had practically ordered the two of them to keep the peace.

She'd call, if only because she felt she *had* to.

Disappointment at the idea of him being relegated to a mere item on her to-do list soured the beer's taste on Angelo's tongue.

His cell screen lit up. The initials MC and a 210 number flashed, indicating an incoming . . . video chat?

Surprised, Angelo quickly scooted to sit up, nearly spilling his beer in his lap. He propped his elbow on the love seat's armrest and held his phone up as he swiped to answer.

Mariana's image appeared, and his evening instantly improved.

With her face free of makeup, lips curved in a sheepish smile, long hair in a high ponytail, and the top half of a UTSA sweatshirt visible on the screen, she looked like a young college coed. One he would have wanted to approach after class or in the dorm hallway if he hadn't had a girlfriend his freshman year, when he'd lived the traditional college student life. In the before times.

"Hi, I, uh, didn't actually mean to video chat," Mariana said. "Cat and I were texting a few minutes ago about video chatting later, and I guess my brain was still on that wavelength." She wrinkled her nose, clearly embarrassed. She looked cute, if also tired, her fatigue evidenced by the faint half moons shadowing under her eyes. "We can hang up and—"

"No, this is fine," he said.

More than fine, actually. He took another sip of his beer and relaxed into the love seat cushion. Pleased with their impromptu meetup and the chance to see her again.

"It's been a long week for you. How are you holding up?" he asked, recalling her text about working an added twelve-hour shift so she could be off both days this weekend for the competition.

"Ay, yes, it has." Her camera bobbled as she shifted, making herself more comfortable on the gray-cushioned sofa or love seat he caught a glimpse of. "I'm getting too old to pull extra shifts like this. Plus, more evening rehearsals since we've changed up our regular set."

"Are you and your sisters ready?"

She shot him a coy grin above the rim of her wineglass. "Let's just say, you better bring your A game, papito."

"Oh yeah?"

Her "mmm-hmmm" hummed from inside her glass as she sipped the red wine. Lowering the glass, she took her time swallowing, her eyes fluttering closed. She tipped her head side to side, stretching out the muscles in her neck, and Angelo could sense the stress gripping her. When she opened her eyes again, worry wiped away the remnants of her teasing sparkle from moments ago.

"Of course, the rehearsals and changed set won't matter if we're no longer in the competition. I'm assuming you saw the video?"

"Yes, as did my uncle. And, I'm betting, the decision makers with the Battle."

"I'd take that bet, too," she said on a heavy sigh. "I'm expecting an email or phone call from the organizers. Probably demanding a retraction, which Cat would give, to a certain degree. She screwed up by mentioning our issues with gentrification, but she made some valid points."

"Such as?" Angelo's ire piqued. His tío might push his weight and influence around at times, but he cared about the legacy he left behind and held high regard for their heritage. "From where I sit, Cat hit a low blow by questioning my tío and Los Reyes's commitment to our culture."

"No offense, Angelo, but from where you sit is at your familia's mansion in a ritzy suburb outside of the city limits. Which is fine, but it's not the minority-dominated neighborhoods that are being bought out. 'Upgraded,' as El Rey Properties likes to say. Which really means the longtime residents get pushed and priced out. Cat's not the first one to say this about your uncle and others. Unless things change, she won't be the last."

"You can't negate the good that comes with gentrification. Spruced-up areas. Booming business. Less crime."

His point was met by her indignant scowl. "At what price to those who call the areas home? A housing voucher to relocate to another area when those areas are fewer and fewer? Often uninhabitable if you're lucky enough to get in. Or where public transportation is less accessible."

"There's another—"

"So, the corner mercado where you bought Bomb Pops and Drumstick cones and Chinese candy as a kid becomes a . . . a hot yoga studio? And the fiestas and cultural celebrations are either tokenized or forgotten?" She shook her head, the motion tugging the end of her ponytail off her shoulder to swing gently behind her. "Or a—"

"Do you really want to debate the issue of gentrification with me right now?"

His calm inquiry stalled her stream of arguments. She drew back and blinked a couple of times, her mouth forming a cute O.

A warm blush climbed her neck, moving higher to tint her tanned cheeks. Angelo heard the clink of her wineglass meeting a surface off to her left, and then she covered her forehead and eyes with her hand.

"Dios mío, what the hell am I doing?" she mumbled.

A rhetorical question. Also, one he had asked himself multiple times in the almost two weeks since he'd first recognized Mariana Capuleta onstage. Been enthralled by her presence and, as they got to know each other better, even more so by her dedication to her familia and their comunidad.

Her shoulders rose and fell as she expelled a rush of breath he not only heard and saw but somehow felt. As if his body were attuned to hers and the exhalation of her stress drew out his along with it.

Brow furrowed, she slid her hand from her forehead to her ponytail. Her fingers picked at the rubber tie until she tugged the band down the length of her tresses. An abrupt head toss sent the black waves cascading onto her shoulders like one of those shampoo commercials. Only no commercial had ever turned him on like she did.

Angelo shifted, adjusting his jeans.

His hands strained to touch the dark strands of her hair, feel their silkiness between his fingers. He wanted to lean closer, breathe in her scent. Discover if her shampoo smelled coconutty like Brenda preferred. Or maybe floral like the one he would always associate with his mom. When it came to Mariana, he predicted it would be something uniquely her own.

Damn, Marco would tease him for being a lovesick fool. Another reason to keep his growing feelings for Mariana secret.

"I'm sorry," she said, mussing her hair as she massaged the back of her head. "I've been doing some research on the topic and . . . ugh . . . I'm wound up a little tighter than I realized." She shook her head again. "But no, I do not want to debate with you."

"Me either," he admitted.

Her hand moved to the base of her skull, where she kneaded her neck muscles. Her eyelashes fluttered, and Angelo swore he heard her muffled moan. His blood instantly rushed south in a flood of pleasure-pain. He wanted his hands on her, massaging her neck and shoulders and . . . and anywhere else she would allow.

"Aaaaanyway." The word sounded like it was dragged out of her, her disgruntled tone pulling him back from the outskirts of Lustville. "Leaving the grab for property on the West Side alone, we have another unpleasant topic we should discuss instead."

Talk about a mood buster. Angelo tipped back his beer, hoping the cool liquid might temper the heat coursing through him.

Mariana followed suit and sipped her wine. "I called instead of texting because I wanted you to hear it from me. There was no malicious intent behind Cat's video. At least, none premeditative."

"Fair enough. She still pissed off some people, though. Some important people."

"She knows she crossed a line. Now I have to figure out damage control."

"Why you?"

Chin tucked, she gazed at him from under her lashes, lips pursed in a classic "you're kidding me, right" wise-aleck pout.

He chuckled, amazed that she could find humor while shouldering the responsibility for someone else's mistake. "Never mind, I think I know the answer to that. Better question: Have you gotten any flak from anyone with the Battle?"

Her pout slid into a frown. "No, but I expect I will. Soon. You heard what Galán said the other day: keep the press focused on Nuestros Niños. I told Cat to let me handle the initial conversation with the competition organizers. We might need to steer clear of social media and the press."

"You know to expect local television stations at the Market on Saturday for our Round One performances, don't you?"

"Like I said, that's assuming Las Nubes is still in the competition. We all signed that morality clause, remember?"

She hitched a shoulder like it was no big deal, but Angelo saw the unease lurking in her hazel eyes. Caught the quick nibble of her lower lip before she pressed them both together. Plus, he knew why the prize money was so important to her. Even though his uncle was in his office willing the organizers to pull the plug on Mariachi Las Nubes, Angelo couldn't wish for the same, knowing how much that would hurt Mariana.

Yes, he wanted to win. Not only because the extra money would bring him closer to finally buying his own place, but because playing with Los Reyes tied Hugo and Angelo to his father in a way nothing else could. Every time he stepped into his dad's place as lead guitarist for Los Reyes, Angelo felt his father alongside him, plucking away at his guitar strings like in the old days. The two brothers may have been completely different in personality, but when they'd played, their shared joy had been unmatched. The few times the three of them had been onstage together . . . man, those were the days.

Love and loss arrowed through Angelo's chest.

Winning the battle would stroke his tío's ego while honoring Angelo's father's memory; that's why Angelo stuck with the band. But did those reasons for taking the crown and its significant purse outweigh the stress Mariana's parents were facing with the loan company and Casa Capuleta?

She had made it clear that the prize money was essential.

"Your plan is to keep a low profile?" Angelo asked, skeptical that a social media blackout would suffice.

"Not really. But . . . I'm stumped by what Galán might expect. Still unsure what he thought you and I could actually do to get our bands to play nicely. Which I obviously flopped at doing," Mariana complained.

Her eyes shifted to something off to her right, then back to him. "Hold on a sec. I cut up an apple for a snack but left the plate on the breakfast bar."

Instead of leaving her phone behind, she carried it with her, inadvertently giving Angelo an over-the-shoulder tour of her home. A surprise peek at the private space of the woman who had invaded his thoughts so often lately. And in doing so, drew attention to a loneliness he had ignored by necessity.

A mosaic of framed family photos hung on the wall above her gray sofa. He squinted but couldn't make out any details, leaving his interest unsatisfied. He spotted a flash of red throw pillows, her glass of wine, and a table lamp topped by a stained-glass shade on an end table. On the far wall, a framed painting with swipes and splashes of rich colors hung next to a filmy curtain that skimmed the hardwood floor. The space looked tidy, the personal touches inviting . . . like the woman who inhabited the apartment. As well as his dreams.

"Giving the press your infamous stiff-arm might not be what Galán wants. How about you do the opposite?" he suggested.

"Meaning?"

She stopped, and then the room behind her blurred as she turned and headed back toward the living room. Now Angelo had an insider's view of a small kitchen with gray countertops—also tidy—and white cabinets. He spotted the breakfast bar she had mentioned, and thought how much nicer this conversation would have been had it taken place with the two of them seated on the black, padded barstools beside each other instead of through a screen. Maybe another time.

A guy could hope.

"Since you won't let me try to help with your parents' loan situation . . ."

Her face scrunched as if the idea pained her, and she gave an exaggerated shake of her head. Probably the same reaction she'd had when he offered his assistance via text earlier in the week and she responded with a thanks, but you know I can't.

He hated the idea of good, hardworking people like her parents being taken advantage of financially. As had happened with his. His father had been swindled into investing heavily in a business without seeking advice from Angelo's more experienced uncle. When it flopped, his parents had found themselves deep in debt. Watching their struggle had led Angelo to initially declare financial planning and business as his major, intent on helping them and others avoid similar mistakes. But when his parents had died, passing along their debt to Angelo, Hugo convinced him to change paths and come work for El Rey Properties.

Even if it might not be the right place for him long term, El Rey Properties was doing good for San Antonio and its residents.

Yes, gentrification would bring change to the West Side, but that wasn't necessarily a negative. More job opportunities and safer neighborhoods meant the potential for a better way of life. He wanted to be part of that improvement by offering financial-literacy workshops once his consulting business was up and running. Being informed could help the people in the comunidad make smarter choices for themselves and their familias.

For now, though, if Mariana didn't want his advice regarding the loan her parents had signed, he'd help another way.

"What do you think about a combined interview with representatives from our two bands?" he suggested. "The assistant director already asked if anyone is willing to talk up the competition and Nuestros Niños with a local radio or news station this weekend. You and I could do it."

"Oooh, I don't know. Cat normally handles our promo."

"After what happened today, I won't be surprised if the Battle organizers don't want to hand her a microphone. If you and I do the interview together, we'll know for sure it won't escalate into another shouting match," he said, liking the idea more and more as he spun it off the top of his head.

Her brow wrinkled with a pensive frown she gave voice to with a mumbled "hmmm." That, plus the lower-lip bite that had him wishing he were the one nibbling on the plump flesh, led him to believe she might be considering his idea.

"We'll show them a united front with Mariachi Las Nubes and Los Reyes," he added.

"You'd be okay with that? Speaking to a reporter with me?" Behind her, the mosaic of wall photos scrolled by like a reel as she sat on the sofa again.

Frustration nipped at Angelo like a teething puppy, pouncing at his ankle and leaving scrape marks. He didn't want to be worrying about the Battle and competing against her. Or this long-standing feud. He wanted to ask about the photographs. When and where they'd been taken. Hear about the memories that would no doubt elicit her affectionate smile or that faraway, enraptured look in her eyes when she shared a story about her familia. Spend time doing something together that would have her adding their photograph to her treasured collection.

"Yes, I'd do that," he answered. "For you."

"Why?"

A simple, softly voiced question tinted with caution.

A not-so-simple answer plagued him. There were countless other single women in San Antonio if he wanted to date. Why this one? Why this particular woman tied to his tío's nemesis?

Angelo couldn't explain the intricacies of this inexplicable connection he felt with her. Not when he didn't quite understand it himself. So, he shared the part that did make sense, without revealing his growing affection and risking her shying away from him.

"Because so much of our lives, yours and mine, has been shaped by the actions of others. Hasn't it?"

Her head bobbed in a slow, barely there nod, remorse and empathy blanketing her beautiful features.

"Hell, it's still happening," he said. "You had nothing to do with Cat's viral video today, but you're the one fixing things. We had nothing to do with whatever actually went down between your dad and mom and my tío all those years ago. Neither one of us is out there taking potshots at each other like our band members. Maybe that's why Galán tapped us as the peacekeepers. As impossible as that sounds."

"Maybe," she murmured.

"And while you won't accept my assistance with your parents' loan situation, I can assure you, I am not the bad guy in your fight against gentrification and what sounds like a bogus power play for Casa Capuleta," he reiterated, desperate for her to believe him.

"I know," she said. "That's what makes this . . . you and me . . ."

She pressed her fingers over her lips as if to stem the flow of words. Confusion clashed with longing, brightening the gold flecks in her expressive eyes.

You and me.

Damn, he liked the sound of that.

Encouraged, Angelo sat up, determined to convince her to go along with his idea. To show that together they made a good team.

"Look, we can keep texting about rehearsal and performance arrival times, and whatever. Trying to keep our band members from crossing paths as much as possible. But, if you ask me, after today, I think the two of us speaking on behalf of our groups is a smart move. I'm sure we can draft and send an email tonight explaining our peace-seeking idea to the Battle's publicist. Then we'll brainstorm some specific sound bites to mention during our interview."

"Like how any rumble between our bands will take place, fairly, onstage Saturday. And we share the same goal to raise awareness and support for Nuestros Niños."

"'Rumble'?" He laughed at her archaic word choice, charmed by her cheeky glare and the "whatever" tilted-head-one-shoulder shrug she gave him. "Dramatic, but if it works for you."

"*This* . . . *us* . . . works for me," she admitted softly.

Her candor surprised him. Sure as hell pleased him.

Mariana lowered her gaze, and Angelo found himself leaning toward his cell, wishing he could reach through the screen to gently tip her chin up. Her lashes fluttered, and suddenly he found himself lost in her mesmerizing eyes.

"I know I'm blessed that my familia's always here for me. This week, though. Tonight. Your support, talking things through with you, it's different. It's . . . bueno, I was gonna say nice"—she laughed at his teasing groan—"but you've made it very clear how you feel about that adjective. Still, I don't know how I can repay you, Angelo."

There were a lot of ways he wanted Mariana Capuleta to feel about him. Indebted was *not* one of them.

"Even among acquaintances, repayment is never necessary," he said, repeating the horrible label he had used to describe their relationship the other day at the Majestic.

"Among *friends*," she corrected.

Yes! Angelo kept the cheer to himself, and instead tipped his beer toward her in a salute, before taking a sip of the now-lukewarm brew.

Progress . . . he would drink to that. And pray for more.

Chapter Ten

"It's wonderful to see our music and culture bringing people together for a good cause like Nuestros Niños. Any final words for our viewers?"

The young reporter flashed an expectant smile, and Mariana slanted a quick glance at Angelo standing beside her. Her partner in crime, who was slowly stealing her heart.

He politely gestured for her to go first, sticking with their plan and allowing her to take the lead.

This morning, Cat had called Mariana "gutsy"—again—for agreeing to do an interview with a member of Los Reyes. Papo had initially refused to allow it, but Mariana had stood her ground, reminding him that they all had a stake in the competition, as well as in Casa Capuleta's future. She had as much to gain or lose if Las Nubes was kicked out and would do whatever was necessary to stop that from happening.

Gutsy, though? Not really.

Unlike her familia, she knew the Los Reyes member pairing with her would be Angelo. That's why she secretly described herself as relieved. Fortunate, even.

She hadn't known what to expect after she and Angelo drafted the email, said a prayer for buena suerte, and hit "Send" Thursday night. And they definitely needed the good luck.

By midmorning Friday, the Battle's publicist had responded, telling them both to arrive three hours before the first band would hit the stage at 1:00 p.m. on Saturday, already dressed in their charros, prepared to plug the charity and downplay any feud.

Those exact orders had been repeated by the publicist moments before Mariana and Angelo went live near the red double doors of the Mi Tierra Cafe entrance facing Dolorosa Street.

Naturally, the young reporter, eager to find an edge that would have her segment going viral, much like Cat's ill-thought-out video, had gone right to the "juicy" angle with her first question, probing into the rivalry between the two bands. Mariana, who never froze in tense situations, froze. Angelo stepped in, his easy deflection and relaxed manner in front of the camera calming the anxious jumping beans in her stomach.

"Bueno, like Angelo mentioned," Mariana answered, relieved the interview was nearing its end, "both Mariachi Las Nubes and Mariachi Los Reyes are excited and honored to be here. This entire event is all about the kids."

Angelo leaned toward Mariana, dipping his head closer to the microphone she held between them. His shoulder lightly bumped hers. Rather than edge aside, she pressed against him, comforted by his stability and strength.

"So even if you can't make it out here to the Market this afternoon," he said, "or if you couldn't get a ticket to see us with our bands for Round Two and the finals at the Majestic Theatre . . ."

She grinned up at him, thrilled by his confidence that they'd both make it to the finals.

He winked. His lips mere inches from hers spread in his cute, lopsided smile, and those jumping beans in her belly started hopping again for an entirely different reason.

Dios mío, dressed in his pale cream charro, its deep bronze embroidery embellishing the snug-fitting jacket and pants, with the late-morning sun glinting off the decorative metal gala, he cut a heart-stopping figure. His crisp white shirt highlighted his tan skin and the dark silk of his billowy tie. Some people claimed they loved a man in a uniform; ay, if you asked her, there was nothing like a mariachi in full charro.

"If they can't get a ticket to the next rounds, what do you suggest?" the reporter prompted when neither Angelo nor Mariana finished his statement.

"Oh yes!" Embarrassed, Mariana shook off her infatuated stupor and faced the camera. She waved her black-and-gold sombrero to indicate the restaurant and Market Square area behind them. The location for this afternoon's first round. "If you can't make any of our performances, you can still donate to Nuestros Niños. The link is on the Battle of the Mariachi Bands website, as well as the rest of ours. Angelo and I, and all the musicians in the Battle, appreciate anything you can give for the kids."

Angelo sidestepped to stand partially behind her. His left hand settled on her hip and she nearly swooned. Right there in front of television viewers across the city. His chest grazed her back as he bent over her shoulder to speak into the microphone and pointed at the camera with his sombrero. "Estamos contando con su ayuda. We're counting on your help, okay?"

"And there you have it," the reporter said, drawing the camera's focus her way.

Good, because between the heat of Angelo's hand on Mariana's hip, the light pressure of his chest against her shoulder blades, and the damn-he-smells-good hint of his musky aftershave in the breath she struggled to take in, Mariana wouldn't have been able to utter a coherent word. As it was, she struggled to keep her camera-ready smile in place while her insides melted with lust.

"Great job!"

Galán's loud clapping startled her. She shoved the microphone at the reporter and shifted away, separating herself from the close-knit threesome she, Angelo, and the young woman had created to keep them all in the camera's frame. Angelo's hand slid off her hip, sending tiny waves of friction across her midsection and lower.

She didn't dare look at him. Not with her face aflame and her mind conjuring images of last night's vivid dream. The one starring her and Angelo and several deliciously compromising positions that had left her throbbing with unmet desire when she awoke.

Silently ordering herself to *get a grip, girl*, she scurried toward the white picket fence lining the flowerbed, stopping near the colorful statue of a mustached man wearing a zarape and straw sombrero.

"Thank you for making this a priority," Galán told the local news team, who had already filmed a short interview with him.

"We appreciate your time, Señor Galán. It's an honor to meet you." Now that the camera was off, the young woman's professional demeanor slipped a notch and she smiled adoringly at the charismatic singer. Given Galán's appeal, Mariana sent the budding journalist a mental high five for keeping it together while recording.

"It's for a worthy cause, no?" Galán answered. "We're open to more interviews with the contestants as the competition continues. Reach out to our publicist."

He shook the reporter's hand, thanked her cameraman for his time, then ushered Angelo and Mariana toward the well-known Mexican restaurant in popular Market Square. Once inside, he quickly guided them past the glass panadería case running nearly the length of Mi Tierra's lobby area, where a line of customers waited to order some of the delicious baked goods. The sweet scent of the pan dulce mingled with the tangy aroma of spices, peppers, onions, and grilled flank steak as a waiter hustled by balancing a plate-filled tray on his shoulder.

Mariana's stomach grumbled a complaint. Too nervous to eat anything this morning, she might have to treat herself to an oreja before meeting her familia in the parking lot across the street. The sugar-and-cinnamon elephant ear–shaped puff pastry was her favorite.

"You wanna grab something?" Angelo asked, as if he'd read her thoughts. Or, how embarrassing, heard her stomach growl.

"It's okay. I'll pick up some orejas on the way out. The girls know I can't come here without buying a box of my favorite pan dulce."

Angelo started to respond, but someone recognized Galán, calling out his name, and the crowd surged toward them. Angelo put his arm around Mariana's shoulders, tucking her against his side for protection. She huddled closer, shocked by the sudden hysteria. Comforted by Angelo's husky "I got you" and the strength of his arms as they embraced her.

Two hulking men in dark suits stepped in to hustle their group through the excited crowd. Galán flashed his famous smile and lifted a hand to greet his adoring fans, apologizing for his inability to stop for autographs or selfies due to the competition's close start time. Thankfully, Galán's record label had reserved the restaurant's entire patio space as his home base to ensure a measure of privacy. The patio overlooked Produce Row and would allow him to hear and see the performances on the nearby stage, while the scrollwork metal railing lining the perimeter would keep adoring fans out of the area.

Mariana had eaten on Mi Tierra's patio countless times over the years. She loved the decor, with its bright yellow wooden chairs, their brick-red cushions matching the background of the tile flooring adorned with yellow and navy floral circles and crosses. The rich colors gave a festive vibe that, along with the friendly service and delicious food and drinks, made the restaurant a local and tourist favorite. They also happened to serve the perfect frozen margarita for celebrating special occasions, as her familia had for Sabrina and Violeta's twenty-first birthday.

The patio was usually packed. Because of today's VIP, the Battle staff had the area to themselves. Several people Mariana recognized from the first meeting at the Majestic were deep in discussion over an open laptop. They waved as Galán ushered Angelo and Mariana to a table for four.

"Please, join me for a few moments." The singer pulled out one of the chairs facing Produce Row for Mariana. "I need to speak with you about what happened this week before you leave to prepare for your shows."

His deep voice was measured, the teasing lilt he'd used with the reporter outside the restaurant now gone. Worse, with his expression impassive and his eyes hidden behind dark sunglasses, it was impossible for Mariana to gauge Galán's mood. She hoped their interview had done enough to appease his displeasure with Cat's rash behavior.

Beside her, Angelo offered an encouraging smile as he took her sombrero to place with his on an empty table.

"Gracias," she murmured.

Thankful they were in this mess together, she sank into her chair and cast a nervous glance at the crowd gathering on the other side of the railing. The brightly colored paper cutouts spaced between the patio's bare light bulbs hanging overhead matched the rectangular doilies strung on lines from the buildings on one side of Produce Row to the other, extending the festive ambiance from the restaurant to the packed brick-paved walkway. Right now, between Cat's screwup, the interview, and their upcoming performance, she was too keyed up to enjoy the celebratory atmosphere.

The portly gentleman who had arrived with Galán at the Majestic strode through the opening connecting the patio to the inside seating area. His unbuttoned suit jacket flapped in the brisk late-March breeze as he held an iPad out to Galán.

"Here are the numbers you asked about earlier." The man tipped his head in greeting but remained focused on business. "Take a look and let me know if you want me to reach out to any of the songwriters. The producers are serious about this. We should move quickly if you want the upper hand."

"Excuse me. This will only take a few minutes. Make yourselves comfortable." Galán motioned toward an older woman hovering in the doorway. "Let Ana know if you'd like something."

Angelo looked to Mariana first. She shook her head, wanting nothing more than to get their conversation over with so she could take a few moments to compose herself. Shake off her own stress and get in the right mindset to give her usual preperformance pep talk to her sisters.

"I think we're good, gracias." Angelo settled in the seat beside her with a polite nod at the server.

"Dios mío, do you think he's still pissed?" she whispered to Angelo as soon as Galán stepped away with his assistant.

"I don't see why. You did great out there," Angelo answered.

Slipping his hand under the edge of the white tablecloth, he gave Mariana's thigh a supportive pat. She flinched, caught off guard by the intimacy. Even more so by how comfortable—how right—the weight of his hand felt on her thigh. He started to pull away, but Mariana grabbed Angelo's wrist.

This close, and without a live camera pointed at her, she let herself drink him in. The deep red nick from his razor blade on his angular jaw. The tiny black circle of his pupils barely visible in his sable eyes. The question mingling with interest in their depths.

With Galán and his assistant occupied, Mariana boldly slid her hand over Angelo's. As if it were a natural reaction, he twisted his wrist, bringing their palms together. His fingers wrapped around hers, giving them a gentle squeeze. The reassuring pressure and the confidence gleaming in his eyes seemed to say "I'm here. We got this."

A warm sense of contentment spread through her, and she squeezed back, holding on tightly to this man who was fast becoming a touchstone. A calm port in the storm that continued to rage around them.

The left side of Angelo's mouth tilted up, a teasing glimpse of the grin that sent delight rippling through her like a harpist plucking their instrument's strings. Dios help her, she wanted to lean in and press her lips against his. Throw caution to the brisk wintry wind and let herself get lost in the rapture of his kisses again.

"I appreciate your patience." Galán rejoined them and pulled out a chair on the other side of the table.

Straightening in her seat, Mariana withdrew her hand from Angelo's. Praying that Galán hadn't noticed her and Angelo's closeness. Also telling herself to ignore the sense of loss releasing him left her with.

Galán removed his dark sunglasses, revealing his grave expression. "I have to say, during our first meeting at the Majestic, I wondered if I might regret my decision to include Mariachi Las Nubes and Mariachi Los Reyes in the competition. On Thursday evening, I began to."

Behind him, fans who recognized the famous singer swarmed along the metal railing, snapping pictures and gawking. Several women fanned themselves, despite the fifty-degree temperature. Had they not been competing, some of Mariana's sisters might have been among the swooning melee.

Given the precarious situation, Mariana didn't have the luxury of fangirling, not that she would have anyway. Instead, she looked Galán directly in the eye and channeled the *Fake it until you become it* mantra, prepared to stand up for her familia's right to compete.

"However, your email Thursday evening showed initiative and goodwill." Galán's arched brow implied his approval, which she took as a good sign. "Donating a private local booking with Las Nubes for the highest donor to Nuestros Niños during today's Round One. Not a bad move."

"That was Mariana's idea," Angelo said.

"But you thought of the joint interview first," she added, shifting on her seat to face him.

"And we drafted our official statement for the press release together," Angelo countered. His eyes lit with a pleasure she felt as well when she remembered how easily they had meshed while brainstorming Thursday evening.

"It's good to see my trust in the two of you was not misplaced," Galán noted.

"No, it wasn't."

"Definitely not."

Mariana and Angelo spoke in unison, each breaking off to let the other continue. When he didn't, she filled the awkward pause. "Like our email mentioned, Cat normally handles any interviews for Las Nubes. As our musical director, she can speak more knowledgeably about the rise of women in mariachi and why we select the songs we perform, a message we think is important for the girls in our all-female music class at Casa Capuleta to hear. As well as those with Nuestros Niños and beyond. But Angelo and I . . ."

She rested a hand on Angelo's forearm, linking the two of them together. The wool material of his mariachi jacket with its ornate stitching scratched her palm, so different from his smooth skin when they'd held hands a few moments ago. When his we-got-this squeeze had bolstered her.

Mariana would have been fine facing Galán on her own. This problem was a Capuleta creation. She was used to triaging for others.

But having Angelo here . . . bueno, somehow, his belief in her, in them, added to her inner strength.

"To be frank, Patricio," she admitted, "no one in our familias knows of our . . . um, our . . ."

"Friendship," Angelo supplied, when she floundered.

His playful wink gave her all sorts of far-from-friendly urges, and for a second she lost track of the conversation.

"Uh, yes. Our friendship is, um, a recent development," she finished.

One of Galán's dark brows quirked again, this time in a move she interpreted as "oh really." His intuitive gaze cut to her hand resting on Angelo's forearm, then back to her.

Busted.

Her fingers twitched, but she didn't slide her hand away. They were a team, and not only because Galán had rashly paired them up.

"We haven't actually said anything about your request that Angelo and I pair up. For the good of the competition and Nuestros Niños," she elaborated.

Angelo mimed zipping his lips shut.

Surprise raced across Galán's face, quickly replaced by a sly smirk she had seen in many of his music videos and endorsement ads. "So, this 'development' is my doing? Your 'pairing up,' as you call it, for the greater good and all."

"Mmm-hmmm. And we're fine continuing to work together," Mariana threw in. Hell, if this was the web of deceit she was spinning and would have to go to confession for, why not go all in?

"Definitely." Angelo slung his arm behind her, resting it on her seat back. His fingers traced the embroidery on her jacket sleeve. A heady distraction she probably didn't need at the moment, but she savored it all the same.

Galán eyed them both, his smirk growing into his megawatt smile. Around them, fans raised their cameras and cell phones, desperate to get a good shot of El Príncipe. Some watched with open interest; others eyed her with flat-out jealousy.

But there was no danger of Mariana trying to steal their crush's heart. Not when she had fast become the number-one fan of another tall, devastatingly handsome mariachi. This one, more affable and approachable and prone to scaling the walls she'd built up around her heart.

"Look, you know what it's like to have a father—or father figure, in my case—with a big personality. One who likes calling the shots," Angelo said.

Galán's expression shuttered, and Mariana could have kicked Angelo under the table for bringing up the touchy subject.

"It's no secret that my father and I have been at odds," Galán answered. "Your point is?"

"My point is that you understand it's not easy reining in machismo pride. This animosity between our familias is decades old, from our parents' generation. Bled down to ours by those who balk at changes and inflamed by social media. Unfortunately, it's business *and* personal." Angelo leaned toward Galán, his expression matching his serious tone. "Mariana and I promise to do our best. Our band members know that we're on notice. And Mariana and I agree, we can't let this so-called war interfere with more lives. Not only ours, but more specifically, the kids served by Nuestros Niños."

"No, we can't," she added.

"War, huh?" Galán drummed his fingers on the table.

"Bueno, that might be a tad dramatic." She nudged Angelo with her elbow.

"Hey, you were the one who said we needed to keep the rumble onstage." Angelo's teasing reminder of their conversation the other night had Mariana rolling her eyes.

"Let's consider this an antiwar council of sorts then, shall we?" Galán suggested. "I will guard your . . . interesting little secret. While you two do your best to calm any animosity that arises. Because, fair warning, if you do wind up making it to the second round, my record label added a new twist in honor of the anniversary year. It's a luck-of-the-draw matter. One in which teamwork will be imperative."

"Twist?" Mariana asked.

"That's all I can reveal." Galán slipped on his dark sunglasses and lounged back, casually crooking an arm over the empty chair beside him. Around them onlookers jockeyed for position again, eager to snap a pic of the legend. "I'm sure your bandmates are anxious to hear about this morning." He raised a hand, and the server hurried over with a glass of tea. "I hope your bands bring it to the stage today. But keep in mind, there have already been two incidents. If there's a third, we'll be left with no choice but to pull you out."

Mariana's stomach clenched at the warning. A reminder of all that was at stake here for her familia. For Casa Capuleta.

Angelo gave a brisk nod and pushed back his chair. By the time Mariana rose, he was holding out her sombrero. She didn't meet his gaze. She couldn't. Not with her emotions spinning like a tumbleweed. Wanting to wish him luck but hearing her father's complaint this morning about her fraternizing with the enemy. And all he knew about was her interview with Angelo. If Papo knew the rest . . .

Ay!

She didn't want to think about that right now. Couldn't let that worry worm itself inside her head. There was no room for error today. Las Nubes needed to make it to Round Two. That's where her focus should be.

Not the comfort of Angelo's hand on the small of her back as they walked through Mi Tierra. Or his murmured "buena suerte" before they parted ways after she bought the box of orejas.

Guilt sluiced through her when she returned his good-luck wish. He brushed a featherlight kiss on her cheek, and she told herself her heart raced out of fear that someone might see them.

A lie.

It raced because her heart yearned for more. She just couldn't see a realistic way for that to happen.

Chapter Eleven

Mariana stepped up to the microphone and stared out at the crowd tightly packed shoulder to shoulder in Market Square. She recognized many friends, a few regulars who often came to their public performances, several familias from Little Flower Basilica, and a group of students in the all-girl music class with their parents. The secret judges were scattered somewhere in the vicinity, identities not to be revealed until the results for Round One were announced tomorrow on a local Sunday morning television show.

On Mariana's left, Cat held her vihuela tucked under her bent arm and stepped to her own mic. Once in place, she tipped her chin in the tiniest of signals. Go time!

"¡Bienvenidos a todos!" Mariana cried. "Welcome, everyone, to the Battle of the Mariachi Bands! I'm Mariana Capuleta—"

Cat leaned toward her mic. "I'm Catalina Capuleta. And along with our sisters, we're excited to bring some powerhouse estrogen to the fiesta courtesy of—"

"Mariachi Las Nubes!" In unison, the sisters announced themselves. A chorus of gritos and cheers greeted them.

Trumpet raised high in the air, Mariana grinned at Cat, then twisted to share an encouraging smile with the rest of the girls grouped by their instruments behind her.

Tucking her trumpet to her chest, she continued with the opening back-and-forth monologue she and Cat had planned. "We're proud to be the first—"

"Pero certainly not the last—" Cat chimed in.

"All-female mariachi in the Battle. And we are ready to bring it!"

More gritos met Mariana's confident cry.

"We've got a special thirty-minute set for you," Cat continued. "As we bring you a taste of the mujeres who paved the way for us. Strong women, talented musicians and singers, who fought hard to make a name for themselves in an industry that, bueno, hadn't made much room for them."

Heads bobbed in the crowd. Mostly women, agreeing with Cat's truth that the female mariachi had a harder go of it, facing machismo and traditionalists along the way. Several of their students raised fists in the air, their youthful faces alight with pride and determination.

"But that's changing," Mariana assured them all. "To get this female-mariachi lovefest started, we're kicking it off with an oldie but goodie. A tribute to the amazing woman whose love, support, and musical skills played a huge role in all of us being up here today. One of our mamá's favorites, often heard while she's cooking in the kitchen or dancing in our sala, also sung beautifully by the great Linda Ronstadt on her best-selling album *Canciones de Mi Padre*. Mamá, this one's for you."

The opening notes of "Los Laureles" brought a resounding cheer from the crowd, and Cat's rich, sultry voice had several audience members clutching a fist to their chests. Pride swelled in Mariana as she backed away from the microphone and raised her trumpet. Gazing out at the crowd, she found her parents near the back on the right. Papo hugged Mamá from behind. Hands clasped in front of her, she stared up at her girls, an enchanted look on her lightly lined face. Mamá always said she felt happiest when her familia was together, sharing their love of music, enjoying the gifts Dios had given them.

Feeding off her mamá and the crowd's enthusiasm, Mariana closed her eyes, sucked in a deep breath through her nose, and blew her first notes.

This was why she kept playing with the band, even with her long hours at work and the extra physician-assistant shadow hours packing her schedule. When Cat's voice mingled with Sabrina's guitarrón, Violeta's and Teresita's guitars, Blanca's violin, and the other teens on rhythm, it took her back to the early days. When she had felt alone and scared, afraid to hope. Finally accepting that she could have a home, with parents and sisters, where love thrived, even through the hard times.

Música. *Their* music. It bound them. It was part of who and what they were. Her familia.

Midway through Las Nubes's set, the crowd's energy was at raise-the-roof level. They were loving Cat's song selection, featuring fan favorites by famous female mariachi, Banda, and ranchera singers from Lola Beltrán to Jenni Rivera, Chavela Vargas to Graciela Beltrán, and more. The song mash-ups allowed Las Nubes to add their own twist to the popular tunes, highlighting their talents. Right now, Teresita was killing it on her guitar solo in the middle of an Ana Gabriel classic. Cheers rose when Cat jumped in on the vihuela, creating a masterful duet. Gritos pierced the air. On cue, Mariana picked up the chorus vocal, motioning for audience members to join her.

As she held the final note, Mariana spotted Angelo, his buddy Marco, and Hugo off to the left, near one of the beer stands. They were already dressed in their charros, even though they'd been given the lucky spot of closing out the round.

The two younger men watched the performance, Marco slack-jawed, Angelo beaming with pleasure. Her gaze connected with his as she finished, chest heaving for breath. Heart swelling with pure joy at sharing this important part of her and her familia with him.

Cupping his hand around the side of his mouth, Marco leaned toward Angelo and said something that drew his attention.

With Cat introducing their next selection, Mariana noticed that, unlike his nephew and Marco, Hugo wasn't paying much attention to Las Nubes on the stage. Instead, he scanned the crowd, stretching his neck to search for someone or something. She followed his line of sight and stopped when she spotted Mamá and Papo still standing with his arms wrapped around her.

When Mariana glanced back at Hugo, his mouth had thinned to a hard line under his mustache. Her stomach dropped. *Por favor, don't let him do anything to ruin this.*

Blanca bowed the opening notes of the next song on her violin. Gracias a Dios for muscle memory from hours of practice because it drew Mariana back to their show before she missed her cue. She forced herself to concentrate, but as the song came to a close, she slanted a look to where the three men had stood. Only Angelo remained.

"Bueno, our time is almost up . . . I know, right?" Mariana widened her eyes in mock surprise as she appeased the audience's groans. Her uneasiness over Hugo's strange behavior dissipated when someone called out "Otra! Otra!" and more joined in the cry for "another one."

"I don't know, should we?" Cat teased. Her grin spread to Christmas-morning size when the cries intensified. "Would you like us to play a special medley we recently put together for a quince?" She put a hand up by her ear, encouraging the crowd's cheers.

"What do you think, ladies?" Mariana angled to include the rest of the sisters. Each struck a different pose, pretending to consider her question.

"We can't have an all-female tribute without including a little something from the Queen of Tejano Music!" Cat announced.

The audience erupted, drowning out the sisters' unanimous cry: "Selena!"

Mariana closed her eyes as she raised her trumpet to her lips and sucked in a chest-and-stomach-filling breath through her nose. The energy pulsing in the air infused her. She channeled it into her instrument as she blew into her mouthpiece, her fingers working the valves to create the opening notes of one of Selena's hit songs.

Just like at Felicia's fiesta, the medley was a crowd-pleaser. And when Cat and Claudia met at center stage to dance a Selena-style cumbia in the middle of "Como la Flor"—something Cat had added specifically for the Battle—everyone went wild.

Minutes later, as their show drew to an end, deafening cheers saluted their performance. Cat and Mariana held hands so tightly as they took their bows she thought they might fracture a bone or two. She didn't care.

They'd done it. They'd brought the house down. The audience loved them. No way—no freaking way—they wouldn't make the next round.

At the back of the crowd, Papo and Mamá blew kisses toward the stage. Around them, whistles of appreciation filled the crisp late-March air. One of their students cupped her hands around her mouth and started chanting, "Las Nubes! Las Nubes!" Soon the cry intensified as more added their voices.

Pride. Joy. Exhilaration.

They vibrated through Mariana with such intensity it felt like she might burst.

She tried not to. Really, she did. But Mariana couldn't stop herself from seeking out the one person she shouldn't. She had shared so much about herself, why music meant so much to her. She couldn't *not* share this incredible moment with him.

Dressed in his charro for his band's set later, Angelo made a striking, virile figure that had others in the crowd taking notice. But what appealed to her more were his magnetic charm and sense of humor, the good inside him that had Angelo clapping along with everyone else. Despite the competition.

His smile widened, just for her, as he signaled two thumbs-up.

Mariana's heart pounded in her chest. She told herself it was only adrenaline, the high of performing with her sisters in front of such a responsive audience, the certainty that this reception had to guarantee their spot in the Battle's next round. But she knew it was at least in part because of him. Because of what he was quickly coming to mean to her.

Several hours later, Mariana stood in the spot where Angelo, Marco, and his uncle had. This time she and her familia were the ones watching their competitors put on an incredible show.

Cat's stoic expression might hide her unease to the average onlooker, but Mariana knew her sister's stress tell. Even a gel manicure couldn't stop Cat from biting her thumbnail, a terrible childhood habit she had mostly kicked. Unless her stress level skyrocketed.

The last band of the night, Los Reyes was kicking ass onstage. Their medley of mariachi classics, performed traditionally, had the audience enraptured. From the older generation to the youngest, people sang along and cheered. Off to the side, an elderly couple danced a Mexican polka to the crowd-favorite ranchera.

While many in her familia looked on with concern, Mariana found herself enraptured by the sight of Angelo masterfully playing the guitar. Having purposefully avoided anything to do with Los Reyes in the past, this was the first time she had seen him perform. She watched, captivated, as the fingers of his left hand pressed and released the strings along the guitar neck, deftly creating the chords.

Eyes closed, he gave himself up to the music and the emotions it evoked. It was sexy and raw and, damn, it had her thrumming with lust and desire. Even when Los Reyes harmonized, she easily picked out Angelo's voice. His rich baritone called to her, and in her mind, he sang for her alone.

Los Reyes neared the end of their set, and Angelo flashed his crooked grin at someone near the front of the crowd. Jealousy, hot and raw, shot through Mariana. Then he looked her way, his grin broadening. She grinned back, hoping he could see her pride in him on her face. Without realizing it, she started to raise her hand to wave, but Cat announced, "I've seen enough. Let's go."

Before Mariana could react, Violeta slung her arm around Mariana's shoulders and practically dragged her off with the rest of the girls.

She craned her neck to catch another glimpse of Angelo. But with the crowd chanting, "Otra, otra!" with fists pumping into the air, and Violeta holding on to her like their lives depended on getting out of Produce Row, Mariana's view of the stage was blocked. She caught a flash of pale cream sombreros with burnished bronze stitching before she and her sisters reached the edge of the crowd. Cat didn't break stride, instead heading straight for the parking garage.

A strange disappointment settled over Mariana as she and the others followed. What would it be like if Angelo could join her and her familia back at Casa Capuleta to celebrate their bands' success today?

Instead, he would join Los Reyes and his uncle. The man who earlier had been staring daggers at her parents, and who might very well be behind the private lender's demand for the balloon payment. Despite their deepening friendship, when it came down to it, Angelo held allegiance to his familia. The same way she did to hers.

That's why, when the top four bands who'd made it into the Battle's next round were announced tomorrow morning, she'd have to hope Los Reyes wasn't among them. She had watched each competitor's show today. The bands with the best audience reception had been Las Nubes and Los Reyes. They were each other's biggest competition. Having Los Reyes out raised the sisters' chances of winning.

Regret carved off a chunk of Mariana's postperformance high like an artist slicing off a chunk of clay in a masterpiece titled *Inevitability*. Heart heavy, she climbed behind the wheel of her car, barely paying attention to who rode with her. She mmm-hmmm'd her way through the conversation home, worn out from the highs and lows of her secret emotional turmoil. Worried about tomorrow's announcement and what it could mean for them all.

Chapter Twelve

A strange déjà vu sensation settled over Angelo as he stood at the back of the Majestic Theatre, observing the musicians and competition staff seated in the orchestra level waiting for Patricio Galán to arrive. This time, the number of bands present was cut in half, and his tío hadn't insisted on making a grand entrance. But just like last time, Mariana Capuleta was avoiding him.

His calls. His texts. Hell, she hadn't even attempted eye contact since her arrival shortly after his.

Yesterday afternoon, just like in the courtyard at Casa Capuleta the first time, he'd been mesmerized by her performance. She and Las Nubes had put on a powerhouse show. He'd walked away awed by their talent, keenly aware that the palpable connection their music created between the sisters was much like the one between his father, his tío, and him. Music as a connector—something he and Mariana shared. Something that could also drive them apart thanks to the competition's stakes.

Later, he'd noticed Mariana surrounded by her sisters in the crowd while he and Los Reyes were onstage. By then she had changed out of her charro, but her hair remained pulled back in that tight low bun, the red flower matching both the scarf draped around her neck and the color still staining her lips. Strumming his guitar and harmonizing with his tío and the rest of the guys, he had struggled with maintaining his stage presence while trying but failing not to seek her out. Afraid someone in her familia would notice. Because her sisters had all been closely watching Los Reyes. In fact, while the rest of the audience cheered, Mariana's sisters had looked on with varying degrees of concern. Even calculation on Cat's part.

For one brief moment, he had thought he'd caught Mariana's radiant smile, and his chest had puffed up with pride. But then, amid the crowd's whoops and gritos and whistles of appreciation, Mariana and her sisters had made a hasty retreat, not even sticking around for the final song.

He tried to blame her aloof behavior now on their need to keep their distance around the others. The stress of the competition. The lingering tension caused by Cat's viral video. While their interview had gone well, Angelo knew that Galán's cryptic warning at Mi Tierra about the next round weighed heavily on Mariana.

And yet, she didn't strike him as someone who caved under pressure. If anything, she faced difficult situations head-on, assuming responsibility, even for the errors of others. After their brainstorm session over video chat the other night, she had seemed more at ease having drafted a plan and gained a sense of control of the situation. Something he ventured to guess she had lacked as a child, shuffled through the foster care system until she had landed at Casa Capuleta.

The competition. The animosity between their bands. Galán's bid for the two of them to keep the peace. The loan problem her parents faced. All uncontrollable situations that more than likely upped her anxiety. Which only made him want to soothe her worries more.

That need had had him ditching the Los Reyes celebration out by his tío's pool last night midway through his uncle's boastful speech proclaiming the inevitability of them moving on to the next round. While the others cheered, Angelo had escaped to the privacy of his room. He wanted to talk with Mariana, share the events of their day. As had become their nightly ritual over the past week.

When she didn't return his texts or answer his call, unease slithered through him like the milk snake he'd come across the last time he'd camped out at Garner State Park.

He'd awoken this morning, even more unsettled to find she still hadn't replied. Anxious to watch the live segment of *Sunday Morning in San Antonio* when Patricio Galán would announce the top four bands who would move on in the competition.

Mariachi Las Nubes had been announced first, followed by Mariachi Los Reyes, and sweet relief spread through Angelo like the syrup Brenda had poured over her pancakes. He pictured Mariana sitting on her gray couch, one of those red throw pillows clutched to her chest in anticipation, watching Patricio on her TV. Then again, knowing her familia's closeness, they'd probably gathered at Casa Capuleta to await the news together.

He nearly sent her his congrats. But with three text messages and one voice mail unanswered, a guy had to hold on to at least a measure of his pride.

Which was why he now stood at the back of the theatre, pretending not to be watching Mariana from a distance.

"You snapped outta your pissy mood yet?" Marco clapped him on the shoulder and gave it a shake.

"Whatever," Angelo grumbled.

"Güey, you look and sound exactly like Brenda when she's pouting because you told her no about something. What gives?"

Sucking his teeth and shrugging off Marco's grip in response to his buddy's dig probably added to Angelo's moody-teen impersonation. He didn't care.

Arms crossed, he stared at Mariana seated near the front of the theatre with her sisters and their father. Angelo knew she couldn't openly greet him in front of everyone. Hell, Los Reyes and Las Nubes had pointedly avoided each other while congratulating the other two bands joining them in the second round. But she could have responded to his texts. Privately offered her own congrats.

What could have possibly happened between the time they left their meeting with Galán and last night that was making her give Angelo her champion stiff-arm?

"Speaking of your little sister, where is she? I thought she asked to come with you to get a close-up look at El Príncipe?" Marco asked, throwing his voice into a breathy falsetto. A fair impression of Brenda whenever she sighed Galán's nickname.

"When she heard he hadn't arrived yet, she decided to explore the theatre. Said something about taking a selfie with the peacock statue on the balcony railing." Angelo waved at the upper-level seating area of the famed theatre. "There was another teen hanging out in the lobby. She must be with the band from El Paso or Houston. The two of them went to poke around."

"Sweet. Oye, looks like he finally arrived. Vente, let's grab our seats." Marco smacked Angelo's stomach with the back of his hand, then headed down the aisle toward the rows Los Reyes had claimed.

Sure enough, Patricio Galán strode down the far-left aisle, calling out a welcome to everyone. Angelo trudged behind his buddy, his patience running low, but it had nothing to do with Galán's tardiness.

"Gracias a todos." The famed singer repeated his thanks to everyone as he reached the front. "First, felicidades! Congratulations to each of you for the fantastic performances yesterday. Our decision was not easy. And you all deserve to be here!"

Angelo settled into his cushioned seat, his ears tuned to what Galán was saying, his attention straying to Mariana several rows up and across the center aisle. Galán and the director explained the rehearsal schedule for the Majestic, mentor coach availability—a new addition this year, publicity opportunities, and other Round Two details. The entire time, Mariana studiously wrote in a notebook propped on her lap, occasionally tapping her chin with a mechanical pencil. Cat periodically leaned on their armrest to whisper in her ear. Mariana either nodded or shook her head and scribbled away, attentively listening to the information.

As Angelo knew he should. Tío Hugo had already given the band their marching orders earlier: whatever it took to win, Los Reyes would do it!

Mooning over the competition was nowhere in his tío's game plan.

"And now, for our exciting twist to this year's Round Two." Galán clapped his hands together, then rubbed them briskly, a mischievous grin matching the gleam in his eyes.

Murmurs whispered among some of the musicians as Galán played up the anticipation with a deliberate pause.

"Do we have the bag with the names?" he asked one of the stagehands. The young man gave him a brown cloth coin bag with a string tie. Galán held the small bag aloft. "Inside here are pieces of paper with each band's name. I will randomly pull names in a 1-2-1-2 order. This will be your pairings for Round Two, where you are expected to perform together. Since this is a double-knockout round, the winning pair will move on to the finals."

Shocked cries blended with surprised gasps and excited chatter at the stunning revelation. Never had bands been expected to mix before.

"Ellos no pueden hacer esto," Tío Hugo muttered.

"Yes, they *can* do this. You read the documents we all signed," David, a longtime member of Los Reyes and Hugo's senior by a few years, warned.

"This is ridiculous," Hugo complained, inciting a few others in Los Reyes, who muttered their frustration.

David patted the air in a calming gesture. "Don't worry. We have a two-out-of-three chance of not being paired with them."

Tío Hugo grumbled under his breath, one fist thumping his thigh with agitation.

No need for David to name the "them" in question. Everyone knew he meant Las Nubes, who had converged in a loose huddle over in their rows. Presumably sharing similar protests among themselves. Same with the other two bands. Even the Los Reyes members in the row behind Angelo had scooted to the edges of their seats, a mix of shock and indignation on their faces.

Ignoring his tío's grumbling, Angelo glanced at Mariana. With one arm wrapped around a teen pressed beside her, Mariana spoke to the rest of her familia in a hushed tone. Her expression serious, she splayed a hand in the center of their circle, clearly attempting to assuage their worries. Cat and one of the twins frowned over their shoulders at Los Reyes. Mariana snapped her fingers at the two of them a couple of times, and they turned back to their huddle.

"Okay, let's find out our pairings!" Galán shook the bag high in the air, his glee too enthusiastic for Angelo's liking. The singer lowered the bag to tug the gathered opening loose. Digging his fingers inside, he withdrew a slip of paper. "Team One, Mariachi Luna y Sol."

The leader of the band from Houston tipped his head in acknowledgment, then gave his members a raised go-get-'em fist.

"Team Two . . ." Galán made a show of digging inside the bag again, drawing out the suspense.

Hugo mumbled a curse. Over in their rows, most of Las Nubes folded their hands in prayer, like Angelo, probably asking for the band from El Paso's name to be called next.

"Mariachi Las Nubes," Galán read.

A collective groan sounded from participants on both sides of the aisle. Mariana shushed her sisters, but Angelo caught her nervous side-eye in his direction. The odds David had mentioned earlier were dwindling.

"Rounding out Team One . . . we have . . ." Galán continued with his torture. "Mariachi Las Aguilas! That means, Mariachi Los Reyes, you're Team Two."

The last part of his announcement was drowned out by Arturo Capuleta's "That can't be!" and Hugo's "Hold on a minute!" mixed with gasps of horror from many, including from some in the two other bands.

"¡Cálmense! ¡Cálmense!" Galán raised his hands as he asked for a calm that Angelo knew half the people in the room were far from feeling.

In a surreal, time-warpesque moment, everything suddenly amplified. His heart pounded a fast bass beat in his chest. The voices arguing around him clashed like cymbals. His attention bounced from his uncle and Los Reyes to Mariana and Las Nubes like a pinball pinging chaotically inside a machine.

Most of Los Reyes and Las Nubes were on their feet with a melee of reactions—frantically, angrily, insistently appealing to each other and the show organizers to make sense out of the incomprehensible.

Hugo's face was red, his jowls tight with fury, fists stiffly at his sides. David and Marco each gripped one of his arms. The older man insisted that Hugo take a beat—or two or, hell, three—before blurting out something they might all regret.

Over on the Las Nubes side, fear stamped the younger Capuleta sisters' faces. The others appeared stunned, one wide-eyed with her hand clamped over her mouth, as they intently listened to whatever Cat and Mariana were saying. Cat gestured wildly each time she spoke. Mariana placed a hand on one of the younger girls' backs, offering comfort. Whatever the two oldest sisters discussed, their father's grimace made it apparent that he did not agree. At one point, Mariana grasped her father's hands and spoke directly to him. Arturo shook his head; Mariana countered with a nod of her own.

Angelo sought out Galán, irked that the singer had only given them that cryptic warning about a "new twist" rather than the full details, allowing them time to prepare for the potential volatile situation. The man knew how this pairing could affect their bands, given the feud. Why would the organizers borrow trouble with this harebrained scheme?

Galán shook the bag in the air as if to indicate that the selection was out of his hands. As messed up as this situation might be, Galán was right—the drawing had been fair.

"Hey, are you listening?" Marco waved a hand in front of Angelo's face, pulling his attention back to their group.

"Uh, yeah. Yes!" Angelo repeated at Marco's what-the-hell's-up-with-you frown, one of many since they had arrived today.

"Look, vato, Las Nubes was a crowd favorite yesterday," David said, directing his words at Hugo. "If this is a one-pair double elimination, we want to partner with the strongest band. Increase our chance of making the finals. I hate to admit it, but after yesterday, the strongest just might be Las Nubes."

"Qué desmadre," Tío Hugo muttered.

Several others grumbled their agreement with Hugo, echoing variations of his "what a screwed-up situation" curse.

David's scowl silenced the younger men's complaints.

"You have to keep your cool during the team-representative meeting they mentioned," the older man advised Hugo.

"I can go instead," Angelo suggested. "They asked me to do the interview yesterday. If we need someone to coordinate rehearsals and exchange information about our sets, let me handle it."

Tío Hugo's frown carved deep grooves in his already-lined forehead, but he tapped a knuckle against his chin as he considered Angelo's idea.

Despite the moderate temperature inside the theatre, sweat gathered under Angelo's armpits. He rubbed his suddenly clammy palms on his jeans. Things could really go south if his tío said no. As codirectors of Las Nubes, Mariana and Cat would surely represent Las Nubes. The friction between Cat and his uncle would create sparks. Sparks that could lead to blowing all their chances in the competition.

Representing their band would give Angelo a valid reason—not the secret one Galán had initiated—for communicating with Mariana.

"Fine," his tío muttered.

Relief sluiced through Angelo like water shooting from a lawn sprinkler across their front lawn.

"Tell their representative that they can learn our set and sing backup," Hugo added.

"Bueno, I doubt that's what the organizers will expect," Angelo said, also certain that, as the Las Nubes musical director, Cat would have her own ideas about the song selection for their combined set.

"Tradición. That is what we are known for. That is what we will stick with," Hugo demanded.

"Tío, we should consider what Las Nubes brings to the stage as well. They've proven they're a force to be reckoned with. They're good. Hell, better than good. We should combine our—"

The director clapped his hands for everyone's attention, interrupting Angelo's attempt to prepare his uncle for the teamwork mentality Mariana and her sisters—as well as the judges—no doubt envisioned. A blending of their talents, not a demotion to backup-singer status.

"Now that our teams are set and ready to get started," the director announced, either choosing to ignore or not interested in dealing with the outcry, "information regarding your mentors and team rehearsal times here at the Majestic will be emailed to you shortly. We'd like a moment with a representative from each band to discuss specifics and expectations with fewer voices in the mix."

"The following mariachi, please stay. The rest are excused to leave," Galán added, motioning toward the back of the theatre. His message was clear—the rest were *expected* to leave. "Mariana Capuleta, Baylor Chavez, Miguel Garcia, and Angelo Montero, please move up here. Everyone else, since I am one of the mentor coaches, I will see you at your first group rehearsal. ¡Felicidades!"

With Galán's "congratulations" signaling the end of the team meeting, the chatter—for some, the complaints—among the contestants started up again. Angelo stepped into the aisle so the band members behind him could file out. Thanks to the roll call Galán had named as those who should remain, Angelo didn't have to worry about Tío Hugo changing his mind.

It took several moments for the theatre to empty. Much of the time for Angelo was filled with Tío Hugo glaring at Cat and muttering gruff warnings for Angelo to watch his back "with that Capuleta girl." Angelo ignored him, instead busying himself with texting Brenda: Time to go.

She answered quickly: My friend is staying. Can we hang out on the mezzanine level, out of the way, until you're done?

He fired off an okay, while surreptitiously eyeing the Capuleta side of the aisle, anxious to make his move to a seat next to Mariana's.

One by one, each Capuleta took their turn hugging and cheek kissing Mariana goodbye. Cat and their dad seemed intent on hammering her with advice. The way she shook her head or waved them off had Angelo betting it ran along the same churlish lines as his uncle's.

Finally, only the four band representatives, Galán, the director, and a few others from the crew remained. Plus, two teens hiding up in the mezzanine. The director waved Angelo and the guy from Mariachi Luna y Sol closer to the front.

Keeping an empty seat between them, Angelo sat in Mariana's row. He tucked his chin in greeting but didn't say anything to her. Oh, he wanted to. Hell yeah, he had questions. But this wasn't the place, or the time, to ask why she'd been ghosting him.

Plus, based on the tight line of her lips and the white-knuckled grip of her hands clasped in her lap, she grappled with how to troubleshoot and make the best of the untenable task ahead. Mariana placed an exorbitant amount of pressure on herself to protect her familia, solve everyone else's problems, and none of them had seen this one coming.

He was racking his brain for what he might say to mollify her worries when Mariana surprised him by scooting over to fill the seat he'd left open between them. She leaned to the side, smoothing the material of her knee-length black skirt under her butt, and her shoulder bumped his. Angelo shifted to share the armrest with her. Sure, he could be a gentleman and let her have it to herself. But he was still irritated by her silent treatment and didn't want to deny himself the pleasure of her touch.

"Dios mío, I feel like we've gone from the frying pan into the fire. Don't you?" Mariana whispered, hunching toward him. She shot him a conspiratorial look from under her wispy lashes. Trust shone in her hazel eyes, and Angelo secretly thanked Galán and his team for their high jinks. "What are we going to do about this?" she asked. "You got any ideas?"

Her faith in him dispelled his frustration. He covered her hand on the armrest, wrapping his fingers around hers in the closest he could come to an embrace. For now.

Actually, he had no idea how they could keep the feud from detonating among some of their band members. But the fact that Mariana thought of the two of them as a team—a "we"—pleased him far more than was wise given the calamity they faced.

The thing was, they faced it together.

Chapter Thirteen

Heading to the lobby. See you there.

Mariana hit "Send" on her text to Nina, then slipped her phone inside her satchel. Her eyes fluttered closed on a bone-weary sigh. Just when they'd gotten past one mess, another popped up in its place. Unfreakingbelievable.

If she didn't know any better, she'd swear the organizers were punking all of them. But Galán and others had made it clear their commitment remained to the charitable organization. Plus, to avoid any semblance of favoritism, the band pairings had been randomly selected in a luck-of-the-draw—or bad-luck-of-the-draw—scenario.

Eyes still closed, she sucked in a deep breath. Needing just a second—or two—to quiet the emotions and thoughts cycloning inside her. The stress of the last twenty-four hours—the interview and meeting with Galán, the competition and awaiting the results, avoiding Angelo to avoid the crush of familia guilt only to feel its elephantine weight anyway because he deserved better—had taken its toll. Add this new, horrifying turn in the Battle . . . ay, all she wanted was a soak in the tub and a supersize glass of cabernet with her phone on "Do Not Disturb."

She had time for neither.

After early mass at the Basilica this morning, Papo had picked up barbacoa for breakfast tacos on the way home. Those who weren't too nervous to eat had filled their bellies, and their entire familia had crammed in the sala at Casa Capuleta. Some on the couch. Papo in his recliner. Several on dining room chairs they dragged over. The rest sprawled on the floral area rug. Everyone anxiously watching *Sunday Morning in San Antonio*, desperate for the segment when the Battle of the Mariachi Bands Round One results were announced.

A millisecond after Patricio Galán's glorious words—"Landing in the top spot, Mariachi Las Nubes"—pandemonium erupted in their house. Shrieks and cheers and cries of "Ay Dios mío!" Group hugs and happy dances and claims of hearts pounding in their chests.

Once the celebration that had no doubt awoken the Gomez familia upstairs finally settled to a delirious hum, Nina had shocked Mariana's socks off by hesitantly approaching her and Mamá to ask whether she could tag along with the band today. Nina was two weeks shy of reaching the end of her grounding, but this was the first time she'd shown any real interest in Las Nubes. More importantly, the flash of yearning in the teen's eyes when Fabiola and Teresita had dog-piled on top of Claudia, the three of them rolling on the floor amid squeals of joy, had empathy welling in Mariana's chest.

It had taken some convincing, but Mamá finally agreed to let Nina attend the meeting, then grab a late lunch with Mariana. Nina's "thank you" and the shy smile that rarely cracked her tough-girl facade had Mariana praying the teen might be finding her way to trusting them.

"You okay?"

Angelo's question pulled Mariana out of her musings to realize everyone else had left the orchestra seating area. Except him, standing in the aisle at the end of their row, waiting for her.

"Mmm-hmmm, I'm fine." A fib that easily rolled off her tongue because she repeated it so often.

His jean jacket clutched in one hand, he gestured up the aisle. "We should probably get going."

Rising from her seat, Mariana ducked under her satchel strap to leave it hanging across her torso. Angelo shuffled back, making room for her to slide out of their row, then fell in step beside her.

The muffled thump of their boots on the carpeted aisle filled the silence. Despite his earlier assurance that they'd "figure something out" and his promise to the competition organizers that there would be no problem with blending their bands, a new undercurrent of unease ran beneath the surface of their conversation.

Guilt coupled with disappointment in herself led Mariana to reach out and draw Angelo to a halt. With the sleeves of his gray sweater pushed up, the corded muscles of his bare forearm flexed beneath her touch.

Questions loomed in his eyes. Ones she knew he had every right to voice after her rude silent treatment. He didn't, though.

She had expected him to ask her about it during the meeting when everyone else was occupied with working out the rehearsal logistics for the other team. There'd been another perfect opening when Galán had stressed the importance of communicating with each other and working as a team to bring out their best—advice that hit a little too close to home for her conscience.

Angelo could have made a snide comment. Instead, he had replied with a simple "Understood."

At the time, she'd been relieved. Unwilling to air their dirty laundry in front of everyone.

Now, his refusal to call her out for her rudeness had Mariana's guilt-laced irritation boiling over.

"Just say it already," she demanded.

"Say what?"

"Aren't you gonna ask me why?"

"Why what?"

Mariana gaped at him, wondering how he could be so infuriatingly calm while she . . .

She wanted to be like Cat and howl at the Fates. Tell someone off. Punch something. Hard.

She wanted to lean on his broad shoulders. Rely on their new unlikely relationship formed in the midst of this madness.

She wanted to give in to her craving for more than friendship. A craving that scared her because it felt too much like a betrayal.

That's why she had ignored his calls and texts. Even though doing so had crushed her.

"Why what?" Angelo repeated.

"Why aren't you mad at me?" The question burst from her as if he'd hooked a fishing line in her rattled thoughts and reeled the words right out of her.

"Do you want me to be mad at you?"

"Yes! No! I mean . . . uuugh." The groan sighed out of her as she dropped her chin to her chest and cradled her forehead in her palms. Flustered by her confusion. Tired of the tug-of-war between what was right for her familia and what felt right for her.

Staring down at the toes of their black boots, barely a foot but what seemed like a mile apart, she muttered a disgruntled "Maybe."

Angelo gently clasped her wrists and lowered her hands. The whisper-soft back-and-forth of his thumbs along the inside of her wrists soothed and tantalized, confusing her even more.

"Hey," he said softly, ducking down to peer at her.

He eyed her curiously, head tilted in question. The motion had the cuff of his oversize turtleneck brushing against his jawline. Caressing the spot she had imagined herself pressing a kiss to late last night when she'd lain in bed, unable to sleep. Her head spinning with Cat's and their dad's warnings about the Monteros. Her body pulsing with unsated desire.

"Aren't there enough pissed-off people around us already?" Angelo asked.

She nodded, dumbstruck by the simple validity of his point.

"Yes, I'd like an explanation," he continued. "Based on our friendship, I think I deserve one. But I won't push—"

"I'm sorry," she blurted, unable to resist giving him the apology he deserved. "Everyone was freaking out about the competition. Harping about the feud and stressing out about our need to win the prize money." She shuffled a baby step closer to him, and his hands slid from her wrists down to weave their fingers together. "Still, I shouldn't have ignored—"

"Oh, are we interrupting something?" Nina called out.

Mariana's breath hiccuped in her chest. Pulling her hands from Angelo's, she spun to face the stairs at the top of the aisle, where Nina stood . . . with another girl?

"You said to meet you in the lobby, but everyone from the meeting came and went. We thought maybe you were waiting for us down here," Nina said.

She and the petite teen looked at each other and shrugged in agreement, then started down the aisle toward Mariana and Angelo.

"Hi, I'm Brenda," the girl said, lifting a hand to give a loose-fingered wave. "I'm—"

"Angelo's sister," Mariana finished. The teen's dark eyes, high cheekbones, and straight nose, plus her similarly engaging grin, made it easy to see the family resemblance.

"And I'm Nina, one of Mariana's younger sisters." Nina waved a greeting to Angelo, who seemed as nonplussed as Mariana to see the girls together.

"What are the two of you—or how did you two—Ay, did anyone see you girls together before they left?" Mariana blurted.

No way would Hugo or Papo, or Cat for that matter, have given their blessing to the girls hanging out with each other. The uproar would have raised the theatre roof!

"We were in the mezzanine when you texted," Nina answered. "I figured you said I could stay, so why chance running into someone who might make me leave?"

Gracias a Dios for Nina's adolescent reasoning.

"I doubt Tío Hugo even remembered I was here." Brenda hitched a shoulder in a typical teen *whatever* shrug. "Even from where we were all the way in the top row, I could tell he was pissed. Believe me, I know to make myself invisible when he's in a snit."

More wise teen rationale.

"If you two are done with your meeting, Brenda and I have an idea." Nina nudged Brenda with an elbow.

"Oh, right!" Brenda bounced on the toes of her dark brown leather ankle boots, her bubbly nature at odds with Nina's usual broodiness. "Well, since Angelo promised to treat me to a late lunch, and Nina and you were planning an outing . . ."

Brenda passed the verbal baton back to Nina with an open-palm gesture.

"Why don't we all grab a bite together—"

"At the Pearl District!" Brenda's voice hit an octave that should have shattered the theatre's decorative stained glass. She clapped excitedly, wide eyes pleading with her brother.

Meanwhile, Nina's pert face was stamped with a strange mix of tough-girl saucy and hopeful longing.

Mariana shook her head, instinct warning this was a bad idea.

"Oh please. Pretty please," Brenda cried.

She raced down the aisle, dragging a surprised Nina by the arm. Amusement tickled Mariana's funny bone. There was a certain karmic humor in seeing Nina, who usually kept everyone at a ten-foot-pole distance, standing arms tightly linked with Angelo's exuberant sister.

"Nina said she's never been to the Pearl District before," Brenda continued, pleading their case. "It's a beautiful day outside. Perfect for ordering takeout and having a picnic in the park."

Brenda laid her head on Nina's shoulder like they were best buds. Nina flinched, shock momentarily glazing her face. Then an awed smile wavered on her lips, evidence of her unvoiced hunger for connection and acceptance.

The problem was, as soon as Mariana and Nina got back to Casa Capuleta, someone would ask how they'd spent their afternoon. Then what?

It was one thing for Mariana to secretly plot with Angelo. That was for the good of the competition and Las Nubes. Fine, and maybe her own, in a damn-it-felt-good-to-be-with-him sense. But no way could she involve Nina in a lie, even one of omission.

"I'm sorry," she said, the girls' crestfallen faces compounding her regret. "It's not a smart—"

"Sounds like a great idea to me," Angelo announced.

"Yes!" Brenda's cry and energetic happy dance had Nina doing a decent rendition of a rag doll being flung around by a gleeful child.

Mariana swung her head around so quickly to gawk at Angelo, a burning sensation hissed down the right side of her neck. "What are you thinking?"

"I'm thinking, the girls and I are hungry. And the director said we should start discussing ideas for how to mesh our band sets. Plus, you owe me."

"Owe you?"

"Uh-huh."

Angelo slipped on his jean jacket, then dug his hands in the pockets with a nonchalant shrug. As if the idea of the four of them—two Capuletas and two Monteros—sharing a meal together, at a popular spot in the city, were no big deal.

"For ignoring me last night. And this morning," he added, correctly interpreting her what-the-hell-are-you-talking-about scowl.

"Oooh, you're gonna love the Pearl District. It's a fun place to people watch," Brenda told Nina. "We can order takeout from different restaurants and picnic on the grass."

"Or we could hit Whataburger again," Angelo suggested.

Nina burst out with laughter. She slapped a hand over her mouth, but the "no way" in her brown eyes was loud and clear.

"Did I miss a joke?" Brenda asked. She looked from her brother, to Mariana, and finally to Nina, who shook her head and waved off her new friend's question.

"Naw, but maybe there's a burger place at the Pearl?" Nina asked. She pressed a hand to her stomach at the same time she shot Mariana a brazen smirk. "'Cuz for some reason, I'm suddenly craving a hamburger and fries."

"I see the two of you are burger fans. Must run in your familia." Angelo winked at Mariana, who found herself flustered by his flirtatious teasing in front of their sisters.

"When we met at Whataburger, I said it was more like my late-night craving of choice. That doesn't mean I eat there all the time," she corrected.

"I knew it!" Nina's screech made Mariana realize her gaffe. The teen leaned closer, her smirk widening as she jerked a thumb at Angelo and stage-whispered, "So this guy must be Whata—"

"All righty then!" Mortified by the very real possibility of Nina revealing the secret name Mariana used for Angelo's contact in her phone, she leaped forward and wedged herself in between the teens. "If we're gonna grab lunch, we should go!"

"Really?" Brenda screeched.

"You're saying yes?" Nina's childlike euphoria was worth the risk of being caught.

"Hold on a sec. Is this guy—I mean—am I what?" Angelo asked.

Giving her sister a stern zip-your-lips glare, Mariana grabbed a fistful of the back of Nina's lightweight jacket and tugged her up the aisle.

"We'll meet you two at the Pearl," Mariana singsonged over her shoulder, feeling anything but bright and cheery.

Nope.

More like anxious to get Nina in the car, where they could set some ground rules for this one-and-done Montero-Capuleta group outing. Starting with an hermana never blabbed the other sister's secrets. Especially when it came to a hot guy she had no business crushing on.

~

"You're right, this place is pretty sweet." Nina wiped her mouth with a napkin, then dropped it inside her paper to-go bag.

"And you haven't even seen the best parts yet. Come on, I wanna show you The Twig. It's a supercute indie bookstore. And Felíz Modern, this trendy art deco shop with all kinds of creative stuff." Brenda scrambled to her feet on the red-and-black-plaid blanket Angelo had spread out for them on the grass earlier.

"Hold up," Angelo ordered before Mariana could swallow her mouthful of ramen.

"Aw, c'mon," Brenda whined. "You two are still eating and you haven't even talked about competition stuff. Half an hour. That's all I ask."

"As if you've ever been in and out of The Twig in thirty minutes," Angelo chided.

Mariana took a sip of her sweet tea, eyeing the brother-sister interplay with interest.

"Hmm, you're right. Thank you, dearest hermano. I'll take your advice and see you in an hour." Brenda sent him a cheeky grin, then spun on her low bootheel as she called a "c'mon" to Nina.

The girl's cheekiness made Mariana laugh, which wound up making her choke on her sweet tea. She sputter-coughed and nearly dropped her drink. Nina scooted over on her knees at the same time

Angelo leaned across the blanket. Both of them pounded on Mariana's back in unison.

"I'm"—cough—"fine," she choked out. Eyes watering, she waved them off before they left her shoulder blades bruised.

Technically, Nina was still grounded and shouldn't be off having fun. Then again, as far as Mariana knew, this was the first time Nina had shown any interest in hanging out with a friend since she'd come to Casa Capuleta. Maybe time with Brenda would be good for her. Give her a taste of how things could be if she was a permanent member of their familia.

Peering up at Nina, Mariana squinted in the early-afternoon sun. "If I let you go . . ."

"I know, make good choices, yada yada," Nina filled in, bobbing her head as she recited another of Mamá's mantras.

Mariana arched a brow, making it clear that she needed more than lip service from her sister.

"I will. We will." Nina hopped to her purple Converse–clad feet to stand shoulder to shoulder with Brenda. No ten-foot-pole distance. "Promise."

Gone was the moody adolescent with a Texas-size chip on her shoulder. Seeing Nina behaving like a carefree teen lightened the constant weight of responsibility in Mariana's chest. As the only other Capuleta sister who had arrived alone, she knew her parents were counting on her to connect with Nina. Today they'd made great strides, in part thanks to Brenda.

Nina flashed Mariana a hopeful smile. "¿Por favor?"

"Okay, go have fun," Mariana said. "Una hora solamente."

"Got it. Only one hour."

"Here, we'll even set a timer for fifty minutes. That way we have time to get back and won't be late." Brenda thumbed her cell screen while Nina gathered their trash. Seconds later the two were beating a fast path toward the well-known indie bookstore.

With the girls off exploring, Angelo uncrossed his legs and stretched them out over the area Brenda had occupied. He set his nearly empty ramen bowl aside and leaned back on his straightened arms behind him.

"I didn't realize there was another Capuleta sister. One not part of Las Nubes."

Mariana nodded as she fished for a piece of broccoli in her bowl. "Nina's been part of our familia for about six months. She's still settling in, finding her place." Hopefully.

"Will she join the band?"

"If she wants. One of the major Casa Capuleta House Rules is that we take up an instrument. Even if we suck. And let me tell you"—she pointed her chopsticks at him, grinning at the memories his question evoked—"there were weeks and months when Blanca and later Fabiola started with the violin that many of us walked around with earplugs when they practiced."

"I bet," he said on a laugh. "The violin makes beautiful music. Except when it doesn't."

"Mmm-hmmm. Thinking about my mom and Cat teaching music lessons to kids and adults in the community center makes my ears hurt."

"Ouch," he murmured, dropping his head back and closing his eyes against the bright sun.

She wanted to slide closer, invite him to rest his head in her lap. Instead, she stayed on her side of the blanket, longing for a closeness she shouldn't. "You and your sister seem to get along well. It's nice."

Eyes still closed, he wrinkled his nose at her use of "nice." She laughed, relieved at the return of their ease with each other since her apology at the Majestic.

"Brenda's a good kid," he said. "That's not to say we don't butt heads. Mostly I try to think of how my mom used to respond, things she and my dad said or did. Kind of honoring their memory for her."

Moved by his admission, Mariana allowed herself to openly admire this man who continuously surprised her. The sun's rays turned his black hair a shiny ebony, and she itched to comb her fingers through the wavy locks. The light kissed the angles and planes of his bronze skin and glinted off a silver button on his jean jacket like his playful wink.

Such an extraordinary man. Beautiful inside and out.

"She's lucky to have you," Mariana said.

"Ah, pues, there was a time when I would have begged to differ. After our parents died, those first few years were pretty rough." He shook his head but continued his sun-worshipper imitation—eyes closed, face lifted to catch the rays. Unwittingly giving her a chance to continue her fantasies starring him.

"I was floundering. Without my tío Hugo's support, I would have botched everything."

"Somehow I doubt that."

"No, it's the truth. I wasn't ready for the responsibility of parenting."

"At nineteen, who is?" she offered.

Heaving a weighty sigh, Angelo shifted, rolling his shoulders and torso in a languid stretch that had her wishing they were in a much more private place enjoying a picnic for two. Instead of a public park with children racing by in a game of tag.

Settling back on his straightened arms again, he stared at his boots stretched in front of him, his handsome face solemn.

"You already know that the accident happened mid–fall semester my sophomore year. But afterward, I couldn't concentrate on school, couldn't study. The two people who had always provided stability in my life were . . . gone. In an instant." The memory pinched his features as he grappled with an old pain that experience had taught Mariana would dull, but never go away.

"Brenda was inconsolable. I tried commuting from here to Austin so I could be with her as much as possible, but in the end, it was too much. I wound up dropping my classes and moving back home. I needed to be here for her and couldn't concentrate on school, and my parents' finances were a mess. Everything was . . ."

A bone-weary sigh blew through his lips, and she longed to comfort him, remind him of the great job he was doing raising Brenda. But he spoke before she could.

"Anyway, when spring semester rolled around, then summer, I just couldn't see the point of going back. Nothing made sense."

"But you figured it out. Eventually. You found the strength of spirit to go on. For yourself, for Brenda."

A dog barked excitedly at the kids chasing each other around the grassy area, drawing Angelo's attention. A bemused smile tipped the corners of his lips, and she wondered if he was remembering Brenda at that age. His ability to break through his own sorrow and find joy in their lighthearted play endeared him to her even more.

"Actually," he eventually said, once the kids were rounded up by their mom, "Tío Hugo is the one who convinced me to register for classes again. He talked me into changing my major from business and finance to accounting so I could manage the books for El Rey. He even paid the difference in my scholarship, which meant I didn't have to get a part-time job and could be there for Brenda after school."

Kudos to his uncle. Apparently, the man had a redeeming quality after all.

"As someone trying to earn a scholarship to counter my PA school tuition and fees this fall, that sounds like a pretty sweet deal," Mariana admitted.

"Yeah, it was. Mostly." Angelo tapped the inside edges of his boots together, his brow furrowed at whatever thought now meandered in his mind. "My uncle and I don't see eye to eye on some things—bueno, many things—but when it counts, he's been good to us."

"I can see why you have such a close relationship with him."

"He's been like a dad to us. Granted, a strong-willed, opinionated one. The opposite of my dad, really. But a father figure all the same. Man, how I miss my parents." Angelo's chest rose and fell on another heavy sigh. The pleasure-pain of reliving memories and if-onlys was something she knew well, too.

"You don't have to talk about this if you don't want to," she told Angelo, trying to protect him from pain like she did with those she cared about.

Because she did care about him. There was no use denying it anymore.

"I don't mind. It feels important for me to share this with you." Angelo tilted his head to look at her, his expression serious but with a sincerity that ensnared her.

She wanted to know everything about him. His past, his present, the future he sought . . . and that she yearned to be a part of. What made him laugh or ache or filled him with nostalgia. When it came to Angelo Montero, she was fast becoming a glutton for more.

"I'd like that," she murmured, scooting closer on the blanket.

"My parents were hardworking, honest people, but they made some costly, inexperienced financial decisions. That's why I initially studied business and finance at UT. When they died, their finances were in shambles. That's how I wound up losing our home after they died. Tío Hugo opened his to Brenda and me. Just like your parents did for you."

"Familia. They help us get through the worst in our lives."

Angelo tipped his head with a shared understanding.

The fact that Hugo Montero, the man who created such strife for her familia, had a soft spot for his own should have buoyed her. It was proof that Hugo wasn't all bad. That maybe they'd get through Round Two without any collateral damage.

And yet, what Hugo had done for Angelo and his sister confirmed the debt of gratitude Angelo felt he owed his tío. Rightfully so. But a debt that would have him siding with his uncle if, more like when, battle lines were drawn between their familias. This feud was about more than the Battle. Papo honestly believed that Hugo might be involved with the private lender's grab for Casa Capuleta. If that was true, any relationship between her and Angelo was doomed.

The best she could do was savor this clandestine time together. Hold it close to her heart. Because once the competition finished, meeting like this couldn't happen again. No matter how badly she may want to.

Sadness crept over her, but she pushed it away. Maybe she couldn't change their future because she couldn't control what others did. Life had taught her that much. But she could grab on to what was right in front of her.

"Thank you for sharing that with me," she told Angelo. "For trusting me."

"I don't normally like to talk about that time in my life. The frustration and fear. The feelings of inadequacy. You make it easier, though. Being with you feels, to use a word you're fond of, 'nice.'"

He rolled his eyes and she laughed, heartened by his playfulness despite having deep dived into the painful details of his past.

"Plus, it's not often I get to spend a lazy afternoon relaxing on a blanket with a beautiful woman I find intriguing."

Tracing the outline of squares in the checkered blanket, she eyed him from under her lashes.

"Intriguing, huh?" Coy wasn't typically her style, but she lapped up his compliment all the same.

"Definitely." He sat up and crossed his legs, swiveling on the blanket to face her. "Usually, it's Brenda and me eating lunch and perusing The Twig's bookshelves. Having you here makes the outing better. But what about you? How do you spend your lazy days?"

"Ha!" The laugh burst out of her at his question. "It's rare for me to ever have a lazy afternoon. If I do, I don't come here. I mean, sure, they did an admirable job with the revitalization of this area."

She looked around at the families, couples, and groups dotting the tables and grassy open park area. Old and young, tourists and locals alike. Even a few pets enjoyed the sunny late-March weather with their owners.

"I just can't help but wonder, especially with everything happening on my side of town, at what cost?" she mused.

"Change isn't all bad. Or it doesn't have to be. Years ago, this whole area was an industrial wasteland. A piece of history being lost." He gestured toward the refurbished Pearl Brewery behind her. "Now Hotel Emma's a hot spot, and the Pearl District has some of the best culinary restaurants and trendy boutiques owned by locals. This green space and others like it draw people outdoors. It's evidence that gentrification can be good."

"Until it takes your home. Your neighbor's home or business." The thought of losing Casa Capuleta galvanized her fight instinct. "I'm not saying no to change. I'm saying no to a loss of cultural history. To pushing people who don't want out, out. People like me and my familia."

"My uncle says—"

"Look, I know you love your uncle, but many of the projects he's been involved with don't necessarily have the best history or track record. Not when it comes to taking longtime residents into consideration."

Agitated by the topic, which now threatened to taint their afternoon together, Mariana moved to push herself to stand. Unfortunately, she planted her hand in the dregs of her ramen bowl in the process. Mumbling a curse, she dug in the paper to-go bag for a napkin. Before she could find one, Angelo loosely grasped her wrist.

"How about a change of subject?" he suggested.

Gently he twisted her wrist to rest her hand in his. Her breath caught in her throat as Angelo drew a napkin over her palm and fingers—once . . . twice—wiping away the sticky sauce. Prickles of awareness flittered across her skin. Slowly he raised her hand to his mouth. His intent gaze locked on hers, he licked a droplet of sauce off the side of her thumb.

Lust raced a fiery trail up her arm. It arced through her, leaving her breasts heavy and achy for his mouth's attention. She imagined his tongue tracing a pleasure-inducing path down her stomach . . . slowly moving lower . . . and she burned with desire.

For months she'd been fantasizing about her handsome stranger, now the tempting mariachi she shouldn't crave but couldn't resist. Her body knew exactly what it wanted.

Him.

Angelo lowered her hand, cradling it in his. Maybe she should have pulled away, broken this dangerous connection. But she didn't. Couldn't.

"There are a lot of things I want to do with you, Mariana. Arguing isn't one of them." He traced the lines on her palm with a featherlight touch and . . . Ay Dios mío . . . her toes curled in her boots, while other parts of her throbbed with desire.

"We'd need a little more privacy for some of the ideas I have in mind," she admitted.

His lips curved in a sexy grin. "That's a topic I am more than willing to explore. Unfortunately, there's something not nearly as fun, and definitely more stressful. But at least it's one we can tackle together."

She wanted to savor their sensual playfulness, but he was right. They couldn't avoid their responsibilities any longer. "The competition. More specifically, our Las Nubes and Los Reyes pairing."

Angelo's expression sobered at her mention of the Battle.

For some reason, his reaction reminded Mariana of Brenda's comment at the Majestic: how she'd learned to avoid her tío when he was in a snit. Cat had complained numerous times about Hugo Montero's hot temper and flair for the dramatic. Compounded by his traditional machismo when it came to women mariachi, his difficult personality could make the coming weeks of competition rehearsal an arduous challenge.

"I'm guessing your uncle isn't pleased about performing with an all-female band. Am I right?" she asked Angelo.

His fingers curled tightly around hers. "Yes. However, *I* am more than pleased by our pairing."

"That's good to hear. I should give you a fair warning, though. When it comes to her music career, my sister Cat's equally as hard-headed. She will not sit quietly and allow your tío to dictate how our combined set will go. Not if she thinks she has a better, a *winning*, suggestion."

"Hopefully with Galán and another mentor at our first practice, they'll provide a voice of reason. Along with ours."

"You're assuming I can be reasonable, huh?" she teased.

Angelo threw back his head with a laugh that had him doubling over and, eventually, even swiping a thumb at moisture in his eyes.

"Hey now, it wasn't that funny," Mariana complained.

"You are the most levelheaded, problem-solving whiz I know," Angelo told her. "I'm confident that you and I will figure out a way to get our bands working together to give us all a fighting chance of making the finals."

He made it sound easy, like bridging the divide between their two camps wouldn't be a problem. She wasn't foolish enough to believe that, but she was willing to try. Because somehow, with him at her side, she felt like anything was possible.

"Despite our differences, we all want to win," she said. "You'd think that would counter ego—Hugo's or Cat's. I mean, if we can't work as a team, we'll all be out."

"Exactly. That's what we need to keep the others focused on. Marco and David will help me herd the rest of our guys in the right direction, even my tío. What about your side?"

"Mamá will speak with Cat and Papo if needed. The others will follow my example." They would most certainly be watching and taking their cues from her. That meant she had to be careful. Working with Angelo, while not giving any indication of her growing feelings for him.

A cool breeze blew over them, dragging a loose lock of hair from her braid across her cheek. Mariana angled her face into the wind, trying to draw the strands away.

Angelo softly tucked her hair behind her ear, then ran his fingertips in a tantalizing, whisper-soft path along her jawline and cheek, stopping when he reached the edge of her mouth.

Mariana fought the sudden urge to lick her lips. Desperate to kiss him. Taste him. Savor him once more.

As if he read her thoughts, Angelo leaned toward her. Anticipation quickened her breath, and her lids started to drift closed. He stopped inches away, not nearly close enough, his breath warm on her face. His gaze met hers. Intense . . . heated . . . seeking her permission.

She swallowed. This powerful need for him suddenly made her nervous.

When he didn't come closer, waiting for her to give him some sign that she welcomed his advances, she bobbed her head in the smallest of nods. Or, bueno, she thought she did. She hoped she did. All her thoughts were focused on one thing and one thing alone. His lips. On hers. Now.

Grabbing a handful of his sweater, she tugged him toward her. Making her consent clear.

"Huck! No, boy, heel!"

The cry came an instant before a small black bundle of wavy fur and energetic wiggles jumped onto Mariana's lap.

Angelo reared back with a "What the he—"

A red nylon leash trailing on the grass behind him, the friendly, if mischievous, Huck set his paws on Mariana's shoulders and proceeded to show his love with warm licks and cold nose nuzzles on her neck and cheeks.

Laughter bubbled up in her throat, and she giggled, enamored by the young pup. If not by his timing.

"I am so sorry." A petite, twentysomething-year-old woman in black leggings and a tee under a baggy windbreaker came running toward them, her brown ponytail swinging in the breeze.

"That's okay," Mariana assured her. "He's such a sweetheart."

Angelo ran a hand over the puppy's back. His fingers intertwined with Mariana's in the dog's thick fur, and the animal clambered around to shower his affection on Angelo, burrowing in his chest.

Grabbing the red nylon leash, the young woman hunkered down on the grass and reached for her puppy. "He's usually much better behaved. Aren't you, Huck? Come here, boy."

The energetic pup launched himself at his owner. After apologizing again, the young woman and her furry friend headed off, leaving Mariana and Angelo in an awkward, post-interrupted-kiss silence.

Angelo settled back on his half of the blanket. A respectable distance away.

"That . . . this . . ." Mariana fluttered a hand between them to fill in the words she had to say, even if she didn't want to. "Bueno, it's probably for the best that we don't, you know. With everything going on. Even if we—"

"I'm not going to deny wanting to kiss you."

His honesty slayed her. And deserved the same from her. "I won't either."

But where did that get them?

Horny but unsatisfied . . . that's where.

"Mariana, I can't promise that everything will go smoothly this round. But I *can* promise you that I'll do my best to ameliorate the drama as much as possible. If us plotting how to achieve that involves a lazy afternoon picnic, or maybe dinner or an evening together? I'm in. All I ask is that if you're worried or upset or anything else, you talk to me about it. No ghosting. Deal?"

He held out a hand. Not to shake, like a business transaction. Palm up, as if asking her to place her trust in him. Like he'd done several times during the short time they'd known each other.

Ay, it was a dangerous proposition. One her conscience told her to avoid. Keep their relationship solely focused on the competition, nothing more.

In the end, she gave him the only answer her heart allowed.

Pulse racing, Mariana sucked in a deep breath, then placed her hand in his. "Deal."

Chapter Fourteen

Early Tuesday evening, Angelo pressed a hello kiss to the crown of his sister's head, then dropped his keys on the kitchen counter and headed to Tío Hugo's home office.

"It's your turn to cook dinner," Brenda called from her stool at the breakfast bar.

"I'm thinking leftovers."

"Gross!" she complained.

He grinned, expecting her response. Obviously, she hadn't seen the package of chicken breast he'd left thawing in the fridge this morning.

Before he got started with dinner, he wanted to touch base with his uncle about tomorrow's combined practice. Cat had emailed song suggestions yesterday. Hugo had grumbled that he had plenty of experience and didn't need her input. Of course, Angelo reminded him of the director's call for *teamwork* and how Las Nubes had wound up in the top spot in the first round. Unfortunately, his salient points in favor of the sisters had landed on his tío's deaf ears.

The tap of Angelo's bootheels on the gray tile reverberated down the hall leading to his uncle's side of the house. As he neared Hugo's office, he heard his uncle's baritone voice drifting through the partially open office door.

"I heard they claimed an anonymous call was made to immigration officials instigating an investigation," Hugo said.

Angelo halted at the mention of the government department.

"What time did authorities arrive at Casa Capuleta?"

What? Fear seized Angelo's chest. A raid at Mariana's familia's property? Happening right now?

He glanced at his watch, his gut tightening with dread when he read the time: 6:13 p.m. Had ICE and Homeland Security officials just descended? Or had they shown up at the community center earlier, brandishing weapons no doubt, at peak time for after-school classes? Right when parents were dropping off their children and latchkey kids arrived on their own. All confronted with the harsh ugliness and often heartbreaking injustice of an ICE sweep.

His uncle didn't even sound surprised! Had he known about this?

Horror filled Angelo at the thought.

"Serves Arturo right," his tío grumbled.

Blood roared in Angelo's ears. Anger sliced him with its sharp blade, compelling him to act. With a loud slap of his palm, he shoved the office door open.

"¿Qué hiciste?" he demanded.

Tío Hugo gaped at him, jaw slack with surprise. Angelo didn't back down.

"What did you do?" he repeated, the words gritty like sandpaper on his tongue.

"Ahhh, let me call you back in a minute, Pedro." Tío Hugo jabbed a finger at his cell screen, then dropped the phone onto the wide mahogany desk with a clatter. Hoisting the leather belt encircling his paunchy stomach, he sauntered around the desk edge. "I don't know what you think you overheard, pero no me faltes el respeto."

"Don't disrespect you? Are you kidding me?" Angelo scoffed. He closed the door to keep Brenda from overhearing, barely controlling the urge to slam it. "You're on the phone talking about an ICE raid. A damn ICE raid, Tío! At a location we both know is crawling with innocent kids and parents right now. Not to mention it's home to the teenagers in the band we're scheduled to practice with for the Battle tomorrow! You don't see a problem with that?"

"Cálmate," his uncle ordered as Angelo strode toward him.

"I'm not going to calm down until you level with me. Tell me, how the hell are you involved?" Fury vibrated through him like a jolt from a live electrical wire.

"I am not 'involved.' So be careful before you go throwing accusations around."

"Then what do you know about it? Who's the anonymous tipster?"

Jaw muscles tightening under his jowls, Hugo folded his arms across his burly chest. He leaned on the edge of his desk, eyeing Angelo with indignation. "Sí, I heard rumors that a fugitive who had been court ordered for deportation might be hiding in one of the Casa Capuleta apartments. But whatever that person did with the information is on them. You cannot blame me for someone else making the call."

"And you didn't think to say anything about this to me?" Angelo countered.

"Why?"

"Why?" Angelo sputtered. He jabbed a hand through his hair, frustrated at his tío's hardheadedness. "Because it involves the Capuletas."

"And what does that have to do with you?"

More than his tío knew. But Angelo couldn't admit that the last person he'd spoken with most nights over the past couple of weeks, and the first person he thought of when he awoke, was the oldest Capuleta daughter. Instead, he settled for part of the truth. "It concerns me, and all of Los Reyes, because we're supposed to practice with the majority of the Capuleta familia tomorrow, remember?"

Hugo's scowl deepened the furrow between his brows and pushed his lips in a sourpuss pout. "This has nothing to do with the competition."

"You're wrong, Tío. This will affect the young girls, probably all the Capuletas. Whether the tip is proven unwarranted or not, for those being confronted by the agents, or with a familia member facing the interrogation, the emotional turmoil will be devastating."

He pictured the sisters huddled together at the Majestic on Sunday after the surprise band pairings. The worry and uncertainty creasing their faces. Even Cat's. What was potentially going down in their home and the community center right now would be a thousand times more shocking. Especially if things went bad with the raid.

Fear pressed on his chest. *Por favor, Dios, let things go smoothly and be over quickly.*

"Most of the time, these tips are baseless," Hugo said with a blasé shrug. "I chalked the news about the fugitive up to wishful thinking on the part of . . . bueno, it doesn't matter who. And if the tip pans out, so much for Arturo Capuleta's clean-cut image."

"If his tenant is hiding someone, that doesn't automatically make Arturo Capuleta an accessory," Angelo argued. "Odds are he's unaware of it."

"And you are an expert on his character all of a sudden, ha?"

"Having met the young women he and his wife have raised, I think it's safe to say that they are decent people, Tío." Hands on his hips, he faced his uncle, unwilling to back down. Not when innocent lives, ones he had come to care about, were being threatened. "I know there's bad blood between you and Arturo, but if you once loved Berta Capuleta . . . to put her familia—hell, everyone at the community center—at risk? That's not right. And if what happened today is someone's method of trying to drive the Capuletas out of that building, El Rey Properties should not be part of it."

Hugo's nostrils flared. Outrage at what he no doubt considered Angelo's disrespect turned his face into a mask of stony condemnation. And yet, he failed to refute Angelo's unspoken but clear accusation.

Was Hugo associated with the private lender who sounded more like a loan shark strong-arming the Capuletas?

Angelo didn't want to believe it. He had defended his uncle countless times, especially to Mariana.

Gut-punched by the potential truth, Angelo turned away from Hugo. He paced to the window overlooking the front of the property. This home, with its expansive circular drive and tall security gate at the edge of the wide manicured lawn, had been a haven for him and Brenda. But did living here, in the esteemed, rarified air of Fair Oaks country-club territory, as Mariana had teasingly called it, allow his uncle, and by default Angelo, to remain out of touch with those living in the older neighborhoods in San Antonio? The ones most affected by some of the deals El Rey Properties brokered?

Angelo didn't want to be involved with the cause of the problem faced by the people residing in places like the home on C Street where he'd lived with his parents as a kid. The same area where Hugo and Angelo's dad had grown up. But he was beginning to think that his tío might be.

"This is going too far," Angelo said.

"Quit being so dramático," Hugo chastised him.

In the window's reflection, Angelo watched his uncle reach for an envelope and a letter opener. His beefy hand practically swallowed the thin gold instrument as he slashed the sharp blade through the paper's folded edge with a quick flick of the wrist. Back to business. Unmoved by the gravity of the situation.

"You know how things like this can go down, Tío," Angelo pushed, desperate to find a crack in his uncle's indifference. Proof of his conscience. "The intimidation tactics ICE will utilize. Weapons visible. If not drawn. And even if the authorities find this one fugitive, at what expense will it be to the innocent bystanders?"

"I was told that government officials arrived shortly after one. The center was closed. Only those living in the apartments would have been affected. If they are not hiding anything, they will be fine."

Stunned by his uncle's casual dismissal, Angelo spun around to face him. "Gracias a Dios for small graces. Is that it? What about when the kids in the apartments came home from school? Or those who showed up for music or dance lessons this afternoon? What were they subjected to?"

"You cannot lay this incident at my feet. I came by the information secondhand. If the Capuleta familia has a problem today, it is not my doing. Now"—Hugo slapped the letter opener on top of his desk—"as far as I am concerned, we are done here. No need for you and Brenda to hold dinner for me. I have my own plans."

Without waiting for a response, his uncle stormed out of the office.

Angelo stared at the empty doorway, stunned by his uncle's callous behavior. Instinct urged him to drive to Casa Capuleta and . . . and what? Would a Montero showing up actually help or make things worse?

"Angelo!" Brenda's cry carried down the hallway seconds before she burst into the office, her face ashen, eyes wide with fear. "Something happened at Nina's place. I just saw it on the news. She can't use her cell phone yet, so I can't reach her. Please, can we drive over to check on her?"

~

Parked a block over from Casa Capuleta on Buena Vista Street, Angelo tapped his thumb on his truck's steering wheel. Anxiously awaiting a text. Praying Mariana and her familia were safe. Pissed beyond rational thought at his uncle.

Beside him in the passenger seat, Brenda craned her neck as she scanned the area around them. Twilight loomed, casting a gray pall and long, somber shadows along the streets and sidewalks.

"No answer yet?" Brenda asked, despite the fact his phone hadn't vibrated indicating an incoming message.

Angelo shook his head. "Keep in mind, it's been a stressful afternoon for them. The building was taped off while authorities interrogated everyone. The sisters probably couldn't communicate much with their parents or anyone else who was inside. I'm sure they're all still freaked out, even though the authorities have left."

"It sounds so horrible. So scary. I can't even imagine . . ." Tears pooled in Brenda's eyes. She pressed a hand to her chest as if it ached. His sure did when he thought about the sisters. The tenants and students.

"I don't think you or I can understand what anyone who was at Casa Capuleta today has been through." Twisting in his seat, Angelo hooked an arm behind Brenda's. "We're lucky. That's why it's important for us to be strong for them and help however we can. Even if it means backing off and giving them some time. That's why we're waiting to see what Mariana says."

"I understand. I wanna be a good friend. Nina was already going through a lot. Being a foster kid and all. Now this?" Tugging on her seat belt strap, she sat up straighter, determination stamping her face while her sad sniffle hinted at her tears. "I know Tío might not approve of our friendship, because Nina's kind of a Capuleta and her mom's in jail. But she didn't make her mom's choices. Nina's just like me in lots of other ways. Like, we'd both do almost *anything* to see Bad Bunny or Maluma in concert. And even though she thinks she might wanna play the violin, she's starting with the guitar, same as me. She's never read *How the Garcia Girls Lost Their Accents*, but she's heard about it, so I'm going to loan her my copy. And neither of us likes all our house rules or sushi. Or math. Bleh!"

He couldn't resist smiling as she scrunched her face in a grimace at the mention of her least favorite subject.

"Are you sure we're related?" he teased. "'Cuz I'm an ace at math."

"For which I am thankful because you make a half-decent tutor."

"Half-decent? Hey now!" He lightly thumped the top of her head at the dig, and she narrowed her eyes in a playful glare. His phone vibrated, rattling in the center console. Brenda snatched it up before he could.

"Yes! Mariana says we can meet in the back courtyard. Let's go!" Brenda reached for the door handle, ready to cut and run. Angelo stopped her with a hand on her forearm.

"Hold up. Remember, don't go in there bombarding her or anyone with questions. Let Nina talk, if she wants to. About whatever she wants to. You listen and be the good friend you are. That's probably the best thing we can do. Okay?"

Brenda murmured a subdued "okay."

As he pocketed his keys and slid out of the driver's seat, Angelo repeated his own advice to himself—*be a good friend*. That's what Mariana needed right now. Ever since their near kiss a couple of days ago, he wasn't bothering to pretend with himself anymore that friendship would be enough. But today, that's what she needed.

He and Brenda walked east down Buena Vista, then crossed the street to make a left on South San Jacinto, heading toward Commerce and the community center. Up ahead at the intersection, two older couples huddled together. Anxious faces, wringing hands, and worried glances toward Casa Capuleta a block down suggested the topic of their heated discussion. Angelo tipped his ball cap in greeting as he ushered Brenda around them. Thankfully the pedestrian walking light blinked, and they crossed Commerce without needing to stop. No need for Brenda to get freaked out by neighborhood gossip about the raid.

Normally fairly busy, the one-way street lay eerily quiet. Most residents were likely staying inside. Away from any potential trouble. Even the corner bodega where Angelo had waited that first night he'd recognized Mariana had a Closed sign on its door.

Yellow police tape sagged across the Casa Capuleta front entrance, a blatant "beware" reminder to all who passed by. He wanted to rip it down, shove it in the graffitied metal trash bin on the corner. Instead, he tamped down his anger and reached for the calm Mariana might need from him.

He pushed open the metal side gate leading to the courtyard, and it squealed in protest, heightening his antsiness. Brenda started to race ahead without waiting for him.

"Slow down," he cautioned, not wanting to barge in and risk interrupting the sisters, who might be seeking solace in their backyard sanctuary.

He and Brenda reached the open area with its strings of white mini lights crisscrossing above. Unlike during Angelo's first visit, tonight the raised stage, dance floor, and tables lay empty. The memory of the partygoers like ghosts lingering in the normally festive space.

On the far side of the dining area, Nina and Mariana sat in one of the bench swings. Nina's shoulders were hunched, her face tearstained. One arm around her sister's shoulders, Mariana glanced up as Angelo and Brenda approached.

"Oh! Hi!" Nina swiped her cheeks with her sweatshirt sleeve, then planted one of her black Converse on the concrete to stop the swing's motion.

Thankfully, Brenda had the presence of mind to rein in her earlier impatience and follow his instructions about taking things slow. She looked up at him, the determined teen who had yelled for him to ignore the speed limit on the drive over, now an uncertain kid, afraid of making things worse for someone she cared about. He understood the sentiment.

"Thanks for coming to check on us," Mariana said, breaking the ice for them.

"I wish I had heard about everything sooner. Brenda saw it on the news." Angelo left out the part about overhearing his uncle's conversation. Hugo hadn't implicated himself, and without irrefutable proof that his uncle was involved, he didn't want to upset Mariana by mentioning it. "Had I known what was going on, I would have—"

Mariana waved off his words. "There's nothing you could have done. The girls and I were stuck waiting on the sidewalk in front of Silva's bodega, praying for it to all be over quickly. Safely."

"Are you . . . are you okay?" Brenda asked, her voice subdued.

Mariana turned to Nina. The two exchanged an unspoken message, and Nina gave a tentative nod. Mariana clasped her sister's shoulder and gave a brisk nod of her own.

"We're made of strong stuff, us Capuleta girls." Mariana's lips curved in a gentle smile, but Angelo spotted the dregs of sorrow dulling the gold flecks in her hazel eyes.

She put up a good front for the teens. Underneath her veil of positivity and strength, he'd bet he'd find a woman as scared as her sister, yet determined to be the rock the others needed to rely on.

"Would you maybe wanna come up and hang in my room?" Nina motioned hesitantly to the metal stairs that led to the second- and third-floor apartments. "Claudia's spending the night at Cat's place, so we have the room to ourselves."

"Sure. If your parents won't mind. I mean, they probably don't know I'm a—"

Brenda broke off with an uncomfortable wince. She didn't say it, but Angelo knew what she meant. *They probably don't know I'm a Montero.*

The need for anonymity had led him to grab a ball cap for cover even with the dusky twilight shadows.

"It's fine." Mariana patted Nina's thigh and nodded again when her younger sister looked to her for reassurance. "Just tell Mamá and Papo a friend came to see how you were doing, and that I said it was okay for you to invite her up."

"Not too long, though," Angelo added. "It's a school night, and the Capuletas might need a little more familia time before bed."

Nina stood from the swing, setting the bench in motion. The metal chain squeaked as it rubbed against the industrial-size hooks screwed into the wooden frame. "Thank you for, you know, driving Brenda over."

Had he not heard about Nina's skittishness from Mariana, Angelo would have hugged the teen. Instead, he gave her a playful wink that was rewarded with a shy smile from her. "We were worried about you. And everyone else here. I'm relieved that you're safe."

The two teens hooked elbows to climb the stairs side by side. A much more subdued pair than they'd been at the Pearl District on Sunday.

As soon as the door closed behind them, he turned back to catch Mariana releasing a heavy sigh. Head tilted toward the darkening sky, eyes closed, she sucked in another breath, held it, then let it go with another audible exhalation.

"May I join you?" he asked.

She peeked open her left eye. "You want to join my meditative breathing exercise?"

He laughed, turning it into a cough when she raised her brows, clearly affronted. "Uh, no. But you go right ahead. Meditative breathing is known for its calming effects. Or so I've heard."

"Mmm-hmmm," she mumbled. Eyes closed again, she sucked in another deep breath through her nose.

Angelo eased onto the wooden bench seat, careful not to rock the swing and interrupt what he figured might be her first moment to decompress on her own. Away from the responsibility of caring for others.

The side of his knee accidentally brushed against hers as he made himself comfortable. He left it there, pleased when she didn't shift away. Silently he watched her—chest and stomach slowly expanding, then deflating, with each measured breath in, then out. After a few moments the strain on her striking features ebbed. The wrinkle between her brows faded, and her shoulders relaxed. Finally, the hands fisted on her lap released their tension.

Only then did he notice her outfit—modestly cut black skirt, light green high-collar blouse, fitted black blazer, low professional heels. Not her usual scrubs or sweater and jeans.

"Was your scholarship interview today?" he asked.

"'Was' being the operative word," she muttered on a loud exhalation.

"How did it go?"

"It didn't." Dropping her chin to her chest, she buried her face in her hands with a muffled groan.

Unable to resist the urge to comfort her, Angelo smoothed his palm along her head, down her loose braid. He gave her shoulder a gentle pat, hoping to soothe her unease.

"I was literally walking out the door to drive to campus for the interview when my mom called," she mumbled, head still bowed.

After another tired sigh, she flopped back in the swing, arms sprawled at her sides. Brow furrowed again, head slowly shaking from side to side as if denying the thoughts tormenting her, she stared up at the sky bleeding with wispy shades of blue and purple. Dejection personified.

"I've never heard my mom like that before," she said, the words laden with anguish. "Frantic. Scared. I could hear people yelling in the background, the Gomezes' baby crying. It was so loud, I could barely hear my mom asking me to pick up the younger girls from school. Keep them safe."

She sucked in a shaky breath and scrubbed a hand over her forehead. "Cat had already started a call chain alerting students and parents not to come to the center for classes. Warning them to stay away to avoid any potential problems."

"I hate that any of you had to experience this," he told her.

"Me too. We're lucky it didn't happen later in the day, when classes were already in session. Still, to have our homes invaded like that. All because of some damn anonymous tip that proved wrong. It's infuriating."

Shifting to sit up, she peered around the empty courtyard. Once a beloved space for fiestas and happy memory making for many. Now a space she probably pictured overrun by government officials and chaos. His heart ached for the loss of security she and those who lived on the premises must feel.

"I usually love it back here," she said, her voice a whisper on the cool breeze. "The hum of cars idling at the corner light or driving past on the street side of the hedge. The strands of lights like stars in a blanket of midnight blue. Late spring and fall, Mamá opens the window, and you can hear her telenovela on the TV or music from whoever's playing the keyboard."

"That first night I walked back here for the quinceañera—"

"You mean the one you crashed? Then got tossed from?"

She nudged his arm. Slid him a side-eyed smirk that had him huffing a rush of air through his teeth on a laugh. The fact that she could poke fun at him was a positive sign.

Playfully, he nudged her back. "As I was saying. That first night, this place felt otherworldly. An oasis in the middle of the bustling city."

"An oasis, huh? I like that. We should add it to our website." Planting her shoe on the concrete, she pushed the swing backward. "D'you mind?"

He shook his head. She lifted her foot and their seat swung forward. As gravity pulled them backward again, her head settled on his shoulder. He tipped his to the side, resting it against her crown, relishing this quiet moment together. Relieved that she was okay. The citrusy scent of her shampoo tickled his nose, and he knew he'd always associate the smell of lemon and orange with her.

"That's what this place has always been for me," she continued. "Somewhere where there's peace and quiet. Spending time back here helps me reset. Believe that someday there will be or can be forgiveness for the wrongs done. Maybe even between our familias."

Her hand found his where it rested on his thigh. Their fingers intertwined, comfortable. At peace. Like being home.

Dios, how he needed to believe forgiveness among their familias was possible. That picnics like Sunday's or nights like this or, hell, even Whataburger dates could be the norm. Not the secret exception.

He wanted to accept his tío's claims that he'd had nothing to do with the raid. That his uncle wouldn't take his grudge to such an extreme. And yet, Hugo had sidestepped Angelo's questions about the neighborhood lender causing the Capuletas' financial problems.

With El Rey Properties business, Angelo had trusted his uncle. But this was twice now that Hugo teetered on the side of something Angelo could not condone. If Hugo had anything to do with the raid or the private lender . . .

Given what had happened with his parents, that wasn't something Angelo could ignore. He would have to strike out on his own. Even if it created a rift.

"Thank you for not peppering me with questions." Mariana squeezed his hand, drawing him out of his worried-thoughts spiral. "Or making me feel like I have to pretend to be the strong one."

"You *are* strong. That doesn't mean there aren't times when you need to lean on someone else, though." He brought their joined hands to his lips. Pressed a soft kiss on the back of hers.

Mariana lifted her head off his shoulder to peer up at him. The reflection of the lights strung above them mingled with wonder in her eyes. She dragged her shoe on the concrete to stop the swing's motion, the scraping sound mixing with the strains of a Mexican polka that danced over the chain link fence and tall hedges from somewhere nearby.

Her gaze locked on his, she slowly dipped her head to kiss one of his knuckles, then another, before resting her cool cheek against the back of his hand. With night falling, the temperature had dropped.

The once crisp air had grown colder, but the flare of desire in her eyes warmed him like one of the gas heaters dotting the courtyard. Drawing him closer.

He cupped the side of her neck, his thumb sweeping over her smooth skin to caress her jawline, the corner of her mouth, the edge of her lower lip. When she lifted her chin, tilting her face toward him, he welcomed what she offered.

Tenderly he brushed her lips with his. Tentative. Butterfly light. It wasn't nearly enough. Not for him. Nor apparently for her, as her free hand fisted in his sweater and pulled him toward her. He crushed her mouth with his, starving for a taste of her. Mariana's moan urged him on. His tongue swept along her bottom lip, savoring her flavor, wanting more.

She opened for him, their tongues tangling and twisting in a sensual dance. One hand still fisted at his chest, her other slid along his waist, hugging him closer. His palm slid to her nape, and he deepened their kiss. She nipped at his lower lip, suckled it between her warm lips. He groaned with pleasure, their tongues teasing and tasting.

And still he needed more. Craved more of her.

Out on the street a car horn blared. Mariana stiffened in his arms, and Angelo remembered where they were. That at any moment a member of her familia could step out onto the stair landing or peer out their sala window and catch them.

Disappointed by the interruption—both the car's and reality's—he eased back to rest his forehead against hers. Their hot breaths mingled in the small space separating them.

"Dios mío, that was—" Mariana broke off on another rush of breath.

"Incredible."

She grinned, the sorrow in her eyes now replaced with humor and desire. "I was going to say foolish. Given where we are."

"I've been wanting to do this since you walked away on New Year's Eve. Nearly convinced myself that I must have dreamed you. Until I saw you onstage. Here," he admitted. "So, I say better than incredible."

"I'd be lying if I didn't agree. But . . ." She trailed off and her lashes drifted closed.

"But?" he pressed, when several racing heartbeats had sped by and he remained in limbo.

She sat up, slipping her arm from around his waist and releasing her grip on his sweater. "There's so much coming at us from so many directions. As incredible—to use your word—as this feels, I can't help asking myself why we would want to borrow more trouble."

"But it's a good kind of trouble, isn't it?"

Tilting her head, she shot him a squinty-eyed glare softened by the amusement curving her lips. Lips he *really* wanted to kiss again.

Instead, he pushed to his feet and held out a hand to help her rise. "C'mon, it's getting late, and you've had a hellacious day. Hopefully you can get some rest tonight. As long as you dream about me, at least once."

Her chuckle rippled over him like a humid summer breeze tickling the surface of a lake.

"Wouldn't you like to know?" she teased.

At the bottom of the stairs, he gave her a gentlemanly kiss on the cheek. She pressed against him, her hands on his chest, sandwiched between them.

"Gracias, for being here. It helped. *You* helped." Stretching up on her toes, she gave him a quick peck on the lips, then hurried up the steps, promising to send Brenda out right away.

At the top of the landing, Mariana turned and grabbed ahold of the railing. She leaned against it and stared down at him, a pensive expression on her beautiful face.

"I'll see you tonight," she called out.

He frowned, not following at first. Then she laughed, sent him a surprising wink, pleasure plumping her cheeks with her smile, before she turned and went inside.

Oh, he'd definitely see her tonight, as he had most nights since meeting her . . . in his dreams. Her intimation that she'd be doing the same had him grinning like a fool.

Angelo stared up at the inky night sky with wonder. Whether a trick of the lights crisscrossing the courtyard or a natural phenomenon, he could have sworn that a star twinkled at him. A sign from his parents, giving their blessing to this precarious relationship?

He sure hoped so. He'd take all the help he could get, divine or otherwise, figuring out how to navigate the troubled waters ahead for him and Mariana. But he was up to the challenge.

Tomorrow night's combined practice might very well be their first chance at brokering a détente.

Chapter Fifteen

"You look good tonight. What gives?" Cat slowed her car for the red light at the intersection of West Market and Navarro Streets and inspected Mariana like a judge on *America's Next Top Model.*

"Gracias . . . I think?"

Cat laughed at her dubious response. "I mean it as a compliment. You're usually in scrubs or comfy sweats when we rehearse after one of your shifts. You even put on makeup tonight. No offense, but this is much better representation for Las Nubes."

"None taken, querida." Mariana singsonged the endearment as she lowered the passenger seat sun visor to peer in the small mirror. "It was a tough day in the ER. Between that and the uproar of yesterday, I needed a pick-me-up. Figured a hot shower, a blowout, and some makeup might do the trick."

"Good to see you treating yourself to a little self-care. You look pretty."

"Gracias." Mariana mimed fluffing her hair and grinned at her sister. "I feel pretty."

Also, excited and—okay, fine—foolishly giddy about seeing Angelo again after their kiss last night. A kiss she had replayed in her mind as she fell asleep. Then dreamed about till morning. And thought about when she'd managed to put up her feet in the break room for a hot second.

The fact that he and his sister had cared enough to drive all the way to Casa Capuleta to check on her and her familia after the traumatic afternoon had truly touched her. Nina, too, who badly needed the reassurance that there were those who valued her.

Mariana and Angelo's private time in the courtyard, the comfort his soothing presence and words brought her, had been a balm to her wounded soul. It was different from the comfort of her familia. In the best way. In a way she was coming to rely on, as scary as that might be.

"You know my motto, 'Love yourself like you want your lover to,'" Cat said with a confident jut of her chin. "Hey, did you hear back from Angelo?"

"What? Why?" Mariana slammed the sun visor shut, her pulse blipping. Dios mío, had someone spotted them in the courtyard last night? No, if that had happened, they would have cried foul already.

"The set ideas I asked you to email him? Did you also mention the new song I wrote?" The light turned green and Cat made the left turn onto Navarro, heading toward the Houston Street parking garage by the Majestic. "What Hugo emailed was a joke. Las Nubes will *not* be relegated to merely playing backup while Los Reyes performs their regular set."

"Don't worry. That's not what the judges want," Mariana reminded her sister. "I'm sure Patricio Galán and our second mentor will shut that down if Hugo tries."

"If not, I will," Cat warned. "The set list I drafted is killer. And with my new song, I purposefully kept the musical arrangement of the duet simple, making it easier for everyone to pick up fast. I'll tweak it for our own set later. Like, it'd be great if Teresita added some of her guitar magic in the musical break, but old-school Hugo might throw a conniption. We'll see. It should only be a matter of deciding who they tap to join me on the main vocals."

It was also a matter of ensuring both sides played nicely. If Cat went in guns blazing, they'd all wind up like the patriots who lost in the Battle of the Alamo.

Cat turned into the dimly lit parking garage, and Mariana broached the touchy subject she and Angelo had agreed to address with their hardheaded familia members.

"Hey, I know how much of a perfectionist you are, especially when it comes to your music. That's what makes our shows unforgettable," Mariana said, buttering her sister up. "Pero, with this gig, you'll have to give up a little creative control. And, I love you, querida hermana, but you've gotta have some restraint. No losing your cool, okay?"

Hopefully Angelo was convincing his uncle to do the same.

Easing into an opening between a blue minivan and a beat-up sedan, Cat pulled to a stop. "If Hugo isn't flying his petty machismo flag, I won't feel the need to rip it down and stuff it in his mouth. Deal?"

She pulled her keys from the ignition, then dropped them into her purse with a sweet-as-sweet-tea smile that was all veneer and no heart.

Mariana didn't know whether to laugh at her sister's kiss-my-ass attitude or groan at the potential impending standoff.

~

Thirty minutes into the combined practice, the dreaded standoff hit its peak.

Cat and Hugo faced each other from opposite sides of the electric keyboard that had been set up stage left. Good thing Mariana had convinced Papo that his presence at the rehearsal would only fan the flames of animosity. It hadn't been easy, but for the good of Las Nubes, he had agreed to stay home. Only because Galán would be present.

As it was, the famous mariachi made a superb firm, nonpartisan referee. At the moment, he stood behind the pianist, attempting to explain to Hugo, again, the value of blending instead of stifling each band's talents.

"Like I said before, I understand that it's important to honor tradition," Galán said.

"Hey, I agree with Galán about that, but this old 'eres más bonita calladita' dicho you subscribe to?" Cat interjected, pointing a finger at Hugo, her glacial tone intent on freezing out the older man's antiquated "you're prettier when you're quiet" patriarchal saying. "It's not happening here."

"Enough!" Galán held up his hands, stopping Hugo before he could fire back at Cat's outrage.

Everyone else on the stage quieted at Galán's gruff outburst.

"Cat!" Mariana hissed, pinching her hotheaded sister through the sleeve of Cat's thin red sweater.

Seated in folding chairs spread across the wide stage, the other girls stared at their oldest two sisters with varying degrees of nervousness and uncertainty.

When they had first arrived, the two bands had immediately separated the chairs into two distinct groups. Then George Garcia, their second mentor and a producer from the recording label, put an immediate stop to the segregation, ordering them to group up by instruments. Violins on the left; guitars, guitarróns, and vihuelas on the right; trumpets and percussion at center stage.

There'd been grumblings. Some skeptical side-eyed glances. Then Angelo and his buddy Marco dragged their chairs across the scuffed black surface to their respective spots. Mariana had joined Marco in the trumpet and percussion section, bringing Claudia and Fabiola with her while glaring Cat into taking her vihuela and the sisters who belonged with her to meet Angelo in the guitar section.

The younger girls, still grappling with the emotional fallout from yesterday's harrowing afternoon, had been visibly intimidated by their older male counterparts. Thankfully, George Garcia's nearly two decades of industry experience proved him more than worthy of his mentor role. The anecdotes he shared about collaborations that had worked, some that hadn't and why, along with his keen perspective on what each band brought to the collective table for the competition, had set a cooperative tone.

When the producer suggested a classic Vicente Fernández song every mariachi knew as a warm-up, the powerful sound of their combined instruments filling the hallowed theatre's space had taken them all by surprise. Even Cat had raised her arched brows, clearly impressed. Angelo shot Mariana a quick wink that, despite her what-are-you-doing shake of her head, had sent a zing of pleasure through her chest.

They moved into another tune with Galán calling on individuals to sing different parts. The antagonistic vibe slowly dissipated, until they moved from warming up to discussing song selection for their combined set. That's when the fireworks display Galán was now trying to douse had started.

"Arguing is not productive, and none of us is interested in wasting our time. Right?" Galán's no-nonsense frown bounced from Hugo to Cat. "As I was saying, Catalina's song selection and the mash-up of your numbers that resonated with the crowd on Saturday is smart. The arrangement of her original song can be fine-tuned, some sections are rudimentary—"

"Excuse me? Nothing I write is rudimentary." One hip cocked, Cat jutted her chin at a pugnacious angle, somehow managing to look down her nose at Galán, though the man stood more than a half foot taller.

Mariana flinched, shocked at her sister's audacity. Pissing off the most influential judge would not help their chances in the competition. Annoyed, she pinched Cat again. Harder.

"Ouch!" Cat sputtered. Jerking her arm away, she glared at Mariana. "It's the truth."

Surprisingly, Galán smirked at her bald claim. Hugo, on the other hand, shook his head with a disagreeable scowl and grumbled a complaint under his breath.

Behind his uncle, also trying but failing to shush his relative, Angelo's bug-eyed frown telegraphed a "what the hell" sentiment that echoed Mariana's thoughts.

"That was a critique, not a criticism, Catalina. If you want to make it in this business, you'll do well to learn the difference." Arms crossed, Galán spoke with an air of superiority warranted by his years growing up in the spotlight with a father known by millions as "El Rey" and having earned his own royal moniker, "El Príncipe." The King and Prince of Mariachi, each successful in his own right.

"Simple may be better given the short rehearsal timeframe," the famed singer continued. "Overall, Cat's set breakdown works well. I would keep the song order, definitely the suggested mash-up of the crowd-pleasers. Hugo, why don't you and George work with the others on learning the transitions while Catalina and I take a look at this duet she's written. See if it's worth adding."

"Oh, it's worth it," Cat threw out.

Mariana closed her eyes and muttered a prayer for patience because she was thiiiis close to throttling her sister in front of everyone.

"Qué fresca," Hugo grumbled.

Cat's *humph* made it clear what she thought about being called fresh by someone clinging to outdated ideas.

Angelo's uncle gathered the copies of sheet music and song breakdowns Cat had brought for the members of Los Reyes, having already given her sisters theirs. He gave Galán a curt nod before striding back to the others.

With the bands practicing on the stage, Galán helped the accompanist move the keyboard to the left stage wing to work on Cat's new duet.

"What happened to giving up a little creative control and playing nicely?" Mariana hissed at her sister.

"Mija, please. Playing nicely does not mean being a pushover. I got this." Lips pursed in a smug moue, Cat flounced after the group moving to the wings.

Angelo sidled up to Mariana as soon as she was alone. His hand settled on her lower back seconds before his warm breath tickled her ear with his whisper. "I suppose that could have gone worse?"

"Don't tempt fate."

His soft chuckle eased the tension seizing her neck and shoulder muscles. As it had last night in the courtyard, his presence calmed her apprehension.

"It's gonna be fine. We're gonna be fine," he assured her.

Ay Dios, she so wanted to believe in his promise.

"Oye, what are you two waiting for?" Hugo called, motioning them over with a jerk of his head.

George and Angelo's uncle led the different musician groups through the proposed song choices, explaining the segues in the mash-ups that combined some of their fan favorites, giving a nod to both male and female greats.

During a short break for her section, Mariana looked over to catch Teresita and Angelo with their chairs scooted closer together. Head bent, Angelo peered intently at Teresita while she played. Her slender fingers lifted and pressed on the guitar strings along her instrument's neck, expertly transitioning between chords, while the fingers of her right hand plucked and strummed the guitar's lower strings. Angelo's lips moved, and though Mariana couldn't tell what he said, it made Teresita smile. Not the shy, polite smile she reserved for those she didn't know well, but the wide, silver-braces-displaying grin that told of her ease with Angelo.

As if she felt Mariana watching, Teresita glanced in her direction. The teen gave a thumbs-up, joy lighting her dark eyes and round face, before she went back to playing.

Angelo pointed at Teresita and mouthed, "She's amazing!"

Pride bloomed in Mariana's chest like a field full of Texas bluebonnets signaling spring's arrival. Witnessing Angelo's appreciation for her sister's talent, the way he so easily set aside the feud none of them had created, gave her hope.

"And we're back. Ready to give this duet a try," Galán announced.

He strode onto the stage, leading the small group from the wings. The keyboard was quickly set up with the accompanist on his padded stool. But when Cat stepped to Galán's side, her back was ramrod stiff, her hands tightly clasped at her waist. Her expression was mutinous, but her demeanor deceptively restrained.

Something had clearly gone down while Cat and the others were offstage. Something—or someone—had her either extremely pissed or, worse, unnerved. This was so not good.

"After listening to recordings of your respective performances this past weekend, Catalina has agreed to humor me—" Galán motioned to Cat with the pieces of sheet music he held. Her lips pressed into a firm line, but she allowed Galán to continue without interruption.

"—by making a switch that creates a better vocal blend for what, I will admit, is a beautiful song."

Mariana caught the faint arch of Cat's right eyebrow at Galán's praise. Still, she remained oddly quiet.

"Angelo and Mariana," Galán said. "I'd like to hear the two of you sing the duet."

"Excuse me?" Worrying about Cat's strangely subdued behavior, Mariana was certain she had misheard.

Galán waved her over, then moved to speak with the accompanist.

Mariana remained frozen in her seat, her trumpet clutched in her lap. Singing lead vocals in a Las Nubes show was nothing new for her. She'd been doing it for years. But performing "No Me Olvides," a duet about two lovers ruing their parting of ways, the title taken directly from the line where each begs the other not to forget them, singing the lovers' lament with Angelo, that . . . Dios mío, that was a little too art imitating life.

Her heart thudded in her chest.

"Pssst, vete." Claudia nudged the side of Mariana's thigh with her trumpet, repeating "go on" under her breath when Mariana didn't move.

Shaking herself out of her stupor, Mariana realized that Angelo already stood at the keyboard. She had to stop overthinking this, making herself more nervous than others would assume the situation warranted. Easier said than done, though.

Her legs wobbly, Mariana stood and set her instrument on the folding chair. Wiping her palms on her black jeans, she hurried to her sister's side, taking the sheet music Cat handed her. Lowering her voice, she asked, "¿Estás bien con esto?"

Cat nodded. "Yeah, I'm fine with it. Galán's reasoning is annoyingly sound. My range might be broader, but I'd have to hold back to not overpower Angelo. Your vocal weight runs lighter and will blend well with his baritone."

Mariana's skepticism must have shown on her face, because Cat put a hand on her shoulder in a show of support. "You'll be great. This is my song we're talking about. I wouldn't hand it off to just anyone and risk them screwing it up."

Hooking an arm through one of Mariana's, Cat drew her closer to the keyboard. The accompanist walked Angelo and Mariana through the music, his fingers dancing across the keys as he played a few bars demonstrating a transition and the location where the key changed. Galán and Cat chimed in with advice, then stepped aside, leaving Mariana and Angelo the center of attention.

She faced him, repeating to herself that this was the same as any other duet she had sung with her sisters or one of her parents countless times. She cleared her throat. Chanced a glance at Angelo under her lashes. His calm gaze met hers. The certainty mixed with sweet affection she saw there sent an arrow straight to a lonely corner of her heart. One he was secretly filling.

The accompanist counted out the tempo, then started with the opening bars.

Her first notes were shaky, but Angelo nodded his encouragement. He entered on the second line, his baritone strong and vibrant. His rich voice wrapped around her like a comforting blanket. It called to her love of their music, bolstering her confidence.

Midway through the heartbreaking lyrics and haunting melody Cat's talent had beautifully woven, there was no doubt that Galán's ear hadn't failed him. Despite this being their first time with the unfamiliar music, Mariana and Angelo harmonized beautifully. Their voices filled in where the other's left off. Both singing with full chest voices as the song crescendoed to the emotional goodbye in the lyrics, then easing back with longing as they held the last note.

Several beats of silence met the song's finish. Mariana sucked in a shaky breath, moved by their performance. Then the stage erupted with applause.

Angelo's lips curved with his engaging, lopsided grin. Love for him filled the worried spaces in her chest, and Mariana smiled back at him.

"See, I told you it was a keeper," Cat announced.

Her sister's quip might have been aimed at Galán, but as Mariana stared into Angelo's eyes, she couldn't help thinking . . . yes, he most certainly was a keeper.

~

"Hold up! I need to ask you a question before you go, and you're going to level with me, got it?"

At her sister's odd request, in a tone that sounded more like a demand, Mariana released the car door handle and swiveled to face Cat in the driver's seat.

"Oh-kaaay." She drew out the word, intrigued by Cat's death grip on the steering wheel and intense stare at the darkened road in front of Mariana's apartment complex.

Yellow light from the streetlamp several yards away filtered through the front windshield, bathing Cat in an ethereal glow.

"I hope I'm off base here. Like, not even in the right ballpark. But . . ." With an exasperated huff, Cat twisted to face Mariana. "What's going on with you and Angelo Montero?"

"What?"

Cat shook her head, her "don't mess with me" glare making an appearance.

"N-n-nothing." Mariana cringed at her stutter, cursing the Catholic guilt ingrained in her from years of catechism at Little Flower Basilica.

She'd never been good at lying. Not even white lies of omission. They reminded her of her birth mother keeping secret the truth about her cancer and her lack of care because they didn't have health insurance. An issue that led to her untimely, unnecessary, death.

"You can't kid a kidder. Out with it." Arms crossed, Cat leaned against the driver's-side door, her glare assuring Mariana that her sister would not back down. The two most important things in Cat's life were her familia and her music. This competition affected both. As did anything that might mess with Las Nubes's odds of winning. Anything like a secret, prohibited romance.

Mariana flicked the magnetic clasp on her satchel open and closed, buying herself some time to consider how much, if anything, she should reveal. Not that there was much—*Ay, stop lying to yourself!*

The need to talk to someone about this tug-of-war inside her stilled her fidgeting. The magnetic clasp gave one final click as it slid into place. Maybe she'd been so on edge lately because what had started out as a kiss with a captivating stranger, then a meal at Whataburger to satisfy her curiosity, had suddenly spun into a web of deception.

Her and Angelo's deepening relationship.

Nina and Brenda's budding friendship.

Galán's pressure for her and Angelo to somehow negotiate peace between their bands.

The multiple reasons why Las Nubes needed to win. Which also meant leaving Angelo disappointed by his loss.

It was all too . . . too . . . Damn it, she was so overwhelmed, she couldn't even find words to express herself. She, who prided herself on being decisive and focused and in control of whatever situation life or her job threw at her, suddenly found herself floundering.

She had to talk with someone. Ensure she wasn't making a mistake that would wind up hurting the people she loved most.

"Okay," she murmured, gathering her courage. "But you have to promise you won't freak out."

Cat's glare moved into the "yeah right" zone.

"At the first all-team meeting, Galán approached Angelo and me with concerns about our feud. He asked us to work together to keep our bands from sabotaging the other, and over the past few weeks, we've become friends. Fine!" She threw the last word in when Cat's scowl morphed into "evil eye" status. "More than friends. But nothing's really happened, I swear!"

Her sister smacked the steering wheel with the butt of her palm. "I knew it!"

"How?" Unbuckling her seat belt, Mariana crooked her left knee on her seat and faced Cat, anxious to hear what had given her away.

Dios mío, if anyone else had figured out their secret, Angelo could be facing a similar inquisition from his tío or Marco. If so, it wouldn't be long before word got back to Papo and Mamá. Dread descended like an evil spirit, and Mariana made a quick sign of the cross, praying she was wrong.

"I hope you're praying for some common sense," Cat grumbled. "I figured out your deplorable secret when the two of you hit the second chorus in the duet. Then it became clear."

"Yeah, right. You were too busy being pissed at whatever happened offstage with Patricio Galán."

In typical diva style, Cat tossed her hair over her shoulder with an irritated huff. "That man. His ego's writing checks his talent and experience can unfortunately cash. But that doesn't mean he knows everything. And you, hermana"—she pointed at Mariana with determination—"you are not changing the subject. I could tell you're into Angelo by the way you sang."

"That's ridiculous," Mariana scoffed, hoping her sister was wrong.

"First of all"—Cat held up a finger—"nothing involving my music is ridiculous. Second"—another finger ticked up—"my song is killer. Even Galán and his two-time Latin Grammy–winning Songwriter of the Year ego had to admit that 'No Me Olvides' has the potential to be a showstopper. Pero ustedes dos . . ." Cat shook her head, awe tinting her words as she repeated, "But you two? The way you sang it. Raw and real. Girl, I got goose bumps."

Shoving up one of her three-quarter-length sweater sleeves, Cat held out her forearm as if the goose bumps might still be there.

"Stop it." Mariana swatted her sister's arm away, embarrassed by how much she may have unintentionally revealed.

"It's true."

"You think anyone else got the same idea?" *Dios, please let the answer be no.*

"Uh-uh. I thought maybe I was overreacting. Not that that ever happens, mind you."

They shared knowing smirks. Cat overreacting *always* happened.

"Anyway," Cat went on, "none of the other girls seemed to pick up on your I-wanna-jump-him vibes. Probably because we rarely see them."

Mariana grumbled at her sister's rude observation. "Now is not the time for that lecture."

With a bratty it's-the-truth-and-you-know-it *tsk*, Cat lifted her shoulder in a *whatever* shrug reminiscent of Nina's. "Everyone seemed pretty clueless. Even that guy Marco. But this . . . whatever *this* is . . . smells like trouble."

Head tilted back against the side window, Mariana stared through the car's sunroof at the night sky. Worried thoughts tumbled through her mind like clothes in a dryer. Especially with her sister echoing Mariana's concerns about her and Angelo borrowing trouble by giving in to their attraction.

"So, this all started because of Galán?" Cat asked.

Mariana closed her eyes at her sister's bewildered question, trying to decide what she should share. How much she should admit. It's what she wanted, right? To confide in someone she could trust. Come up with a plan that made sense. One that managed to please everyone while leaving her free to explore where things with Angelo might lead.

A pie-in-the-sky dream that might wind up leaving her with nothing but a pie in the face.

But who better than Cat, the Capuleta sister who bucked authority and went after what she wanted, to help Mariana figure out how to make this work?

"Remember the New Year's Eve bash, when I hurried you off the dance floor right after midnight and you asked if something was up?"

Cat frowned. "Uh, yeah, so?"

"I kissed Angelo Montero that night."

"Hold up, you did what?"

Any other time, Mariana would have laughed at her sister's open-mouthed double take.

"But I didn't know who he was! Not until he showed up the night of Felicia Bonavilla's quince!"

Cat gave another confused double take, and Mariana realized how bad her explanation sounded.

"Let me get this straight," Cat sputtered. "New Year's Eve. You kissed a guy you met at the rooftop bar, and it turns out he was Angelo Montero?"

Mariana nodded mutely.

"Daaaamn, girl. I didn't know you had it in you." Cat grinned, a strange admiration lighting her eyes. She unbuckled, then shimmied in her seat, leaning toward Mariana. "Okay, tell me everything."

"I'm not proud about kissing a stranger I just met in a bar."

"Whatever. Live a little. But a Montero? Mija, I've gotta give you some pointers on how to pick 'em."

One palm pressed to her suddenly throbbing forehead, Mariana glared at her sister. "This is no time for jokes. I don't need your pointers anyway. I'm not interested in picking anyone else."

Cat drew back, her shock evident. "Oh shit! You really like him."

Mariana stared at her sister, wanting to say yes, afraid of what admitting her feelings out loud might bring.

Somehow Cat picked up on Mariana's turmoil. Reaching for Mariana's hands, she held them tightly, her expression worried. "It's going to be okay. Just, tell me everything."

A relieved sigh whooshed from between Mariana's lips. "New Year's Eve was like this surreal dream. I couldn't stop thinking about him. Then the night of Felicia Bonavilla's quince, Angelo and Marco snuck in to watch our show and everything kinda snowballed from there."

By the time Mariana finished with the whole story, Cat had sunk back against her car door again, her face a mix of awe and horror.

"Girl, you two kissed in the courtyard? Talk about asking for trouble," Cat murmured. "A boy like that? It would kill Papo if he found out."

"I know." Despair engulfed Mariana like steam rising from a pot of tamales on the stove.

"I do have to say, I caught Angelo intervening to shut down Hugo's egotistical bluster several times during rehearsal tonight," Cat pointed out. "Those two might be familia, but they don't seem to be cut from the same cloth."

Biting her lip to stem the flood of his good qualities that wanted to rush out of her mouth, Mariana nodded.

"When we were getting ready to leave," Cat continued. "I heard Violeta telling Sabrina that he was really sweet with Teresita during practice. Asking for tips with one of the mash-up transitions. Complimenting them both on how we kicked ass last weekend."

Of course he had. "You should have seen him with Nina and his sister yesterday and on Sunday. It's obvious Brenda adores him."

"It's obvious that you do, too."

The truth seared its brand on Mariana's heart. She couldn't lie. Didn't want to lie about something so beautiful, if also unexpected.

"I do," Mariana whispered. "He's a good man."

"Who's also a Montero." Cat's lip curled at the name. "Why, of all people, did it have to be him?"

Heaven only knew the answer. Unwilling to give up, Mariana pressed her sister. "Any suggestions?"

"Other than run—fast—in the other direction?"

"Not helping."

"Talk to Mamá."

Mariana winced.

"I know," Cat said with a wry laugh. "A week ago, I would have told you to lose his number. Block his calls. But Friday night, the day after I posted that reckless video, I came over for familia dinner and stuck around for a while. After Papo and the younger girls went to bed, Mamá opened a bottle of wine. Two glasses later, she brought up the feud."

"Two?"

Mamá rarely drank. That much alcohol must have really loosened her tongue.

"Surprised me, too," Cat answered. "I'm betting the competition dredged up the past. Back when Papo and Hugo played together and the short time Mamá joined their band. I think she feels a little responsible for having come between the two friends. Wishes things could have turned out differently."

"Interesting how neither of the men involved appear to have similar misgivings. If anyone should, it's Hugo, who backstabbed Papo by cutting him out of that property deal because of jealousy."

"Dios deliver me from machismo pride," Cat bemoaned.

"Amen."

Shaking a fist at the sky through the car's sunroof, Cat grumbled something under her breath that sounded a lot like "freaking Galán."

They sat in a commiserating silence for several moments. Mariana squinted under the glare of an approaching car's headlights but still caught her sister's worried frown.

"If you're not going to follow my advice and run," Cat said, "I'm begging you: don't screw things up with the competition. Talk with Mamá. If there's any hope of this not blowing up in your face—in all our faces—it might have to come from her."

Letting her eyes drift closed, Mariana prayed her sister was right. That Mamá would have a solution to help Mariana and Angelo save this relationship that had barely begun to sprout.

But oooooh how she wanted her love for Angelo to have a chance to bloom.

Chapter Sixteen

"Oye, güey, I have to take a rain check on pool tonight." Angelo tucked his cell phone between his cheek and shoulder to push the F-150's "Start" button.

"What the hell? I thought Brenda was at a sleepover and you had the night off kid-sis duty?" Marco complained. The sound of a car hood slamming shut alerted Angelo that his buddy was still at work. "I told the guys we could meet up around nine. Give me time to close the shop and clean off the grease."

"Something's come up."

"It's Friday night. Work can wait, man."

"This can't," Angelo said, not refuting Marco's assumption that it was work curtailing their fun.

Male voices jabbered in the background, calling "adiós" and "hasta mañana, vato," signs the men at the auto body shop were heading home. Angelo waited while Marco updated his boss on a repair job, then came back on the line.

"I'll catch you next time," Angelo promised.

"Güey, you been acting so cagey lately, if I didn't know your sorry ass any better, I'd think you were hooking up with someone on the sly."

Angelo cringed at the bull's-eye analysis and his phone slid off his shoulder, clattering onto the WeatherTech floor liner at his feet. Marco's cheesy picture, snapped over beers at their favorite dive bar, grinned up at him as if he knew he'd caught Angelo up to no good.

Muttering a curse, Angelo scooped up his phone, then quickly buckled his seat belt and switched the call to Bluetooth. Mariana's text had said she'd be ready by eight if he wanted to swing by her apartment. An invitation he didn't plan on missing.

"Get your mind outta the gutter," he told Marco. "I'll catch you later."

Marco muttered a crass version of the "all work, no play" warning in response. Angelo laughed and hit the button on his steering wheel to end the call.

Moments later, a right onto Ralph Fair Road had him heading toward I-10, praying traffic was light and he'd be with Mariana soon. Between her twelve-hour shifts in the ER the past two days and their separate band rehearsals last night, they hadn't had much time to talk since Wednesday evening at the Majestic. And even then, it'd been impossible to get a quiet moment alone. Her text an hour ago suggesting they meet to practice the duet before tomorrow's combined rehearsal had been a welcome surprise.

If he got lucky, after he and Mariana practiced the song, he'd convince her that food delivery and a movie streaming on her TV were the perfect way for them to cap off a stressful week. Then he wouldn't have to worry about Marco's warning. Angelo's night would find him and Mariana enjoying work *and* play.

~

A gust of wind zipped through the open hallway, and Mother Nature's frigid fingers brushed Angelo's hair onto his forehead as he knocked on Mariana's second-floor apartment door. He hunched his shoulders in his black leather jacket and tucked his chin under his scarf, fighting off the cold weather that had blown in earlier in the day.

Hearing movement inside the apartment, he shot a shivery smile at the peephole. Two lock clicks later, the gray door opened. Mariana peeked her head around it, then waved him in with an "Ay, it's cold out there." She shuffled backward, opening the door wider for him to enter.

Angelo stopped in the short entryway while she locked up behind him. When she approached, stepping close and lifting on her toes to kiss his cheek, it was like coming home. One of her hands grabbed his jacket sleeve near his biceps, the other flattened against his chest. Instinctively he curved an arm around her waist in a tight hug.

Mariana pressed her cheek against his, infusing him with her warmth. Her hand slid from his chest, up his leather jacket to settle at his nape, drawing him closer. She smelled like citrus and spring, and holding her in his arms thawed the cold that had seeped into him. Both from the chilly weather and the years of being on his own without a partner. Mostly because of his responsibility to Brenda, but also because no one had drawn his interest.

Until Mariana. He couldn't *stop* thinking about her.

"It's good to see you," she murmured.

"I'm glad you texted." Understatement. Her days had been packed with work and rehearsal, and she had begged off their nightly phone calls. A move that left him missing their conversations.

Far too soon, she stepped out of his arms.

"Would you like something to drink before we start?" she asked, ushering him into the L-shaped dining, kitchen, and living area of her tidy apartment.

Angelo removed his jacket and scarf, then settled onto one of the black, cushioned stools at the breakfast bar. "Got anything warm?"

"Hot chocolate? Coffee? I was so cold when I got out of the shower, I made myself some peppermint tea but also have ginger lemon. Both decaffeinated." She pushed a button to turn on the Keurig, then opened a cabinet and reached for a white ceramic mug with a bouquet of Texas bluebonnets stamped on the side. "If you're a hot chocolate lover, I can even toss in some mini marshmallows."

Opening another cabinet, she pulled out a half-filled bag of the puffy white treats. "I keep them on hand for Claudia and Teresita. With them it's more like, would you like some hot chocolate with your marshmallows."

He laughed. "I'm good with ginger lemon, thanks. My sister's the one with the sweet tooth in our house, though my uncle's a close second."

Mariana's smile faltered. A frown dipped between her brows.

"You okay?" he asked.

"Hmm? Oh yeah, I'm fine."

She spun away on her airy, unconvincing response and busied herself with a flurry of activity: exchanging the marshmallows for a box of tea and a container of honey, sliding the mug onto the Keurig's tray, and pushing the button to dispense the hot water. The machine hummed and got to work. Mariana remained standing with her back to him.

Angelo waited, her soldier-stiff spine and death grip on the edge of the gray counter giving him the sense that she was far from *fine*. For some reason, mentioning his uncle had cooled her warm welcome.

Sure, Hugo had been gruff and testy at the beginning of Wednesday's rehearsal, but once they'd started playing, even his tío had recognized the rich sound of their blended instruments and voices. Cat's mash-up brilliantly highlighted both bands' talents, and the Capuleta women brought a new dynamic to the Los Reyes set. One his uncle had grudgingly complimented . . . once they'd gotten home.

Had something happened with Casa Capuleta? Maybe there'd been an issue with a patient? If so, she had kept it to herself with the distance she had put between them the past couple of days. Until her invitation tonight.

The machine made a gurgling sound, and water began flowing into the mug. Angelo slid off the stool to step around the breakfast bar. "I can go if you're not up to this or if you're uncomfortable with me being here," he offered.

"No, we should practice."

Not exactly the reason he wanted to stay. And damn, he hoped definitely not the only reason she had asked him over.

"Mariana."

She spun to face him. The motion sent her curtain of black, wavy hair cascading over her shoulder. A curl settled along the edge of her breast, teasing the lust he held in check when he was around her.

"I'd like to believe that we've always been truthful with each other. Am I right?" he asked softly.

She nodded. Uncertainty and yearning clashed in her hazel eyes, confusing him as to what had caused the first.

"That's good to know." Gently, he tucked her hair behind her ear. Let his fingers linger along the smooth column of her neck.

Mariana's eyes drifted closed, and she leaned her hip against the counter on a soft sigh.

"I've got a sneaking suspicion that your definition of 'fine' is different from mine," he told her. "And probably Webster's, too."

Her lips curved in a self-deprecating smirk. "It's more a relative term."

The coffee machine quieted, and she turned to pluck the tea bag string, dunking it up and down in the hot water.

They reached for the honey at the same time, and his hand covered hers on the bear-shaped plastic bottle. Mariana stilled. But she didn't move away. Angelo wrapped his arm around her waist from behind, holding her loosely in his embrace.

Her hand encircled his wrist, and for a gut-punching moment, he thought she might push him away. Instead, she leaned back, tipping her head to rest on his shoulder. The scent of her citrusy shampoo teased him, and he pressed a kiss to her temple.

"What's going on?" he asked. "Let me help you."

"I don't know if you can."

"Try me. I'll do my best," he promised.

She sighed and her body went slack in his arms. Angelo tightened his embrace to hold her weight, accepting her trust in him. Welcoming it.

"So many things are suddenly out of my control. I hate it." Her fist thumped the counter. "The ground I'm walking on feels unsteady. Like the life I've tried so hard to build might fracture if I can't make everything right."

"It's hard to tackle everything. Maybe ask yourself, what can you *actually* control? Figuring that out might lessen your frustration over your inability to have a say in the other matters."

"That would mean giving up something that has become important to me. More than it should, probably. Still, I'm not sure that's what I really want to do."

"Can you set it aside for now? Pick it up again later?" He assumed she was talking about PA school. Maybe canceling her interview had tanked her chances of earning the scholarship she needed.

"Cat figured out that you and I are seeing each other."

Angelo swore his heart stopped at Mariana's unexpected revelation. It sputtered, tripped, then seemed to hit high-blood-pressure-alert levels.

His arm around Mariana's waist tightened as he replayed her words in his head.

That would mean giving up something that has become important to me.

Did she mean him? Them?

With the threat of others finding out, would Mariana end things before they had ever really begun?

No. This wasn't over. They weren't over. Not yet. Not before they'd had a chance to build on what felt so right. Without interference from those who couldn't see past the line separating their familias.

"She had already left the other night, so she didn't see us in the courtyard. How does she know?" he asked.

Mariana turned in his arms to face him. "She claims it was when you and I sang the duet at rehearsal the other night."

"Are you kidding me?"

Mariana laughed. Which surprised him because he didn't see anything funny about this new wrinkle in a situation already as riddled with wrinkles as a shirt he'd recently pulled from a basket of clothes Brenda had forgotten to fold.

"I told Cat the same thing. But she swears that watching us perform her song, she could just . . . tell."

Angelo thought back to Wednesday evening at the Majestic. His surprise when Galán had asked Mariana to take the female vocals instead of her sister, who typically sang lead for Las Nubes. The horse kick to Angelo's solar plexus when he scanned the lyrics and recognized how they echoed an ending he couldn't bring himself to accept for the two of them. The intensity of their connection as the song crescendoed to the final line . . . the final goodbye.

"I'm thinking this is partly how she guessed." Mariana smoothed her fingers across his brow, and he realized he was frowning at the thought of the song's lyrics in relation to the two of them. Being forced apart by circumstances beyond their—damn, that phrase again—beyond their control.

He shook his head, stymied by Cat having pegged their relationship so easily. Worried about what her knowing might mean for him and Mariana.

"What did she say?" he asked.

"After she warned me that I was asking for trouble? And that it would kill Papo if he found out?"

The blunt truth had Angelo dropping his forehead to her shoulder with a murmured "damn, that's bad."

Mariana caressed the back of his head. Craving her touch, he nuzzled her neck, soaking up her warmth. Her fingers flexed, fondling the short hair at his nape, and desire kindled inside him.

"Then she suggested I talk to our mom."

"What?" He straightened, stunned.

Sandwiched between him and the counter, Mariana gripped the edges at her sides. Arching her back, she peered up at him, her expression thoughtful. As if she was actually considering her sister's mind-boggling suggestion. "Cat thinks the competition stirred up old emotions tied to the feud's genesis. That Mamá might want it to end as much as you and I do. I'm trying to figure out how to broach the topic. How I reveal"—she tugged his sweater at his stomach—"this. Us."

Us. He liked the sound of that.

"Would it help if we went together? So you're not facing her alone."

A pleased smile curved Mariana's lips. The warm confidence that had drawn him to her that first night lit her face.

"What?" he asked, when a few seconds went by and she continued staring at him with that secretive smile.

She combed her fingers through his hair, then cupped his cheek. "Why am I not surprised by your thoughtfulness?"

"Let me guess, because I'm a nice guy, huh?"

The flicker of delight in her eyes had something else igniting lower in his body.

"In part, yes. Also, because you've shown me what's in here." She placed a hand over his heart. "And that's worth fighting for."

Her admission had him wanting to howl at the moon.

He set his hands on either side of her on the counter edge and leaned closer. His thumbs grazed her hips through her leggings. Her pupils flared, and an answering desire arced through him.

"You and I, we're definitely worth fighting for," he assured her.

"I'm glad you agree." She skimmed a hand up his cheek to the back of his neck in a tantalizing caress. Tipping up her chin, she let her eyes flutter closed. He willingly obliged, covering her mouth with his.

Mariana's tongue swept over his lips, and suddenly they were devouring each other. Tongues twisting and grazing. Hands exploring, caressing, kneading. She moaned with pleasure and tugged his waistband, bringing his body flush with hers. It wasn't enough. He needed more. Wanted all of her.

Breaking their kiss, he grasped her hips, easily lifting her to sit on the counter.

"Yes," she murmured, wrapping her legs around his waist.

Blood pulsed low in his body, his jeans growing tighter as desire and lust raged through him. Her mouth sought his again. Tongues and lips, heat and fire. He cradled her jaw with both hands, angling her face as he eagerly took what she gave.

She moaned again, her knees tightening on either side of his waist.

"I want you so bad," he murmured. He dug his fingers in her hair, brushing it aside to expose her neck, impatient to taste her smooth skin.

"Sí." It was more breath than word, her hips bucking, seeking what she wanted, too. Another moan echoed from her throat as she rubbed against his erection, the sound of her pleasure a match to his flaming desire.

He kissed a trail along the column of her neck, down her chest, stopping at the V of her sweater to lick the swell of her delectable cleavage. Reveling in her gasp. Appreciating the arch of her back as she gave him better access to her luscious curves.

Her fingers fumbled with the bottom edge of his sweater, grabbing and tugging it up. He released her long enough to help her pull the sweater over his head. Seconds later the navy material dropped to the gray tile floor at his feet.

They stared at each other. Chests heaving. Her lips kiss-swollen. Desire turning the gold flecks in her eyes a burnished yellow. Pink splotches on her neck and chest from the scruff along his jaw. He feathered the pads of his fingers over the marks he'd left on her, intent on soothing them.

His crotch throbbed with the need for release. Aching to bury deep inside her. But if they continued and the rest of her familia found out about them, she risked getting hurt much worse than these angry scratches from his scruff. As much as he craved her, keeping her safe took precedence.

"Mariana, if we don't stop now . . ." Angelo eased back to give her some space. Allowing her to put a stop to their foreplay.

Instead, she grabbed a fistful of his undershirt, keeping him from moving farther away.

"I don't want to stop," she told him, her voice firm, her expression determined. Hungry. "Do you?"

~

I don't want to stop. Do you?

Mariana's own words echoed in her head as she stared into Angelo's sable eyes. If he decided to go all Mr. Nice Guy on her now, she would respect his good intentions. But you better believe that as soon as he left, she'd be satisfying herself in her bedroom. With the image of him hot and ready, like he was now, driving her orgasm.

Angelo cupped her jaw, his long fingers splaying over her neck. If his thumb swooped lower, he'd find her pulse beating a frantic pace. Instead, his thumb swept a delicious arc of heat across her cheek. It flirted with the edge of her mouth, and she turned her head to nip the pad of his thumb with her teeth. Her gaze locked on his, she grasped his wrist, flicked the tip of her tongue over the fleshy area she had nibbled. Suckled the tip of his thumb into her mouth.

"Mariana."

Her name was a husky groan on his lips. Lust seared through her, arrowing to her breasts, pebbling her nipples, and pooling lower, where she throbbed for his touch.

Angelo leaned in to rest a forearm on the cabinet above her head. His handsome features taut with desire, he watched as she took more of his thumb into her mouth, then slowly drew it out. She trailed her tongue to the center of his palm, where she placed an openmouthed kiss.

"Are we stopping?" she whispered, eyeing him from under her lashes.

He swallowed. His jaw muscles tightened as he visibly struggled to gather himself. His restraint, his will to do the right thing when the proof that his body craved the opposite was evident in the bulge filling his jeans, made her want him even more.

"If we don't halt things now, I'm worried you might . . ." The words were gruff, guttural. A man holding on to his self-control. Barely. But putting her needs first.

"I'm okay with this," she promised. "More than okay."

"I want you to be sure," he answered, his eyes fixated on hers as if searching for any sign of doubt. "I don't want there to be any regrets."

Hooking her legs around his waist, she slid her butt to the edge of the counter until his crotch nestled at the juncture of her thighs. Even through his jeans and her brown leggings she felt him throb, ready, eager. Exactly like her.

"Didn't we just agree that this"—she rolled her hips, imitating the act she knew they both craved—"that *we're* worth fighting for? I'm tired of holding back. Of worrying what others will think or do. For once can I put myself first? Put you first? Do what feels good, instead of what we should—"

His mouth crashed down on hers, his hand cradling the back of her head to keep it from banging against the cabinet behind her. Surprised by his fervor, she gasped, and his tongue swept in to tease hers. His other hand grabbed her ass, the fingers digging into her flesh as he held her lower body intimately against his. She ground into him, desperate to be rid of the clothes separating his flesh from hers.

Seeking more of him, she wrapped her arms around his shoulders, let her palms revel in the play of muscles along his broad back while their mouths mated. Tongues and lips. Moisture and heat. Raw and real. Leaving her heady with an eagerness only he could satisfy.

Her fingers clawed at his undershirt. Desperate to inch it up so she could touch his bare skin. As if he sensed her aim, Angelo broke their kiss to cross his arms and grab the shirt hem. In one fluid motion, he tugged the T-shirt over his head, then let it drift to the tile floor, where it joined his sweater.

Eyes blazing with desire, nostrils flaring with each heaving breath, Angelo stood before her bare-chested and sinfully gorgeous, the reality of him far surpassing her vivid dreams. As a nurse, she was accustomed to seeing the human body. But Angelo's . . .

Ay, he made her want to enroll in the school of Angelo Montero and register for Anatomy & Physiology I. Thoroughly enjoying the A-plus effort she'd been raised to tackle every endeavor with as she took her time studying his physique. Memorizing every dip and curve. Each shadow and edge. The sensitive spots and erogenous zones that excited and drove him wild.

Lightly she traced her fingers over the curves of his pecs, down the muscular swoops to the top of his rib cage. His swift intake of breath heightened her awareness, urged her to continue. Her exploration moved lower as she traced his washboard abs. Marveled at the superhero build he'd been hiding under the cover of his laidback button-downs and conservative sweaters and nice-guy charm.

His muscles trembled under her touch, fanning the flames of her lust. She bent to drop a tender kiss in the valley between his pecs. Moved higher to place another over his heart. Higher to test the racing pulse at his throat. He smelled of musk and deep woods and a spice she couldn't name but would forever think of as *him*.

His fingers delved under her sweater hem to stroke her sensitive skin along the waistband of her leggings.

"I need to feel you," he growled.

"Yes."

The word had barely sighed out of her mouth when his hands traveled higher, skimming her rib cage, caressing the swoop of her under-breasts through her lacy bra. He cupped her fully in his palms and her breath shuddered in her chest. His thumbs circled her nipples, the friction turning them into pebbles that strained for his attention.

"Taste you," he murmured, ducking down to lick a trail along the edge of her V-neck sweater.

She moaned with pleasure. Leaning back against the cupboard, she offered herself to him, her body crying out for Angelo to do exactly what he craved.

"Ay, por favor," she murmured, grinding against him. Driving herself over the edge. "I want you. Now!"

Angelo scooped her off the counter and she yelped in surprise. Her legs squeezed his waist, her hands grabbing on to his shoulders as he strode around the breakfast bar, then drew to a halt in her living room.

"Which one?" He looked from right to left at the two bedroom doors on opposite sides of her small apartment.

"On the left," she directed, busy skimming her nose over the warm skin below his ear. Drawing the lobe into her mouth. Relishing the shudder that shimmied his shoulders when she blew on his skin.

She knew they were crossing a line they couldn't uncross tomorrow. That she was allowing him closer in a way she didn't take lightly.

But she couldn't deny herself anymore. Didn't want to.

Angelo pushed open the door to her bedroom with his boot. He stopped in the threshold, and Mariana paused her delectable trail of kisses along his neck to find him staring at her intently.

Heat smoldered in his dark eyes. Still, he waited, giving her another chance to change her mind.

Instead, she stretched up to press her lips to his, giving free rein to the love for him taking root deep in her soul.

Chapter Seventeen

Sunlight streamed through Mariana's bedroom window, casting white lines and gray shadows over the daisies dancing across the bottom half of her comforter. The alarm on her phone hadn't trilled its usual wind chime tune, so it had to be earlier than eight thirty.

Rather than kick off the sheets to jump-start her day like she normally would, she burrowed under the covers and snuggled closer to Angelo's warmth, loath to let the outside world intrude on their private interlude.

Head nestled on the crook of his shoulder, she traced a finger along his left collarbone to the dip in his sternum, then back again. Down the curve of his left shoulder, over the rise and slope of his biceps. The human body really was a true marvel. Sinew and bone, fragile and strong, science and nature combined. And his . . . bueno, his was a study of perfection.

Angelo roused, a low growl of pleasure rumbling from his throat. His arm around her waist tightened, drawing her smile. He palmed her hip, his fingers splaying across her lower belly. His pinkie tucked under the hem of his white tee, which she'd slipped on before falling asleep. Heat arced through her at the memory of the magic his fingers had worked last night. Lust-filled magic she was more than ready for him to conjure again.

"Buenos días." The husky timbre of his gravelly early-morning voice awakened parts of her that should have been sore from all the recent attention. Instead, she throbbed for more.

"Good morning." She propped up on her elbow to peer down at him. Her heart squeezed at his sleepy-eyed grin.

He finger-combed her hair out of her face and softly tucked it behind her ear. "I see you're an early riser."

"Job hazard."

"And looking this beautiful so early in the morning? That's due to . . ." His fingertips moved from the sensitive shell of her ear to trail along her jawline. They brushed a whisper-soft back-and-forth under her chin, a sensual caress that had her breasts growing heavy, her nipples straining for his attention.

"Good genes," she answered, pleased when he laughed. "And a good night's sleep. Thanks to you."

Desire flared in his dark eyes. His hand drew a slow, titillating circle on her hip. "Did I miss your alarm going off?"

"No."

"So, that means we've got some extra time to fill before you have to get ready to volunteer at the clinic, and I have to pick up Brenda at her friend's house. Any ideas?"

The naughty quirk of his brow had her grinning with salacious glee. Oh, she had ideas all right.

She splayed a palm over the curve of his pec muscle, glorying in the feel of his smooth skin and steely strength.

"Maybe this?" She circled his nipple with a fingertip. "Or this?" Bent to swipe the tiny pebble with her tongue. "Or this?"

She rubbed his erection through his boxers with one hand, desire cresting through her as she stretched up to nip at his lower lip with her teeth. Hungry for more of him, she crooked a knee over his thighs and pressed the length of her body against his.

A low guttural sound rose from Angelo's throat. His hand slid from her hip to her lower back. The other one cupped her nape, deepening their kiss as he rolled to his right, taking her with him.

Arms and legs and sheets tangled. The T-shirt she had appropriated and his black boxers were tossed aside. The sound of a nightstand drawer being opened, followed by a foil wrapper ripping accompanied her demand for him to hurry. Sighs and moans, cries of "sí" and "more" and "there, oh, there" joined the early-morning sunlight filling the room.

Later, when she lay sprawled across his chest—their bodies sated, their breathing slowing from heaving pants to calm, satisfied inhalations—a traitorous *what happens next* thought sneaked its way into the room. Into her bed.

A troubled sigh trembled out of her.

"A peso for your thoughts?" Angelo murmured.

"Oye, they don't even warrant a dollar?" she complained, swatting his arm playfully. Delaying the inevitable conversation.

He chuckled, the vibration in his chest tickling her ear.

"It's not your thoughts I don't buy into. It's the thoughts of others. The ones I imagine you're starting to stress about."

His uncanny perception had her twisting to prop her chin in her palm, elbow bent on the mattress, to face him.

"The ones causing this." The pad of his forefinger rubbed at the spot between her brows. The place several of her sisters warned would have a perpetual stress line if she didn't lighten up. Live a little.

"Problem-solving. It's what I do. Sometimes, with my familia, that translates to worrying. It's hard to turn off."

"You don't have to explain yourself. I get it." Craning his neck, Angelo kissed the spot between her brows. Her heart melted.

He settled back on the pillow, his tousled hair, scruffy angular jaw, and sexy maleness somehow looking oddly at home with her dancing-daisies bedding, chosen because the design made her feel happy. Like being with him did.

He caressed her forearm where it lay across his torso, and Mariana realized she had quickly become a fan of Angelo's love language. His propensity for physical touch both soothed and aroused.

"The way you take care of your familia and go out of your way for your patients are admirable traits," he told her. "They're part of what makes you so incredible. But I hope you remember, you don't have to fight every battle alone. Talk to me."

Talk to me.

It seemed like lately she'd been avoiding doing just that with far too many of the important people in her life.

How much of what her parents had learned yesterday about the raid and the bank loan they'd been denied should she reveal to Angelo? Much of it was secondhand. Some conjecture. They had asked her to keep the information to herself, to not even share with her sisters. But more and more it sounded like Hugo Montero was . . . bueno, *probably* was . . . involved with the loan problems.

Torn, she heaved another troubled sigh and sat up. Angelo followed. He drove a hand through his tousled hair in that uneasy tell she'd noticed the night he'd waited for her in front of Casa Capuleta. Still, he didn't say anything. Didn't push her.

Their reflection in the metal-framed mirror above her distressed wood dresser—his expression serious, troubled; hers uncomfortable, with hands twisting in her lap—emphasized the need for Mariana to make a decision. Trust him or stop before someone got hurt. It wasn't fair to either of them.

Nervous about his reaction, she pulled the comforter and sheets snugly at her waist, smoothed a few wrinkles in the daisy pattern dancing over their legs.

Angelo covered her fidgeting hand with one of his, threading their fingers together. "This isn't like you. I've seen you with your sisters, heard you on the phone with people from the hospital and your volunteer clinic. You're direct but caring. You don't beat around the bush. Why now? What aren't you telling me?"

He was right.

Even when the prognosis was dire for a patient, she leveled with them, then took the extra time to help them come to terms with whatever they faced. For her and Angelo to have a real chance, she had to be honest with him, no matter the outcome.

"You already know about the balloon payment for the private loan my parents had to take out when the building's faulty wiring was discovered after Nina started that fire in the community center's kitchen. But we—"

"Hold up, Nina started the fire?"

Mariana winced at her inadvertent slip of the tongue. "Actually, that piece of info hasn't been widely shared. The fire department ruled the incident an accident, and we wanted to protect her from the neighborhood chisme chain."

The way gossip flew around their comunidad, in no time the story could morph into Nina nearly blowing up the building while making drugs instead of mistakenly catching a kitchen towel on fire while trying to light a cigarette. Smoking was a major Capuleta House Rules infringement. But not one worthy of the nosy neighbors' condemnation when Nina was already struggling to fit in.

Tugging her hand from Angelo's grasp, Mariana scrubbed it over her face, wishing she could scrub away the guilt over spilling Nina's secret. "Please, keep that between us. Nina's come a long way from the surly teen merely biding her time before she got sucked back into the system. Afraid to trust in the familia we want her to be a part of."

"Understood," Angelo assured her.

"Thank you. Bueno, the thing is, my parents were forced to accept the private lender's bogus terms after the bank denied their application for a second mortgage. We thought it was because of their credit and the amount of the loan. Turns out . . ."

She paused, hating that the information she shared might taint Angelo's relationship with the man he considered a father figure.

"Turns out, what?" He shifted on the bed to face her.

"We found out that someone may have influenced the bank's decision. Someone with a vested interest in gentrification on our side of town. And . . . and an unpleasant history with some of the residents." Mariana watched for his reaction, hoping he read her subtext. Unwilling to outright accuse his uncle.

Within seconds his questioning frown morphed into shock, followed quickly by a tight-jawed fury.

"We haven't been able to confirm anything yet," she cautioned.

"But fingers are pointing in my tío Hugo's direction, aren't they?" The question was a low snarl that matched the anger hardening his handsome features. But she saw the pang of anguish in his eyes, and her heart ached for him.

"Yes, they are," she murmured, wishing she didn't have to say the words.

Shoving aside the covers with a muttered curse, he sprang from the bed to pace the carpeted floor. "A couple weeks ago I would have said you were wrong. That despite his beef with your parents over what happened in the past, my tío wouldn't risk the legacy he's built with El Rey Properties. I've always thought the rumors about him tiptoeing the line of ethical business dealings were sour grapes from those he beat in the bidding wars."

"And now?"

Her softly voiced question stopped his caged-animal pacing. Swiveling toward the mirror, he splayed his hands on top of her dresser. One of his fingers nudged the framed five-by-seven photograph of her familia taken after midnight mass last Christmas. The same familia his uncle's actions threatened.

Shoulders hunched, head bowed, he released a heavy breath that had the muscles in his broad back rippling. "Now I have to decide, do I confront my tío today, in the midst of our paired performance? Risk pissing him off, so he makes things more uncomfortable, or worse, for you and your sisters? Hell, how do I even know if he'll even level with me if I ask? It's not like he has all these years."

She knew his questions were more rhetorical than meant for her to answer, so Mariana kept quiet while he combed through the turmoil he wrestled with. Frustration vibrated in his bunched muscles. She wanted to go to him, soothe him as he'd done countless times for her. But she was the one who had brought this ugliness to light. He might very well hold that against her.

If their situations were reversed, who's to say she wouldn't? Her familia loyalty ran deep. As did his.

Angelo's chin lifted. He stared at her in the mirror, his expression troubled yet resolute.

"I'll find out what I can without creating any fallout that might risk our bands' place in the competition. I'm playing for my father, and your reasons for needing to win affect countless others. I'll be damned if this feud or my tío's grudge takes that chance away from us."

The sound of tinkling wind chimes trilled from her cell phone alarm. The outside world with its responsibilities and expectations called. She could only hope that when she and Angelo answered, the outcome didn't wind up tearing them apart.

Chapter Eighteen

Midafternoon on Wednesday, Angelo slowed his steps as he neared the entrance to the emergency room at Baptist Medical Center. He eyed a trio of hospital employees wearing scrubs and tired expressions, standing off to the side of the double-wide sliding glass doors. Two of the women sipped from paper coffee cups. The other chugged a bottle of water, then tossed it into a recycling bin nearby. Hopefully the fact that they weren't clamoring around a line of ambulances, curt instructions and indecipherable medical terminology bandied about as they wheeled patients into the ER, was a sign that he'd gotten lucky.

If he'd caught Mariana during a momentary lull in the action, she might be free to chat. Join him in the break room she had mentioned or a bench outside to nibble on one of the two dozen orejas he'd bought at the pastry counter at Mi Tierra after his business lunch. He was hoping the bribe—sure, he'd own what they were, especially if they worked—would entice her to grab whatever time they could together.

Each of the past four days she'd worked twelve-hour shifts at the hospital. Afterward, she had either headed to Casa Capuleta for rehearsal with her sisters or stayed on to shadow one of the PAs. The two of them had texted and spoken briefly on the phone, but he hadn't seen her since their combined band rehearsal Saturday. Hadn't touched her, kissed her, since leaving her house earlier that morning.

Tonight's final combined practice at the Majestic before Saturday's Round Two elimination meant they'd have twenty-odd chaperones again. No chance of sneaking a kiss, or even a hug, to appease his insatiable appetite for her.

The whoosh of the automatic doors greeted him, and he was swept up in the cacophony of noise. Crying babies, an afternoon talk show broadcasting on a television high on the far wall, the buzz of conversations peppered with an occasional moan, and the squeak of gurney wheels rolling down a hallway. He quickly scanned the crowded waiting area. No Mariana.

Tucking the pastry box under one arm, he approached a counter where a woman with a short brown bob and a no-nonsense demeanor held court.

"Did you check in online? If so, your last name and date of birth, please," she said by way of greeting. Her fingers continued pecking away at a keyboard, eyes not even bothering to look up from her screen.

"I'm not here to see a doctor. I'm actually looking for a nurse."

That got the woman's attention. Swiveling her neck, she eagle-eyed him over the silver metal rim of her glasses.

Angelo smiled invitingly—he hoped—and held up the white pastry box. The flimsy clear plastic cutout on the top crinkled with the motion. "I'm a friend of Mariana Capuleta's. Thought I'd swing by to drop off an afternoon snack and say hello. If she has a minute."

The woman's authoritarian disposition didn't waver.

He cleared his throat. Tugged uncomfortably at his tie. Her stern expression had him feeling like a teen knocking on his crush's front door, trying to sweet-talk her overprotective mom into letting him inside.

"Is she expecting you?" Curt. No nonsense. Unmoved by his charm.

"Uh, no. I thought I'd surprise her."

It had seemed like a good idea at the time. When a display case of sweet breads had a guy craving the woman he couldn't stop thinking about, what else was he supposed to do?

The lines around the older woman's mouth deepened as she pursed her lips, clearly unimpressed by his spontaneity. "Your name?"

"Angelo Montero."

A slight flare of her thinning eyebrows met his response. He couldn't tell if that was a good flare or a bad one. Talk about stoic bedside manner.

"What did you bring for her to share with the rest of us?" The woman pushed her rolling chair away from her computer and held out her hand, fingers motioning in a "gimme" sign.

Something told him that winning over the gatekeeper would be key to successfully connecting with Mariana. After four days of relying solely on technology for contact, he'd offer to make a coffee run as well if doing so increased his odds of having even five minutes of privacy with her.

Dutifully, Angelo handed over the box. "Two dozen of her favorite pan dulce. Orejas from Mi Tierra. Feel free to try one . . . Nurse Hettler."

His use of the name he spotted on her badge as she stood earned him a twitch at one corner of her mouth before it resumed its straight-line impression.

"Oh, I will. Come with me." Without waiting for his response, she pivoted on her rubber-soled shoes and headed down a short hallway on the right.

Angelo didn't have to be told twice. Weaving around a runny-nosed toddler who'd gotten away from her parent, he followed Nurse Hettler and the box of orejas down the bustling hall.

Halfway down, she stopped at a door with a long, thin window running along the right edge. Pushing down the metal handle, she opened the door and poked her head inside. "Mariana, there's a fine-looking young man out here with decent taste in pan dulce who says he's your friend." Nurse Hettler glanced back at Angelo and surprised him with a wink before poking her head inside the room again. "Mija, I say he should be more than that. If you don't claim him, maybe I will."

Pleased to have met with her approval, Angelo murmured a "gracias" and took the pastry box the older woman held out to him as she opened the door wider for him to enter.

Inside, he found Mariana alone, seated at a round table in the corner of the small break room. The metal legs of her plastic chair scraped the checkered gray-and-white flooring as she stood. Tired shadows darkened the skin under her eyes, but the smile that spread her full lips had him punching a mental congratulatory fist in the air.

"Hey, you," he said softly, relief melding with the anticipation of finally seeing her again.

"Hey yourself."

The door clicked shut and Mariana hurried toward him. Angelo barely had time to move the pastry box out of the way before she wrapped her arms around his waist in a tight hug. Instinctively he welcomed her embrace, his free hand splaying on her shoulder blades as he held her. Breathed in the scent of her citrusy shampoo mixed with a medicinal, antibacterial hospital smell.

"I wasn't sure if you'd be free, but I was at Mi Tierra for a lunch meeting and—"

"And decided to come bearing delectable treats." Arching back, she grinned up at him.

"I hope that's not the only reason you're happy to see me," he teased.

She scrunched her face as if she were actually pondering his question. Then she stretched up on her toes and dropped a quick peck on his cheek. "Not the only one, but I will happily accept your gift. And set aside two treats for me before the locusts I work with descend and devour them all. C'mon, join me."

She started to slide out of his arms, but Angelo snagged one of her hands and pulled her to him. A peck on the cheek was better than nothing. But this was the first time they'd been alone in days and he planned to take advantage of it.

"This side's feeling left out." He tapped his opposite cheek.

Mariana rolled her eyes, but her playful grin warmed him. "It is, huh? Let me see if I can take care of that for you."

Stretching onto her toes again, she kissed his left cheek. Another chaste, innocent peck that did little to satisfy his hunger for her.

As she started to draw away again, Angelo placed a hand on the small of her back. She cut a glance at the door behind him a second before she tucked her hands inside his suit jacket and leaned against him. Desire heated the yellow specks in her eyes to molten gold. Slowly she slid her palms up his chest and around his neck, tugging him down for a sinfully delicious kiss that nearly had him dropping the box of pastries at their feet.

"Damn, I've missed you," he murmured moments later when they came up for air, mindful that one of her coworkers could enter at any moment.

"I knew it would be tough taking back-to-back shifts so I have the weekends off for the competition. Still, it's been a tough week," she admitted. "I'm sorry I haven't been up to chatting much in the evenings."

Linking their hands, she led him over to a worn leather sofa butted up against the far wall. Angelo set the pastries on a wooden coffee table that had probably propped up many tired feet in its day, then leaned back, looping his arm on top of the sofa cushion behind her.

"This is the first time I've seen you in a suit. You clean up pretty well," she teased, snagging his tie and sliding it through her fingers. "You had a meeting at Mi Tierra?"

His pleasure at finally finagling some alone time with her dimmed.

"Yeah, I did. With a friend who works at a local bank." Specifically, the one where Arturo and Berta Capuleta held their accounts.

Her hand stilled on his thigh, where she'd been busy brushing lint off his navy suit pants.

"I figured, before I talk to my uncle, I should do some digging on my own. Have facts instead of just my conjecture," he told her.

"And?" She hadn't pulled away from him, but there was a sudden stiffness of her spine. Her hand clenched in a reflexive fist on his thigh.

"And I still don't have definitive proof that Tío Hugo pulled any strings. Though apparently the bank president is a new member of our country club as of several months ago."

Mariana's shoulders sagged on a rush of breath. "Damn, I was hoping we were wrong. That the chisme was just that, gossip from those with nothing better to do."

"Me too."

She laid her head on his shoulder, and he hugged his arm around her. Treasured her trust in him, especially when he was beginning to lose trust in someone he had always relied on for guidance.

"If it's true . . ." Mariana murmured. "If your uncle convinced the bank to deny our loan, forcing my parents to accept the ridiculous terms from the private lender, this feud will never end. It'll go beyond the past and the differences between our bands today."

The truth of her words filled him with dread.

She sat up and splayed a hand over her heart, her face creased with pain. "We're talking about my familia's home. The community center. You mentioned Hugo's legacy with his properties and gentrification efforts to boost run-down parts of San Antonio. But Casa Capuleta has its own legacy. One that's rooted in pride for our comunidad and cultura. Generations have celebrated important moments at our place. That can't be lost."

"I know. I get it." Angelo cupped her cheek, hating that the uncle he once admired could be causing so much agony in the life of the woman he loved.

His heart sputtered like an old truck backfiring.

Love?

It was far too soon for him to be thinking—feeling—in terms of love and commitment.

And yet . . .

Dazed, he drove a hand through his hair, thoughts whirring in his brain. There was no denying that when his college classmate had divulged the country-club information over lunch, plus the fact that his tío had been seen golfing there with the bank president, Angelo's gut reaction had been to protect Mariana at all costs. No matter who was involved on the other end.

But . . . love?

"What are you going to do?" she asked.

"What I promised you I'd do. Find out the truth." For her. For them. Because he loved her.

The thought settled in his chest, expanding to fill the achy desolation he hadn't revealed to anyone, not even himself.

A sad smile curved her lips and she sandwiched one of his hands with hers. "Maybe we should wait until after Saturday's competition. It's just a few more days. My parents are the only ones who know I have a friend doing some digging. This news would blow up our bands' already shaky partnership. Let's win this round and get our bands to the finals. Back on competing sides."

Frustrated by how screwed up things were when they didn't have to be—shouldn't be—Angelo lolled his head on the sofa's edge behind him and groaned up at the pockmarked ceiling tile.

"I've buried my head in the sand for too long," he admitted, despising the truth but intent on facing it. "That makes me an accomplice. I can't be on anyone's side when unethical, unfair practices are taking place. It doesn't matter who that person is."

"We don't know for sure yet," Mariana said, remorse clouding her beautiful eyes.

Angelo appreciated her attempt to cheer him up, but his gut, and mounting evidence, told him the truth. For years he'd been wanting to strike out on his own. He simply hadn't intended to end his time at El Rey Properties disgruntled with himself and potentially estranged from his uncle.

"Hey," Mariana whispered. Raising their joined hands to her mouth, she kissed the back of his. "We'll figure this out."

He tugged her to him and wrapped her in a tight hug, silently praying she was right.

Chapter Nineteen

Late Saturday evening, Angelo stood alongside his uncle, Marco, and the rest of Los Reyes, squinting and sweating under the bright stage lights at the Majestic. An excited hum vibrated through the audience as they waited for Patricio Galán to come back onstage and announce the winning pair of bands who would move on to the final round next weekend.

He sought out Mariana, but she was surrounded by her sisters, faces brimming with excitement, their red-tinted lips accentuating their broad smiles. Performing in the second half of the show, Los Reyes and Las Nubes had wowed the crowd. His and Mariana's duet had brought the house down, just as Galán and Cat had assured everyone it would, despite their sniping over Cat's last-minute tweaks.

The other two bands had put together a solid set. But if the winner was determined by audience cheers alone, Mariachi Las Nubes and Mariachi Los Reyes won hands down. Unfortunately, the judges had an opportunity to weigh in, too.

"Oye, who's that girl sitting next to Brenda?" Hugo asked, tipping his head toward where Brenda and Nina sat in the third row with Berta Capuleta.

"A new friend Brenda met recently," Angelo answered.

"Pero, she's not with Berta Capuleta, right?" Even with the mariachi music piped through the theatre speakers to fill the brief lull while the judges conferred, the accusation in his tío's voice was clear.

Marco leaned in closer to be heard over the music. "Isn't she the newest Capuleta? The one who started the fire in the community center?"

Angelo reared back, bumping into a bandmate standing behind him. "Where the hell did you hear that? They were trying to keep that quiet."

"They who?" Marco asked.

Hugo's thin mustache trembled with his sputter, and he angled to put his back to the crowd. "Any Capuleta is trouble, pero si esa nena es una delinquente, Brenda will not associate with her."

"Nina's not a delinquent," Angelo argued. "The fire she started was an accident. The authorities made that ruling in their report. Enough already. This is not the time or the place."

Damn, Marco and his big mouth. Later, Angelo would have to find out how Marco had heard about Nina and the fire. If someone on the Casa Capuleta staff was talking, the familia should know about it.

The mariachi music switched to a canned drumroll, and Patricio Galán sauntered onto the stage from the left wing. The audience roared as if the pope had arrived to bless them. Instead, it was mariachi royalty. El Príncipe stopped at center stage, flashed his megawatt smile, and preened for the admirers of all ages swooning in their seats. After encouraging their applause and whistles—and lapping up their adulation—he quieted the crowd with a raised hand and got down to business.

Moments later, the audience roared with approval when Mariachi Las Nubes and Mariachi Los Reyes were announced as the Round Two winners! Angelo was immediately engulfed in backslapping hugs and high fives. Gritos pierced his eardrums.

Mariana and her sisters politely shook hands with the Los Reyes band members, even his uncle. Teresita, who had slayed her guitar solo in the Selena remix, gave Angelo a tight hug. He returned her embrace, thrilled for the sweet, extremely talented kid. Secretly hoping they'd have other opportunities to play together.

Mariana gave him a long, wistful look as others chatted, congratulated, and commiserated around them. He wished he could wrap his arms around her, whisper his congrats in her ear. But that couldn't happen in front of everyone. Not yet. Not until his uncle admitted his duplicity and found a way to make things right with the Capuletas' loan. Angelo and Mariana had agreed to wait until after the competition before he confronted his uncle. The waiting had Angelo's stomach tied in uncomfortable knots.

For now, the two of them planned to celebrate with their familias and friends on their respective sides of the Capuleta-Montero dividing fence, then meet up later tonight at her place for their own private party.

It wasn't ideal. But he'd take it.

~

"Did you hear me? Are you deliberately trying to sabotage our chances of winning the competition?"

At Cat's churlish inquiry late Sunday afternoon, her third since they'd finished rehearsal fifteen minutes ago, Mariana slid a pissed-off glare at her sister. She refused to have this argument with the three teens following them out of the community center's large music room.

"You left our celebration early last night, for *whatever* reason. You can*not* miss Tuesday night's rehearsal," Cat insisted. "We only have one week to prepare. Every minute counts before the finals on Saturday."

"Which I managed to get off for by taking a double shift on Tuesday."

"So, swap with someone else."

Frustration clawed at her with sharp nails, and Mariana shoved open the glass door leading to the courtyard with more force than necessary. "First of all, it's not that easy. And second, I can't swap because the only other day I'm off is Thursday, when my scholarship interview was rescheduled for noon."

"I'm sure they'll let you reschedule again. This is important."

"And my scholarship isn't? Is that it?"

"Of course that's important. But this is different."

"Because it ultimately affects your dream. So, mine should take a back seat?" Hanging on to her patience by a quickly unraveling thread, Mariana halted a few feet into the courtyard. "That's pretty crappy, Cat. Even for you!"

One hand planted on her jutting hip, Cat tapped the toe of her red boot with a huff. "Look, don't go putting words in my mouth. You're already messing with things by messing around with—"

"Madre de Dios, enough already!"

Cat's haughty demeanor slipped at Mariana's uncharacteristic outburst. "Whoa-kay!" she sputtered, then quickly recovered, crossing her arms with an annoyed huff.

Mariana blew out a puff-cheeked breath, annoyed at her inability to remain calm in the face of her sister's understandable, if rudely expressed, apprehension. She glanced at the younger girls standing near the center's back door, gawking at her.

Claudia eyed the argument with interest. As the oldest teen, she lived with the same parental expectation as Mariana to keep the peace among her younger sisters, not be the cause of their squabbles.

Poor Teresita's dismayed "deer in the headlights" expression said she'd rather be anywhere else but caught in the middle of the bickering. And Fabiola, classic middle-child pleaser, worried her lower lip and cut a look up at the second-floor landing. Probably praying for a referee to arrive in the form of Mamá since the other older girls had left through the front already.

"We should discuss this in private," Mariana muttered to Cat.

Her sister answered with a temperamental *humph* and a dismissive wave at the younger girls, telling them to beat it up the stairs.

"Please let Mamá know that Cat and I will be up shortly," Mariana told Claudia.

The oldest teen nodded before edging past the most temperamental of them all. The other girls scurried past Cat to follow Claudia. Halfway up, Teresita peeked back at Mariana, concern puckering her brow.

"It's okay," she reassured the youngster. "Cat and I are going to have a calm, rational discussion. We won't be long."

Flouncing away, Cat slid the backpack straps of her vihuela case off her shoulders and set it on one of the mesh metal tables near the stage.

Mariana waited until the upstairs door shut behind Teresita before closing her eyes and sucking in what she hoped would be a calming breath. It wound up turning into a sigh of resignation.

She identified with Cat's drive for perfection when it came to her music and their performances. The need to be her best, do her best, mirrored Mariana's dedication to her patients. It was the impetus behind why becoming a PA was so important to her.

Winning this competition felt like a life-and-death situation. So much was riding on it. Money for the balloon payment. Adding another crack in that damn glass ceiling barring women and young girls like them. For Cat, it also meant notice by those with influence in the music industry.

Mariana understood where Cat was coming from—the pressure her sister felt, as their musical director, for Las Nubes to win. Still, Cat's people skills needed some serious work.

The *thomp thomp thomp* of Cat's boots pacing the wooden stage broadcast a warning of their continuing discord.

"We can't have a conversation with you making all that racket," Mariana complained.

"Fine." Cat stomped over to sit on the edge of the stage. Legs and arms crossed, one high-heeled boot swinging with an agitation that matched the scowl on her face, she squinted at Mariana under the late-afternoon sun. "You slept with him, didn't you?"

Mariana jerked to a stop several steps away. Apparently, Cat wasn't pulling any punches. Not that she ever did.

"That's not any of your business."

Cat sucked her teeth and swung her boot faster. "Have you at least spoken to Mamá like I suggested? Found out how this dalliance of yours—"

"It's not a dalliance. Don't cheapen what Angelo and I have."

"What you have? What you—Ha!" Cat hopped off the stage to pace a new path, this one toward a table near the back entrance, before she spun on her heel to make the return trip. "Is it worth hurting Papo for? Pissing off Hugo Montero so he'll find another way to come after Casa Capuleta? Mamá told me about what they believe happened with the bank. Convenient how you didn't feel the need to let me in on that piece of news."

"She made me promise not to say anything. Plus, we don't know for sure if Hugo Montero's involved with that."

"Says who? Angelo? Hugo's nephew?" Cat scoffed and spun to continue her pacing, her black hair fanning out behind her as it caught on the cool breeze. "Someone we don't really know all that well. Other than you, apparently, in the carnal way."

"Stop it! Please!" The entreaty ripped from Mariana's throat in a burst of pain-filled disillusion.

Cat's pacing halted, but she didn't turn around.

Hands fisted at her sides, Mariana blinked away the tears of anger burning her eyes. "That's low, Catalina. I know you're stressed about the Battle. But you're going too far."

Head tipped back, Cat heaved a guttural groan.

"For the first time in my life, I'm not toeing the line and playing it safe," Mariana said. "I'm taking a page from the Catalina Capuleta playbook and going off desire and instinct."

Cat twisted to shoot her a sideways glance heavy with "kiss my ass" attitude. And a measure of respect.

Mariana wasn't sure she deserved the latter. Not until she and Angelo figured out how to convince Hugo to make things right with the private lender. Or, if it was still possible, the bank. Her insides quaked with fear for the consequences of her choices. The fallout if somehow Cat was right, and Mariana was proven wrong for putting her trust in Angelo.

No, she couldn't—wouldn't—think that way.

Ay, a tsunami wave of self-doubt crashed over her, dragging her confidence into a death spiral with its vicious undertow.

The door to the second floor opened, and Nina stepped out onto the landing. Coatless, she hugged herself against the late-spring chill biting the late-afternoon air.

Angling away from the stairs, Mariana swiped a tear from her cheek and hid her face from the teen. She needed to pull herself together before she went inside or the questions and prodding would multiply. Her tears were too near the surface, but she couldn't leave without going up. Mamá had said she needed to discuss something their Child Protective Services caseworker had called about earlier in the day.

The metal landing squeaked, alerting Mariana that Nina was still there.

"Mariana, can I talk to—"

"Not right now." Her voice hitched. Another tear slid down her cheek. Dios, she was tired of being pulled in so many different directions. If she could just get a few minutes to—

"I was wondering if you—"

"I don't have time to deal with you right now, Nina." The harsh words fueled by the venom of Mariana's own self-recrimination slipped out like evil vipers. In her peripheral vision she caught Nina's recoil at the biting castigation.

"Forget it. I should have known better."

The stony mask of indifference the teen had worn until recently slid into place as she backed away from the railing.

Mariana stepped toward the stairs, ashamed by her harsh outburst. "Nina, I didn't mean it like—"

"Whatever. I can take care of it myself."

Fumbling for the handle, Nina tugged the door open and stumbled inside. But as she turned for one last glance at the courtyard before disappearing inside, the teen's mask slipped, revealing the hurt caused by Mariana's gruff dismissal.

Guilt stabbed like an ice pick buried deep in Mariana's chest. Pain sluicing through her, she crumpled to her knees and buried her face in her hands, cursing her selfishness.

"Hey, come on. She's gonna be okay." Cat crouched beside Mariana, gently resting a hand on her back. "We all say shit we don't mean when we're upset."

Mariana shook her head. "I know better. She's fragile, on the verge of believing in Casa Capuleta, and I let my frustration with myself and, and—"

"And with me. I'll own it. I was being a bitch. Mostly because I'm afraid for you."

The candor of her sister's rare admission of fault drew Mariana's. "I'm afraid, too. I want to fix everything. Instead I might be making it worse."

"Talk to Mom. If there's anyone who keeps calm and thinks straight in a storm better than you, it's her. Now come on." Cupping Mariana's elbow, Cat pulled her to stand. "If I'm going to apologize, I refuse to look like I'm groveling."

"That'll be the day."

Their soft laughter turned into murmurs of apology and a tight hug. Above them a door opened, and the metal stairs warned that someone headed down.

"Oye, qué pasó con Nina?" Mamá called out.

"Here's your chance. Good luck," Cat whispered before grabbing her vihuela case, then hurrying to meet their mom at the bottom of the steps. "I'll let Mariana tell you what happened with Nina while I go check on her."

"No, leave her alone." Worry pinched their mom's face, accenting the lines that had begun to lightly trace her forehead. "She asked for some privacy, and after the disturbing news she received today, we need to respect her wishes."

A knot of dread tightened in Mariana's stomach. "What news?"

Mamá motioned for the girls to join her at one of the tables. "Nina's mom alerted DFPS that she wants to sign away all parental rights."

The screech of their wrought-iron chair legs grating on the concrete floor drowned out Mariana's and Cat's shocked cries. This was a first for any of the Capuleta sisters. All the others had lost their birth mothers to sickness or an accident. Their fathers were either never in the picture or had tragically perished with their birth moms.

"When she gets out of jail," Mamá went on, her concerned frown deepening, "her mother made it clear that she doesn't want Nina back."

I don't have time for you right now.

The hateful words Mariana had spoken moments ago swooped over her like hungry buzzards circling a dead carcass, anxious to peck and claw at her bleeding chest. "I need to go talk to her."

She started to rise, but her mom grabbed her sweatshirt sleeve to stop her. "No, mija. She specifically said she did not want to talk to you. That's why I came out here to see what happened."

"The two of us were arguing about, um, about our rehearsal schedule," Mariana hedged, tipping her head to Cat.

Cat gave her a pointed "do it now, girl" stare.

The conversation about the feud and Angelo could wait until another day. Tonight, they needed to make sure Nina was okay. That she understood she was wanted and welcomed and loved by everyone here.

"I was frustrated, and I lashed out at Nina when she interrupted us," Mariana told their mom. "I knew I was wrong as soon as I snapped.

But I had no idea about her mother's decision. Me pushing her away probably made Nina feel even worse."

Dios mío, her heart ached for the girl she had seen giggling and joking around with Brenda at the Pearl. Cheering from her seats in the Majestic last night. The real Nina. Not the withdrawn, surly teen who kept herself behind a wall of stoicism as a means of hiding her pain.

"Perdóname, Mamá. I messed up," Mariana apologized.

"Ay, mija, we all make mistakes. Nina will understand eventually. Give her some time." Scooting to the edge of her chair, Mamá cupped Mariana's cheek. Winter's unseasonable return had chilled her mom's hand, and it cooled the flush of remorse burning Mariana's face. "You two go on home. Papo and I are here for Nina, when she's ready."

"Are you sure?" Mariana asked, hating that her careless words had compounded Nina's feelings of rejection. "I could wait a bit and see if she—"

"No, vete, mija." Mamá patted Mariana's cheek, her smile softening her suggestion that Mariana go.

A brisk breeze shook the leaves of the potted plants scattered among the tables and the tall hedges bordering the courtyard. Dressed in one of her comfy, short-sleeved batas, Mamá shivered and stood. "Maybe you can come for dinner tomorrow night."

"We should have familia pizza night before practice. It'll be a nice show of support for Nina. And as an apology for missing rehearsal on Tuesday, Mariana can treat us to Devici's." Cat's smug grin widened when Mariana growled at her sister's maneuvering.

Undeterred, Cat's grin turned pure Machiavellian as she added, "You can apologize to Nina tomorrow night, then ask Mamá for advice about your duet."

Their mom tilted her head in question. "Tienes un problema, mija?"

"No. There's no problem. Well, not really, but . . ." Mariana hesitated at Cat's sotto voce "do it already" through her gritted teeth. "But

I could use your help with something. If there's a chance for us to talk in private."

"Bueno, let's plan for pizza, and hopefully Nina will join us. Then you and I can chat, mija. Come, my viejita bones are getting cold, and you girls need to get home and rest. You have a busy week."

"Viejita? You're not old, you're like fine wine, Mamá—you improve with age," Cat teased.

"Suck-up," Mariana grumbled.

They hugged and kissed goodbye. But not even the warmth of her mamá's love or her assurances that all would be well relieved Mariana's shame as she pictured the anguish on Nina's face.

If her selfishness in getting involved with Angelo, no matter how right it felt . . . if her ego thinking that she could solve what for decades and across generations had been unsolvable . . . if she ultimately wound up hurting Papo and Mamá like she'd done with Nina today . . . Dios mío, Mariana would never be able to forgive herself.

Fear clawed at her conscience as she drove home, praying that tomorrow she could make amends. That Nina would accept her apology and Mamá possessed the answers Mariana so desperately needed.

Instead, an hour into her shift the next morning, her glass-ball juggling act came to a shattering, horrifying halt with a single text message in their familia thread.

Mamá: Nina ran away. Early this morning, an El Rey Properties building nearby was vandalized. La policía are here. Please come as soon as you can.

~

Angelo was in the middle of a tense conversation with Raul Vega, the assistant manager at El Rey Properties, midmorning Monday when a notification flashed on his cell indicating an incoming call from Mariana.

His instinct was to click over. He and Mariana hadn't been able to connect with each other since their private celebration at her place Saturday evening, and he knew she had a killer work schedule the next few days. Even a quick "can you call me after your shift" would allow him to hear her voice. She'd be a calming influence in the literal firestorm he'd been dealing with since the row of El Rey Properties town houses had been engulfed in flames early this morning.

They'd spoken briefly on the phone last night, but she'd been subdued, dealing with a headache she said would be "fine" with some rest. Still, he hadn't been able to kick the niggling sensation that something else was wrong. That the pressure of keeping their relationship a secret weighed on her as the evidence pointing toward his tío's negative influence on the bank's loan decision grew.

Now that he knew his uncle had sponsored the bank president's VIP country-club membership in exchange for refusing the Capuletas' loan application, Angelo couldn't keep quiet anymore. Even if it affected the Battle's final round this weekend. Making things right for the Capuletas was more important.

Angelo had blocked off time on his and his uncle's work calendars later today, intending to confront Hugo with the information. Unfortunately, dealing with the early-morning blaze now took precedence. Making matters worse, between the fire department investigating potential arson and the police combing through an exhaustive list of potential suspects with a grudge against the company or Hugo himself, his uncle's rage had reached out-for-blood level.

Angelo's phone beeped again with a second call from Mariana. Raul was midexplanation about the terms of the company's insurance policy, so Angelo had to send her call to voice mail. If he was lucky, she might still be on break at the hospital when he tried to reach her later.

"I'll contact our insurance agent to confirm," Raul said. "Be prepared in the event the authorities request financial records involving any suspects they bring in for questioning."

"Everything's in order. We've got nothing to hide," Angelo assured the assistant manager.

The pause on Raul's end of the line had doubt dragging a bony finger across Angelo's shoulders.

"Raul?"

"Your tío would never run afoul of the law. ¿Pero ya tú sabes?"

"No, I don't know. What are you implying?" Anger bit at Angelo. What the hell else was his uncle hiding?

A heavy sigh blew through the phone before Raul answered. "Your tío has a reputation for playing hardball because he does. But you have nothing to worry about. Like I said, we have never done anything technically illegal."

The qualification—"technically"—had Angelo plopping back in the leather desk chair with equal measures of disbelief and indignation. The chair hinges protested, rocking under his weight.

"Answer this for me, Raul: Has Hugo been involved with the loan trouble Arturo and Berta Capuleta have had after the fire at the community center a few months ago?"

"It's best you ask your tío about that."

¡Madre de Dios! Anger detonated inside Angelo like a stick of dynamite with a lit fuse, rocking the foundation of the life he had struggled to rebuild after his parents' death. All those times he had defended his tío over the years, wanting to believe in the man who had been there when Angelo and Brenda had needed him the most, despite his faults.

"Remember, if the fire investigation unit contacts you, feel free to give them any documents they request. Answer any financial questions they may have," Raul finally said. "Your tío and I will handle the rest."

Angelo's phone beeped and Mariana's name flashed on his screen again.

She rarely called while working. Now this was three times in—he checked his watch—in less than ten minutes? A strange foreboding prickled the back of his neck.

"Raul, I need to take this call. I'll get back to you if I have any questions."

"Go! I should touch base with your tío. Reporters were circling the property earlier, and we need to draft a statement or at the very least talking points. Hugo speaking off the cuff when he's this pissed is not a good idea."

"Keep me posted." Angelo didn't wait for a goodbye before clicking over to Mariana. "Hi, I hope your morning's going better than mine."

"Ay, thank God you answered."

He straightened in his seat at Mariana's shaky whisper. "Everything okay?"

"No. It's not. We—I—Is Brenda home from school yet?"

"Yeah, I think she's in her room. I've been holed up in my tío's office all day."

"We heard about the fire. I wouldn't bother you when you're busy, but we're desperate and there aren't many people we think she might reach out to. Nina's—" Her voice broke on the teen's name, and alarm bells clanged in his head.

"Mariana, what's wrong?"

A shuddered breath carried through the phone line before Mariana whispered, "Nina's missing."

"What?" Fear for the teen pushed Angelo to his feet. The rolling desk chair banged against the wall behind him, rattling the framed pictures. "Since when?"

"She ran away sometime in the middle of the night," Mariana answered, her voice cloaked in trepidation. "She left a note for my parents saying she was better on her own. And I'm part of why she feels that way."

"Don't do that. You can't blame yourself. You're a good sister."

She took on so much responsibility for others. Sometimes, like now, too much.

"Let me go find Brenda. Maybe she's heard from Nina."

He left the office, calling out to his sister as he reached the foyer and open familia room, where the sun streamed through the glass windows overlooking the empty back patio and pool area. A deceptively bright, sunny day unlike the catastrophic storms their familias faced.

Brenda met him in the hallway leading to their rooms.

"Where's the fir—Never mind." She held up a hand at his frown, probably attributing it to her poor word choice, unaware of Mariana's terrifying news. "What's up?"

"Have you heard from Nina?"

"Not since yesterday afternoon, when she got her phone for an hour. But she's supposed to have it for good starting today." Brenda grinned, her eyes sparkling with the excitement of a teen who knew firsthand the delight of having their phone privileges reinstated after a punishment.

"Can you hand Brenda the phone? Or put it on speaker, please?" Mariana asked. "I'll do my best to not alarm her."

"I know you will." He changed the audio setting, then held out his cell between him and Brenda. "Go ahead, Mariana, you're on speaker."

"Hi, sweetie, it's Mariana. I don't mean to pry, but this is really important, okay?"

Her expression solemn in response to the gravity in Mariana's voice, Brenda nodded, then added, "Okay," as if realizing Mariana couldn't see her.

"Are you really sure that Nina hasn't contacted you? Not even through DM on social media or some other way?"

"Yes, I'm sure. She said she'd call as soon as your mom gave her permission, but I haven't heard from her yet today. Why?"

"Can you think, is there anyone else she would reach out to if she had a problem? Anyone from her old school or neighborhood that she might have mentioned?"

Brenda's gaze met his, uncertainty creeping into her eyes. "Um, not that I can remember. I mean, she talked about her mom some, but not really any friends from where she lived before. Is something wrong?"

Angelo wrapped an arm around Brenda's shoulders and tucked her against his side. "Nina ran away sometime last night."

"What? No!" Brenda's shocked cry filled the hallway. Panic stamped her round face. "She could be in danger. Or worse! We—we gotta find her!"

"The police are looking for her and we are, too. It's going to be okay, sweetie." Mariana's reassuring calm, when Angelo knew she was freaking out herself, epitomized her selflessness. One of the many traits he admired about her.

"Brenda, I know Nina's your friend and it's right that you'd want to be loyal to her. But if she contacts you, for any reason, por favor . . ." Distress quivered in Mariana's voice, fear making its presence known.

Her steely resolve was crumbling, and all Angelo could offer were platitudes over the phone. Damn it, he should be there offering her comfort and a shoulder to lean on, not here, a pawn in this game of smoke and mirrors his tío played.

"We'll contact you right away if Nina calls or texts or anything," he assured Mariana.

He hugged Brenda tightly. When she looked up at him, he tipped his head at the phone and mouthed the words "Tell her."

"Oh! Yes, I will. Of course I will! But, um, does she have her cell now? Or I guess she could pick up a burner phone if she needed?" Brenda asked.

"She took her phone when she left," Mariana answered. "It's turned off right now, so we can't track it, but we're keeping an eye on the app."

"That's smart," Angelo said. "If we—" He broke off when he heard someone yell Mariana's name in the background.

"I should go," she said, the stress and pain in her wan voice ratcheting his worry.

"I'll keep Nina and all of you in my prayers," Brenda called out, tears shimmering in her eyes.

"I appreciate it," Mariana answered. "Try not to worry. We'll bring her home."

Her warmth carried through the phone line. Angelo easily pictured her smile, the curve of her generous mouth. Her tender, caring expression. He had witnessed them when she walked him out of the ER the day he surprised her with the box of orejas at work. Halfway through the waiting room, she had stopped and hunkered down to reassure a young patient. Her demeanor comforting and calm, focused on helping someone else, as she was now.

He dropped a kiss on the crown of Brenda's head, then held up a finger to indicate that he'd like a minute of privacy with Mariana. Brenda nodded, and he strode to the living room, where he took his cell off speaker mode.

"It's just me now," he told Mariana.

The noise at Casa Capuleta quieted, as if she had moved to a more private area of the house.

"Same here," she murmured. "I only have a few minutes, though."

He'd grab on to them like the greedy man he was when it came to her. Always craving more—more time, more privacy, more *her*. More *them*.

"I know your familia's there for support, but I have an inkling that you'll take care of everyone else before thinking about yourself," he said.

"They need me to be strong."

"You always are. I respect that. I also don't mind being the one you lean on. So, if you need anything. *Anything.* Hell, even a Whataburger delivery if that would perk you up. I'm your guy. Always."

There was a beat of silence on her end, and he prayed it was because she took his words to heart. "How did you get to be such a ni—"

"Don't say it!" he warned, though he'd willingly accept her teasing if it eased her distress.

She rewarded him with a raspy chuckle. "It's the truth. You *are* a nice guy. Although if a burger could make me feel better, I'd be stuffing my face with a double patty and large fries."

"And I'd happily join you. I'd even share my fries if you wanted extra."

There was so much more he wanted to share with her. Before that could happen, they had to find Nina. Then he'd figure out a way to convince his tío to do right by the Capuletas. Whatever that meant. If not, there was no way Angelo could reconcile his tío's actions.

"That's very generous of you," Mariana answered. "I should go, though."

"Are you still on the phone with him?" The question came from someone at Mariana's house.

"Yes, but—"

"Give it to me," one of her sisters ordered.

"Cat! What are you—"

A rustle sounded on the other end. A muttered "damn it, back off" and a "give it to me" told him the sisters must be fighting over Mariana's phone.

"Is this Angelo?" her sister demanded, apparently the winner of the skirmish. "Look, I get that your uncle's pissed about someone setting fire to his precious property. But to insinuate that it was my sister? Blathering on about how you told him that Nina set fire to the community center? The two of you are a real piece of work!"

"What are you talking about?" Mariana asked.

No! No-no-no-no-no! Angelo bit down on the cry as he stumbled to the kitchen and collapsed on a barstool. The tangled web of lies and missteps and machinations between their familias and them threatened to smother him and Mariana.

Saturday night at her place, he'd been so wrapped up in celebrating with her, he'd completely forgotten about Marco mentioning Nina and the fire and revealing it to Hugo onstage at the Majestic. All he'd thought about was hugging her close like he'd yearned to do all night.

Now, his tío was pissed about the destruction to his buildings, looking for anyone he could blame. But he wouldn't stoop so low as to accuse a teen.

If that girl is a delinquent . . .

His uncle's words in reference to Nina shrilled like a banshee's wail in Angelo's head.

"There has to be some kind of misunderstanding." But even as he uttered the platitude, doubt seized him.

"A misunderstanding?" Cat challenged. "Then you must not have seen Hugo's interview online yet. Let me share this gem with you."

Seconds later, Angelo's phone flashed with a text notification. He tapped the link Cat had sent at the same time he heard Mariana's "let me read it." A window opened to an article on a local news station's website. The caption Arson Suspected at Property Owned by Well-Known Local Commercial Broker filled the top of the screen above a video that must have been shot this morning. The still image showed his tío Hugo in his black trench coat, jowled face ruddy with anger. The charred facade of the row of town houses loomed behind him.

Angelo's pulse slowed to a dull, dread-filled thud as he scanned the "developing story." Like a fish ensnared by an angler's hook, his gaze caught on his uncle's direct quotes.

". . . a runaway from Casa Capuleta my nephew confirmed had started a fire on those premises."

". . . this investigation is ongoing, pero given the teen's history, it's clear who the main suspect should be . . ."

". . . with the neighborhood revitalizing efforts, in the right hands, Casa Capuleta could be what the comunidad deserves."

All damning accusations. All rooted in decades of discord, not facts. All threatening to sabotage any chance of Mariana's familia ever accepting Angelo.

Worse, if Nina was thinking about coming home but saw clips of this interview, she might get spooked. Convinced she should hide from the police.

If his tío's angry tirade put Nina in more danger . . .

Fury exploded through Angelo like a Texas oil well spewing black gold into the sky. Devastated, he collapsed onto his forearms on the kitchen island. His cell clattered to the granite countertop.

"How could you?" Mariana's embittered voice was a tinny sound on the other end of the line. Already moving out of reach. His own mistake in not telling her about Marco widening the divide created by the years of their familias' animosity.

Desperate to explain, he snatched up the cell and pressed it to his ear. "Mariana, this is all a misunderstanding. Someone else shared Nina's secret with my uncle and I inadvertently confirmed it while trying to defend her."

"I point-blank asked you not to say anything."

"It was an accident. You've got to believe me," he begged.

"I'm not sure I can." Her pain-filled whisper made his blood run cold.

"Please, we can still figure out a way to make things right."

"I trusted you, Angelo." Her anguish burned a trail of guilt deep in his soul. "I gave your tío the benefit of the doubt because you continually assured me that he wouldn't do something like this. I know how much he means to you, so I ignored my instincts. But look at everything he's done. Everything he keeps doing. It's hurting my familia. I can't . . . I can't do this anymore."

"Don't say that." He jabbed a hand through his hair in frustration, struggling to find a way to convince her.

"I should go. My familia needs me." The finality in her tone scared him.

"Don't give up on me. On us. You said we were worth fighting for."

"And you said this was good trouble. It's not, Angelo. Not from where my familia lives and hurts." Her voice caught. She drew in a trembly breath, and his heart bled with the realization that he was the cause of her pain. "If Brenda hears from Nina, I'd appreciate you letting us know. Take care, Angelo."

Before he could respond, the call disconnected.

Seconds later, a low beep in the home alarm system signaled the garage door lifting. His tío had returned.

Anger, disappointment, and disillusion roiled in Angelo's stomach. He thumped his fist on the granite counter and straightened, bracing himself for the impending confrontation.

Chapter Twenty

Angelo stood in front of the living room fireplace, waiting. Fists clenched, boots planted wide, fuming with rage.

Tío Hugo entered through the garage, head bowed as he unbuttoned his trench coat. He came to a stop near the foyer when he spotted Angelo.

"¿Qué pasa?" Hugo's gaze darted around the open living space, then toward Brenda and Angelo's side of the house. "Where is your sister?"

"In her room."

After a curt nod, Hugo moved toward his wing.

"That's it?" Angelo demanded.

Hugo slowly turned, his face stony. "Is there something specific you wanted?"

"An explanation seems appropriate. Credible rationale for why you would say all that nonsense to a reporter?" Angelo accused.

"Raul warned me you would be upset. Though I don't know why. I only repeated what you yourself had confirmed."

"Bullshit!"

"Cuidado." Hugo's eyes narrowed at his stern warning for Angelo to be careful. God forbid his nephew cross the line into disrespect.

Ha! Screw that line. Respect had to come from both ways. And for too long, Angelo had bitten his tongue or kept his head down rather than make waves at the office. But in doing so, he'd been part of the problem.

"What is it about the Capuletas that still pushes you over the edge after all these years? Why can't you let go of the past?" Angelo asked.

"That is none of your concern."

"This feud of yours affects all of us. So, it *is* my concern."

Hugo scoffed, backhanding the air as if the topic were a pesky mosquito he could swat away. Not this time. Angelo advanced on his uncle, intent on finally getting answers.

"If Nina didn't have anything to do with the fire, you've now put a target on her back, Tío. Probably spooked her from coming home. Like the kid doesn't have enough problems."

"Nina? Ahh, sí, the Capuleta runaway. I have no idea about her problems. Tell me, how is it that you seem to know so much about her?"

It was Angelo's turn to swipe away a pesky question. "That doesn't matter. What does is why you're putting the screws to Arturo and Berta Capuleta. Why you'll find any angle, any way you can to take them down. Even now, when both familias are dealing with terrible circumstances. Should we not show each other some compassion?"

"¿Compasión? Compa—" His tío let out an animalistic growl as he spun on his bootheel and stormed toward his office.

"Don't walk away from this!" Angelo called, following in his uncle's frothing wake. "Implying that Casa Capuleta is a waste because it's poorly managed? That's a lie meant to damage their reputation! We both know the good the Capuletas do in their comunidad. Hell, people from across San Antonio praise their center."

"¡Basta!" Hugo shouted, continuing his retreat.

But it wasn't *enough*. Not nearly. Not for Angelo. Not when a teen's life, a decent familia's livelihood, and the childhood home of the woman he loved were at stake.

"I told you, that fire Nina started in the community center kitchen was an accident. The police need to look elsewhere for last night's culprit. *You* are the one causing trouble. Not the Capuletas. First convincing the bank president to deny their loan. Then by not trying to stop that bogus anonymous ICE tip, even though you knew about it ahead of time. And I haven't yet, but I'm sure if I keep poking, I'll find a connection to the private lender forcing them to come up with the balloon payment."

Hugo's palm hit his office doorframe with a sharp smack. His fingers curled around the wooden edge in a tight grip. "Mijo, you think I have far more power than I actually possess. Like I have also already told you, I have no control over whether or not someone chooses to make a call to the authorities. As for the loans, the Capuletas are not a good investment. The bank's president did not need my influence to make his decision."

"But you greasing the wheels by putting him on the fast track for VIP membership at the club didn't hurt, ha? All's fair in love and war. Is that it?"

His tío cut a sharp glare over his shoulder. A fierce warning to back off. But rather than the roar of anger Angelo expected, a wounded expression clouded the older man's black eyes. The glimpse of his tío's softer side—the one that had counseled and supported Angelo when everything seemed lost—gave Angelo a glimmer of hope.

"Why, Tío?" he asked, hands outstretched in supplication. "How has holding on to pain from the past made your life better?"

His uncle's jaw tightened with indignation. He smacked the doorframe again and straightened. Shoulders back. Head high. "Because it assures me that while Berta may have chosen Arturo over me, ultimately I have come out on top."

Without another word of explanation, Hugo strode into his office, locking the door behind him.

Disillusion ripped a ragged hole in Angelo's heart.

All these years he had followed his tío's plan, denying his own dreams out of a sense of familia loyalty.

Was this seedier side of his tío the real reason why Angelo's dad had always refused Hugo's offers to come work for him at El Rey Properties? Had this been his parents' rationale for making Angelo, barely an adult, his sister's guardian?

All this time, Angelo had been kidding himself thinking that he was giving Brenda the comfortable life their parents would have wanted for her by staying at their tío Hugo's mansion. Instead of figuring things out the hard way on their own, had Angelo settled for the easy route?

The doubt-filled questions pelted Angelo like balls of sleet, leaving him burning and raw. He paced the living room, amped for a fight he was loath to have. But the hate his tío held on to from the past bled into Angelo's and Brenda's futures. His belief in his uncle might very well have cost Angelo the woman he loved. And he realized with finality, he couldn't live like this anymore.

~

"How long do you intend to try carrying the weight of the world, mija?"

Perched on the padded kneeler in the second row at Little Flower Basilica Thursday evening, Mariana peeked her eyes open midprayer to find her mamá standing over her. Her mom waved for her to scoot over so she could join her on the end of the dark-stained wooden pew.

Mamá's red-rimmed eyes told of her sorrow and fear for Nina, now missing for four days. Days filled with prayer and phone calls and social media posts asking for helpful information. The white, lacy mantilla draped over Mamá's short black bob and the rosary beads clutched in one hand were signs of the deep faith she clung to during this gut-wrenching time.

Tipping her head to receive her mom's cheek kiss, Mariana spoke in a similarly hushed voice. "I don't carry the world's weight, Mamá. Only that from our little corner of it."

"Ay, mija, I worry about you." Mamá smoothed Mariana's hair, then gave her a quick hug.

"Don't. You have enough already with Nina. I'll take care of the other girls. Try to somehow get us all in a frame of mind to compete on Saturday." She shifted on her knees to face the front of the church, not wanting her mom to see the doubt gnawing at her. "If we lose, we won't have the money to make the balloon payment."

"Las Nubes *will* win. I am sure of it. As for the payment, your papo and I are working on it."

"Por favor, let me dip into my tuition money," Mariana pleaded. She leaned her shoulder against her mom's, desperate for her to say yes. "There are more scholarships I can apply for."

"That money is for your dream. We couldn't be more proud of you, mija."

"Pero—"

"No buts. You can help us by following your plan and continuing to pray for Nina's safe return."

Mamá dipped her head toward the altar, admired by parishioners and visitors for its gleaming white facade, detailed paintings, and elaborate wooden sculpture of Our Lady of Mount Carmel with the child Jesus on her lap. Kneeling at their feet, Saint Thérèse, the Basilica's namesake, reached for the roses Jesus held out. Petals rained down the sculpture, symbols of the heavenly graces Thérèse had promised.

Oh, how Mariana prayed one of those graces was for Nina's safe return. And for her sister's forgiveness.

"I messed up, Mamá." The whispered confession, the admission that her belief in Angelo had been misplaced, scratched Mariana's throat like sandpaper sloughing off the veneer of calm hiding her uncertainty. "As hard as I've tried, I can't figure out how to make things right."

Squeezing her eyes shut against the burn of tears, she bent over her clasped hands, sending up a desperate prayer for guidance and strength of spirit. Begging Saint Thérèse for her intercession.

"Does this 'mess up' perhaps have something to do with them?" Mamá motioned toward the rows of pews behind them. More than half were filled by neighbors, friends, fellow parishioners, many of the young girls in their music class, and even a few strangers who had heard about the vigil for Nina's safe return on the early-evening news.

Their faith in the power of prayer was humbling. Moving and reassuring. Yet it didn't completely assuage Mariana's increasing dread that precious time was ticking by.

Per protocol with runaway situations, an Amber Alert had not been issued. Those crucial first forty-eight hours had passed, and they were now beyond seventy-two. Studies showed that for many witnesses, memories had begun to fade by that time, making it harder for investigators to gather potential key details. Decreasing the odds of locating Nina.

Over the past few days, all Mariana had been able to do was painstakingly comb the streets in Nina's old neighborhood and trust the police. Faith bolstered her. But putting her sister's fate in the hands of others dredged up old insecurities from her childhood, rattling her composure.

"Them? I'm not sure who you mean," Mariana said.

"This mistake you are hung up on, are you really sure that it is one? Here, come with me."

Reaching for one of Mariana's hands, Mamá led her out of the pew, toward the back of the Basilica. They bowed their heads and murmured a smattering of "gracias por venir" or "thank you for coming" along the way. Near the door leading into the vestibule, her mom stopped.

Drawing Mariana close to her side, she whispered, "Perhaps a special word with those two? Sentados en el último banco a la derecha."

Mariana followed her mom's directions, seeking out whoever sat in the last pew on the right. She gasped as she recognized Angelo and Brenda. Eyes closed. Hands clasped in prayer.

Brenda had sent a string of concerned texts over the past few days, each punctuated by some combination of prayer hands, crying face, broken heart, and horrified emojis. Mariana had replied to the teen, doing her best to calm the girl's fears. But the multiple voice messages Angelo had left, pleading with her to give him another chance, remorse weighing his deep voice . . . those remained unanswered.

The yearning to believe him warred with her responsibility to her familia. It was too great a risk for her to take.

Her heart ached with the inevitability that her love for Angelo could never be.

Tears threatened again, blurring her vision. She took a step toward them, the need to comfort Brenda, to soak up the comfort Angelo offered, overwhelming her. But she couldn't allow herself the latter. He had abused her trust.

Even here, in the church where she had learned the concept of turning the other cheek, she couldn't bring herself to forgive and forget. Too much was at stake for her familia.

"I'll go ask them to leave before Papo notices them," she said, resolute in her responsibility.

Instead, her mom's clasp tightened. With a firm shake of her head, she led Mariana into the empty vestibule.

"Two Monteros coming to pray for a Capuleta," her mamá said, her voice still pitched low to avoid it carrying into the sanctuary. "That is something I did not think possible. Perhaps my years of supplication have finally been answered."

"Mamá, I can explain."

Her mother held up a hand, stalling what Mariana knew was a lame defense.

"I thought Brenda looked familiar when she came to see Nina the night of the raid. She reminded me of another young woman I knew years ago." Mamá fingered the crucifix hanging on her gold chain, her expression pensive. "Brenda mentioned that her brother was waiting for her outside. Of course, I checked the courtyard from the living room window. A mamá's old habit . . ."

"And you saw us together," Mariana deduced.

Mamá's lids fluttered closed on her slow nod, as if she couldn't bear to look at the daughter who'd been lying to her for weeks. Lies of omission but lies all the same.

Shame pummeled Mariana like the barrage of stones that once threatened Mary Magdalene.

"I shouldn't have kept this from you and Papo. We met by accident a few months ago. Then Galán asked us to keep the peace between our bands, and as we got to know each other better, it . . . we . . ." She cupped her mother's elbow, hating that she had disappointed the woman who had given her so much. "But it's over now. I'm done with him after he told Hugo about Nina. It was silly for me to ever think something between us would be anything but hopeless."

Sorrow pinched her mother's features as a soft sigh blew through her lips. The visible proof of the distress Mariana's deceit caused brought humiliation raining down on her.

"Mamá, please forgive me. I—I got swept up by my emotions. In the idea that maybe together he and I could . . . I don't know, bring an end to the feud. Instead, we made things worse."

"Mija, you are too hard on yourself. Your ability to empathize and put others first is a beautiful gift. Pero, hay veces . . . yes, there are times it can be a detriment to you. We cannot control everything. Trying to do so will leave you unsatisfied and unfulfilled. Or worse." Mamá grasped Mariana's hands tightly, her sorrow giving way to a benevolent smile. "That is not what I want for you."

"I'm fine. Or I will be," Mariana assured her mom, praying that if she said the words often enough, they would eventually be true.

"I hope so, mija. And if Brenda and her brother are anything like their parents . . ." Her mom stared through the open vestibule doors into the sanctuary, her eyes glazed, focused on a distant memory.

"Kindhearted, faithful people, full of love for each other and those in our comunidad. If their children are the same, then I know Brenda will be a good friend for our Nina. And Angelo, a good partner for . . . someone."

Someone. But not her. Was that what Mamá meant?

"There was a time I prayed for an end to the animosity. For a way to go back to how we once were—Arturo and Hugo compadres, me a besotted girl thrilled to join their band. Your papo and I falling in love so fast, we failed to notice Hugo's feelings for me. None of you children deserve to pay for the decisions we made back then. Or the mistakes we continue to make today."

A wistful sadness filled her eyes as she cupped Mariana's cheek. "Unfortunately, as thankful as I am for Angelo and Brenda's prayers, you are right. Before your papo sees them, it is better that we go give our thanks and politely suggest they not stay long."

The agony of wanting so desperately what she could not have tore through Mariana. Mamá must have read the pain on her face, because she softly patted Mariana's cheek.

"Have faith, mija. All will work out as it should," Mamá said softly.

With a shuddery breath, Mariana nodded.

Together they walked to the last row, where Angelo and Brenda sat, heads still bowed in prayer. Angelo looked up as they approached. Surprise, hope, and concern flashed across his handsome face.

He stood, dipping his head as he murmured, "Señora Capuleta, we have been praying for Nina's safe return."

"Gracias, mijo, te lo agradezco."

Because, yes, even a Montero's prayers were appreciated.

Brenda rose from the kneeler to exchange cheek kisses with Mamá, and Angelo stepped into the aisle near Mariana to give them more room.

She hadn't seen him since early Sunday morning, but her gaze devoured him as if it had been months. A thin, cream sweater hugged his torso the way her arms longed to do. The black scarf he'd left dangling around his neck begged for her to grab ahold of it and tug him closer, burrow in his chest, and lose herself in his kiss.

Lustful wishes she couldn't allow herself to crave anymore. But she still did.

That's why she hadn't answered his calls or returned his texts. Because while distancing herself hurt, she couldn't trust herself to not give in to her desire to be with him.

"Can we step outside to talk?" Mariana asked.

Her gaze darted to the front row, where Papo sat with the rest of the girls, then back to Angelo. He nodded, his lips a tight line of worry.

Once they all reached the privacy of the vestibule, Angelo splayed a palm on his chest and dipped his head with respect for her mother. "My sincere apologies, Señora Capuleta, if our presence creates any problem. That was not my intent."

"There is no need for you to apologize, mijo." Mamá held out her hands for Brenda and Angelo to take. "I do not know how, but I pray that one day there can be peace between our familias. Gracias, both of you, for caring about our Nina enough to be here."

A tender, maternal smile momentarily soothed the anxiety puckering her brow. She hugged Brenda and Angelo goodbye, then returned to the vigil inside the sanctuary.

Mariana motioned at the main door, and they walked in a weighty silence out to the parking lot.

"I'll wait in the truck, so you two can talk," Brenda suggested.

Angelo clicked the key fob to unlock the doors, then guided Mariana toward the truck's tailgate, away from the glaring lamppost a few parking spots over.

She shivered in the unseasonably cool night breeze, having left her cardigan sweater in the pew. Angelo slid his windbreaker off and draped it over her shoulders. His gesture reminded her of New

Year's Eve, when his chivalry, engaging smile, and heartwarming comments about his sister had wooed her. And his kiss had completely disarmed her.

Just like then, the warmth from his body clung to his jacket, enveloping her. Closing her eyes, she savored the sensation, recalling with bittersweet pleasure the small ways he showed he cared. His tender caresses and gentle touches. The pleasure-filled nights when they let their desire take the lead, and the mornings after when she awoke wrapped in his arms. Last Sunday, after Round Two's win, she had rolled over and awakened to find him watching her sleep. He greeted her with a hungry kiss, and she had nearly confessed her love.

Angelo adjusted his jacket on her shoulders and shuffled closer. "I could tell you that Brenda bugged me to bring her. And that would be the truth. But not all of it."

His thumb brushed the bottom of her chin. A slow, sensual caress that sent waves of heated awareness rippling down her neck . . . across her chest . . . arrowing to her heart.

"I've been worried about you. About Nina and your entire familia." Bending closer, he touched his forehead to hers. "I couldn't stay away. I had to see you. Apologize in person."

Her heart aching, Mariana forced herself to back away. She shook off his jacket and handed it to him, immediately missing his warmth. "I can't do this, Angelo. Not now. Not . . ."

The word "ever" lodged in her throat. The finality of it leaving her raw and bleeding. Unable to say it.

"Mariana—"

"I trusted you. I let my guard down and, ultimately, let my familia down in the process."

In the shadows of the tall streetlight, she caught the clash of disappointment and pain in Angelo's eyes. "Please give me a chance to make this right."

"All my energy is focused on finding Nina and bringing her home. Making sure she's not blamed for the town house fire out of spite and retribution for decisions and mistakes others have made."

Angelo reached for her, but she shied away. If he touched her, the facade of strength she had to keep in place—for her sisters, her parents, and herself—would crumble.

"Nina won't be blamed," he promised. "We all know there's no way she would have done it. The cops told my tío's lawyer today that they have some leads."

A car door closed several rows away. A reminder that people might start leaving soon. Papo would wonder where she had gone.

"I should go," she said, but she couldn't bring herself to leave.

"I won't give up on us. I still believe we're worth fighting for."

His certainty should have buoyed her spirits. Instead, the despair of inevitability squeezed her heart in its painful grip.

"I am not my uncle," Angelo asserted. "I'll do whatever it takes to prove that to your parents. And you. I promise."

She had thought he'd been proving that since the first night they'd met. But after his uncle's deceitful revelation, she wasn't so sure.

Or maybe it was herself she doubted. Her judgment. Her rash behavior where he was concerned.

The self-recrimination of either option made it difficult to look at herself in the mirror.

"I need to head inside before someone comes looking for me," she told him. "I wish it were different, but there's too much between us. There's nothing we can do . . . Please, just go."

A sob tore from her, opening a floodgate of tears, and she raced toward the Basilica. Back to her familia, leaving him to return to his.

Moves that put them in the same place they had started. On separate sides of a feud that continued to rage.

Chapter Twenty-One

Brenda stayed uncharacteristically quiet on the drive home from the Basilica. The silence and light traffic gave Angelo time to run through his conversation with Mariana. His promise to prove himself to her familia.

Somehow, he'd do it. Starting with convincing his tío to use his network around the city, especially in the West Side, to help locate Nina.

Once that effort had begun, the more difficult task would commence: compelling his uncle to rectify the damage he had done by interfering with the Capuletas' loan. Pushing out good people couldn't be the legacy Hugo wanted to leave behind. If so, his tío should be aware that it was a legacy Angelo would deny.

By the time he turned into the long driveway at his tío's house and the truck's headlights trailed over the meticulously maintained grounds, Angelo had come to a decision. His days in the place he'd once considered a refuge were numbered.

He slowed his truck to take in the familiar view. The escarpment of live oak and cedar elm trees towered over the smaller Mexican buckeye and mountain laurel trees that would soon pop with their pink and purple flowers. In years past, on warm spring days, Angelo had sat studying in their shade, the mountain laurel blooms sweetening the breeze with their grape-bubblegum scent while Brenda kicked a ball around the yard or wheeled her pink bike up and down the long driveway.

"Whose car is that?" Brenda sat up in the passenger seat and pointed at a maroon BMW parked in front.

"I think it belongs to Frankie Ruiz, Tío's lawyer."

The older man had mentioned his "new toy" during a strategizing conference call with Hugo yesterday. Angelo had been asked to join in so that Frankie could advise him on the financial documents the investigators had requested.

"It's kinda late, isn't it?" Brenda asked.

9:06 p.m. shone on the truck's dashboard display screen.

If they were lucky, a visit this late from the lawyer meant some kind of break in the arson investigation. With the real culprit behind bars, maybe Hugo's trusted confidante and legal counsel would be an ally in Angelo's bid to convince his tío to lend his resources to the search for Nina.

"It might be best for you to say hello, then hang out in your room," he told Brenda while they waited for the garage door to open.

"Believe me, I'm still so pissed at Tío for being a jerk about Nina, I'd skip the hello if I could."

Angelo bit back a sigh. The annoyed glances, mumbled criticism, and conversation sidestepping his sister had given Tío Hugo weren't new reactions to some archaic patriarchal comment or expectation from him. In the past, Angelo would privately talk with Brenda about how to deal with those she would inevitably encounter who, like Hugo, touted old-school ways of thinking. Leaving their tío to stew on his own until the disagreement blew over.

Not this time.

This time their tío had crossed a line by targeting a defenseless teen with his obsessive hatred. Days later, the hard feelings had not blown over. Depending on what happened when Angelo confronted his uncle, they might not.

Angelo and Brenda entered the house and found Hugo and Frankie sipping mezcal in the sala. Both men appeared to be in jovial spirits.

Far different from the somber mood shared by those at Little Flower Basilica.

Brenda politely paid her respects, ignoring their tío's "where have you two been" and excusing herself on the guise of it being a school night.

"Fill a veladora and join us for a drink, mijo. We have good news to celebrate." Hugo motioned toward the bar with his traditional votive candle–style sipping glass. The irony of his uncle drinking mezcal from a vessel originally used to hold Catholic prayer candles, similar to those being lit for Nina tonight, wasn't lost on Angelo.

He skipped the drink and lowered to sit on the sofa's armrest on the opposite end from Frankie. "I'm listening."

Apparently reading Angelo's irritation, Hugo sniffed with distaste. His grin slid into the twisted-lips glower he'd been wearing around the house all week, and he tipped his veladora at his drinking companion.

Frankie took Hugo's cue for him to explain, and the lawyer sat up, adjusting his gray pants legs with a tug at the thighs. "Ah, sí, great news. The police arrested a former tenant of the town houses today. He denied involvement, but there are incriminating texts and a voice mail decrying El Rey Properties for pushing him and several other familias out after we finished renovations."

"So, the fire was in retaliation for unfair treatment?"

Frankie frowned at Angelo's blunt question. His hesitant gaze darted from Angelo to Hugo, whose glower intensified.

"Actually," the lawyer drew out the word, ostensibly gauging whether Hugo preferred to answer. When Hugo stayed mum, his glare intensifying, Frankie continued. "Everything with the purchase, renovation, and relocation options provided are per the regulations. I think this is more a case of poor judgment and alcohol overconsumption."

"And the police are certain the culprit wasn't the fourteen-year-old who was initially *incorrectly* tapped as the potential pyromaniac?" Angelo asked.

He knew he was poking an angry bear, but the image of Arturo and Berta Capuleta on their knees at the church, despairing over the safety of their daughter, drove him to try and make his tío recognize the severity of his actions.

"Where were you two this evening?" Hugo repeated, eyeing Angelo over the rim of his veladora. Wily. Testing.

He knew, Angelo realized.

His tío was already aware of exactly where Brenda and he had been. Angelo didn't know how; frankly, he didn't care. But the antagonist in Hugo—that infamous ego of his—demanded he hear the truth directly from Angelo himself.

Unbelievable. Shaking his head, Angelo barked a sharp laugh. It was either that or rage, and he intended to keep his wits about him when he went toe to toe with his tío.

"Fine." He slapped his palms on his thighs, ready for the reckoning he had sensed coming since the morning of the fire. "We went to the prayer vigil for Nina Capuleta. Brenda and I felt it was important to show our support. And I wanted to extend my apologies, seeing as how you threw me under the bus in that initial interview."

"Maybe I should go." Frankie set his glass on a stone coaster on the aged wood coffee table.

Hugo nodded slowly, his attention still zeroed in on Angelo.

After a mumbled "Buenas noches, I'll touch base tomorrow," the lawyer let himself out.

Tension crackled in the sala like the orange-red flames engulfing the logs stacked in the fireplace. Hugo sipped his mezcal, then tapped the veladora against his lips. Waiting.

Angelo knew the move. Had been coached by his tío on the maneuver intended to ratchet up an adversary's unease. Pushing them to fill the silence and potentially throw off their game.

Heaving an impatient sigh at his tío's futile tactics, Angelo laid all his cards on the table. He had nothing to hide. And someone really important he didn't want to lose.

"I know about your involvement with the bank denying the Capuletas' loan. How that move forced them to seek out the private lender in their comunidad, who's involved with another one of our properties and is now putting the screws to them. Add Frankie's news about how and why the fire was started, and . . . I can't do this anymore."

Hugo's lips pressed into a hard line.

"Tío, I respect your drive and, sometimes, even your ambition, pero El Rey Properties isn't the right fit for me. It's time Brenda and I got our own place and I figured out my own path. I've buried my head in accounting to appease your wishes and avoid details about land-development deals I'm not sure are the right moves, or that I don't necessarily agree with."

"Meaning?" his tío grunted.

"Meaning, there has to be a way for revitalization without erasing what makes an area like the West Side so unique. Without hurting good people in the process. Or involving old grudges."

Hugo's condescending scoff pushed Angelo off the sofa armrest in frustration. Pacing to the fireplace, he stared at the flames devouring the pieces of dried wood. Suffocating them with red-hot fingers until they were nothing but a shadowy pile of soot.

A charred chunk broke off a log and tumbled to the base, shooting sparks up the chimney. He didn't want his tío's hatred to wind up engulfing their familia the same way. Leaving their relationships blackened and in ruins.

"You have it all figured out, ha, mijo?"

"No, I don't. But I'm certain that progress can't mean squeezing out people like the Capuletas. Those who embrace the West Side's rich history of arts and activism. And by staying quiet all these years, I've been part of the problem. That's on me, but it stops today." He swung around to face his uncle, who somehow looked smaller to him now. No longer the strong, imposing figure. The one with all the answers and a confidence Angelo had once envied.

"I love you, Tío. I don't want this hatred you've held on to for so long to consume you. It's already pushing Brenda and me away."

Hugo balanced his empty glass on the leather chair's rolled armrest. He traced a finger around the rim, a frown puckering his jowled face. "Amor. Odio. Love. Hate. Two sides of the same pinche coin. A damn coin that has created problems for many across the centuries." His frown faded, acceptance mixing with it. "I made my decision years ago. After Berta chose *him* over me. What good will regret do me?"

"It could lead you to make a different decision now. Tonight."

"¿De qué hablas?"

"I'm talking about putting your business connections to good use. Seeing if any of your contacts on the West Side can help the Capuletas find Nina. Asking your new golf buddy from the bank to reconsider the Capuletas' loan application. Or getting the private lender to back the hell off."

His uncle laughed. A gruff, roaring guffaw that filled the open sala and foyer. "You're kidding me, right?"

"No, I'm not. Show Brenda, show me, the man who silently cried at my side when my parents died instead of telling me to suck it up. The tío who opened his bachelor pad to a dazed and overwhelmed college kid and who sat awkwardly at pretend tea parties with a four-year-old who mourned for her parents. He's in there. I have to believe that."

Hugo swallowed. His chin trembled as the corners of his mouth curved down to match his thin mustache. "It's not like the Capuletas would accept my help, if I offered."

"At this point, I think they'd—"

"Angelo! She texted! Nina texted!"

Brenda's house slippers slapped the hardwood floor, her messy bun wobbling on top of her head as she raced into the sala, holding out her phone like it might explode. "She's in trouble. We have to go help her!"

"Hold up. Do you know where she is? What did she say?"

"What I just told you! She's in trouble!" Fear enhanced the wide-eyed "duh" glare Brenda shot him.

Heart pounding, he grabbed her cell to read the message thread himself.

Nina: Are you there? It's me, Nina.

Brenda: OMG! It's so good to hear from you!!

Nina: I think I need help.

Brenda: Where are you?

Nina: Been staying at an abandoned building. Squatters showed up a while ago so I hid in a closet.

Nina: They're arguing over drugs I think. I'm scared they'll find me.

Brenda: Tell me exactly where you are. We'll come get you.

Brenda: Please, Nina. You can trust me.

Nina: On S Brazos. The corner at El Paso.

Brenda: Stay hidden. We'll be there soon. Promise.

"South Brazos and El Paso." Angelo repeated the text out loud, trying to picture that part of the West Side.

"That's the Los Courts area," Hugo said. He frowned at his empty glass but didn't elaborate.

"You mean the Alazán-Apache Courts?" Angelo asked.

The eighty-year-old government-housing area was listed as a top US endangered historic site. It had been in the news for years, with most residents and activists decrying the city's plans to demolish the buildings and create mixed-income housing.

"Sí. Over by Guadalupe and Apache Creek. It's not the best area for a teen on her own, left to the elements, nature and human—especially at night," Hugo added, his expression grim.

"That's why we have to go. Now. I told her we'd come." Brenda tugged on Angelo's arm.

He shook off her hold. "There's no 'we' gettin' in my truck. You stay here, safe."

"Pfff, yeah, right." Brenda stomped to the coatrack by the double front doors. Grabbing her jean jacket, she slipped it on over her night-shirt and sweatpants, then shoved her feet in a pair of sneakers she'd kicked off after school. "Nina's my friend. She's scared. I'll stay in the car if I have to, but I'm gonna be there to give her a hug when you find her."

"Brenda," Angelo warned.

"I won't get out of the truck unless you say I can. I promise. Please, let me go with you. I can't stay here." Squinting her anger at their uncle, she squatted to tie her sneakers as if Angelo had already agreed to her ludicrous plan.

"She is strong willed, this one," Hugo muttered. "Just like her mamá."

"Gracias, Tío. I take that as a compliment. Now, let's go, hermano. Before it's too late."

Angelo strode over to grab his windbreaker off the rack. "Okay. But you follow my instructions once we arrive."

"You should call the girl's familia. Let them know you heard from her. I'm sure you still have the oldest Capuleta daughter's number."

Hugo's advice had Angelo pausing in the doorway to the garage. There was no way Hugo could know about Angelo and Mariana's relationship. And yet . . .

"It's not the worst area, but it's not the best. Call if you need my help. Ten cuidado."

"I will," Angelo said, mindful of his tío's advice to be careful as he raced to his truck.

~

"Mariana, you cannot drive there alone. Let me swing by and pick you up."

Her exasperated sigh was not the response Angelo wanted as he sped down I-10. His gaze flitted from the road ahead to the side view and windshield rearview mirrors, scanning the area for cops.

"This time of night, on a weekday, I can be there in less than thirty minutes," he said.

"And I can be there in less than ten."

He heard a door close on her end of the line, then the sound of her footsteps running down the stairs from her second-floor apartment. Brenda threw him an "oh shit" glance before shifting to face the passenger-side window. Probably to avoid his fear-fueled, quickly rising frustration.

"Mariana, it's not a safe place—"

"I've been combing the streets around there the past few days, flashing Nina's picture. Asking if anyone's seen her," Mariana insisted. "Besides, people from the Los Courts area are in my ER all the time. I've even run into a few who remembered me. I'll be fine."

"I'd feel better if you waited for us."

"And I'd feel better having Nina back at home where she belongs. Thank you, Brenda, for being such a good friend to her."

"You're welcome!" his sister called out.

He tightened his grip on the leather steering wheel, praying Mariana's propensity to be her familia's problem solver didn't put her in danger. Hating how the clock seemed to tick faster than the miles passed. "Mariana, I know you're anxious to find her. I'd be the same if it was Brenda. But please, don't do anything foolish."

Brenda grabbed his arm, her anguished "Dios, no" echoing his silent pleas.

He tried to offer her a reassuring smile, but with his stomach tied up in herculean knots, it probably looked more like that gritted-teeth emoji she usually sent with an "oops, I goofed" apology text.

"I'll park by the intersection and get a lay of the area," Mariana answered. "If it's clear, I'll poke around. If not, I'll wait."

"Promise me."

"Ay, Angelo, por favor." Her irritation matched his. For completely different reasons.

"Just, stay on the line until I get there. We should be there in"—he took his eyes off the road ahead to check the GPS—"about twenty-five minutes."

"Fine."

Conversation was minimal as they both broke the speed limit, desperate to get to Nina. Mariana, navigating city traffic from her nearby apartment. Angelo, switching lanes to pass cars on I-10, watching for police, counting down the miles to exit 155B, Frio Street / West Cesar E. Chavez Boulevard.

Too soon for his liking, Mariana was making the left turn off South Frio onto Guadalupe, then a few blocks later a right onto South Brazos. The same route he would take in fifteen minutes.

"It's pretty quiet," she told him.

"Good."

"Wait a sec . . . hmm . . . what's happening over there?" she murmured, as if talking to herself out loud. "That doesn't look . . ."

"What's going on?" Angelo asked. "Tell me what you see!"

The fear of her running headlong into a dangerous situation . . . of something harmful happening before he could arrive to stop it . . . of losing her like he'd lost his parents, sank its claws into him and thrashed like a rabid beast.

No! This could not be happening again!

Rational thought fled and he floored the gas pedal. Screw any cops between here and Mariana. They could follow him to this abandoned building and arrest the squatters who were scaring the crap out of Nina. And *then* give him a damn speeding ticket if they wanted. As long as Nina and Mariana were safe, he didn't give a shit.

"Mariana? Talk to me!" he called when she didn't answer.

"Hold on. I'm making a U-turn on El Paso so I can park. There are two guys hanging out on the corner. I think I . . . Hey—hey, you!"

Her voice calling out to two strange men Angelo couldn't size up or protect her from yet echoed through the cab of his truck.

"Mariana, what the hell are you doing?" he screeched.

"Shh!" she ordered.

Brenda slapped a hand over her mouth. Her eyes widened with trepidation and shock he doubted came anywhere close to matching his own.

"¡Oye! ¡Ven pa'ca!" Mariana shouted.

She was calling them over? Dios mío, his entire chest seized, and he swore he was having a heart attack.

"I'm getting out. Let me hang up," Mariana mumbled into her phone.

"No! No! Stay on the line!" Angelo yelled.

Her car door slammed as she yelled, "Hey, you remember me?"

"¿Chica, que tú haces aquí?" a gruff voice asked.

Angelo gritted his teeth to keep himself from voicing the same "what are you doing here" question.

"I'm looking for my sister," she told the guy.

"You better leave. There's some shit about to go down over there. And it ain't good."

"I think my younger sister is inside. I have to—"

"¡Vete!" another male voice demanded, repeating the first man's order for her to leave and emphasizing it with a "Now!" when she rebuffed him.

"Mariana, get inside your car. I'm almost there," Angelo shouted, uncertain whether she could still hear him.

"I need to find Nina! Just give me a—"

The sound of a car backfiring or—damn it, was that gunfire?—rang through the truck's speakers. Mariana screamed. Male voices shouted. She yelped in pain; then her call disconnected.

Brenda gasped. Her hands cradling the sides of her head, she gaped at him in disbelief.

Tears brimmed in her eyes, and Angelo wanted to comfort her. Tell his baby sister that everything would be okay. That Mariana and Nina were okay. But he couldn't.

Panic like he had never felt before gripped him. His blood turned cold. His heart pounded with dread. Light and shadow flickered into his cab like an old *Twilight Zone* episode as he zoomed by streetlamps edging the highway.

Por favor, Dios, he prayed, *let her be okay.* Let her be okay.

Let. Her. Be. Okay.

~

Mariana's elbow stung. Her back and shoulder blades ached. She winced and gingerly touched the back of her head, relieved to not find any blood. Though she'd probably have a goose egg after banging it on the damn road when one of the men she'd recognized from the ER had linebacker tackled her to the ground.

Now all six foot plus, two hundred and fifty pounds of him loomed over her. They sprawled in the middle of El Paso Street as footsteps pounded nearby. The guy grumbled, "Stay down," and leaned closer to shield her from whoever ran past them. Mariana peeked under his bulging biceps and saw the group that had been arguing in front of the abandoned one-story, cinder-block building scattering like cockroaches. Probably as spooked by the gunshot as she and her surprising protector.

The footfalls faded and the guy shifted.

"You okay, nurse?" He pushed to his knees and swiped his hands together to rub off the gravel and dirt, then held one out to help her up.

Gingerly she rolled her shoulders and patted down her lower back, testing for new aches and pains.

"Are they all gone?" she asked, groaning as he pulled her to her feet.

"Looks like it." The other guy who had tried to warn her rose from his crouch near her front driver's-side tire. He palmed his balding head, pushing his sweatshirt hoodie off.

Far back on the empty lot, the hinges of the building's wooden door screeched in protest as it banged open. Someone wearing a baseball cap poked their head out, craning their neck as if checking to make sure the coast was clear. A small figure emerged. In the shadowy gloom, Mariana made out a dark jacket over jeans and what looked like a pair of Converse sneakers.

"Nina?" she called out, praying the blow to her head wasn't messing with her vision.

The person froze. Their head jerked around, knocking the ball cap askew as they turned in the direction of El Paso Street, where Mariana had parked. With the cap's bill no longer shading their face, the dull yellow glow from the lone streetlight and the half moon shining above cast their beams across a familiar oval face with a pointy chin.

Sweet relief pooled through Mariana like honey dripping off a breakfast biscuit. Tears clogged her throat and she swallowed past the sudden tightness to yell, "Nina! Over here!"

Mariana raised her arm to draw her sister's attention. Pain shot down her right scapula. She yelped and hunched over, reaching across her body with her left hand to grab her shoulder.

"Oye, estás bien? Someone yelled 'gun' and I reacted. But we hit the asphalt pretty damn hard, man," the big guy said.

He clasped her upper arms and bent to peer into her eyes as if checking for concussion signs. Same as she would have done if their situations were reversed.

"I'm-I'm good. Thanks. It's Benji, right?" she asked.

He'd been in the ER about a month ago, suffering with kidney stones but managing to keep the jokes rolling even through his intense discomfort.

"Yeah." One of his beefy hands slid down to her elbow. She winced in pain.

"Hey, get the fuck away from my sister!" Nina yelled as she ran across the dusty lot.

An F-150 truck careened around the corner, coming to a screaming halt in front of Mariana's car. Its bright headlights blinded her, making it impossible to see who the idiot, unsafe driver was. She winced again as she lifted a hand to block out the headlights' glare.

The driver's-side door flew open. Through her squinting eyes she made out a broad-shouldered man, his dark jacket unbuttoned and billowing in the wind as he ran toward them.

"Back the hell off!" Angelo roared.

His steely, guttural voice shocked her, and she stumbled backward.

Benji shoved her behind him to stand feet wide, fists raised, ready to fight. "I don't know who you are, güey, but we don't want any trouble."

"We cool, man." Benji's buddy held up his hands in a conciliatory gesture.

"Then you better leave her the hell alone," Angelo ordered, continuing his approach. "Mariana, you okay?"

Angelo tried to reach around Benji to grab her, but the big guy dodged to his left and pushed Angelo's arm out of the way. The slap of their hands and muffled grunts as they shoved each other snapped her out of her stunned stupor.

"Stop! I'm okay!" She wedged herself between them before either could throw a punch, sucking in a sharp breath at the ache in her elbow and shoulder blade when she flattened her palms on their broad chests to push them apart. "We're all good!"

Nina reached her side and threw her arms around Mariana's waist from behind.

Benji's muttered "whoa" accompanied the scrape of road gravel as he backed away.

"I'm sorry. I'm so, so sorry." The teen's anguished cry had Mariana grabbing Nina's wrists to loosen her hold so Mariana could twist around to hug her.

The words she'd been praying for the chance to say spilled from her like a can of Big Red shaken and then popped open. "Me too. I was mad at myself and took it out on you. I hope you can forgive me."

"I shouldn't have run. It was stupid." Nina's voice broke, and the tears Mariana had been holding back broke the floodgates. She squeezed Nina tighter, whispering prayers of thanks to have finally found her.

Angelo wrapped his arms around them both, and her tears turned to a sob of relief. His warm breath brushed Mariana's cheek as he kissed her and murmured, "Gracias a Dios, you're safe."

"Oye, you three don't wanna hang around here," Benji advised. "No telling if those punks'll be back."

Mariana craned her neck to smile at him over Nina's head. "I can't thank you enough. Not that I hope you have to, but if you're ever in my ER again, Mariana Capuleta a su servicio."

He gave her a thumbs-up, sent a macho chin jut at Angelo, and then he and his friend crossed the intersection at El Paso to head down South Brazos toward Los Courts.

Angelo smoothed a palm over Mariana's hair. His fingers tucked into her french braid at the base of her head and he ducked closer to press his lips to her temple. She breathed in his familiar scent and closed her eyes, love for him quieting the fear that had held her in its grasp.

"I should have believed in you," she admitted. "Instead, I let my self-doubt get in the way, and that wasn't fair."

"I messed up, too. Forgetting to let you know about Marco telling my uncle, and me tripping up while trying to defend—"

"My sister," Mariana finished. "You don't know how much that means to me. Thank you."

Relief—and did she dare hope, love?—swam in his eyes.

She thought about Mamá's advice earlier this evening. Words Mariana had prayed over when she'd gone back inside the Basilica after Angelo and Brenda had left.

"I know you're not your uncle," she said. "And it was unfair of me to hold you accountable for his mistakes. You wanted to believe in him because you love him. I get that. I would do the same."

"It's okay." Angelo pressed another kiss to her temple, and she leaned into him, thankful he was here with her.

"Can I get out now?"

Brenda's hesitant voice startled Mariana. She squinted through the truck headlights to find Angelo's sister peering out the open front passenger window.

Angelo groaned but waved her over. With a squeal of delight, Brenda hopped out of the cab to join the hug fest.

Tears streamed down Nina's face as she blubbered, "Thank you so much for coming."

"I told you we would," Brenda assured her.

"We're relieved you reached out." Angelo ruffled Nina's tangled hair. "You gave us all a scare, kid."

"Yes, you did." Mariana cupped her sister's cheeks, palpated her shoulders and down her arms. "Are you hurt? Did anyone hurt you?" Dios, she hated to even ask, but if they needed to get Nina to the ER for an exam or to report someone, they had to stop there first before going home.

Nina stilled Mariana's ministrations. "No. Nothing happened. I knew what to do. Lie low, keep to myself. I didn't run into any problems. Until tonight, and then I hid."

A breath she hadn't realized she'd been holding whooshed out of Mariana. The fisherman's knot of anguished guilt that had tied her insides since early Monday morning finally loosened.

"Dios mío, girl, you're lucky. Being street smart paid off, but don't you ever do this again," Mariana warned, tugging Nina in for another tight hug.

Angelo's hand traced comforting circles on Mariana's back. He didn't say anything. He didn't have to. His presence here. The fact that he had jumped in his truck the moment her sister cried for help. That he'd confronted two potential assailants in a bid to protect her when he arrived on the scene. It all spoke volumes.

She looked up at him, his handsome face a mix of shadows from the truck lights and the garish yellow glow of the streetlamp. Angelo Montero was a good man. She loved him. And she no longer wanted to hide it.

Mariana held out her hand. A ghost of his engaging grin tugged at his mouth as he linked his fingers with hers.

"We should get her home," she said. "Will you follow us and come inside to share the good news?"

Angelo drew back. A worry line appeared between his brows. "I'm not sure that's a good idea."

"I am." She brought their joined hands to her chest, holding them close to her heart. "You and Brenda are an important part of bringing our familia together again. I think we should all share the good news."

Chapter Twenty-Two

After 10:30 p.m. on a weeknight meant the small parking lot alongside Casa Capuleta sat empty. Angelo slowly pulled into a spot two down from Mariana's sedan.

"Are you sure it's okay for us to go upstairs with them? This should be a happy time for their familia." Brenda leaned forward in the passenger seat and tipped her head back to peer at the apartments above the community center.

The strands of white lights were off, but above the chain link fence and hedge, several floodlights illuminated the back courtyard and the path leading to the front street. Welcoming those who belonged. And those who, like him, yearned to.

"Just so you know, I told Tío Hugo that you and I will be moving out soon. Getting our own place."

"You did?" Excitement danced across Brenda's round face.

Angelo nodded. "I haven't gotten it all figured out yet. But soon. Okay?"

"Better than okay!" Unbuckling, she lunged across the center console to hug him.

Outside, a car door shut, then another.

"We'll go up because Mariana invited us," he told Brenda. "But if it's clear they'd rather it be familia only, especially not, you know, Monteros . . . if I tell you we need to go, no trying to finagle more time."

"Understood."

Angelo glanced out the front windshield and spotted Nina and Mariana waiting for them on the sidewalk. One arm slung around her sister, Mariana beckoned for him and Brenda to join them.

In a strange, relieved, yet also tense silence, they walked to the front of the building, where Mariana unlocked the glass door and led them to the lobby elevator. As soon as it opened, Brenda hooked elbows with Nina, and arm in arm they stepped inside.

Mariana must have sensed the apprehension inching its way across the muscles in his shoulders and neck. Or maybe she noticed his fingers nervously *tap tap tapping* the sides of his legs. Either way, she slid her palm slowly over his to weave their fingers together.

Her simple touch was a much-needed balm. His shoulders lowered. Breathing felt natural instead of his forced three-count-in, three-count-out meant to help slow his racing pulse.

He had said his piece to Tío Hugo and the world hadn't ended. Officially meeting her parents was a necessary step. One he wanted to take.

The elevator dinged their arrival, and his stomach lurched. The doors creaked open, and he waited for Mariana and the girls to exit first. He motioned for Brenda to fall in beside him, allowing the sisters to take the lead.

"I texted the older girls that I had good news and they should hurry over. Doubtful they've made it yet, though. Everyone's going to be thrilled that you're home." Mariana wrapped Nina in a one-arm hug, then spun around to walk backward a few steps. "And they'll be extremely thankful for the two of you."

She pointed at him and Brenda, her sharp features softened by a delighted glee he hadn't seen since their private Round Two celebration Saturday night. And Sunday morning. Damn, happiness looked good on her.

Brenda elbowed him in the ribs and shot him a brow-raised grin brimming with a hope he wanted to feel. Mostly, though, he felt a little nauseous, worried that Arturo and Berta Capuleta might consider him an undesirable interloper. But if he wanted their approval at some point, he had to brave their doubts and convince them of the sincerity of his feelings for Mariana, as well as for the rest of their familia.

They reached the apartment door and Mariana withdrew her ring of keys from her jacket pocket. While she was still fumbling to locate the right one, the gray door flew open.

Berta Capuleta yelped in surprise when she saw them. The yellow-and-white-checkered dish towel she held dropped to the woven MI CASA ES SU CASA mat.

"Qué pasa, vieja?" Arturo's question reached them before he appeared behind his wife. "Nina!"

Both parents simultaneously reached for the teen, drawing her in for a group hug. A chorus of "gracias a Dios, you're safe" and "our Nina is finally home" and "I'm so sorry, Papo and Mamá" jumbled on top of each other.

The girls' mom leaned back to cup Nina's cheeks. Tears trailed down their faces, and even Arturo swiped at his eyes with the sleeve of his gray Dallas Cowboys sweatshirt.

"We should get out of the hallway," Mariana said, shooing her parents and Nina inside.

"¡Sí! Everyone come insi—" Arturo stopped short, still blocking the doorway, when his gaze landed on Angelo. Confusion played across his craggy features, quickly usurped by glowering resentment.

"Angelo and Brenda are the ones who helped me find Nina," Mariana announced. "She actually texted them when she was in trouble."

"I did," Nina admitted, her usual prickly disposition tempered by remorse. "I was afraid you'd be so angry with me you might not want me to come home, even though I desperately wanted to. Brenda and Angelo had promised that I could always count on them, so I did."

Berta sandwiched one of Nina's hands with both of hers. "Ay, mija, no matter what, this is your home. Yes, I may be angry at a choice you make, pero I will always love you."

"Sounds like what my brother says to me," Brenda mumbled.

Angelo nudged her booted foot with his. Now was not the time to draw attention to themselves.

"That is a wise brother you have." Berta smiled at Brenda. Despite the tears that streaked her cheeks, Berta's expression radiated with a mother's peace and understanding. She extended a hand for his sister to take, while still holding on to Nina with the other. "I am happy my daughter has a good friend like you."

Elbowing Arturo aside, Berta drew the two teens into the apartment with her, wrapping them both in a group hug. Arturo remained standing in the doorway, eyeing Angelo with unease and a hefty measure of distrust.

Instead of following her mother, Mariana stepped to Angelo's side. "Papo, please. Give him a chance. Angelo has shown that he cares about me, and Nina. He's a good man whom I care for deeply."

Completely caught off guard by Mariana's admission, Angelo froze. He fully expected Arturo to curse him for being a hated Montero and slam the door in his face. But Mariana looped an arm around his, squeezing it tightly as she rested her head on his shoulder. Humbled by her trust, he silently swore to prove himself worthy of her love, of her father's acceptance.

Arturo's shrewd gaze shifted from Angelo to Mariana and back again.

"Arturo, es tiempo para dejar el odio."

Berta's calmly spoken words, advising her husband that it was time to leave the hate behind, were fertilizer to the seed of hope buried inside

Angelo's heart. She spoke the truth. It was what he so badly wanted for all of them, but would Arturo agree?

Bowing his head in deference to the Capuleta patriarch, Angelo laid his heart on the line. "I won't come inside, if you'd rather I didn't. I respect your daughters and your wife, and you, Señor Capuleta, too much to intrude. Especially at a time like this."

He gestured to Nina. At the three younger Capuleta girls who had come running from somewhere inside the apartment amid shrieks of joy and now eagerly awaited their turn to hug their sister.

"But know that I love Mariana," Angelo continued, conviction strengthening his resolve. "I love her strength of character. Her devotion to your familia, and the comunidad Casa Capuleta serves. Even her patients. I love her need to take on everything for everyone. It makes me want to do all I can to support her. And be the someone she knows she can always rely on. No matter what."

Mariana squeezed his arm tighter. He pressed a kiss to the crown of her head, then faced her father again.

From behind her husband, Berta Capuleta beamed at Angelo. Her eyes glistened with happy tears.

Arturo stared at him for several interminable beats. Then, with a *humph* of suspicion and a brow arched in warning, he jerked his head to the side, indicating that Angelo should enter.

~

"He came through big-time, didn't he? Guess he really did have it in him to prove that not all Monteros are made from the same cabrón mold as Hugo."

Mariana chuckled at Cat's snarky commentary. "Yes, he did. And I'd definitely say that Angelo is not an asshole. Quite the opposite."

Side by side, she and her sister leaned against the kitchen counter, watching the others in the sala. Mariana mostly watched Angelo with

Teresita, who'd brought out her guitar after the conversation had turned to the Battle and their disappointment at no longer playing together. More heartwarming was the fact that they wished each other good luck in the finals this weekend.

The older Capuleta girls had all arrived earlier, and the entire familia, along with Brenda and Angelo, had gathered to give thanks. Some crammed on the sofa, some on dining room chairs. Others lounged on large throw pillows on the floor. Papo held court from his recliner. They all shared smiles and laughter and the sweet sense of relief.

Once the tears had dried and the hug fest had dwindled, her parents alerted the police and Child Protective Services about Nina's safe return. There would be paperwork and consequences for her decision to run away. But the Capuletas would get through it. Together.

"Now that he has Mamá's blessing, and Papo's no longer giving him the evil eye, what's next?" Cat asked.

As if he felt Mariana's gaze, Angelo glanced her way. He grinned, that infectious, slightly crooked grin that made her belly flip and her heart flutter.

"You know me, we'll take it slow," Mariana told her sister. "But he makes me feel good. Happy. Horny." She laughed at her sister's cackle. "I figured you'd appreciate that one. Truth is, the stressful stuff isn't as stressful when I talk things over with him."

Cat playfully bumped Mariana's shoulder with hers. "You deserve it."

"We all do."

"Happy and horny, that's me all right," Cat teased.

Mariana playfully swatted her sister's arm. "Seriously, though, I know the Battle was a chance for you to maybe get some notice in the industry. After not rehearsing this week, do you think we even have a chance on Saturday night?"

"Mija, please, do not doubt our talent, nor my ability to whip you girls into shape over the next two days. There's no doubt we're gonna kick ass Saturday night. But even if the judges screw up"—a mischievous smirk tugged up the corners of Cat's mouth—"I've got a plan B to cover the balloon payment."

"What? How?"

"I didn't want to say anything while we were all freaked out about Nina. And it's not finalized yet, so I—"

"Ay Dios mío, quit stalling!" Mariana complained, excited but also afraid to hope.

Always a fan of the spotlight, Cat giggled and leaned forward, lowering her voice to a conspiratorial whisper. "Are you ready for it?"

Mariana scowled with impatience.

"Galán's label asked if I'd be interested in writing some songs for them. Like, a paid gig. My work, on someone's album."

"Are you serious?!" Mariana screeched.

"Shhhhh!" Cat pounced, covering Mariana's mouth with her hand. "I don't want to say anything until I've seen the contract. But I've been dying to tell someone."

"Wuh-wu-hm?" Mariana mumbled, her question garbled by Cat's hand.

"You have to keep the news between us until it's a done deal, okay?"

Mariana nodded and tugged on her sister's wrist. Cat didn't budge.

"It's kinda fun not hearing you lecture me about whether I've thought this through," she teased.

Mariana licked Cat's palm with the tip of her tongue, eliciting the "ewwwww" she'd known it would.

"What are you, in fifth grade still? Yuck," Cat sputtered, swiping her palm down the side of her black leggings.

"Whatever. It worked!" Mariana threw her arms around Cat's shoulders for a celebratory hug. "That's freaking incredible, girl!"

"I know, right?"

"Everything okay over here?"

Cat and Mariana broke apart at Angelo's question. He strolled over to Mariana and tucked a loose strand from her braid behind her ear.

Cat rolled her lips between her teeth, a signal for Mariana to keep her mouth closed about their secret.

"Everything's great," Cat said. "I was just telling Mariana that the weather's perfect for enjoying the courtyard."

She winked, put a finger to her lips when Angelo turned to Mariana with a quizzical frown, and then went to join the others in the sala.

"It's hard to tell when she's teasing or being straight with me," he told Mariana.

"Well, you'll definitely know when she's pissed."

He chuckled. She linked her fingers with his and pulled him toward the apartment's main door. "But Cat's right, it's a nice night to swing out back. I doubt they'll miss us if we sneak down for a bit."

Outside, the air was crisp, but no longer as frigid as it'd been the past few days. Mariana unlocked the double doors leading into Casa Capuleta, where she flipped a switch to turn on the strings of white lights.

Instead of moving to one of the bench swings, she pulled Angelo into the shadowy area under the stairs. Away from potentially prying eyes peeking through the sala windows.

He leaned back against the brick building and wrapped his arms around her waist, drawing her to him. She shuffled her boots in between his, her hands gliding up his strong chest to lock at his nape.

"I don't think I've properly thanked you for riding to my sister's, and my, rescue tonight." She pressed a kiss to his neck. Another under his square jawline.

"Just like another night I recall, you didn't really need saving, gracias a Dios, but I'd willingly come to your rescue anytime."

His words warmed her heart. His musky scent as she nuzzled the area below his ear had other parts of her tingly and heating up with desire. She nipped at his earlobe with her teeth. Laved it with her tongue and savored the salty taste. His hands splayed along her lower back, urging her closer. She obliged.

Going up on her toes, she laid her body flush against his. Their hips almost aligned, and she rocked her pelvis, rubbing the bulge in his jeans. A low groan broke from his lips.

"Damn, I wish we were somewhere more private," he murmured.

She tugged his head lower and tipped her chin for his kiss. Angelo captured her mouth with his. Their tongues thrust and withdrew, entwined and teased, mimicking the dance their bodies craved. One of his hands slid down to cup her ass, holding her tightly as they bucked in a sensual rhythm. Both of them hungry for a satisfaction they could find with only each other.

He broke their kiss to trail tiny love bites along her jaw.

"You taste so damn good," he whispered.

"Mmm," she murmured, angling her head to give him better access to her neck. "I swear, your scent clung to my pillows. Made me crave you even more after you left."

His low, husky chuckle rumbled over her in titillating waves. Her nipples pebbled, straining for his touch.

She wanted to rub up against Angelo, indulge her craving for him. But it was almost midnight, which meant they didn't have much time out here. The younger girls had school the next day, and most of the rest of them had work. She fully expected one of her sisters to either open the window and call out a "time's up" or simply head on down without warning.

So what if they interrupted a girl trying to enjoy a little foreplay in the shadows. Or work up the nerve to ask an important question.

Her fingers toyed with the short hair at his nape as she drew back. "About what you told my father earlier. When we first got here."

Angelo tucked his chin to peer down at her intently. The light from the sidewalk streetlamp and the second-floor landing shone through the metal stairs, casting shadowy lines across his face and the wall behind him.

"I meant every word."

Awed by how easily, how confidently, he declared his love when she so often guarded hers—afraid to let someone close and risk losing them—she stared up at him in a daze. Lightly, she traced the pad of a finger along the outline of his lips. He nipped at her fingertip, gently biting the padded flesh, then sucked it into his warm mouth. Lust shot straight to her core.

He clasped her wrist, brought her hand down to his heart. "Look, I know we both have full plates right now. I've gotta find a place for Brenda and me to move into and start the search for a new job. Who knows how long—"

"Wait—you what?" Her head shook in a double take, certain she had misheard.

"I told my uncle tonight. I'm ready to go out on my own. Brenda's excited. Granted, she has no idea the logistical nightmare involved. But you and I are professional glass-ball jugglers, aren't we?"

Mariana blinked a few times, still processing his news. "You aren't doing this because of me. Or because of us. Are you?"

Dios, that would be the wrong reason. This was a major change. Two of them! He had to make these choices for—

"No, this is for me," he assured her.

Mariana dropped her forehead to his chest in relief. Talk about an immense amount of pressure to put on their relationship.

"And for my sister," Angelo added. "I love my tío, but he makes decisions I don't agree with—at work and home. It's time I pursue what I really want to do. Financial consulting, not accounting and taxes. I also told him he needs to find a way to make things right with your parents' loan."

"You did?" She straightened, shocked by his news. "Damn, you're full of surprises tonight."

"Good ones, I hope."

"The best ones."

Angelo pressed a kiss to her forehead, then drew back again. "I agree with your mom. We need to put the hate behind us. On Saturday night in the finals, there are two incredible mariachi competing. Doesn't matter all-male, all-female, mixed. We all deserve to be there. As much as I hate to say it, I'm not sure if my tío's capable of changing. I hope so. I love him. I'd like him to be in Brenda's and my lives, but it has to be in a healthy way."

"Wow," Mariana murmured. "That had to have been a tough conversation with him."

Angelo nodded and slid his hands in her back jeans pockets. "About as nerve-racking as facing your dad."

"Which you did marvelously." Stretching up, she placed a chaste, closed-mouth peck on his lips, then lowered her heels to the ground. "Thank you for being so vulnerable and brave."

Cupping the back of her head, he gently guided it to his shoulder. She slid her arms around his waist and sighed with contentment.

"I'd do it again, for you," he said.

His sweet words gave her the courage to finally share her true feelings with him. Removing the barriers she had erected to protect her from the old fear of losing her loved ones after her birth mom died, or of being yanked away and separated from someone she had started to care for if CPS decided to move her to a different foster home.

If she trusted Angelo with her life, with her sister's, she could trust him with her heart.

"I love you," she whispered.

Once the words were out, a buoyant euphoria infused her, and she didn't want to stop saying them.

"I love you." She grinned up at him, praying he saw the truth in her eyes. "I love your good heart. How much you adore your sister, and mine. Your sense of decency. The way the sound of your voice on the phone relaxes and excites me. I love that you're an all-around ni—"

He kissed her. A slow, sultry, knee-weakening kiss that had her swooning in his arms.

"Don't say it," he mumbled as he traced the shell of her ear with his nose.

"All-around nice guy," she teased.

He growled, his teeth grazing her neck and sending ripples of desire down her chest, arcing over her breasts.

"You said that we both have a lot on our plate," she told him.

Angelo nodded.

"How about we tag team at juggling? I'm going to be busy when PA school starts in the fall. I might need help remembering to unwind, let go of my need to control or manage everything."

"And starting a new job or maybe even my own consulting firm will be difficult. I'd love some help destressing." He tugged her against him, making his favorite destressing activity clear.

"Mmm, I can totally help you with that."

He grinned. That disarming, crooked smile that tripped her pulse and filled her with joy.

"And if one of us happens to drop a glass ball, it'll be okay," he assured her, bending to kiss her forehead, her cheek, her lips. "Because we'll pick up the pieces together."

"Together. I like the way that sounds."

Epilogue

"¡Bienvenidos a todos!" Papo cried into the microphone. His pleased grin widened when his welcome was repeated in a wave of voices.

Neighbors, parishioners, students, comunidad members, and fellow musicians filled the Casa Capuleta courtyard late Sunday afternoon. All here to commemorate the fantastic news—for the familia and their neighborhood.

Standing on the dance floor in front of the stage, Mariana craned her neck to look over her shoulder at her father. Pride gleamed in his beaming expression. It puffed his chest and straightened his shoulders as he waved at the crowd. He gestured toward her and her sisters, lined up alongside Mariana. The tears glistening in his eyes brought an answering tightness to her throat.

The crowd quieted and Papo spoke into the microphone. "Gracias to all of you for being with us to celebrate the first-ever all-female Battle of the Mariachi Bands champions! ¡Arriba Las Nubes!"

Cheers and gritos pierced the air. Her sisters bent forward and backward, looking down the line at each other, sharing ecstatic grins. Pure unadulterated elation swelled within Mariana until she felt like it might shoot from her pores.

Dios mío, last night . . . being onstage at the Majestic, standing under the falling cannon-fire of confetti after Patricio Galán proclaimed

Las Nubes the winners and pandemonium ensued, her sisters swarming in a group hug amid raucous cheers . . . ay, it still felt like a dream. She fully expected to wake up and find it was really Saturday morning, hours before the final round.

Beside her, Cat reached for Mariana's right hand and squeezed it. Hard. Cat's eyes closed as she blew out a rush of air. Relief. It hovered around their collective euphoria. Especially with Cat.

Admiration for her sister wove like warm ribbon around Mariana's chest. For all Cat's cocky diva attitude, she'd been so stressed about the competition's outcome that she'd taken to biting *all* her manicured nails, not just her thumbs. Wanting so badly to win. For themselves, for the young girls scattered around the courtyard with them now, for their parents and home.

All the Capuleta girls felt the same. But Cat yearned to do something more with her talent, and winning the opening-act spot for Galán's upcoming concert meant an opportunity to shine under a much bigger spotlight. Her determination and dedication to craft, the way she doggedly pushed her sisters to do their best—as obnoxious as it could be—had paid off. Not only had they brought home the gold trophy and prize money, but then Galán had sweetened the pot by inviting Cat to perform her new duet with him during *his* set in his concert.

Talk about an unexpected twist!

Of course, Cat had played it cool, politely thanking the famed singer while reminding him that she'd need a say in the final arrangement. Ay, the audacity of that one. Galán had laughed as he left Las Nubes's dressing room at the Majestic. As soon as he was gone, Mariana and her sisters had squealed with glee. Happy dancing like they were kids who'd learned they were going to Disney World.

"Before we ask Las Nubes to treat us to a few songs," Papo continued, "I want to congratulate those from Los Reyes who were able to join us today."

Angelo slid his hand from the small of Mariana's back to wave at the crowd, who clapped and whistled their approval. Nearby, his friend Marco and several other Los Reyes members acknowledged the crowd and Papo. Hugo had stayed away from the festivities, but he'd been surprisingly gracious last night, going so far as to offer Papo his congrats and gratitude for Nina's safe return. A small yet appreciated olive branch.

At the moment, though, Mariana had eyes for only Angelo. No longer worried about hiding her true feelings. Still awed by the way he had stood up to his uncle. From the moment they'd first met, she had sensed something special about Angelo. An undeniable connection between her and this compassionate, strong, generous man.

As the cheers quieted, he draped his arm around her waist again. His hand splayed over the gold gala trailing down the side hem on her charro skirt. His touch sent an excited tingle racing through her. Teasing her with a memory from their private after-party at her apartment last night. His palm caressing her bare hip, forging a sensual path lower. His fingers working their delicious magic until she cried out with pleasure.

For now, she settled for leaning her head on his shoulder, content to be in his arms. He hugged her close to his side, and a deeper sense of home, security, and love enveloped her. She wanted to offer the same to him, and his sister. Having them here, welcomed and accepted at Casa Capuleta, was a start. Just as it had been the start for her.

"Mijas, come on up and sing a few songs for us." Papo motioned for Mariana and her sisters to join him onstage.

Angelo pressed a kiss to Mariana's forehead and patted her hip before she eased away. Hand in hand with Cat, Mariana strode toward the stairs off to the side.

"Bueno, mi gente," Cat said, once they had all taken their positions. "We've come a loooong way from the three, then five sisters playing for anyone who would listen at church and here at Casa Capuleta."

Laughter met Cat's teasing reminder of their band's early days.

Mariana leaned toward her mic, her gaze seeking out her parents, who had moved with Nina and Brenda to join Angelo in front of the stage. "Mamá and Papo, you brought us all together. Us girls. Everyone gathered here. What we accomplished last night—"

"Wait a sec! Can we just repeat exactly what that accomplishment was again?" Cat teased, waggling her brows.

"You mean, when Las Nubes earned the title of Battle champions?" Mariana paused for the gritos and whistles, grinning with glee when Angelo stuck two fingers in his mouth to contribute an earsplitting whistle to the fray.

Cat encouraged the crowd by cupping a hand around her ear. Mariana tipped her head in gratitude for the adulation. She let the rowdiness continue for a few moments longer, then raised a hand to calm the cheers.

"As I was saying"—she side-eyed Cat playfully—"Mamá and Papo, what we accomplished last night is a testament to your devotion to our familia and our comunidad. Change may come to our neighborhood, pero, because of you, pride for our heritage and culture, and love for each other, will remain."

Mamá laid her hands over her heart. Papo blew Mariana and the girls a kiss. Cries of "Arturo y Berta" and "viva Casa Capuleta" rained down on them.

Mariana slowly raised her trumpet to her lips, preparing to trill the first notes of the opening song Cat had selected earlier. Seconds before her eyes drifted shut, as her lungs filled with a deep breath, her gaze caught on Angelo. Tall and proud, he stared up at her, his flutter-inducing, lopsided grin tugging up the corners of his mouth.

She took a page out of his book and shot him a wink. His grin widened, and though she hadn't thought it possible, she fell for him a little more.

Later, as they cuddled and kissed in the bench swing under the stars, they talked about their future. Her plans for school in the fall. His to start a consulting business and offer free financial-planning classes at Casa Capuleta, to help people like his parents and hers. Brenda's desire to start music lessons with Nina, maybe join Las Nubes when the two girls were ready. And Angelo's appointment with the leasing manager at Mariana's apartment complex. The house he was saving for, maybe even their house, would come eventually.

"And your uncle?" she asked, tucking her head into the crook of Angelo's neck, relishing in his familiar scent.

Angelo rubbed a hand up and down her upper arm to ward off the evening chill. "Tío Hugo's a work in progress. It's been a tough weekend for him. Losing the Battle. Brenda and me moving out, and me giving notice at the company."

"Any regrets?"

"Not a single one."

His answer came quickly. Confidently. But familia was familia. Hugo was Angelo's closest connection to the father he had adored. Mariana's heart ached for him. For the loss Angelo would suffer if his tío couldn't forgive him for wanting to forge his own path.

"Are you sure?" she whispered, slipping her arm around his waist and burrowing closer.

He gathered her in a tight embrace. Held her in the cocoon of his arms as the bench gently swayed and the strains of an old bolero drifted from the open sala window in her parents' living room.

"Yes, there's a lot of uncertainty ahead. There's a lot we can't control. But there's one thing I am definitely sure about." Tucking a knuckle under her chin, he tipped her face up to look at him. "This." He brushed a butterfly kiss on her lips. "You." Another peck that had her wanting more. "You're the best thing that's happened in my life. As long as we're partners, the juggling, the band playing, the familia drama . . . we'll get through it. I love you, Mariana Capuleta. Para siempre."

For always.

Two words she'd been afraid to rely on for years. Somehow, with Angelo, she found hope in them.

She cupped his cheek, consumed with love for this amazing man who'd stolen her heart and given her his in return.

"I love you, too," she murmured, stretching up to meet his lips for a kiss that held the beautiful promise of their future.

ACKNOWLEDGMENTS

It's the same with every book . . . My fingers may be the ones tapping on the keyboard, but many others help me get the words on the page and bring my beloved characters to life. In 2020 and early 2021, when I was writing the proposal for this series and then began working on *West Side Love Story* (*WSLS*), times were hard for everyone. Social distancing made the solitary life of a writer even more so. I'm not gonna lie; it was hard to get lost in my story world when the real world was a mass of worry and stress and fear for the lives of our loved ones, neighbors, coworkers—even strangers.

I couldn't have finished this book without the emotional and mental support of many, so please indulge me as I share heartfelt gracias to some special people . . .

Farrah and Kwana—without our daily pep-talk texts, prayers, video chats, and even a surprise package in the mail . . . oh gosh . . . I would have been an even bigger mess of emotions! Our friendship means so much to me, ladies!

Alexis, Mia, and Sabrina—you talked me off a precarious ledge while I was writing this proposal, ultimately helping me envision something even better than before, and then encouraged me the whole way till "The End." Our amiga-hermana relationship is a true blessing!

Zoraida, Adriana, Diana, and Lydia—along with Alexis, Mia, and Sabrina—over two LatinxRom retreats, you all listened and chimed in with ideas and more as I took the Capuleta sisters from a seed of an idea to a beautiful book (with another blossoming soon); whether in-person or virtual, I'm so thankful for our time together, building each other up while sipping bubbly and snacking on plátano chips. ¡Las adoro mucho! #LatinxRom

Sonali and Jamie—your feedback on the proposal for the series truly made it shine and helped me shape the beginning of the novel. And Sonali, your pep talks and critiques during revisions helped pull me out of the weeds and silence those pesky doubts. *WSLS*—and I—wouldn't have gotten this far without both of you!

Aunt Cathy and Aunt Terry—for the insight and ideas about San Antonio, Tex-Mex lingo, and mariachi music, and for your continued support with all my books. I'm super thankful you're my beloved tías!

JoAnn—thanks for answering my random texts about life in SA! Love ya, prima!

The friendly woman (who wished to remain anonymous) at the Texas Department of Family and Protective Services Office of Consumer Relations who answered the phone, then patiently answered my questions and shared advice on different scenarios I presented—any errors regarding the Capuletas serving as foster parents and adopting the girls are all mine.

My agent, Rebecca Strauss—for her input and guidance from the genesis of the Capuleta familia to this point of sharing them with readers; I'm super thankful you're on my team!

My editors Maria Gomez and Lindsey Faber—for the fantastic teamwork with *WSLS* and for understanding how important it is to me that my work represent my comunidad well and con mucho orgullo (with much pride). Thanks so much for helping me bring the Capuleta sisters to life!

My big sis, #1 brainstorming partner, and beta reader, Jackie—your confidence in my writing and in me boosts me when those impostor-syndrome doubts whisper their negativity. I'm so thankful to have a #1 positivity partner by my side, for everything! #YOLOsisters

My baby brother, who gifted me with a beautiful writing desk, where this book took shape and went from an idea to words on the page! I appreciate your love and support!

Mami and Papi—a part of you is in every matriarch and patriarch I write: all the good, all the loving moments, maybe some of the chancla-waving ones as well. Like Grandma and Grandpa, you're role models for the loving relationship my characters and many of us seek. ¡Los quiero mucho!

Alexa, Gabby, and Belle—for the "how's your word count today" texts and the "so proud of you, Mom" messages, and the "let me know if you need my partner and me to be your cover models" chuckles . . . for urging me to go after my dreams and telling me "it's your time now." As proud as I am of the opportunity to share my books with readers, I'm more proud of the three amazing, strong, accomplished Latinas you all are! I'll love you forever! XOXO

And finally, in the romance genre, we write stories about heroes and heroines. In *WSLS*'s fictional world, Mariana's an ER nurse, but the frontline workers everywhere putting their lives on the line to care for others during this global pandemic are *real-life* heroes and heroines. Gracias for your hard work and dedication and the care you've given to countless patients. My prayers are with you and your loved ones.

ABOUT THE AUTHOR

Photo © 2015 Michael A. Eaddy

Priscilla Oliveras is a *USA Today* bestselling author and 2018 RWA RITA double finalist who writes contemporary romance with a Latinx flavor. Proud of her Puerto Rican–Mexican heritage, she strives to bring authenticity to her novels by sharing her culture with readers. Her books have earned starred reviews from *Publishers Weekly*, *Kirkus Reviews*, and *Booklist* along with praise from *O, The Oprah Magazine*, the *Washington Post*, the *New York Times*, *Entertainment Weekly*, Frolic, and more. She earned her MFA in Writing Popular Fiction from Seton Hill University, where she currently serves as adjunct faculty while also teaching the online class "Romance Writing" for ed2go. A longtime romance-genre enthusiast, Priscilla is also a sports fan, beach lover, and Zumba aficionado who often practices the art of napping in her backyard hammock. For more information, visit www.prisoliveras.com.